TRAITORS' PROMISE

BOOK II

LAUREN
PARKER RHODES

WILDFUL WRITINGS

NSW, Australia

This is a work of fiction. Its characters, places and incidents are a product of the author's imagination and any resemblance to actual persons, living or dead, or real events or locales, is entirely coincidental.

www.laurenparkerrhodes.com; Instagram: @laurenparkerrhodes

© Cover design: Holly Dunn Design

Paperback ISBN: 978-1-7637346-1-6

eBook ISBN: 978-1-7637346-2-3

Also by Lauren Parker Rhodes

Access Lauren's other books here, or at:
www.laurenparkerrhodes.com/books

DRIARN DUOLOGY
The Wife (short story prequel)
Amber Wolf
Blue Pointed Star

WHEN SECRETS BECKON

TRAITORS DUOLOGY
Traitors' Creed
Traitors' Promise

Author's note: Each of these books, with the exception of Traitors' Promise, were previously published by Lauren Searson-Patrick and have been republished, with permission, by Lauren Parker Rhodes. Traitors' Promise has only been published by Lauren Parker Rhodes.

Content Warnings

This book is intended for adult audiences and contains mature themes and relationships. There is a threat of, and actual (off-page), sexual assault, discussion of sex trafficking and child abuse, and torture.

This one's for you. You who sees the wrongs in the world and is ready to take your first step to righting them, no matter how small. Remember, you don't have to be the biggest or most powerful to make a difference — you need to believe you can and start where you are.

CHAPTER ONE

For a moment – just a moment – the freedom that fills me is almost enough to take me soaring through the open space. As if my magic might have finally—

I plummet.

My cheeks are forced back from my teeth by the wind. A scream rips from my chest, wrenching the oxygen from my lungs with it as the sound is swallowed by the force of my fall. My mind empties.

Just one thought remains.

This is how I will die.

No. I can do this. I *chose* this.

Something sharp cuts into the back of my hand, and I drag my focus to the weight attached to me – the one that came with me as I leapt. Blossom is curled around my body, fingers and nails digging into me like I'm her sole remaining life line. Which ... perhaps I was.

Until I led her off the island.

Fuck. Blossom.

Why did she come with me? Why did I let—

I choke on the tiny amounts of air I can gulp down, my vision blurring as tears whip free of my eyes, gone too quickly to even wet my cheeks. The skin on my face feels like it might tear straight off.

Blossom squeezes my shoulder as we tumble through the sky, clinging to each other hard enough for every muscle in my body to ache. She grips my fingers, pointing our joined hands downward, against the force of the wind, to where the sky is tinged blue and gold. More vibrant than the natural sky. A shimmering bubble that encapsulates Zanteera Island.

The wards.

As we hold tight to each other in free fall, Blossom's unwavering strength and support is like a railing I can hold on to in this otherwise expanse of nothing. Instinctively, I narrow my body, arms by my side, my left awkwardly where Blossom still hangs on. But I don't want her to let go. I bite back all the thoughts of what I will never get to do now. What I have robbed Blossom of through her loyalty to me.

Because we will die this way, but, if we can bring the wards down for the others to get through unmarked, more than us will live. Including Nix and River. Janly. Emeris.

Quillian. A sharp pang runs the length of my chest.

Looking over my shoulder as best I can, I see the smaller island Nix has created above us – a mass of dirt so dark it's almost black from here. Are they too far above us? Will they make it through in time?

The shallow breaths I take aren't enough for me to think clearly. But, in the back of my mind, I know there is no out from this. No *collection* scheduled to rescue me from my duty. No magic in my veins that will manifest wings, or power over the earth. No portal or healing to save me from what's at the end of this fall.

Nothing to help me.

And that's the point. No magic means we can, temporarily, bring down the wards.

Perhaps that will be the greatest service of all. I know Nix and River won't let this go unanswered. They will get to the bottom of why the *prisoners* were treated so lavishly for doing unspeakable things. I wish I understood what led them here, what they saw, were ordered to do. But we don't have time now. All I can do is trust they will make sure this sacrifice of mine and Blossom's isn't for nothing.

Something small and grey appears to the side of me, and I try to blink to see what it is.

A single heron.

Wings tucked in tight, in free fall along with me and Blossom. A tiny part of me wonders who sent it. If it's a sign from Claudius that we are doing the right thing.

The lining of the shimmering, gold bubble races towards us, and I stop trying to drag air into my lungs.

I hold Blossom to me as the world flashes around us. It seemed so subtle from Claudius's office. From here, the explosion of sunlight is almost blinding. But there is no snapping against my skin, no ripping sensation as we go through. Nothing that would immediately tell me we've been marked.

As I look over my shoulder, the iridescent bubble gently recedes, like a curtain being drawn away.

The air rushes in my ears, my hair stinging my face as the tiny, shrinking island lowers itself through the gap, leaving everyone on top unmarked.

I hope.

I think I hear Blossom's startled yelp as we tumble through the open air.

The grey heron opens its wings just below us, arcing out into a wide sweep of the sky.

Then the mainland suddenly seems too large.

So close.

So ... blue and green. The capital sparkles like a jewel in the distance.

This is as close as I have been to my city, and Akira and Zale, in five years. I can almost—

The wind is knocked out of me as something hard slams into my back, forcing Blossom from my grip as I tumble through the air. A wild nausea claims me as I spin. Catching glimpses of buildings—

The sky—

The river—

Clouds—

The chunk of floating dirt in the sky. And, somewhere beyond that, Zanteera Island.

Finally, I have enough air to scream.

'I've got you.' Quillian's deep voice rumbles through my back, reverberating in my chest before it's carried away on the breeze. There's something off about it, but I can't focus as we start to soar again, the abrupt change in direction creating a surge in my stomach, and I squeeze my eyes shut.

'Bloss?' I choke out, my voice ragged as I swallow down the vomit that's desperate for release.

'River,' he says, shifting me around, and I blindly clutch at anything I can find to hold onto.

A gasping sound fills my ears.

'Breathe,' Quillian says over my head, pulling me harder against his chest, and I'm surprised to find that I can, dragging huge lungfuls of air into my chest as if I am breathing for the first time.

Going up is so different to going down. My stomach starts to settle in time with the deep, rhythmic sweep of Quillian's wings – a stark contrast to the chaotic pounding of Quillian's heartbeat under my cheek.

He lands us back on what can only be Nix's island, slowly releasing me down his front until my feet touch earth and I sink onto my knees, the wobble in my legs too much to keep me upright. I just fell – and flew – through the sky. A tremble starts in my fingers and travels up my shoulders until my teeth chatter uncontrollably. Quillian steps up behind me, framing me with his legs and maintaining physical contact. Perhaps he thinks I'm a flight risk. I bark a short laugh—

We *flew*. I missed his wings.

Curling my fingers in the dirt, I force my eyes open and immediately meet Cortane's. Her sharp, grey gaze flashes with something hard, but it doesn't cover the hollowing out there, too. Is that pain?

I find Blossom where she has sunk to the ground, much the same as me, pale, even a bit green, like she is also refusing to vomit right now. We stare at each other, eyes wide, before she smiles slightly. The enormity of what we've just accomplished filling the space between us.

'Get us the fuck out of here,' Quillian demands sharply, and my heart stutters a little.

As the others look back at him in silence, I realise, for the first time in five years – even longer, if I'm honest – I have no idea where I'm going.

'We're going to fall,' Nix grinds out, his teeth clenched as sweat pours off him.

'Everyone get down,' River shouts, standing between Nix and Blossom, holding onto each of them.

Emeris sneaks a look over the side before shaking his head at me, the drop stealing the colour from his face.

I try to stand, but the island lurches beneath us and I stumble. Quillian pulls me close as Janly cries out and the nameless Hunter starts to chant to himself. Emeris crawls to Janly and she clings to him, his arms roping around her.

'Options?' I ask Quillian, clutching at his bare forearm.

He glances at Cortane and Finn quickly before he replies, 'None—but you don't leave my side.' His fingers dig into me, in reflex or emphasis, I'm not sure.

'Well, fuck me,' Cortane says, dropping to her knees, 'this is not how I thought I'd go.' She presses herself towards the ground, not mentioning the fact she could surely portal herself – and a few others – to safety. Something about the way she's holding herself makes me wonder if her time in Vana has taken more of a toll than she's let on. Claudius did say it would weaken her, and she confirmed as much, but what else has she endured?

I give instructions to the group as best I can, almost word for word what I would tell new concierges before their first ascension to the marble receiving plane: breathe, stay close to the ground, and hold onto something. Emeris stares back at me the whole time, Janly's face buried in his shirt; I try to infuse him with confidence with a thin smile.

Nix groans, the muscles in his neck and arms straining as he presses his hands into the ground, his magic clearly almost depleted.

A nervous skitter races along my limbs, lifting the hairs on my arms and the back of my neck.

'Listen up,' Quillian says, projecting his voice while keeping his gaze trained on Nix. 'We have about fifteen seconds before we drop like a stone. It won't be a long drop, but the force of the impact will be brutal. When we land, you'll likely be winded. Don't panic. We'll get you off as soon as we can.'

When he looks back at me, a little of his facade falls away, and I know we're unlikely to come out of this unscathed. But as the wind tears at his short hair, I also see what no facade can hide.

A commander.

A man who is taking up the exact space he was born for, the air around him thick with purpose.

'In ... position.' Nix spits through clenched teeth, knuckles digging into the earth.

I focus on Quillian's face as we stand in the middle of our group, the others clutching the ground and each other in any way they can. Except Nix, River, and Blossom, who make their own little group at the edge where Nix kneels.

'Go,' Quillian says, and I gasp as my stomach loops over itself with the sensation of the island dropping away from my feet, and we're free-falling through the sky once again.

Quillian draws me into a crouch, and I've barely drawn my next breath before he lifts us slightly off the island as it slams into the ground, the world shuddering around me in a cloud of dust. All I can hear is the muffled cries and curses from the others, until the force of Quillian and River's wing beats clear the air and it all swims back into view as Quillian plants our feet on what's left of the tiny island.

More than one of our passengers stumbles off the side, vomiting in the grass. But they all seem to be here—alive. I scan our surroundings, trying to take in as much as I can, but the space that stretches out around me, scattered with tall, willowy trees, seems impossible to absorb after the clearly defined edges of Zanteera Island.

'Check the perimeter,' Quillian barks. I'm surprised to see Holland join Cortane and Finn as they leap off Nix's island to fan out around us.

River drags Nix off the side, sweat still pouring down the edges of Nix's now pale face. A spike of alarm sends me scrambling after them, running through the small clearing to grab Nix's soaking face in my hands.

'Nix?' I ask, turning his head and aware of how frantic my voice sounds. But his eyes remain closed, his arms hanging limply. He used so much magic ...

I didn't do all of this, didn't risk Blossom, him, just for him to—

'Nix!'

A low grunt is all I get in response, and I look madly at River.

'He's just about drained,' he says, voice tight, 'I need to heal the burns he'll have internally. Blossom's setting me up a spot.'

I suppress a whimper. 'River—'

'I've got it, but'—he narrows his eyes at me—'we need to have a talk, you and me, once I'm done.' He says it in the same tone he used to scold me when Nix and I had done something stupid. Or dangerous ... like diving—

'You can practice your response on them,' he says with a subtle jerk of his head over my shoulder.

Cortane's scoff sounds from behind me and my chest tightens. I watch River walk away before I turn to face Cortane.

Only to find Quillian staring at me like he's holding back a tide.

And losing.

His face is dark, his green eyes even darker, as if his own personal shadow has descended. I don't know what's worse – that look from him, or the almost unhinged smile on Cortane's face where she stands a step behind him.

'Everyone accounted for?' I ask, knowing they already are. I counted them myself. I do another quick glance to make sure they are all getting to their feet or being assisted in one way or another.

'Yes. Thanks to you,' Cortane says, her voice dripping with distaste, 'we now have an entire island of strays to manage. Loose fucking ends to take care of.'

My heart climbs into my throat. How can she possibly still see any of us as 'loose ends' after what we went through to get here?

'We'll work it out,' Quillian says tightly, still staring at me a little uncomprehendingly. 'Right now, we need to get out of here—make sure we weren't followed, that our landing hasn't drawn the attention of every military surveillance Nuntainia has in the area. Cort,' he says, turning his attention to her. 'Can you get us to camp?'

She swallows, seeming to grow paler even as I look at her.

'All of us?' There is more vulnerability in her voice than I'd imagined she was capable of, and a sting whips at my chest.

I glance around the ragged looking group. The original traitors – Quillian, Cortane, Finn, Nix, and River – are now joined by the concierges I brought with me, Janly, Emeris, Koko, Shiloh, and Blossom. Not to mention the Hunters, Holland and Casey.

Our numbers have more than doubled.

Quillian's expression starts to splinter a little before his mask returns – for his benefit or hers, I don't know. 'Yes, Cort. River will be on standby for when we get there. I just need you to get us there, okay?'

She nods slowly without saying a word. As if she won't make him promises she can't keep and my stomach hollows. How much harder have I made it for Cortane to get her loved ones to safety in her weakened state because I was too focused on my own priorities? Did I just risk that jump, save my friends, only to be found because I didn't understand how it would work from here?

To my right, Emeris and Janly whisper urgently, gathering the others together. Holland and his offsider are among them. I find Finn off to the side, watching both the group and the edges of the clearing. He nods once at Quillian.

'We need to go,' Quillian says, gaze still on Finn.

CHAPTER TWO

Cortane whistles softly and everyone turns towards her as if this is something that happens every day. Quietly, River and Finn gather everyone and herd them towards her, Nix staggering a little behind. There's something unnerving about how the traitors move together.

'Split into two main groups,' Quillian instructs, a little unnecessarily, from where he still stands beside me, elbow touching my arm.

There already appears to be two distinct groups, concierges and traitors, with the Hunters falling somewhere in between – though I don't miss how they watch everything. I don't understand how Finn fits into all of this yet, but given how seamlessly he blends in, there is no doubt he's an integral part of the team.

'Finn and River,' Quillian continues, 'stay back with the second group. You'll take Janly, Blossom, Emeris, Shiloh and Koko.' He turns to the Hunters without breaking contact with me. 'Holland and Casey, you're with me.'

I start a little as he says the second man's name and catch his gaze. I didn't know his name until now and it feels more real, somehow, that he drove his sword into Zenaton's ribs. That he killed for me. I muster a small smile, unsure what else to do. The moment stretches between us until he gives me a shallow nod, then we both return our attention to Quillian. He didn't say my name in the groupings.

'You'll be with me, I assume,' Cortane mutters, her focus concentrated on the space in front of us.

Quillian gives her shoulder a squeeze and mutters something I can't hear.

'River,' he orders, and Finn takes over supporting Nix before River pushes to the front. Flicking his attention between Quillian and Cortane, he seems to immediately understand she's going to need him.

Cortane starts to gently wave her hand in the air before her, the movement mostly coming from her wrist as her fingers point straight up towards the blue sky. The space in front of her starts to shimmy gently, increasing in its intensity. Cortane stares at the space as if she can see straight through it, to where she's sending us. Something I know most Shaides do to anchor their portals to the right destination.

As it opens up into a rough oval shape, just a fraction above ground level, I can just make out what looks like a collection of smallish, white brick buildings.

'Luka,' Quillian says, his voice low and broad shoulders turned completely to me. 'Please don't do anything crazy in that portal. Just walk through and let me see you on the other side, okay?'

'Where are we going?'

He glances behind him to where everyone else is waiting. 'Further away from the city – across the border.'

Quillian waits for a response as my mind tries to catch up – for reassurance, maybe, that I will step through the portal and not disappear. He sighs gently and starts to turn away, but I grab his bicep, letting my fingers run over his muscles slightly. Feeling the difference in texture where they find his shirt and warm, bare skin.

'I'll be on the other side,' I say quietly.

He stands a little straighter and turns back without another word, trailing his arm through my hand until his fingers reluctantly leave mine.

'Move,' he says to Holland and Casey, and I watch the three of them step through.

It reminds me a little of waiting to be collected by Nix, and I glance at him now, the colour slowly returning to his cheeks. He's all business, despite his obvious weakness from getting us here alive, and it's impossible not to see him and River as the soldiers they are. Two brothers guarding our backs while we escape to this new place, wherever it might be. As we not only leave any sort of proximity to the life I once thought I was going back to, but Nuntainia altogether.

The gnawing in my tummy shifts, an unfamiliar kind of stirring that maybe I am right where I need to be – at least, I will be once I step through the portal.

I think I see Holland and Casey move away.

Blossom takes a deep breath before glancing between River and me and stepping through on her own, her concierge dress trailing behind her. Absently, I realise I have no idea what sort of clothes she'd choose for herself. Dresses and activewear were pretty much all we had on the prison island.

The portal swirls gently, its pale green oval edges wavering and the air around it making a soft scream.

Cortane trembles as the others all step through at last, the outlines of them blurring on the other side.

I step up to the portal.

Cortane blocks my path. Blocks me from Quillian and the people I love.

An urgent fluttering starts behind my ribs. Surely she's not going to stop me from getting past?

'Claudius might have thought you'd be good on our team,' she says, a waver in her voice. 'But we don't need a princess with a saviour complex getting in the way. We've worked too long, sacrificed too much. You cannot possibly understand all we've done to—'

I drag in a lungful of the cool breeze, my nostrils flaring with the force. The nickname rankles down my spine, along with the accusation that I haven't sacrificed enough to prove myself worthy.

'What, *exactly*, have I done so far to make you think I'm not fucking helpful, Cortane? When will I have hurt enough, seen enough, *done* enough to be here?' A small part of me wonders if it's wise to push this clearly lethal woman, particularly when she's struggling – and currently standing between me and people I love. But I can't help but think if she wanted to kill me, she would've already done it – or left me on the prison island to burn. I may have inadvertently lumped her with a few 'loose ends', but I saved her and her closest in the process.

Cortane's chest falls a little, as if she is purposefully trying to make herself soften – though it doesn't change the intensity in her stare.

'He has a responsibility,' she says. 'It's critical he's not distracted.'

It sounds like a question, so I nod slowly, unsure exactly what I'm agreeing to. Quillian's words and actions during the whole ... process of getting off the island tell me I'm a massive distraction.

And he wants it that way.

'Hurt him, and I will get to know you from the inside out. Understand?'

A sudden vision of Cortane slicing through my middle looms in my mind. I push it away, stomach swirling uneasily.

Without waiting for me to respond, she grips my arm and drags me almost through the portal, but she pauses just before we enter, yanking me to a stop. She fixes me with a cold stare.

'And it's not about not being – or doing – enough. This is a shit life in more ways than I will ever be able to explain. In the face of what you could have had, what I am told you wanted, will it be enough for you?'

She shoves me away from her and through the tear she's made in the world. I've barely drawn my next breath before Nix scoops me into a hug.

'You fucking did it,' he says into my hair. There's a levity to his voice I haven't heard in a long time, but when I press back to look at him, he's serious.

As I look at his sad face, the events of the last couple of weeks start to sink in. Especially the last few hours. I have broken us out of Nuntainia's infamous prison island. We may not be magically marked, but we will be wanted – hunted – all the same.

The faces of the people around me start to swim as I take them in. So many of them looking to me with something that feels a lot like a question in their eyes. Hunters among them.

'What now, Luka?' Emeris asks, stepping towards me, his gaze searching.

A surge of nausea grips me. I have no idea what happens now. No board to look to, no school administration to answer to. No Warden.

I glance at River, who takes less than a second to see my panic rising—

'Cort!' Finn exclaims as he rushes to her, her limp form crumpling to the ground in his arms.

I press my hands to my mouth as River and Finn grip her between them and race her off to some other location.

'We need to debrief.' Quillian addresses the group, even though I can tell a good portion of his attention is on Cortane. 'We'll move to the meeting hall, assess where we're up to, and allocate rooms so you can all get some rest. At that point, you will need to decide if you stay or go,' he says. 'I'll explain more once we're inside, but you need to start considering where your loyalties lie. Anyone who wants out of here will leave in the morning, but you don't get to come back.'

My stomach skitters as I watch Cortane, River, and Finn disappear into a nondescript building. As we're gently guided towards the meeting hall, I feel that herded sensation I noticed as Finn and River moved everyone towards the portal. Like they're making sure no one makes a break for it.

Once again, Holland and Casey are closely flanked by Quillian, Nix not far behind.

The dirt road we walk down feels like a back lane, only one side has buildings on it. The other opens out into a shaggy looking meadow of some kind, the grass coming to at least my waist. Curiously, I run my hand over the top of it. The fluffy white tops are soft against my palm, and it sounds like they sigh as I brush gently past.

The buildings are mostly whitewashed brick with worn, red tiled roofs. A colour I notice almost matches the road we walk on. As I imagine what this part of the world would have looked like from Claudius's office, I wonder if the colour of the roofs was purposely chosen to blend in.

No one talks as we walk towards the meeting room, nor as we turn a right-hand corner to what looks like the back of a weatherboard hall. The old, pale timber doors creak as Nix pulls them open and we file in. I expect to find a musty, dust-filled space. But the hall is light and bright, sunlight streaming in from the room-length, high windows on all sides. Filled with tables and chairs, it's spotlessly clean, even if the furniture is a little tired, and it feels like a space that's frequently used. If it had a massive window looking into the sky, and a glass board that I'm almost starting to miss, it feels like it could be used for similar purposes – gathering and organising.

This is a place decisions are made.

Quillian glances at me once, his green eyes filled with something I can't identify, before he strides to the front of the hall – much like he did in our concierge room. Standing at the front, feet planted slightly wider than his hips, he shows no sign of the fatigue running through me, making each thought and movement feel like I'm wading through treacle. He just radiates a sense of authority, of unwavering commitment to his cause, that makes the hair on my arms stand up.

'Hey,' Blossom says, bumping gently into my side. We haven't really spoken since we left the prison island, and I feel heavier for it. My inability to give Emeris direction also pulls at me. I led them all here, why shouldn't they expect me to have answers?

I also think of Akira and Zale, who are likely going out of their minds having not heard from me, and an urgency settles into my chest at the need to let them know I'm okay. But I have no idea what happened to my phone.

'What do you think about this?' I ask Blossom in a whisper as we watch Casey and Holland have their hands bound by Nix and hauled to their knees before Quillian.

'That we might have been playing with fire in the prison,' she says, 'and now we're standing in it.'

I blow out a breath, letting my lips puff out, not caring who sees my uncertainty.

'Have you changed your mind?' I ask, my heart rate picking up to a nervous rhythm.

'No.'

I can't help but look away from the Hunters at the certainty in her voice.

Quillian clears his throat, his dark t-shirt stretched tight across his chest.

'This is it,' he says, surveying our small group. 'If you want out, say so now. We will help get you safely back to your families. Set you up with a new life as best we can. To be clear, though, I won't be able to control what happens to you afterwards. If you're found, or if your new identity is called for duty or not. But we will be monitoring you and any hint – *any* – that you have breathed a word about those who stay, we will come for you.'

He doesn't look at me, but a shiver runs down my spine nonetheless.

'I'—Koko tentatively raises her hand—'I have a grandson. Please. I want to go to him. I swear—'

'You're free to go,' Quillian says softly. 'Thank you, Koko.'

'Sleep here the night,' River says, barely looking over his shoulder at her. 'We'll help you get set up when we're all a little less shaken.'

'Come with me,' Janly says, and I start. 'Assuming you don't mind.' She pauses, looking at Quillian. 'I have been here with Claudius before.'

Quillian inclines his head and my mouth drops open as Janly leads Koko from the hall as confidently as if this was just another day on duty.

'What the fuck?' I breathe. 'I mean, I knew she and Claudius ... but how ...'

'No idea,' Blossom mutters.

'Anyone else?' Quillian asks, and I think he's purposefully avoiding my gaze.

Nix turns completely away from the Hunters and stares at me, his champagne-coloured eyes wide and expecting. Encouraging, even.

I shake my head at him and those beautiful eyes shutter.

'Give me a minute,' he grumbles to Quillian before stalking to me. 'Lu, please. There's nothing ... safe here.'

'Are you staying?' I ask.

'Of course,' he says without hesitation.

'Then you can be damned if you think I'm leaving. This conversation is getting old, Nix. Claudius thought I could be helpful for whatever this is, and I have been so far, haven't I?' I hope the question sounds confident and not conveying the slightly desperate need for confirmation I can feel skimming under my skin. 'I have seen too much to go back to living ignorantly. Not to mention three of my best friends in the world are here, and ...' I stumble, completely unsure how to refer to Quillian.

'Lu—'

'You're here, I'm here. Get used to it.'

My skin prickles all over, and it takes much more strength than I'd like to not look at Quillian to see how much of that he heard. I fail, glancing up at him anyway.

Quillian looks at me for a beat, hands clasped behind his back, before continuing. 'For those that remain, you are now shifting to the other side of Nuntainian law. We have been cast as rebels, traitors.' He pauses, looking around at those of us left. 'A role we fulfil proudly, as we endeavour to shine a light on the injustice and inequity that is the lifeblood of our current system. We traitors have proved, often with our blood, or our lives, that we will do anything to seek truth, equity, and fairness. We welcome those who are aligned with our purpose to lift up those that need it. Those committed to bettering our world for everyone in it – not just those who can manipulate it.'

I hold my breath as Quillian looks out at the people in front of him before, finally, his gaze lands on me. The fire in his face makes my heart pound, and there's a slow moment in the hall where it feels like the whole world, not just Quillian, is waiting for my response. It's Claudius's face that comes back to me, to spur me on. How he looked when he asked if I would be happy to keep working with him. Perhaps this isn't what Claudius first intended – Cortane did say we're on a different path, too. But I know this is what I'm supposed to do.

Where I am supposed to be.

'Tell us how it works,' I say.

CHAPTER THREE

The doors behind us open, cutting across the quiet that's fallen over the room, and everyone's attention turns to Finn as he enters the hall.

His face is impassive as he strides to the front of the room, like it almost always is.

I wait for news of Cortane, but he only nods at Quillian and takes up position next to him. I think that's all the confirmation we'll get of her health in this room.

'Finn will take you through the high-level details,' Quillian says, hands still clasped behind his back. 'But we operate on security clearances not dissimilar to what you'd find in most enforcement or military organisations. You're the entry-level intake, and you'll be treated as such.'

I blink. I don't know exactly what I expected but *entry-level—*

'Luka, a word?' He gestures off to the side, his face unreadable. Every inch the formal commander.

'I'll fill you in,' Blossom whispers, as I walk to the edge of the small group and follow Quillian outside.

'Welcome to camp one,' Finn says behind us, his voice fading away as I focus on Quillian's broad back, and the dirty, black t-shirt he still wears. The walk out feels heavier somehow, the almost-forgotten throb in my thigh now a constant beat in the background that's draining my energy along with the dissipating adrenaline of the fall.

But 'camp one' is interesting. I wonder how many others there are.

The sun is stretching across the sky when we reach the open field behind the building, a space of land that seems to curl around this small township, when Quillian turns to face me.

He clears his throat. 'I assume you have an explanation for *diving* off a perfectly safe island?'

I stare at him as the moments since we left Zanteera Island clearly catch up with him. With me too. His shoulders are still taut, like the stress of the last few days, and watching those under his command push themselves to the brink, is finally starting to expand within him.

I'm not quite sure how to explain the rush of certainty that came over me. That the throbbing in my leg, from the broken glass of that framed picture, was a beat telling me there was only one way for the wards to come down. A beat that throbbed in time with a heron's wings as they moved freely through the wards.

I wince as I shift my weight. There's a cool breeze that runs along the ground here, stirring the bottom of my ruined dress. I'm suddenly desperate to get it off, it's seen too much.

A swooping sensation fills my chest as Quillian and I watch each other, as he waits for me to respond.

He came for me. After I fulfilled Claudius's wish – escape the island, and take Cortane with me. Quillian carried me—*flew* me back to safety. Then brought me ...

A slow smile grows on my face and I step into him, but the tension doesn't leave him.

'I dove off that island,' I say, unable to keep the triumph from my voice now I know Cortane will be okay, 'to prove the colour of my soul.' My skin breaks out in little bumps as I say the words out loud. 'I did it because there wasn't a single person on that little island I was prepared to have marked by the wards – we will be hunted anyway, we did not need to make it easier for them. I did it because ... I could. And I'd do it again.'

Quillian curses as he drops his forehead to mine on an exhale, his soft breath brushing across my face.

'You came for me,' I whisper against his mouth, unable to keep the words just in my head anymore.

'Of course I fucking came for you,' he says. 'And I'd do it again.'

I smile against his lips and take a kiss I didn't realise I needed so badly. One that's claiming and full of possibility. One that makes me feel so alive, my skin burns.

He pulls back as I slide my fingers into his hair and I stifle a protest, but there's obviously more he needs to say.

'Finn is giving our standard induction in there'—he jerks his thumb over his shoulder—'but I want you to have mine.'

Quillian threads our fingers together as he leads me through a square and into a small townhouse that doesn't appear to be inhabited. I don't see a single person on the way, and an eerie sense of being watched follows me.

'This,' he says, opening the dark, worn front door, 'is our second command room. We mostly keep it just in case the other is compromised in some way.'

The room just looks like a virtually empty home office – until Quillian lifts the pale-blue rug. Opening a hatch in the timber floor, he removes a large, heavy-looking black box and pulls out a computer. Setting it up on the long, plain white bench that serves as a desk, he drags the two chairs together and gestures for me to sit down.

'What I'm about to show you,' he says, turning the chairs so we're facing each other, our knees touching, 'isn't pretty. It's not censored, and there are parts that are graphic.' My stomach falls over itself. 'I will keep it to just the bit that will give you enough of a … flavour for what's led us here.'

'Okay,' I breathe, not sure how to prepare myself for whatever I'm about to see. 'Why is this not in Finn's version of the induction?'

Quillian swallows. 'Because you're not everyone. I know you feel like you've had a lot of choices taken away from you and – while I know you have chosen to be here with us – the truth is, having Nix and River already on this side must have influenced your decision. You told me you wanted to know where home is, and I don't want our involvement'—he reaches out and tucks some of my hair behind my ear—'to have any bearing on what you do after today. Because there is no "home" here, Luka.'

I frown. 'I've already chosen to stay.'

'You have, but I will give you as many outs as you need—Cortane knows we will have a big problem if she touches you.'

A gentle ebb of relief works its way through my limbs. I didn't really think she'd hurt me after everything on the island, but knowing Cortane's inner workings is not something I can lay claim to.

'I want you to see both why I'm here, and what that sometimes means. So you can decide if this is really what's right for you. Okay?'

My heart swells with the choices this man is making sure I have. I am resolute, but it's clearly important to him that I see whatever is on the computer currently powering up. So I turn fully towards it and watch what looks like a small village load onto the screen.

Or what was a village.

Most of the buildings are burning, with screaming people running everywhere. Some of them drag other people with them, some are collapsed on the ground over others who are clearly dead. The camera bobs slightly through the village as if it's attached to someone. I hear them swear as they open a door. More bodies than I can count fill the screen. The camera turns away again.

Quillian freezes the image. I remain staring at the screen, trying to absorb the scale of death and destruction.

'That's quite typical of what we find after a village in Tae has been raided, especially if they hear of rebel activity and want to send a message.'

I nod numbly, tears burning my eyes as words fail me.

Quillian's chest expands in my peripheral vision, as if he's bracing himself. 'And this is what happens when we arrive during the act.'

He shifts forward a fraction and presses the bottom corner of the screen, skipping the footage forward. It's immediately filled with a row of six soldiers. All on their knees, hands bound – some with what looks like cord, others with green vines like the prisoners would arrive with on the island. Binds perhaps Nix has put there. Most of the soldiers stare resolutely ahead. Defiant. One has his head bowed towards the ground.

A flash of wings comes into the left of the screen, blades out and bloody. Quillian pauses the footage someone has obviously captured as they, too, stand and watch.

'What happened to them?' I whisper.

'They were executed.'

His bluntness is jarring. But I'm not naive enough to think we are still in the world of mysterious, undercover conversations like we were on the island. Not anymore.

'Who took this footage?' I ask thickly.

'We did,' he says. 'As a reminder of the reasons. And the costs.' He sits back in his chair, elbows finding the arm rests as he laces his fingers together loosely. 'It's the only one we have. In a way, it's stupid to have such direct evidence of our crimes – particularly when it could be so easily used in isolation to take us all out. At the same time, I can't move past thinking it's important we remember. None of us like this part of it. We try to take targeted actions to move our agenda forward where possible, rather than resort to broad-brush, indiscriminate violence.'

I think about the prisoners who died on the island, about their careers.

'They were all connected,' I say. 'The deaths on the island. More than the fact they'd each committed awful crimes. They were part of your bigger picture.'

Quillian stays quiet for a moment, as if he's remembering whatever it was that led them there.

'Yeah,' he says. 'They were all on Nuntainia's Defence Committee – the group responsible for overseeing both the strategic and operational arms of the country's defence. The people who order raids like this one.'

I knew at least Nix and River served in the Nuntainian military and were asked – ordered – to do things they couldn't abide by. But, seeing it like this, the images of the dead, dying and burning seared on my mind creates an unsettled churn in my belly. If this was 'typical' of what they'd find, what happened after Nuntainia raided ... how many times were they the ones doing the raiding before they reached their limit? What ask was it that finally tipped them all over the line into being traitors? Just how extensive is the damage that's done to them in the meantime?

'So were those deaths on the island revenge or strategy?' I ask, and Quillian gives me a long look.

'Both. As well as a test, I suppose. To see if it would create any ripples. Any change.'

Silence settles over us and I wonder if Quillian is thinking the same as me. How will we know enough has changed, if anything?

'What was the committee's goal with these attacks?' I turn back to Quillian, feeling like someone else is speaking as my mind still whirls through what we're discussing. What I've seen.

His jaw flexes beneath his slightly gaunt cheeks, the tiredness in his face clear, as he slowly lifts his gaze to mine.

'To take the women and destroy as many of the men as they could. At least those that refused to bend and be sent to the Coprath front under Nuntainian orders. Tae is renowned for its strong Karaylia lines—some women were taken for those reasons, others to supplement the sex trade. And the so-called "defecting" men ... Well, I guess they were destroyed to stop how many could rise up, like we have.'

The world seems to tilt underneath me. All the emotions I felt when Davorous looked at Blossom flood to the surface. Finding her on the floor, Nix ordering me to get River to heal her. How Aiten Gall was selling people from Tae for sex. Freya's fear when she fled the playroom. How it felt to have Zenaton almost stop me from getting off the island.

The back of my throat burns.

There is nothing in me that is surprised that the men here, in this group, had to walk away from that. Turned to taking the lives of the people who ordered those actions and tried to stop them, even when that meant more death.

'Quillian,' I say quietly. 'I can't know all of this and *not* stay here.'

He sits forward abruptly, and runs a hand through his hair before leaning towards me, twisting the chair a little and dropping his elbows to his knees.

'You could have died on that island, Luka. You went—you went *back* and ... I could have lost you.' His voice is strained; it pulls painfully at my chest. 'There is so much I have to compartmentalise to get through each day, but you— I can't box you up, Luka, you're ... everywhere.'

I cup the side of his face, running my thumb over his high cheekbone and taking in the deep furrow between his brows.

'So don't,' I breathe. 'Let me be everywhere. And I will be *here,* with you, doing whatever I can to help stop them.'

He closes his eyes for a moment, then nods.

'I'm going to stop them,' he says. 'Whatever it takes.'

I press my forehead to his and kiss his nose.

'*We're* going to stop them. So you better tell me your plan.'

Quillian sits back again slowly, a weary sort of focus settling in his features as he pulls his broad shoulders back a little.

'The immediate need,' he starts, 'is to recalibrate this camp and then the others. We've been away for some time, some of us more than others, and I have had to be careful not to be inadvertently exposed. So, particularly Finn, Cort, and I need to spend some time with the teams here—ideally Nix and River, too. Then, we will get everybody set up here for the evening and reassess what our next steps are. But as for the *actual* plan, in terms of how we stop the Nuntainian Government taking extreme advantage, that will need some ... tidying.' He rubs the back of his neck. 'We've managed to take out key members of the Defence Committee so far but, without our contact—you—in Parliament House, finding the creator of the prison program and verifying different things we're hearing will be harder. None of those that were taken out on the island knew, or at least weren't prepared to give up, anything we could use for either issue. That means we need to find the remaining members of that committee and get one of them to talk.'

I turn it over in my mind. The people on the Defence Committee will be easy to identify - all that information will be publicly available. The creator of the program, though, that will be much harder. Given the secrecy surrounding the island, if any records exist at all, they will be buried somewhere impossible to get to.

Quillian's expression is hard when I look at him, not unlike the mask he would wear on the island. 'I want every member to pay for the decisions they've made, to bring the person who brought the prison program into reality to justice, and hope that's enough for the Nuntainian government to finally put an end to its corruption. The people who decided, and *continue* to decide on its usage, cannot hide behind the fact it wasn't their brain child.'

'What if you don't find who started it?'

He shakes his head a little. 'I'm not sure I can live with that. I can't risk that the thought-leader behind this can be left to germinate something else. And ... I want them to know what their policy has enabled—has kept hidden away behind gilded prison walls.'

I look back at the screen, as if I can see all the death still playing out on it. Like I can see the women being dragged away and their fathers, brothers, husbands, and sons being murdered.

'And the other things you're hearing?' I ask.

A darkness settles in the space under his eyes. 'The Karaylia breeding program.'

My stomach falls away, a hollowing taking its place.

'I thought we'd succeeded in ending it—we took out all the sites. Or thought we did. Now, I'm not sure. And the number of women and girls Aiten Gall is reported to have coordinated the abduction of from Tae, doesn't match those that have appeared in brothels or in private service. Not that we've found.'

Quillian's phone buzzes where he's left it on the desk, and he scans it quickly.

'I'm needed in the meeting hall,' he says. 'They're going to start gathering the teams together—are you okay if I get Nix to take you to where you'll stay? Give me some time to get them all used to having us back, and you some time to rest up and recover?'

'Of course.' I give him a small smile, my mind already running through what I can remember of the Defence Committee and who we might be targeting next. How we will be able to get underneath the issue of the breeding program to know if it's started again and, if so, how to stop it.

Walking from the small room with Quillian I feel raw, like I've been flayed, stripped of any place to hide, and the reality of our conversation is infecting my exposed flesh.

At the same time, leaving the confined space and sucking in the open air, my chest pinches at the hopes and wants that were so much of my focus not so long ago. How can I even dare to hope to have any of those things with Quillian in the face of what he needs to do here? That there would be space in his commitment to this group and what they – we – are trying to achieve for anything else?

How can I dare to have any right to be a *distraction* from correcting these wrongs?

CHAPTER FOUR

Our rooms are almost like a run-down version of the prison we've just left, but instead of being contained in a single, huge building, they're assembled in uniform rows of small, adjoining units. The whole setup clearly forms the barracks of a base, but as I look over my shoulder and back at the street, it's much more like a small town. Perhaps that's part of the cover.

Much like a small town, I know there must be other people here, Quillian said as much. There's a lived-in – or maybe camped-in – feel to this place, a pulse of energy. Like they're waiting for something behind every building. Like those who are based here aren't ready to show themselves yet.

Or have been told not to.

I try not to notice how barren the landscape is compared to the island. How dry the heat is, that even the air doesn't feel as luxurious on each breath I draw as on the island.

'Are you happy to share?' Nix asks Emeris and Shiloh, who each nod gently, and I'm belatedly relieved I will still be with Blossom. 'I'll be over soon,' he says to me before taking Emeris and Shiloh next door.

River motions us up the short set of front steps. I follow Blossom through the front door that probably matched the white-washed brick at some point, but now it's worn and dirty; I wonder how many people have been in and out of these houses. Quillian said there is no 'home' here, and that's clear. These feel more like what I imagine safe-houses might be like. Trying, but lacking any sense of character—or permanency.

My legs feel heavy. The constant throb in my thigh is quickly sapping what remains of my energy as I walk down the narrow, short hallway with slightly yellow walls, past the open-plan kitchenette into the pale green living room, a floral couch on the far wall. Mentally, I do a quick head count and drown out the quiet conversation between River and Blossom as they bustle around the living space. Koko is leaving to give her family a new life, Janly escorting her somehow; Emeris and Shiloh are next door with Nix; River and Bloss are with me; and Quillian, Finn and Cortane are with the Hunters, Casey and Holland.

I wonder what Claudius would have made of this?

I think on the 'J' I found engraved on the back of his watch and wonder how many times Janly has been here before. He obviously had no qualms about having Blossom and me here, but would he have welcomed Emeris and Shiloh? The Hunters? People who aren't military but still under Nuntainian control, would they have been welcome if Claudius was here? I think on the line of soldiers in that footage, imagine Holland's face among them ...

'They saved me, Riv,' I blurt.

His brows quirk down before understanding pushes them back up, and he runs a hand over his dark-blond hair, remaining standing while Blossom moves to sit. He watches Blossom make herself comfortable on the blue-checked couch placed perpendicular to the floral one I sit on, creating an 'L' shape so we both face the centre of the room.

River, who is obviously trying to work out how to respond to me, stands in the middle of the room and looks back at us.

'We've had so much death,' I say quietly. 'I just—can we not start our time here with more? Not after what they did to help get me here.'

I don't know how to voice that I feel a connection with both Holland and Casey – like we've shared something very few people experience, and now I am as bound to them as I am to the others.

River eventually sinks into the couch next to me, his knees spreading wide as he places his forearms on his thighs, and I wince a little as he bumps my wound.

'That's not my call to make, Luka. I take orders, not make them—mostly.'

'But you can make suggestions, I assume?' Blossom asks, pink spots appearing on her cheeks. 'We've seen the way you and Nix interact with the others, you have more influence than just "taking orders". You're more like a round table of leadership.'

River sighs. 'Maybe. Although perhaps less than it seems to have appeared.'

I mull that over. While Quillian is clearly the leader – though I wonder if it's less 'leadership' than the devotion of his entire being – Cortane would only be fractionally behind, so close it's sometimes hard to tell who any final decisions rest with. But my thoughts keep snagging on Finn. Quiet, respectful, but also obviously *respected*, and I wonder where he fits in. He doesn't strike me as simply a 'follow orders' sort of man. And neither are River and Nix – even if they seem more willing to accept direction than the other three.

I rest my head on the back of the couch and close my eyes. 'How *does* the chain of command work, then?'

River shifts a bit next to me, settling in with a sigh before gently tugging the remains of my dress. 'Let me look at this.'

He pulls what used to be the hem of my dress all the way up to expose my thigh. I breathe hard through my nose. The gash in my flesh is smeared with dried, cakey blood, and an oozing, brighter red a little further down.

'Ouch,' Bloss says, sitting up tall and peering over so she can see.

'This is ... not the official version. So don't repeat it.' River says, clearly concentrating on my wound, gently pressing his fingers against my skin, and I sigh at the instant relief his Arkanan abilities bring. 'Cortane is supposed to be in charge here, at least outwardly. She's the intelligence lead and the teams report directly to her ... but Quillian has more sway than they'd have the other factions believe at times. He's the quiet leader in the back, the one really running this operation, but we keep the truth quiet.'

That setup isn't so different to what I thought. 'I suppose having Quillian openly leading would have jeopardised his position in the Nuntainian military and his attempts at infiltrating the government?' River nods.

'Where does Finn fit in?'

'Finn is second in command – to both of them, really – but you'll almost never find him anywhere Quillian isn't.' I open my eyes so I can try to focus better, and examine the white ceiling as he continues. 'The units Nix and I led before we went to the prison have been consumed by this group. There are different factions all over, so we're not in a single concentrated area.'

'And you, officially, report to Cortane too?' I ask, trying to visualise how they come together like a flowchart I could map on the glass board I used so much on the island.

'Yep,' he says, leaning forward to inspect my leg. 'We're like ... tier two or three of the command. We do a lot of direct contact with the other camps.'

'So ... we're part of a network?' Blossom asks.

I turn my head to River as he nods. 'With this being the lead faction, yes.'

'And this dinner they're all attending, will it be okay?' I ask.

'Yes. Nix and I will be there too. It's a combination of things—a celebration of our return, a reminder of who is in charge and what we're fighting for, and a moment for Cortane to get a feel for what's been happening while we've been away and establish the next steps.'

'And we'd be a distraction?' Blossom asks.

Distraction. The same word Cortane used to describe me before we stepped through the portal.

'Essentially, yes,' he confirms. 'But it's more for the others, not because of you. They deserve to know they still have our appreciation for all they're giving for our cause, without feeling like they're old news. I'm sure Quillian or Cortane will be telling them we've acquired new members and to look out for you, the same as they do when any new person or people arrive.'

'Are they old news?' she asks.

'Definitely not—every single person in this network is valued. It's partly our job to make sure they know that. We need as many people as we can get to not only infiltrate and report on the Nuntainian government, but to take action against it.'

'So Casey and Holland could actually become assets?' I ask, remembering the unsettled look on Holland's face when he mentioned his time at Vana.

River's shoulders tense a little as he glances at Blossom.

'If they can assure the deadly trio they have no ill intent towards any of us *and* that they will fight for what's right, then ... maybe.'

I don't have to ask who the 'deadly trio' are, but I wonder if it would be more appropriate to include River and Nix in that too. A deadly ... quintet?

Abruptly, River sits forward and stands.

'Right, if I sit any longer, I won't want to keep moving. Someone will bring you dinner and clothing while we're out. You're obviously not prisoners here, but I'd really appreciate it if you stayed put until tomorrow morning so our teams know we have new members before they see you wandering about. I don't want either of you to be mistaken for a threat. Tomorrow they'll all know, and you'll be fine.'

Slowly, Blossom stands.

'I'll ... walk you out,' she says without looking at him.

I can't help but strain my ears to hear what they talk about on the way to the front door, but all I can make out is Nix meeting them there and the three of their voices murmuring quietly. Even if I wanted to go out and see what else is here, I don't think I have the energy to get back down even those few steps.

Regardless, given the importance Claudius put on me being here – or getting off that island, at least – I don't intend to compromise that on my first night.

'Do *not* move from here,' Nix calls at me from the front door, 'until I come for you in the morning.'

I'm mock saluting him, hiding my grimace, as Blossom comes back into the room. She smiles, taking a seat next to me and resting her head on my shoulder.

Something softens in me a little as her weight settles against my side. I feel like everything since we took that dive has been a whirlwind, with no moment to properly connect with her. My stomach lurches as my body recalls the sensation of freefalling through the sky, my heart thudding at what Blossom was prepared to do with me.

'Why did you decide to jump, too?' I ask, staring into the foreign living space around us.

I can feel the pressure of her chest on my arm as it rises and falls.

'Where you go, I go, you know that.'

'But—'

'Luka, you're my best friend. I could see your plan written all over your face. You know I was in this before we jumped—I just gave us all another shot.'

'Meaning?'

'What if your magic is starting to come in and we don't know? What if mine is? Having us both go through doubled our chances of having someone without magic bringing down the wards.'

I let the truth in what she's said wash over me. And the questions about our magic that it highlights – something neither of us have really had room to consider since before we stopped taking the tipples. But she's right – we were able to get through unmarked, which means no magic. Statistically, we should both manifest within a few months – less – given how long we've now been off the suppressants. But when I search for *anything* that might give me a clue that I'm changing, I just get ... silence.

'If you could choose,' I ask, 'what would you pick?'

'Not fucking Karaylia, that's for sure. I am never doing that again.'

We laugh together and a little more lightness sneaks into my chest. But it's dragged back by the knowledge of the breeding program.

'No,' I whisper, unable to voice what I have learned in this quiet moment with Bloss. It's a practice I don't know how to reconcile yet, and doubt I ever will.

'Really, though,' she says, her soft laughter falling away. 'I don't mind. I just want to do good with it.'

I make a sound of agreement, but I'm too tired to think about what my answer would be. We sit like that for a few moments and I think I might almost be on the verge of sleep when Blossom draws a deep breath, as if she's preparing herself for something.

'There was another reason,' she whispers, 'for the jump.'

I fumble for her hand and squeeze her fingers when I find it, in a way I hope conveys that she can tell me anything.

'I knew he would come.'

Her words are barely audible, but I know she's not talking about Quillian. I pull her arm across my body so I can hold her hand in both of mine, thinking of all the ways River has been there for Nix and me, how clearly he has added Blossom to that list.

'As long as he's drawing breath, he'll come, Bloss.'

Her next inhale is wobbly, as if she's about to sob, but it doesn't come. 'But if you think this means I will forgive you for making him restrain me while you burnt the fucking prison down, you are sorely mistaken. You're just lucky I'm choosing to ignore it this very second.'

I can't help but smile, even though she can't see it. 'I'd apologise, but it would be a lie.'

'I know.'

Eventually, she settles into sleep. I rest my head on hers where it still lies on my shoulder, and wait for clean clothes.

A knock at the door startles me and I jerk myself up to seated, Blossom falling a little sideways on the couch. Gently, I guide her to lay down, covering her with a crocheted blanket and rubbing my eyes before I head down the narrow, darkened, hallway. The large, round door knob fills my palm as my heart pounds a little harder. We should be safe here, right? Was I wrong about the wards? Were we marked? Have the Hunters found us? Worse, have Holland and Casey given up the location of the camp somehow?

The thumping in my chest kicks up a notch as the door opens all the way to reveal Quillian and Finn, Finn a step behind.

'You're here,' Quillian says, more than a hint of surprise in his voice.

My eyebrows shoot up. 'Is there somewhere else I should be?'

He searches my face. 'Given I'm quite confident you are much smarter than me ... yes.' Mischief sparkles where his gaze locks on mine.

'Well,' I say, 'they rarely choose rebel wardens for their smarts, so I hear.'

The corner of Finn's mouth picks up as he turns to Quillian.

'You'll be staying here?' he asks.

'I'd suggest that's up to Luka,' Quillian says quietly, a richness to his tone that sends a shiver down my spine.

His gaze, the dark green colour of which I can only just make out in the dark, starlit sky, is wholly consuming and I force myself to remember Finn is still standing here.

'He'll be safe here until morning,' I tell Finn as I step to the side of the door, gesturing for Quillian to enter. 'Do you want to come in, too?' I ask, suddenly conscious of my manners. 'I'm not sure what I can offer you food or drink wise but ... I'm sure there's something in here.'

Finn crouches and picks up two large bags that were tucked to the side of the porch.

'Thank you, but no,' he says in that gentle voice of his. 'There will be food and clothes in here, we'll get you organised with more in the morning. In the meantime,'—he turns to Quillian, any trace of a smile dropping—'you don't leave here until I'm back in the morning.' The tiniest trace of a smirk brushes his features, as if he's saying 'don't mess it up and have an awkward night'.

'Apparently I'm not the only one with a keeper,' I say.

'Nix, River, or both?' Quillian asks.

'Well, both probably. But only Nix's instructions sound like yours.' I nod in Finn's direction.

'Goodnight,' Finn says, but remains standing on the porch.

Quillian steps forward. 'Night,' he says, closing the door on Finn and locking it before we listen to him jog lightly down the stairs.

The inky hallway contracts around me as we stand here, looking at each other.

'Lu?' Blossom calls from the couch.

I clear my throat. 'Coming. We've got supplies.'

Quillian wraps a hand around my side and I shiver as he pulls me into him.

'Luka,' he whispers into my hair, 'just—just give me a moment.' There's a rawness to him in this darkness that I can only answer by winding my arms around his waist and pressing myself against his chest, as if we could become one.

He exhales heavily, threading the fingers of one hand into my messy hair and holding me tight around my back with the other. We stand like that for long moments, our breath rising and falling in time—I will stay as long as he needs me to.

Finally, some of the force goes out of his hold and he pulls back a little, dropping his forehead to mine.

'No more diving, okay?' he asks in a whisper.

I might not have thought about it before the jump like Blossom, but I, too, have no doubt Quillian would come for me again. Though I hope whatever comes from here definitely doesn't require such a – potentially – monumental sacrifice.

'No more diving ... unless you're there,' I say, pressing my head a little harder against his to emphasise my point, before leaving him to bring the bags so Blossom and I can finally eat and change.

CHAPTER FIVE

'I'm going to sleep,' Blossom says, her eyes barely open as she pushes herself to standing. 'What time do we need to be—'

'Oh, crap,' I say, my hand flying to the empty pocket in these new-to-me tracksuit pants. 'My phone ...'

The one I would normally set my alarm on. The one I would contact Zale and Akira on. The one I have only just noticed is gone, and suddenly I feel so cut off from them.

'We'll organise you another one,' Quillian says from next to me on the couch, pulling his phone from his pocket and handing it to me. 'Do you want to ask Nix to contact them? It would be best they don't have my details.'

Cortane's copious warnings sound in my ears as I gently take the slightly worn, warm, black device from his hand and watch Blossom disappear down the short hallway that runs away from the front door and up the stairs. Looking down at the sleek screen, I feel ... a little awed at the intimacy of using his phone -- is that weird?

Opening the messaging function, I find Nix's name and their history is much as I would expect. There are only three or four messages, mostly coming from Nix, but they all say the same thing: *done.*

Hey, it's me, Luka. I've lost my phone, can you message Z and A and let them know I'm okay? Check on them for me?

The phone lights up in my hand before I even look away.

Nix K: This is ... new. I've already been in touch. They're fine. Z is trying to keep Teddy focused on her upcoming duty, not her 'other' interests. A is planning a get-together I've told her we can't promise to be at. Pretty sure it's a cover for her worry but they'll be fine, Lu.

Thank you, see you in the morning.

I hand the phone back to Quillian. My heart sinks a little at the thought of Akira and whatever she is planning. Will I be able to do those things now that I've committed to being here? I have no idea what Teddy's 'interests' are, but—

Actually, I do recall Zale saying she wanted to join a vigilante group at one point. Something I hope she didn't do, for Zale's sake. I clear my throat, unable to work out how to feel about that one way or another. On one hand, being part of something that sounds so dangerous was never on my agenda. But it doesn't feel like that. On the other, there is something sort of liberating about living what some would see as a dream – and realising it might be mine, too.

It's empowering to know I have been part of making some of those horrible people on the island pay for their crimes. What sort of person does that make me, if not a vigilante? And shouldn't I want others to join us? Not wanting Teddy to 'run away' with us, makes me as bad as Nix and all his protesting about my involvement.

'All good?' Quillian asks.

'I think so.' I shift a little lower on the couch, resting my head on his shoulder. 'Just ... processing.'

Quillian shifts beneath me so he can toy with the ends of my hair.

'Me too,' he says gently, and a little tremor of nerves snakes down my spine. 'I'd never considered I'd have ... someone like you here and I–I hope it's not something you come to regret.'

I turn further into him so I can look up into his eyes, lifting my fingers to feel the stubble on his chin. '"Like me" how?'

'Not a soldier.'

I nod. 'Yeah,' I breathe. 'That feels like it would be a useful skillset to have here.'

'You have no idea. I worry about the soldiers, don't misunderstand me, but ... having civilians—having you—I don't ...'

My heart clenches and I twist completely into his body, raising myself to sit astride him.

'I'll be okay,' I say against his mouth. 'We're all going to be okay.'

I hope I'm not lying.

Quillian makes a fist in my hair that's still slightly damp from the shower, pulling my head back a little and arching my back. 'I'm going to hold you to that.'

The tension on my scalp sparks a fire, and heat spreads the length of my body, all the way to my toes. 'Do you want to hold me to anything else first?'

A wicked grin kicks up on his face, pressing his dimple back into existence.

'Always,' he says, before kissing me.

Quillian's tongue gently swipes the seal of my mouth, as if asking me for permission, and I open gladly, sucking his bottom lip between my teeth until he groans. Dragging his lip from my mouth, he drops his head to the soft juncture of my neck.

'I'm going to taste every piece of you before tomorrow comes,' he says into my skin, his breath hot.

My inhale catches, my cheeks heating. 'Then why are we still sitting here?'

He chuckles as he stands, pulling me with him and tucking me tight against the front of his body. He walks me to the stairs, where I squeal when he carries me up them and into the only bedroom with an open door. I bounce a little as he sits me on the bed. The way he stands over me, blocking the light from the single bulb in the ceiling, sends a race of flutters under my skin.

'Where shall I start?' he asks, bending to take one of my feet in his hands and bracing it against his chest.

'Here,' I say, shuffling up the bed and patting the space next to me. 'But not with that get up on.' I gesture to his clothes.

Quillian's gaze is focused so intently on me, I think I might combust on the spot. Slowly, he takes his dark shirt over his head, exposing his rich, medium-brown skin that explodes in colour across his ribs, the tattoo that dances across his scars racing around the back of his shoulder and up his neck. I stare at him as the shirt falls softly to the rug and his hands go to the band on his black pants.

'Oh—' I make a strangled sound as they come off and it's *very* clear he's not wearing anything underneath.

I didn't think it was possible for his predatory grin to get wider, but it just about splits his face as he climbs onto the bed and positions us both under the heavy covers. Gripping his face in both hands, I take his mouth in a hungry kiss, all of my worry and desperation to be off that island making itself known in the suddenly frantic need to have him. I don't know what any of it really means yet – being here, being with Quillian, or me being a distraction – but the rush of being able to discover at least some of those things for myself is like wildfire in my veins. For every touch Quillian gives me, every time his tongue moves on mine, that he drags his large hand across my skin, I only want it more – freedom, justice.

Him.

Quillian's need matches mine, and he presses the full length of his body against me, running a hand down my back, over my ass and thigh, and dragging my knee over his hip. Leaving me half splayed open to him, the length of his cock pushing against my entrance hard enough for me to whimper in anticipation.

'I want—' I whisper.

'Tell me.' His breath comes in short bursts between kisses.

'Everything. Consume me, Quillian. Please,' I beg.

Sliding his arm between us, he parts my folds and drives himself straight through my core. I call out, digging my nails into his shoulder.

'I will need more than one night to give you everything,' he whispers, holding us still for a beat. 'But however many nights you give me, I'm going to fucking try.'

Then he moves again, hard and commanding, one hand pressing down on my lower back to keep me close even as he pushes me into the mattress. My vision blurs and I have to drop my forehead to his shoulder, my hand falling away from his face and snaking around his back, the feeling he's building in my core so overwhelming, I think I'm starting to burn.

'Come for me, Luka,' he says, his deep voice rough with desire and running over my skin. He thrusts against me – once, twice more – and I sink my teeth into the firm expanse of his chest, coming so hard I scream into his skin. My whole body shudders and I curl my leg harder around his hip, pulling him deeper. I smile into his kiss when his own release finds him, swallowing his gasping breaths as he kicks inside me, body tense, until we're both languid, sinking into each other and the pillows around us.

'Time to get ready,' Blossom calls from the hall, and I groggily, reluctantly, open my eyes into Quillian's colourful ribs. Somehow, in the night I have squirmed myself under his arm and lie on the bed, eye level with the largest section of his tattoo.

I run my finger over it, over and around the scars, and watch the goose-bumps that appear on his skin.

'*For those that prove the colour of their soul*,' I whisper. It's a message that calls to me somehow, makes my chest feel tight and free at the same time. That purpose, and how steadily it beats in him, is something I want.

'Will I get one of these?' I ask by way of greeting.

Quillian rolls onto his side and looks down at me. 'The tattoos? Yes,' he says, kissing my nose. 'It's not just about confirming your alliance to what and who you fight for, but they're infused with magic the Nuntainian government can't track—it's come out of Coprath—that will allow your magical duty contracts to be overridden.'

It's like a light goes on in one of the shadowy parts of my mind. 'That's why Nix and River *could* actually tell me things when they finally got on board, sort of, with my involvement.'

'Yes,' he says. 'Anything they didn't share will genuinely have been to protect you. Are you ready for yours?'

I smile, even as my stomach turns over when I think about the vileness of those that died on the island. 'I'm ready, but I have no idea how to choose a design.'

The meeting hall is buzzing with activity when we arrive; Finn not far behind us. The group I came with fill the front of the space, but there is a large group of people taking wooden, folding seats that I've never seen before. Quillian gives my hand a single squeeze as he leans down towards me.

'Even if you change your mind, I'll be here at the end, okay?'

'Okay,' I say, smiling up at him. Just the sight of his dark green eyes, so full of faith in me, sends a warmth down the centre of my chest. 'But I'm not changing my mind.'

I watch Quillian make his way to Cortane, Finn still hot on his heels, and find Blossom.

'Ready for this?' she asks.

'Yep,' I say without hesitation. 'I think this is what we're meant to do.'

The thought of Casey and Holland pushes its way forward, and it's hard to swallow past the sudden thickness in my throat. Did River manage to keep them from being killed like I hoped he would?

Multiple voices weave around me as I survey the room with Blossom. It feels not unlike when we'd stand watch in one of the grandrooms in the prison, quietly observing and waiting to be needed. But there is a difference. Today, I think they're waiting for us. Still, there is part of me that's quite content to watch the interactions happening before me in the white brick room: River talking quietly with someone I don't know, his gaze subtly on Blossom and me; Quillian greeting most people he passes with far more warmth than he did the prisoners; and how the rest of the group – people I don't know – start to quiet and look to the front of the room expectantly.

Nix doesn't appear to be here, and a little ball of worry starts to gnaw in my gut. To my left, the large doors creak as they open and Janly, Emeris, and Shiloh spill through the gap. I wave at Emeris and subtly beckon them to join us.

'This is, by far, the most badass thing I've ever done,' Emeris says, grinning when he reaches Blossom and me.

Blossom smiles. 'Let's hope it won't be the last.'

'Shut it!' Cortane's voice echoes around the meeting hall as she comes through the same doors the former concierges just came through, dragging Casey and Holland behind her by the binds on their wrists.

I suck in a cool breath of relief, even as Cortane stares daggers at me.

Holland nods, seemingly at ease with his current predicament, which can't possibly be true. Casey's face shows nothing. Cortane shoves her prisoners towards the front of the room and they stumble against each other, coming to a stop on their knees before Quillian.

'Right,' she says, stepping around Holland and Casey, up beside Quillian. 'Hopefully, after last night, not only do you all now realise you can't leave here without serious consequences for you, your family and friends'—she looks at me as she says 'friends', and I stare back—'but you're also connected to the reason that you stayed. Your personal belief in what we're doing here—exposing the rot in the Nuntainian government.' She pauses a moment to look around at the small group of us newcomers. 'None of us can guarantee the road will be easy, and it is likely you will need to draw hard on that belief. But know this—we are not a collection of individuals striving for our personal revenge. You are joining an organised, structured movement in which you are expected to play a role, take decisions as they're made, and contribute to our goals as a whole. The difference between here and being a citizen of Nuntainia, or one of the peoples they look to destroy, is that you have a voice.'

Quillian looks steadily at me. I know Nix's personal reason, and as my heart aches for him, I wonder if that's why he's avoiding this today, too. For the first time, I also truly wonder what Quillian's personal motivation is.

'Today, you get to commit to us and the cause—justice and equality,' Cortane pauses and the room falls silent as she seems to look at every person individually, and they at her. As if she's silently getting her own commitment from them that they will stand behind what these markings will mean. What we will all now stand for. She's not as warm as Quillian, she does little to soften her usual hard lines even now. But there's still something almost magnetic about her being in front of us like this, and it's clear I'm not the only one who feels it.

The whole room watches her, waiting for her to look at them next, some nodding in response to her gaze. She draws a deep breath. 'Whatever you have heard before now'—she surveys the group once more, flicking a quick look at me—'even from me, we will not force you to be here. You will give up a lot and we don't have the time or the resources to hold your hands through that. So you need to know your own motivations are enough.'

I press my lips together at the echo of the warning she gave me and I wonder what hers, and Quillian's, lives would have been like outside of this. What they would have chosen instead.

'What you *will* get in return,' she continues, her voice thawing a tiny bit, 'is a family that will back you all the way.'

She tucks her hands behind her back and widens her stance. 'Leaving now will be ... tricky. But we don't want, or need, anyone we have to convince to be here—you will just be a liability.'

Nobody moves.

'This,'—she gestures around the room, but I get the sense she means something bigger—'is about fighting for what's right. Fighting for those who can't fight for themselves. But, above all, fighting for transparency.'

Holland glances at Casey, whose shoulders are slumped.

'It doesn't sound glorious,' Cortane continues, 'but it's the lack of transparency that has allowed so many awful events and heinous deeds to be swept under the rug by the Nuntainian government. Those of us here are committed to stopping that practice.' Her face falls, just a fraction, and I can't help but feel like I want to be closer to her. To hear what she has to say. There's a haunted quality to her features that's hard to shake. 'If the wrong person finds, or reads, your tattoo, it's a one-way ticket to Vana. I *promise* that is not somewhere you want to end up.' She swallows. 'And just to be *very* clear, if you end up behind those tortured walls, I cannot get you out. I barely got myself out, and coming back here almost killed me.' The image of her collapsing into the dirt when we arrived flashes in my mind. 'My magic is not yet strong enough to travel back there, and it may never be again.'

Finn moves to the side of the room and drags over a small table, the sound of its legs scraping on the floor filling the space, so at odds with the quiet he normally exudes. Cortane watches him until he stops next to her, pulls up a chair and takes out a large, needled device. Finn presses a button on the top and the whole thing starts to vibrate.

My insides shimmy as I think about Claudius's tattoo, and Quillian's, even if that's in a completely different way.

'Who's first?' Cortane asks.

Blossom steps away from me. 'I am.'

I reach out and grab her arm, twisting her back to look at me.

'Bloss,' I say, uncertainly. 'Are you sure? Sure this is for you?'

She draws a full, pained sounding breath. 'It's for me. And for Frank, who always wanted the best for everyone.' She gives me a sad smile. Frank. The man she married well before I knew her, but one I almost feel like I know.

'For Frank,' I say, pulling her into a tight, fast squeeze.

She takes the seat in front of Finn in silence. She gives River one quick glance before holding my gaze the entire time Finn etches the prettiest cursive text I've ever seen just under the length of her left collarbone.

Eventually, the room starting to fill with gentle whispers, Finn makes the final wipe across her skin with a now slightly bloody cloth and stretches his back out.

My chest swells with pride for Blossom, my fearless friend. Eagerly, I step forward, ready to take my turn. Ready to make a stand with those who want better than the people in that prison, and are willing to do something about it.

Emeris steps up at the same time I do and smiles at me, his perfect white teeth reminding me of the vest he used to wear on the island. We laugh at our eagerness to get our marks, and Emeris winks at me.

'You get the sexy Warden, I get the next tattoo.'

A flush of heat races across my cheeks and fills me with an immediate warmth at the thought of having Quillian – and I'm sure the smile on my face says exactly that. I roll my eyes at him, gesturing to the chair. 'After you. I'm happy to keep the Warden.'

He barks an even louder laugh and takes his seat.

But as I watch him, part of me wonders how much I can really 'have' Quillian while ever he is ... this.

The seat is warm where Emeris sat as I take my position, my chest sparking with the knowledge I am choosing this for myself.

'Where do you want it?' Finn asks.

My heart skips a little at this permanent decision I am making. I think it over for a moment, wanting to have something that's all me, not a mirror of Blossom or Quillian.

'My spine, between my shoulder blades,' I say, lifting my shirt and turning my back to him.

'That'll hurt a little—what did you have in mind?' Finn asks with a kind smile in his voice.

I spin so I'm sitting backwards on the chair and brace myself against the back, dimly aware of the sound of the doors opening again.

'I think I'd like the creed wrapped in jasmine,' I say over my shoulder. Jasmine, like the prison was covered in – a reminder that's where it started for me. That even pretty and fragrant things can be insidious.

'Sounds perfect,' he says quietly, his hand coming to rest on my back.

I can't help but smile into my arms where I rest my head. For the first time in a long time, I feel proud of myself, and not like I'm searching for that pride from someone else. I can just feel the vibration of the pen he holds through his skin before he brings the tip down—

'Wait—' Nix's voice rings out, and the strange sensation on my back ceases. 'I've got mail. For Luka.'

CHAPTER SIX

Cortane starts, but it's River that closes the gap between he and Nix in a few short strides.

'Show me,' he says to Nix, holding out his hand.

Slowly, Finn pulls away from me and I let my shirt drop back down as I sit up, twisting again to face them. The only person who has ever sent me letters is Nix, and that was only after my duty selection, when I was on the island. Akira and Zale message me, they don't ...

So who knows to send me mail on the mainland?

The gnawing in my tummy that started as I watched Blossom formally join the fold doubles in size – am I about to be denied that same privilege? Whatever that envelope entails, it made Nix stop me getting my traitor tattoo. That can't be good.

'River,' I say, drawing myself to stand. 'Give it to me.'

I'm vaguely aware of Quillian edging a little closer, but I don't acknowledge him. I can only focus on the letter.

River hands me a thick, cream envelope. One that looks and feels disturbingly similar to the one that arrived five years ago, called me to serve on the island. Something Nix obviously realised.

I let the weight of it sink into my fingers as I finally look up at Quillian, who is now right beside me.

'We're right here, Luka—I'm right here,' he murmurs. 'Let's see what it says.'

Wriggling my forefinger in the small gap at the top edge, I tear open the envelope, plucking out the letter. It's a single page, with one fold across the middle, and I stare at it for one moment before flipping it open.

Dear Luka,

The Ministry of Domestic Affairs is delighted to advise you have been selected for National Duty. Given you have previously served, and that assignment has now come to its conclusion, we will not be inviting you to the selection ceremony to await your next position.

Instead, based on the recommendation we have obtained from your last duty, you will be placed directly into a role in Parliament – details to come.

Please make yourself available to attend Parliament in two days from the date of this letter. We look forward to meeting you and discussing the details of your new duty and its five-year term.

Sincerely,

Office of the Chief of Staff to the Prime Minister of Nuntainia

The paper starts to shake in my hands as I stare at it, the walls feeling like they're pressing closer.

'What is it?' Blossom asks, the worry in her voice clear.

'I—' My skin feels too tight.

Duty ...

Five years. I can't—another five*—I—Parliament House? But what does that mean they think happened to me after the fire I started at the prison? Am I not now a wanted traitor? Is that why they've sent for me in this way? In Parliament House with people like—*

My head starts to swim. Blossom gently takes the letter from me and I stare at her as she reads, hoping she might read something different to me, regardless how stupid that is. Quillian takes my elbow and I lean into him a little.

'Cort,' he says. 'We need to get into the systems.'

I watch as Blossom passes the letter to River and Nix reads over his shoulder.

'Fucking bastards,' Nix snaps, moving in and drawing me into his chest. Quillian's fingers slip off my arm as I let Nix squeeze me tight, closing my eyes against the tears that threaten.

'Five years, Nix,' I whisper. 'I've already done that. I want—I thought—this is my *life* we're talking about.' A sob shudders deep in my chest and he holds me tighter. 'If I give them another five years ... what if they work out what I—I wanted a *choice*, Nix. *This* was supposed to be that choice. What if—' I can't voice the worry that it's a trap winding its way along my veins. A way to coax me back into the fold and then force me to give up information on the rest of the team here.

Surely getting a request for duty to the very place the traitors wanted me to be is too convenient?

'We're here, Lu,' Nix says.

I laugh hollowly. 'That's what Quillian said.'

'Well ... he does seem to have a knack for some of this shit.' Nix releases me, gently pushing me back towards Quillian and giving a subtle nod. As if he was waiting for Nix's okay, Quillian takes my hand and stands beside me once more.

'Cort?' he asks.

'Yep, systems,' she says curtly. 'Assuming you're all finished your hug-fest.'

The 'systems room' is an insulated office off the meeting hall. The door is thick, made of several layers of some kind of metal, and it sounds like a vault sealing as it closes behind us. Cortane insisted most of the audience in the meeting hall stay behind, and on guard – including Holland and Casey who now have four people watching over them, as well as Finn.

Cortane flicks the light on and those who might as well be my family – Blossom, Nix, and River – are immediately illuminated, the soft, yellow light finding the different highlights in their hair. Absently, I notice Blossom's dark curls seem to absorb the light far more than River's deep blond. Quillian stands at my back, a hand on my hip and his firm chest pressing against me gently.

Rubbing her palms together for a moment, Cortane takes a seat at the terminal and the centre of the room is suddenly split by a translucent, pale-purple glow. Words and icons roll over the screen as Cortane searches for whatever she's looking for.

'Here,' she says, the flickering of the screen reminding me of the images of Traelen when he'd sometimes virtually call the Warden's office from Parliament, rather than using the phone.

That letter was sent by his office, but was it him? Did he make it off the island as the prison burned? Is he still Chief of Staff?

'This is the sealed records of the fire ... and escape from the prison,' Cortane says eventually.

Before us are lists of names under headings that read 'dead on scene', 'recovered', and 'unaccounted for'. I scan the list, looking for any names I recognise.

And there's mine – under 'recovered'.

Blossom is listed as 'unaccounted for', as is Quillian. Nix, River, and Cortane are all listed as 'dead on the scene'. I can't see Finn's. Or Holland's.

The names start to blur before me and I spin to Quillian. 'What is this?'

His gaze is sympathetic when he looks down at me.

'Please don't tell me you're really surprised?' Cortane asks. 'Not after everything you saw and did up there?'

The room stills, waiting for my response, and I will away the wave of inadequacy that rises in a slow burn in the depths of my throat. She's right, it should be obvious they can do whatever they want. It's clearly obvious to Cortane.

Quillian tucks a strand of hair behind my ear. 'This is a pretty standard government approach, Luka. They can't change what happened up there, but they can rewrite it and make their version the only one that's ever believed – if it's ever dug up.'

The room spins around me and I close my eyes. I don't want it to make sense, but it does. How would it look if the general public got wind of the 'fact' that Nix, River, and Cortane – supposedly three deadly criminals – had not only escaped Nuntainia's worst prison, but two of them spent most of their time in a luxury prison-resort that's not supposed to exist? As did the Warden that was charged with treason?

So now they're apparently dead. As if the government simply erased them by adding them to this list. Quillian and Blossom's listings as 'unaccounted for' seem a little more plausible, but mine – *recovered* – makes no sense at all.

'Where'd you get the letter?' I ask Nix and has face shutters a little.

'Zale gave me a heads-up she'd collected your mail. I thought it was unusual ...'

I nod. Zale going to my house to check isn't that unusual. But with the letter going to my house and my 'recovered status' ...

My stomach feels like I'm back in the open sky, but I'm less settled about it. At least then I had a fair idea how it would end, until Quillian dove down for me. Just like the heron.

I'd like to recommend you for Parliament, Claudius's words come back to me along with the memory of the heron. *I'd like the opportunity to work with you again, Luka,* he'd said.

While there is nothing about another five years of duty I can wrap my mind around, here I am being officially requested to go exactly where he wanted me. Exactly where this group of traitors – *my* group of traitors – need me to be so I can be their contact. That swooping sensation in my stomach turns slightly acidic.

Is it too convenient that I've been called to the one place I was aiming for before ... all of this?

Maybe. Probably. But perhaps this 'convenience' is a gift.

But I never got to understand *why* Claudius thought I'd be good in there. Not the real reason. Not why he thought I'd be useful to the traitors undercover in Parliament House. Was it because I can navigate complex situations, or because I know how to fade into the background? My inability to focus on what was going to come following the destruction of the prison, from a bigger, more strategic, perspective about what the public understands, would suggest it wasn't the former.

I clear my throat, breaking the silence the others have fallen into as they watch Cortane manipulate different files onto the screen before us, none of which I have been paying any attention to.

'Is Traelen still in Office?' I ask.

Cortane nods without looking at me. 'Found his sign-in from yesterday.'

Pulling out the one spare chair next to Cortane, I sink into it and resist the urge to drop my head into my hands. Five years. It's not as long as others have given for this fight. My first five probably don't count for this, but they do for how long I have been waiting for my life to properly start. Now, just as it's started to feel like it was going to – albeit in a direction I never would have guessed – it feels like it's being ripped out from underneath me. Five years to survive in the House that created, or enabled, the likes of those I served on the island. People who should have been in Vana. If I'm not immediately outed as a traitor as soon as Traelen lays eyes on me.

But then ... it was likely him that signed the letter?

'Is there any way we can alter the request? Waltzing straight on in is risky as fuck now,' Nix says as he stands at Cortane's shoulder.

The weight of his question drags on the loss of Claudius that sits in my bones. It feels wrong to take the option of an out. He'd looked at me with such faith in his gaze when we talked about my recommendations—about anything, really. Maybe the herons that helped us get through the wards were a coincidence, or—

'Not without leaving a data trail,' Cortane says, and I don't miss the weariness in her tone. Like she's also tired of having this conversation with him. 'I can access some of their systems, but those for staff in the House are much more closely monitored. We can't amend them without an alert of a breach being activated.' She looks over her shoulder at him but she's turned away from me so I can't see her expression. Just the back of her cropped-blonde hair.

'If it was anyone else,' she says in a low voice, 'would you even question whether their time was worth more than the advantages of us having a plant in the House who can *waltz the fuck in?*'

Now, that *is* something I hadn't considered. If it was a question of trading my time for my loved ones' safety, I wouldn't think twice. The same as I leapt off the island. Swallowing the sharpness of the idea of losing another five years, I think of another challenge: could I actually pull it off without getting us all killed?

I think again on my conversation with Claudius about me taking a recommendation for Parliament. Even then, when I didn't know what he was really asking, I had some of the same doubts – can I do it?

The conversation around me stalls, and I know I need to say something. I look up at Quillian, but he shows no sign of rushing me. Blowing out a long breath, I make myself think of Claudius and the heron. He had faith I could do what was needed, and the heron helped get me here. So it's his faith I draw on when I finally open my mouth—

'Lu,' River starts but I hold up a hand to halt him.

'I'm going,' I say. 'We have two days for you to tell me as much as you possibly can about how you got here, what you want, and what you need me to do to get it. We're going back to plan A.'

Quillian's chest expands with his breath and something like regret spins in his eyes. Along with a sparkle of something else.

'Just ... please help me find a way to not be stuck in there for another five years.' I hold his gaze as I say it, my chest tight. Or Vana. But I don't say that bit - the most likely outcome - out loud.

'We can give you that,' he says, his voice gentle. 'Whatever happens, I'll get you out before five years is done.'

Cortane spins in her chair to face us, the huge screen looming over her shoulders.

'Alright, Princess,' she says slowly, like she's about to watch something disastrous she can't look away from. 'Looks like we have no choice but to send you—and you're going to need to sign that duty contract *before* you get your tattoo.'

A flicker of protest snags in my chest, and not just at her ridiculous nickname. That tattoo was going to represent something to me – the decision to follow my own wants and desires, to no longer be bound by the rules and expectations of everyone else. To finally be doing something, by choice, that I felt like I was meant to do, and to nurture the seed Claudius planted all that time ago.

I don't respond. It makes sense, but I can't deny I'm disappointed.

'Right,' Cortane says. 'Let's get some food and meet at Blossom and Luka's in half an hour – I need to deal with the Hunters, and that place has the largest living room.'

'I think they're onboard,' I blurt. 'Holland helped me get to you on the island, brought Casey along. Casey killed Zenaton when he tried to ...' I trail off, finding it difficult to meet Quillian's gaze. I don't know exactly what Zenaton was going to do, but it certainly wasn't going to be good.

When I finally look at him, he's sharing a dark look with Nix.

'We'll put them in the holding cells until we can sort this through,' Quillian says, a tic in his jaw. 'River, can you and Blossom find Janly and organise the food? Nix, you go with Finn and the Hunters. Cort, gather the background we'll need to bring Luka up to speed.'

'And me?' I ask.

'You're with me.'

The townhouse we're staying in doesn't feel anything like 'ours', but I still warm with appreciation that I get to share it with Blossom. Quillian did say there is no 'home' here. How long has it been since he's had one?

He runs his hand through his short, dark hair before clearing his throat and moving to the kitchen, taking a carafe of dark liquid from the open timber shelf above the bench. I lift a brow, it's not quite mid-morning but drinking something that burns suddenly seems like an excellent idea.

'Make mine a double,' I say.

Quillian slides his gaze to me momentarily, but there is no joy in his face. He closes the space between us slowly. Purposefully. As if he's approaching something he needs to prepare for and my heart starts to race.

'Did he hurt you?' he asks, his voice low. 'If you don't want to tell me, I—that's o—'

I place my palm on his chest. 'He didn't get a chance.'

His chest collapses and he drops his forehead to mine, my drink still held in his hand.

'You were just supposed to be a contact, Luka,' he murmurs. 'I always care about the people on my team—them and our goals, they're the priority—but this ... this is new for me.'

My stomach turns over itself and I take my glass from him, placing it carefully on the bench, where it lands with a soft clink as I release it. I spread my fingers around the sides of his neck, his skin soft under my touch, before I loop them around the back, ducking a little so I can meet his lowered gaze.

'I can be both,' I whisper, desperately hoping it's true. 'I can be the contact and do this.' I press my mouth to his and the moment stretches before he sighs quietly and kisses me back.

'You know,' he says when he pulls away, 'Claudius was more right about you than I think possibly even he realised.'

I frown and tilt my head in question.

'He knew you'd be an asset, knew your academic background and foundation in social justice would help guide you through. But I don't know that he could have predicted how you and I would come together, too.'

Smiling at him and the way his words have bolstered my floundering confidence in how I'll manage being in the House, I press another kiss to his mouth. 'Told you I could do both,' I say, hanging onto his recollection of Claudius's view harder than he probably realises.

'Okay,' he says, nodding to himself as he repeats, 'okay.'

I collect my glass and raise it to him.

'Here's to both,' I say, taking a long sip as a knock at the door sounds, voices filtering through the entry.

'Bit fucking early for that, isn't it?' Nix asks, indicating our glasses as he places containers of food on the counter.

'Not when you're about to plan a takedown,' Cortane says, nudging past Quillian and me to grab the carafe and more glasses. 'We're all going to need this—this moment has been coming for a long fucking time.'

My stomach rumbles a little as the warm smell of fresh, sweet breakfast pastries fills the kitchen. Not something I thought I'd ever eat with hard liquor, but here we are. Never thought I'd be about to go into Parliament as a spy either. My mind snags on that thought.

'Am I a spy or a traitor?' I ask.

Nix barks a laugh.

'Or all of the above?' River suggests.

Blossom looks at me, brows raised, and I share the look.

'And the answer is ...?' Blossom asks.

'A traitor is probably the best definition,' River says. 'We're standing in opposition to the current government regime and stepping outside the traditional structures to do so. But you're going to spy in your role as traitor. So ... both.'

'Okay,' I say. 'I can do both.' I look at Quillian again as I say it. 'Let's work out how.'

CHAPTER SEVEN

Now that I have been served my second set of duty papers and have a legitimate way into the House, there is one less issue for the traitors to resolve. The shift in the energy of the group is palpable.

The once empty-feeling townhouse Bloss and I occupy is now full of briefings, strategising, and a growing sense of purpose – of direction. Our arrival had a tinge of defeat about it for the original traitors, I can see that now; the messy end of a plan gone awry. But this has renewed them, given them a focus point to channel all that we went through on the island, and the things they experienced even before their time on the island. The air throbs with an undercurrent of excitement that I can't seem to catch.

The flaky pastry I made myself eat for breakfast sits heavily in my gut as I try to absorb as much as I can from the conversation. It's in sharp contrast to the vague, half-discussions that filled much of my time with them on the island, but it's information that I can place in my own understanding of our government and how it works – or is supposed to work. While some of what I know is dated, the understanding I gain from our discussion is both bolstering and worrying. It's bolstering that I know more than I thought, and worrying to understand just how far wrong it has all gone.

'I know most of that,' I say, interrupting Cortane's overview of the large and small ministries, giving her what I hope is a politely apologetic look. 'What I need to get clear on is the priorities for my time in the House.

Obviously, I don't want to spend five years there for my own reasons, but the reality is that we don't have that kind of time anyway. We might not be marked, but the Hunters are most likely looking for you all the same.' I take a gulp of my cold coffee. 'And once I show my face in there, it's anyone's guess how quickly that's going to motivate them to find you—and try to use me to do it.'

Quillian shifts forward next to me, the old dining chair creaking a little as he turns so he's facing me completely. He gently places his fingertips on my thigh, but otherwise he's all business.

'The prison program you know about—you lived one side of it. We need to know who created it.'

I nod, he said the same at his version of my induction. There's more, I know it's not just that, but he seems to be giving me the space to add it to the conversation myself.

'And I assume you want me to confirm—or, hopefully otherwise—any movement on the breeding program?'

Blossom turns to me almost comically. 'The what, now?'

Giving her a rundown on what Quillian told me, including Aiten Gall's involvement, is met with silence from the room. From Bloss as she processes, and the others, I assume, as they are reminded of the depths of the abuse of power our government has sunk to.

'I need a coffee.' River stands abruptly, and I watch him rise from his seat. It's not often he will find things too much, but I can understand why the breeding program would be. It should be for anyone.

But, as I look back at Nix, who's clearly grinding his teeth together, I wonder how exactly they came to be part of this inner circle. I know their service to Nuntainia, and role in recruiting Tae citizens to be soldiers used as battle fodder, is what led them down the path to becoming traitors. Was that what got them in this room, though?

'Right,' I say, pulling myself back to the list of priorities facing us now. 'Two things. Do you have any thoughts on how, or where, I start?'

'Starting with the third thing would be easiest,' Cortane says, and I lift my brows at her.

'We used to have another contact—a source, really—in the House,' she continues. 'That's how we got the breeding locations the first time. But they've gone dark and have been for some time. If they're still in there, we know they are sympathetic to our cause and, given what they were able to share last time, I can only imagine what they've had access to in the meantime. We need that contact back.'

I look around the group before me. Somehow, that last task seems like the hardest. The first two I can research, find papers, look for evidence. Finding a contact with no description, no name, and no idea where they might fit into the scheme of things ... that feels like a game of chance with a Vanan sentence behind every door.

'So,' Blossom says from where she sits in the cane dining chair next to River as he sits back down stiffly. 'Luka goes into Parliament House as our contact while the rest of us do—what? And how do we manage those of us who are "unaccounted for"?' She does air quotes with a single hand before pinning her gaze on Quillian.

'The easiest solution is for those of us currently dead or missing to stay that way,' River says before glancing between Blossom and me. 'Which means Blossom will have to stay here while you go, Luka. For both of you to suddenly appear back in the capital would just be reckless. You might be listed as "recovered", but the reality is we all got off that island in a way that would get each of us a one-way ticket to Vana. Us'—he indicates the original traitors with a wave of his finger—'because we are essentially escaped inmates. The two of you because you abandoned your duty and aided us.'

'Of course,' I hear myself say as my heart sinks a little. I'd tried not to focus on the fact that I'd be leaving Blossom behind, not after we took that literal leap together, and everything that led up to that moment. Or, really, perhaps she's the one leaving me behind to start her life while I return to another duty, another pause. Given how badly I wanted her to find a new purpose, the twinge of discomfort I feel seems unfair. Especially because she will have a good support network here in River, Janly, and Emeris. But it's still there.

One day, it will be me.

One day.

Although, it's not like she's quite free to live how she likes, either.

'So I'll be on my own?' I ask, forcing any semblance of quaver from my voice.

I've spent so much time in, or close to, the company of others, the idea of going back to my empty house and living alone feels ... cold. Like I've drunk a glass of iced water and it's chilling me from the inside out. Add to that the fact that turning up in Parliament House, where it seems Traelen still works, makes me horribly exposed. Surely, he would know I wasn't actually 'recovered'? Who made that determination on the records anyway? What will they do when I turn up in the House? Will I be welcomed, or escorted to Vana with my hands bound?

'You can resume your normal life with your old friends—it would be suspicious if you did otherwise,' Cortane says, cutting into my spiralling thoughts. 'But your contact with us will be limited. We need the information you have to find, and we can't be compromised when you do. We want evidence we can use, not take to our graves.'

I nod slowly, trying not to let the way my mind is swirling show on my face.

'And exactly what am I looking for, evidence wise? How much detail is enough for your purposes?'

Quillian shifts again, withdrawing his hand from my thigh and placing it on the pale, timber table. He shares a quick look with Cortane, his throat bobbing as he swallows. 'Ideally, I want copies of any physical records on the breeding program, anything that they can't publicly deny. Same on the prison program. Names, crimes, so-called sentences, and how they were really treated on the island. Our time in the prison was like picking off flies.' His gaze shutters for a moment. 'With you on the inside, we have a shot at getting the records and exposing the roots of the corruption instead.'

'So we'll use those records to show that the current government is corrupt? How?'

I think of the different exposés I have seen and even researched a little in my time. They can be pretty damning, but do they affect change? I don't know.

He sits back in his chair. 'By using the systems they already have in place, that the most powerful have conveniently kept themselves exempt from. We take the information public, make it so widely known it will be impossible for the government not to finally root out those responsible and initiate real reform. One piece of information won't be enough, we need to create a wave.' He clasps his hands on the table. 'But most importantly, we want who initiated and implemented it. That seed of poison that started it all. The only place we're going to find that, and everything else, is in the Parliament archives.'

The room falls silent around me as I think about what else the archives could hold. Now I know of the existence of these two programs I could never have even imagined—even as I served inside one of them. The women from Tae who are captured against their will, and children Kasera had as slaves ... The weight of that knowledge is a hard notch in my breastbone that never goes away.

I send out a quiet, perhaps naive, wish that's the worst of what I uncover.

Cortane clears her throat, dragging her gaze from the table before sharing a loaded look with Finn and Quillian that none of them explain.

'As for what we will do while you're in there,' she says. 'We have business in Tae and rallying the rest of our camps but, with all due respect Princess, as you're about to walk straight into enemy territory, the less you know, the better.'

The pit of unease in the base of my stomach grows, but I nod. 'How will we keep in touch?'

'We'll give you an untraceable phone,' she says. 'You will smuggle it in, photograph everything you find, and send it to me. You can use it to contact us as needed, but it's best you be ... conscious of the things you say. Just in case. Try not to use it unless absolutely necessary.'

'That's it?' I don't ask if that means I will have no way to physically reach anyone in this room again.

'Under exceptional circumstances, you can use the portal I'll create for you,' she says. 'But it has to be really fucking serious—making my magic untraceable is hard, and there are only so many risks we can take. No one here wants to end up in Vana for life without at least a proper fucking attempt at bringing it all down.'

I swallow. 'Okay.'

What else can I possibly say?

'Luka,' my eyes start to burn a little when Nix says my name. 'You won't be completely on your own—we're right here.'

The time to leave comes too fast, two days disappearing in the blink of an eye. I lie awake before the sun rises, enveloped in Quillian and one dark-grey wing, admiring the texture without touching. I vividly remember how sensitive they are, and I don't want to wake him just yet, don't want him to see the self-pity on my face as slow, quiet tears leak towards my pillow.

However we're dressing it up, I am still about to be contracted to another duty, sealed into another five years of servitude. And this time, I will be even more up close and personal to the sickening people behind the corruption. Will have to be at their beck and call, fulfil their every whim. Because, whatever my exact role is to be, it's certainly not going to be running the fucking place.

On top of that, I assume I will also be required to take the magic dampener again. A thought that only serves to remind me that I have felt nothing new, or strange, or ... anything that could be described as magical since I stopped taking it on the island. Even though I'm a traitor now – a concept that brings a significant warmth to my insides, particularly when I think of Kasera and Davorous – I can't ignore the reality that the signs indicate I will probably never know what my magic could have been. Will never know if I would have had wings like the ones cocooning me now, or Clayti magic like Nix, who can literally move the earth, or heal like River with his Arkanan abilities. I'll just ... have nothing.

Nothing but an untraceable phone, another duty to complete or illegally extract myself from, and distance. Distance from all the people I wanted to do this with.

Beside me, Quillian inhales deeply as he starts to wake, pressing a kiss to the top of my head.

'Hey,' he mumbles, and I smile gently, sneaking a hand up to wipe my tears. I love him like this, his mask removed, all warmth. 'I feel like I should be worried how quickly I've gotten used to waking up with you.'

I roll onto my side, letting his wing brush over my bare arm as I snuggle into his chest.

'Me too,' I breathe, pressing a kiss to his sternum. 'How long do I have to miss this for?' I ask.

He drags a palm up and down my spine. 'Only the same amount as me.' One large hand cups my backside and scoots me closer, flush against his front where I can feel ... everything. 'Would it be unfair of me to ask you to find something I can use so I can have you back here as fast as possible?'

I huff a laugh. 'No. I thought "as fast as possible" was implied in the job description.'

His palm lifts and his fingers start to trail my skin instead, leaving goosebumps in their wake along the side of my breast, teasing my nipple briefly. Taking my chin in his hand, he lifts my face, bringing my mouth to his, and he kisses me lazily, eyes still closed, sparking fire in my belly.

Quillian's eyes are still closed when the kiss ends, and I watch him, drinking him in. When he finally opens his eyes and notices, a flicker of concern finding its way into his expression. 'Are you okay?'

'Yeah.' I sigh. 'I'm ready, and I want to do this. I just ... I thought my life would be starting by now. The one I'm in control of.'

He releases a slow breath.

'I can understand that,' he says. 'My life hasn't been my own for a long time, either. Even now, when I have explicitly chosen this life that ... sits on the outside of the rest of the world, I feel like I have no choice but to keep going. Sometimes ... I feel the weight of hope I carry for others might crush me.'

'Why is it all on you?'

'Everyone here has sacrificed something—some more than others, but everyone all the same—for the dream of a better, fairer future. I have a history that makes it easy for me to be the face of the movement to seek retribution. That history also set me on this path and makes me uniquely positioned to be the figurehead of what could lead to a revolution – with the right conditions, of course. We're right on the brink of me stepping completely into that role and, right now, there is no one who can do that.'

I trace the explosion of colour on the side of his neck. *For those that prove the colour of their souls.*

'I never considered I'd be part of something like this,' I admit softly. 'I've always ... followed the rules.'

He laughs softly. 'You certainly weren't following any rules on Zanteera Island.'

I smile up at him, my heart warming. No, I didn't follow the rules on the island in the end. I followed my instincts, put my trust in key people around me – and I have zero doubt that was the right thing to do. I stopped Nix, River, and Quillian from ending up in Vana permanently, and I gave Blossom the chance at the life I so desperately wished for her.

So, yes, I have another duty to do – or start, at least. But, in the light of what I've given my friends, and what I might be able to gain for the movement, I'll take it. Quillian's right. Whatever happens from here, it feels like we're right on the brink of it. It's certainly not going to take five years to unfold. I take that thought and try to let it comfort me, instead of increase the pounding of a different sort of deadline. Like the very real possibility of being sent to Vana on my first day in the House.

I'd just like to have freedom over all of my life choices.

My magic, too.

But maybe I can still get that. I just have to get in – and out – of the House first.

Saying goodbye to Blossom feels eerily like when I thought we were saying goodbye on the island. Except, this time, I don't know when I will see her again; I hope like crazy it's sooner rather than later. Her deep teal eyes are rimmed with tears.

'I thought I might get to keep you this time,' she says, sniffing.

'Me too,' I say quietly.

She grips my upper arms and pulls me towards her. 'You be fucking careful, Luka. I don't care about a possible trace on the portal—you use it if there is *any* doubt of your safety.'

My immediate reaction is to brush away her concerns, tell her I am going to be working with a bunch of men and women in suits. How dangerous can they be? But then I think of Davorous, of Zenaton's face when he found me trying to escape, and I know they might be the most dangerous of all.

Nix spins me carefully from Blossom's hold and hugs me hard. 'I'll watch her,' he whispers in my ear, and I grip him harder, so thankful he knows to do that without my asking. 'Although I probably won't need to, given how attentive River's being.'

I press my smile into his shoulder. 'Don't you dare tease them,' I say. 'You'll spook her.'

'Noted,' he says. 'But I make no promises for when I have him on my own.' He presses me back to look me full in the face. 'You know, however this goes, no one is leaving you in there for five years, right?'

The relief I feel at that statement is raw. Not because I wasn't hoping that would be the case, but having him say it out loud is still a balm I want to take with me.

'Ready?' says a familiar voice that I can't quite—

I release Nix and my gaze lands on Holland. He's not in uniform today, but he still holds the posture of someone who wears one regularly. Not that that says much – everyone here looks like that except Blossom and me.

Finn steps forward, too. 'We're going with you,' he says in that soft, steely voice.

'Ah ...' I can't help my gaze flicking to Quillian to see what he might make of this, and there is definitely a level of unease in the set of his shoulders. But he says, 'As far as anyone there knows, Holland is still a Hunter, so his presence shouldn't raise suspicions. Having him there will help you navigate who is who and learn the layout of the building.'

'Interestingly,' Cortane adds drily, 'the Hunters' status in the system was marked as "recovered – on medical leave".'

My quiet sense of alarm that this is all just too convenient grows more insistent.

'But only this group—and Casey—know I have this,' Holland says, lifting his shirt and showing the tattoo that peeks from his low slung pants. It appears to run from hip to hip underneath his belly button.

'Finn is the best there is,' Quillian says as Holland drops his shirt, 'and he will make sure nothing goes ... awry with Holland. Or you.'

A faint breeze starts to my left as Cortane moves her hand in the air and gently begins to open the portal. My stomach knots. Time to put on my duty mask. Go back to my townhouse I've barely thought of in the time I've been away. But also back to Zale and Akira. Yet, away from this group and Blossom. This time, though, I don't have to wait until five years is up. This time, I can find what I need and get out. It no longer matters if it's an illegal way out of the duty contract, that's a choice I've already made.

Finn and Holland move to either side of the portal and look back at me expectantly.

Quillian steps up beside me, slips his fingers between mine and moves in front of me, blocking my path to the portal. 'You know I would never force you to do this, right? If you don't want to go, tell me now and I *will* find another way.'

I suck in a breath, bolstered by his words, by the choice he is making sure I feel I have. Even if I don't really, not from the perspective of the Office of the Chief of Staff. Not turning up for duty is as good as getting marked by the wards – it's additional attention we can't afford. And, on the chance I can get what we need without putting the lives of the people here at more risk ... that's definitely no choice for me.

'I know,' I whisper. 'And I'm going. But don't you need Finn here?'

'Finn protects what's sacred. He goes with you.'

My cheeks burn with the warmth that fills my chest. He bends his head to mine, bringing our foreheads together.

'You can contact me on this,' he says, handing me a phone that looks like an earlier version of my lost one. 'I've saved our numbers in there with initials only. Even still, you will need to be extremely careful with it and *never* leave it unattended.'

He looks at me through his thick lashes. 'Will you wait for me?' he whispers.

I virtually launch myself at him, wrapping my arms around his neck and capturing his smile in my mouth.

'Of course,' I say against his lips. 'Providing you wait for me to get what we need to expose it all.' I smile as I say it, knowing his answer will be 'yes'.

Now, the only thing I need to focus on is getting into Parliament and finding any and all information I can on the prison and breeding programs – and uncovering the traitors' anonymous contact. As a woman on a duty, I will be just about invisible in that House. Getting someone to inadvertently show me, or let me overhear, the details shouldn't be that hard. I could fill several books with the things prisoners on the island said in front of me as if I didn't exist.

I think back on my conversation with Quillian this morning. It's true, I didn't ever think I would be part of something like this.

But retribution feels so much better than following the rules.

CHAPTER EIGHT

Finn and Holland each hold one of my elbows as we move through the portal. My nerves skitter as if they might be portalled somewhere other than my body as Cortane's magic moves over me, then it's over. I blink as I take in where Cortane has sent us.

A deserted car park.

But beyond the starkness that mirrors the pit threatening to open within me, and the fallen down fence that's meant to keep the public out, is a view I'd forgotten I missed.

The skyline of the city fills my vision.

Klades.

Home.

Or what was once home.

I stare at it a moment, a wash of familiarity coming over me and dropping away. I was never one to pedantically memorise the layout of our capital, I just ... knew it. Could make my way around by gut feel. A little like I could navigate the island, I suppose, although it was significantly smaller. But it's immediately apparent the skyline has changed somewhat, and there's a pang in my side at the realisation that the city itself has grown without me. Grown while I was on pause.

The realisation solidifies something in me. I won't wait for a city – or a country – that hides the true nature of those meant to represent its citizens, uses the trust put in them merely to fuel their sins. Not anymore. And just like that, on top of the conversation I had with Quillian, I no longer view this as a repeat of my 'duty'.

It's an assignment – one that only I can fulfil.

For better or worse.

I tap my thigh, forcing myself to shove the risks out of my mind. I just need to stay focused on what I *can* do. Not what might happen if I fail. No. I can't focus on the breeding program that might continue, or that the Hunters will still be after my friends, or that Vana—

Stop. I tell myself. One step at a time. Get into the House, accept my duty contract. I can do that.

Early morning sun reflects off the tallest silver building and those that surround it, making me squint. To the right of the central business district is the Academic Quarter, just a bit further out than I can see, shielded by a run of tall, thick pines not unlike those that created the forest *up there.* I don't look in that direction for long. Despite what my future now holds, it's still an uncomfortable reminder of what my life could have been. Had I not been 'almost' good enough, even though I pretty well single-handedly grew that Academy from the ground up, only for the top job to be given to someone else ...

Had my father given me a recommendation for it.

Had I not been selected for duty.

'I'm going to need a hearty fucking breakfast before we do this,' Holland says, breaking into my reflections. 'There's a great little place on the water-front.'

I glance at Finn, his quiet profile almost in direct contrast to Holland's sunny ... ish – I don't know that I would call how he operates as a Hunter 'sunny' – demeanour, but it's heading in that direction. Finn nods once, looking at me sideways, and we cross the expanse of the carpark and to-wards the pod station on the other side of the road.

My stomach grumbles. The food at the camp hasn't been *bad*, but Koko's cooking is incredibly hard to replace, and a breakfast out actually sounds nice. Particularly if it means I can get to know the people who have clearly been chosen to watch over me, including one that risked exposure by helping me – then, a stranger – to burn the prison.

No one seems to care as we slip into the busy foot traffic and follow the flow of people to the station. Holland assured me that new duty intakes always turn up in casual clothes, even when it's in Parliament. So, for now, I'm wearing a pair of jeans that are, thankfully, more accommodating than the ones I left on the island, and a navy, floral shirt. But it's the white sneakers I love the most and their lack of ties that dig into my calves like the sandals from my island uniform.

For all the world, with Holland and Finn each in t-shirts and dark jeans that fit unfairly well, we look like mature-age students headed for the Academic Quarter. Maybe this time, I will be even more impactful than I was there.

This time, there is no one but me positioned to deliver what we need.

Looking closer at the city around me, the number of Hunters patrolling does seem a bit higher than I recall. Akira mentioned at one point that their presence was making things harder for civilians – we'll have to make extra sure not to draw attention to ourselves.

Curved, silver and faded blue pods whizz past the open-air, street-level interchange, people entering and exiting the round, driverless vehicles in a steady rhythm. The pods that aren't stopping gently move, in single file, around the ones that have stopped, awaiting their next passengers. I smile at the memories of late night trips home with Akira and Zale, Nix and River with us more often than not, as I step into a vacant pod and take a seat on the front-facing bench.

Finn sits next to me, keeping a polite distance between us. Holland slumps backwards opposite us, running a hand down his red beard and leaning his head against the clear plastic that creates the top half of the Pod.

'Wow,' I breathe, looking out the window as the city peacefully races by. 'So much has changed, and yet ... so little. Is that weird?'

Have I changed? I wonder. So different, yet somehow, still me? What version of me will I be if – hopefully *when* – my magic comes in?

I don't expect an answer, really, but Finn's gentle voice fills the pod. 'Not weird,' he says. 'That's exactly what makes this regime so dangerous. All the quiet changes and cost to people's lives, the erosion of human rights – along with the issue of cycling the same biased authorities back into government, even when they acted disgracefully; all of that is swept under the shiny rug of clever messages, sparkling buildings, and the general lack of attention to detail the common person has. Especially to what they can write off as the 'boring' workings of government.'

My heart gives a heavier thump at his words. At the memory of how distracted I was by the glossy veneer of life on the island until Nix and River were arrested. I was exactly the sort of citizen Finn is referring to, and I *have* an understanding of how government is supposed to work. Persuading the people that one, what's happening under the surface is real, and, two, that they don't have to accept it is going to be a challenge.

Holland studies Finn as he talks, his head cocked slightly. 'That's our job now, Luka,' he says without taking his gaze from Finn, 'lift the rug and beat out the dust.'

The view of the Klades River that's visible through the white-framed window of Holland's favourite little café is serene. The banks have been developed into a beach-style landscape, and families are starting to gather for the day with picnic rugs and baskets. It doesn't feel quite warm enough for that just yet, but I guess, like anyone, they also have to take the opportunities as they arise.

'Oh,'—Holland says around his first bite of smoked salmon and eggs—'this is divine.'

A ghost of a smile graces Finn's face. 'You should have eaten more of the food on the island,' he says, gesturing to Holland with his fork.

'Yes.' Holland laughs. 'Only the best for our nation's worst, right?'

The memory of enchanted chocolate balls fills my mind and I think of Koko. My heart brims with the knowledge she is now free to spend her time with her grandson, even if she has a different name now.

'Do we know what happened to everyone else?' I ask, taking in the wide river bank and the sandy shore that tips into the increasingly dark waters behind Holland. The sun glints on the tiny ripples on the surface.

'From the island?' Finn asks, and I nod, chewing my muesli and vanilla, coconut yoghurt.

'We have a team trying to establish the status of everyone who was present at Zanteera Prison, including the concierges.'

My muesli loses some of its appeal, and I look away from the otherwise idyllic view as I process the possibility that my setting fire to the prison may have had unintended results, alongside the intended. I trust Emeris and Janly to have gotten everyone out, but then what happened to them? I curse myself for not asking either of them before I left.

'Can you let me know?' I ask. 'I'd also like to know where each of the surviving prisoners ended up, and if we think that's reasonable.'

Thankfully, I know what happened to Davorous and Zenaton. But, presumably, I will need the records on the prison program to know the rest with certainty.

'Of course,' Finn says, a softness in his gaze as he looks down at me. 'I'm quite confident you're part of the inner circle now.'

My insides warm – that was definitely not something I felt on the island. Holland makes a strangled noise in his throat. 'And I'm what? Just here to look good?'

Finn surveys him from across the table. The moment stretches out long enough for my face to heat, and I could swear the air just got tighter around my shoulders. 'Perhaps,' he says. 'That's yet to be decided.'

Squashing a smile, I let the moment settle, tucking away how they are with each other to examine another time. I also push away my unfinished breakfast and try to ignore the knot my nerves are currently weaving in my liquidy stomach.

'We need to go,' I say, turning to Holland and Finn, my chest swelling with gratitude that they're here with me. 'I don't want to be late for check-in.'

Part of me doesn't want to go at all, but as I look back to the families on the riverbank who remind me of Akira and Zale, I know it's them I am doing this for, along with myself. For the children who deserve to grow up in a safe world, not one that's rotten from the inside out.

It's for the children of the women taken in Tae and all they have witnessed, too. To try to make a better world for them.

Parliament House rises up from a green knoll that's almost entirely covered by a multitude of flowers, like a carpet of petals. Once I thought of this building as stately, with its tall columns and black and grey marble steps that cut through the flowers. Commanding of respect. Now I know it houses people like Zenaton, Aiten, Miana, Kasera, and Davorous ... the colourful petals make my skin itch.

Finn, Holland, and I hover in the small crowd on the street at the bottom of the rise, many of whom take photos of the House and its view over the river.

'Quillian asked me to give you this,' Finn says, holding out a storm-grey feather. My heart skips as I reach out and let it tickle the pads of my fingers.

I'm not really sure what to say, fighting an insistent burn in my eyes. Quillian thinks of me often, that's clear. But, as I look at the men in front of me, and listen to the tourists bustling on the foreshore, I hear Cortane's warning once more, like a broken record in my mind: *it's critical he's not distracted*.

How much is his worry for me, here, impacting his focus there?

Holland gently takes the feather and slides it down the front of my shirt, a move that feels very much like what Nix would do.

'You've seen what those things can do, I assume?' he says, stepping back, and I lift my brows in question at Finn.

'Only if you need it,' he says. 'And don't let anyone else know you have it. Karaylia feathers are only ever supposed to remain with their owners, and this government covets them too much.'

'How do I use it?' I think of the thin, pale scar on my tummy, courtesy of my first meeting with Quillian. How little I knew back then.

'It will respond to your blood,' Finn says, and I pull a face, suddenly a bit queasy. 'He set it up that way. Just nick your finger on the end and run the drop down the spine.'

I stare at Finn, turning the weight of this around in my mind. It's a weight that fits, I think, as I readjust the feather through my shirt. He clearly meant me to only use it if I need it; I'm sure he hasn't forgotten how I feel about blood.

'We can't go in with you,' Holland says. 'But my shift starts not long after you will start your duty induction, so I'll be around. Finn,' he says, looking him over almost appreciatively, 'will be at your townhouse unless I call him in.' A wicked smile splits his face, and Finn looks at him sideways.

'Just until you get settled,' Finn says. 'Then I have my own work to do while you're in the House. But we'll both be staying with you.'

Holland rocks back on his heels. 'Alright, Miss Luka, duty calls.'

The walk up the flower-bordered path feels long, and I force myself not to glance back at Finn and Holland – or where they were. Up ahead, I catch a glimpse of long, silky black hair that snags something familiar in my mind, but it disappears just as quickly.

The people around me start to thin slightly as those just here to take photos fall back. I share a nervous smile with the man next to me as we make our way through the three-storey tall, glass entrance doors.

'Two lines,' a tired-looking woman in a security uniform barks.

Silently, the group I am in moves into two orderly lines to wait our turn to walk through the scanner. I watch as the blue light runs slowly over person after person as they step through the other side and disappear around the corner to the right.

My ears throb in time to the thump of my chest as I take my turn, closing my eyes as the line of blue light runs over my face.

But the feather doesn't register so much as a flicker against my skin.

There's a group of about ten people milling in the hallway as I turn the corner, the woman with the black hair among them. Her almond-shaped eyes find mine and light with the same sense of familiarity I felt when I first saw her. Her cheeks flush pink as she makes her way to me.

'Luka?' she asks shyly.

'Yes ...?' I say, not sure why it comes out as a question. I frantically scan my mind for anything to tell me who she is. I *know* I have met her before, have seen her in photos, but ...

'Oh! You're Teddy!' I blurt.

She grins widely. 'Yes! I feel like we should hug. Can we hug?'

I laugh and draw her in, my arms around her shoulders.

'How is Zale?' I ask when we release. 'Wait—are you *here* for your duty?' I drop my voice to a whisper as a shadow crosses her face. I knew she'd been called up, but I'd never considered ...

'Yes,' she says slowly, then narrows her eyes. 'But before I'm contracted to this, let me tell you this is the very last place in the world I *want* to be—some things just have to be done.'

Her tone hits me right in the breastbone. I glance around quickly, but no one seems to be listening. I think on Teddy's desire to join a vigilante group. That, and being here, seem, on the surface, quite in opposition in terms of values. So the flash in her eyes makes sense.

But it adds a weight to my already heavy load of must-dos and watch-outs. It's one thing to worry about myself in here, watching my every move in case it impacts anyone trying to find or hurt those I left at camp. Now, I'm staring at someone I have an immediate obligation to protect, who's right in the middle of the fire with me.

Still, I don't think we should be talking about this here.

'We should have lunches together while we're here,' I say, giving her a look and hoping she understands.

She loops her arm in mine. 'Yes. Lunch. Definitely. Much to talk about.'

A Hunter leads the eleven of us down a darkly carpeted hallway. The air is hushed, like the sound has been locked away somewhere, and no one talks as we are escorted into a small waiting room. If I were being 'sentenced' to the prison on Zanteera Island, I would have arrived on the marble plane in the sky, before being taken to the receiving hall. There, I would be supplied with any wardrobe I'd care to request, the best food in Nuntainia, and a concierge available to me at any hour of the day or night.

As it is, though, I am here to serve a duty – at least on the outside – and the best I can get is over-brewed, cold coffee and a biscuit that comes wrapped in plastic.

'Help yourself to snacks and a hot drink,' the Hunter says. 'A Parliamentary Official will be with you shortly.'

The whole room watches him leave, but I watch the room.

'Ugh,' Teddy crinkles her nose, and I swear Zale has sent me a photo of one of their children pulling that exact face. 'I *loathe* these.' She drops her half-eaten biscuit in the metal bin. 'Note to self,' she whispers, leaning in to me as we move to the back row of chairs, 'bring own coffee and breakfast.'

There's a mix of people here, although most are younger than me – like Teddy, or younger – so I assume they're all on their first, and probably only, duty, which is much more common. I would imagine, on the surface, this service designation must seem particularly fortunate. It's in the heart of Klades and, while it's been a long time since I have lived here, I don't believe anyone serving a duty in the city is required to stay on-site. Meaning these people can do their duties during the day, or night, and see their families the rest of the time.

Unless they don't live in the capital, of course. In that case, I have no idea where they will stay. Still, less restrictive than the island that houses the second 'prison' that isn't supposed to exist. I'm momentarily grateful I kept up my repayments on my townhouse while I was on the Island. I certainly never had any intention of selling it, but it did feel a bit ... superfluous after a time. And now ... I'm not sure I'm very attached to it. At the same time, the thought of returning there tonight makes the insides of my stomach dance a little. I was such a different person the last time I stepped through that door.

But, truth be told, I'm a different person to what I was a year, even a few months, ago, so perhaps it's unfair to expect my little house to have kept up with me. And I need to remember, it's not the current 'me' that's expected here, but Luka-the-dutiful-concierge.

I lace my fingers together.

Unlace them and rub my arms.

'Zale is beside herself to see you again,' Teddy whispers.

'I can't believe I am finally going to see them,' I say, a small smile tugging at my cheeks as I think of Zale and Akira – two people who have been there for me through so much of my life. 'And your kids!' I look wide-eyed at Teddy. 'I can't even imagine how much they will have grown since I saw them last.' A small weight settles on my shoulders. 'I haven't even met Aleira.'

'No,' she says, 'but she knows you. Zale and Akira talk about you all the time.'

I inhale deeply as Teddy takes my hand and squeezes it in her lap. It's more comforting than she probably realises to know that they haven't completely moved on without me.

'It's good to have you home, Luka,' she says. 'Everyone has been expecting you.'

Her words remind me who else might be expecting me, and my smile suddenly feels false. Who wrote that letter requesting my presence here, and what questions will I be expected to answer about my time on, and departure from, the Island? As Teddy gives my hand another squeeze, I wonder if there is more to her words that I should understand.

A door to our left swings open, and I stifle a gasp as my nails dig into the back of Teddy's hand.

'Welcome to Parliament House,' Traelen says, eyes on me.

CHAPTER NINE

I knew this would happen, everything was too neat – but it doesn't stop the chill in my veins as we come face to face. There was nothing to indicate Traelen was anywhere but in his role as Chief of Staff, and judging by the lack of surprise on his face, I'm right ... he was expecting me. But is that because I was a lucky draw for duty, and he saw my name? Or did he organise to have me here? And how will I work out which one it is, so I can react accordingly? Not to mention the untold number of questions it will raise if he brought me here intentionally, despite everything that occurred on the island.

A coincidence seems highly unlikely, and the ache in my chest recalls when he arrested Quillian. How readily would he do that again?

I smile tersely. It's all I can think to do, and it is, at least, in line with what we talked about at the rebel camp. If I run into Traelen, act normal. Like I am happy to be here, right where I am supposed to be.

Sweat thinly coats my palms, and Teddy glances over, giving the hand she still holds a cautious squeeze. I gently remove it from her grasp and clutch my fingers in my lap, using the pressure to ground me.

Traelen. He's never showed me any ill will, nor anyone else. At least that I am aware of. Arrests aside, of course. He's simply the ever-efficient right-hand of the Prime Minister.

I just need to trust that he doesn't know enough to know my true motives here. If he does, then I will get Cortane to portal me out. Urgently. I resist the urge to touch my fingers to Quillian's feather pressed against my skin. Could I really bring myself to use it in its weaponised form?

I swallow the thought, along with the memory of Casey stabbing Zenaton that rose unbidden – I'm just not convinced I can do that. But I need to know what Traelen knows. Now.

'Welcome,' Traelen says again, this time scanning the group. Some of whom smile eagerly at him, one even waves. A smaller number try to look away entirely, and another, standing at the edge of the room, just stares back, expressionless.

'Your duty here officially started about ten minutes ago. But, before you can take up your posts, I will need each of you to sign these contracts.'

At his words, an attendant of some kind wheels in a trolley stacked with paper contracts, and I am abruptly taken back to the room I signed my first one in. It was much drabber than this and, at that time, I was genuinely worried about where I was going to end up. It turned out, of course, to just be the room they use before sending us into the sky.

Knowing what I do now, and how close Davorous came to seriously hurting Bloss, perhaps that fear was justified. But I was lulled by the illusion they wanted me to see.

Today, despite the relative finery around us, I know more about what I am walking into. And I'm now quite confident that the things I don't know will be worse.

Traelen gestures for the group to line up and sign their contracts. It doesn't take long for the ten in front of me to go through, but Teddy hesitates long enough that I give her a gentle poke in the back to encourage her along. When it's my turn to bend over the silver trolley, I scan the words quickly.

Confidential ...

... IP belongs to the Government of Nuntainia ...

... breach of this contract will result in trial and possible sentence to Vana Prison.

I swallow, the pen shaking in my hand.

It's still hard to make myself officially sign the next five years away, even when I know I have an out. But didn't Claudius also have an out for me? One that was completely blown to pieces by the events that followed his death?

But there's no choice here. Not for Luka the concierge, nor Luka the traitor. Whatever the outcome for each of those parts of me.

And so, under the searing gaze of Traelen, I sign.

The Hunter starts to check names off a clipboard and compare them to their now-signed contracts, before sending them out the door Traelen came in; where I can only assume another Hunter will be to direct them to the next stop. Assuming we all have different jobs here anyway.

Teddy and I fall into the back of the line, and she glances back at me. 'Dinner—we'll see you at yours whenever we're done here. I'll organise food.'

She's definitely staying at home with Zale and the kids, then. I try not to let a small stab of jealousy strike too hard under my rib cage. What would my life be like now, had I been able to do my duty *and* continue my own path at the same time? Instead of being sequestered on the island – or not having done a duty at that time at all. If I'd stayed in the academic sector and had a family, or ...

My thoughts trail off. If I'd done anything different, I wouldn't have what I have now: a solidified purpose; Bloss; Holland and Finn; Nix and River; Quillian ...

I breathe into that acknowledgement. Let it fill me. Bolster me. I didn't get what I thought I wanted. But I got what I needed.

I watch as Teddy leaves the room without looking back, grateful she seems to have caught on about being a little more subtle here, and lock eyes with Traelen. Each step towards the Hunter with the clipboard feels heavier, as it takes me closer to Traelen as well, my heart ricocheting around my chest.

'I can finish up here, Maron,' Traelen says smoothly.

The Hunter glances up briefly before saying his thanks and handing the clipboard to Traelen. It's not something I would have ever presumed on the island – that Traelen would help with administrative tasks – but the Hunter doesn't seem fazed at all.

Act normal, act normal, act normal.

My throat feels like it's too tight, my breaths sawing too loudly.

'Traelen, sir, it's lovely to see you again,' I say, my mouth dry, hoping the waver in my voice isn't obvious.

He turns slowly on his heel, gaze dragging across my skin, before he strides from the room, leaving me frozen for a beat before I understand I am probably supposed to follow him.

He says nothing as he leads me through a maze of hallways and grand rooms full of paintings, columns, and mezzanines. Although, I note there doesn't appear to be any half-naked women draped on lounges in these frames. Mostly just portraits of suited men with engraved, gold plaques underneath.

Now, the idea of being so free I could drape myself on any lounge I please seems particularly appealing, not like when I cringed at it on the island.

'After you,' he says, holding a tall, narrow, but otherwise nondescript, door open for me.

Holland tried to give me the basic layout of the House but, so far, nothing seems straightforward and I can't even guess where I am. I came here in my elementary years as part of a school excursion, as every school in Nuntainia does at some point. But I'm fairly certain we didn't see anything I have walked through this morning, including the security process at the entrance.

The room is off-white, from the walls to the furniture and the tall floor lamp in the corner, although it has a brass post. It's slightly tired looking compared to some of the gilded rooms I have passed through, but it still fits as part of the House. Just a pared back version.

'Take a seat,' Traelen says, settling himself into one of the two bouclé armchairs and crossing one knee over the other in a move that takes me straight back to the Warden's office on the island.

I clear my throat, scrambling for what to say. The conversations – briefings – I had with the team before I left spin through my mind before I settle on the feather at my chest, use it to anchor me. I can do this.

I was in the group that was rescued.

No, I don't know what happened to Quillian and the brothers sentenced to Vana.

No, I didn't see Zenaton during the fire.

Yes, I was escorted by a Hunter, I think his name was Holland.

My friend Blossom (cry here if I can) is missing.

'The emergency portal off the island was chaotic, yes?' Traelen says, and I search his brown-grey eyes.

'Yes ... it was. There were people everywhere.' Well, if I wasn't already committed by signing the contract and the magical terms and conditions which will bind what I can and can't share, I certainly am now.

Traelen nods slowly.

'And the Hunter who helped you escape ...'

'His name was Holland, I think. He said he works here?' I swallow.

'Ah, yes, Holland—one of our best.'

The conversations stalls as Traelen seems to sort through his thoughts, but I don't volunteer anything to fill the silence, hoping with every fibre he can't hear my heart pounding from across the small room. If he knew I wasn't part of the retrieved group and escaped instead, he wouldn't have sent for me for duty, let alone allow me to get this far into the House. Of that, I'm sure. He's far too smart to knowingly enable that big of a security breach. But I don't know what his motives are, and I'm not going to talk myself into a hole voluntarily.

There's a quick rasp of fabric on fabric as he uncrosses his legs and leans forward, elbows pressed into his thighs as he pins me with his stare.

'Let me level with you, Luka. I know who you are and who you're involved with. I also know *precisely* how you got off that island. Leaving a gaping hole in the side of the earth didn't help you cover that up.'

I suppress the urge to clear my throat, clenching my teeth slightly instead, desperately willing the sudden surge of nausea to abate.

Act normal. Let him talk. Think.

'I wouldn't normally risk approaching new parties regarding this ... topic,' he continues. 'But I think I have gathered enough about you and your disposition to understand that your goals here are likely to involve sourcing information. Should I continue?'

We watch each other for what feels like an eternity. How do I get any real read on whether I can trust him or not?

Is this a trap like Cortane's when she tested what I would share about Quillian?

Shit.

Another wave of bitter nausea grips me as I realise I don't know. And I won't know for sure until it's too late. But he has proven he already knows enough to send me to Vana, and hasn't.

Yet.

'Possibly,' I admit, willing the urge to vomit to disappear, continuing to hold his gaze as he studies me.

'There are a number of projects happening in this House that are very important to me,' he says, 'the details of which you may not be aware of. I can't promise you that will change, but ... I think we can help each other.'

'Yes, sir,' I say, hoping that's true.

'There may be times I will call on you for assistance, and you may do the same, but never with an audience,' he says. Then, 'There are three people in this House you can trust—me, Holland, and Teddy.'

'Teddy?' I blurt, unable to mask my surprise.

Holland? He knows about Holland, too?

'You didn't really think that was a coincidence, did you?'

I open my mouth, but he continues as words fail me.

'If you trust nothing else, understand I bring people together for a good reason. Unknowingly bringing traitors into the House is not something you will ever find me guilty of.'

Staring at him, listening to the words he's saying, it seems abundantly clear. Traelen sent me that duty letter. Got me here.

'Yes, sir,' I whisper again.

He continues to survey me for a further minute, still sitting forward, his pale-blue suit jacket framing his legs.

'I'm pleased we understand each other. You will be stationed in the Prime Minister's office along with me.' The air whooshes out of me. 'You will be an attendant, a handmaiden, if you will'—I try not to cringe at what sounds like a demotion from 'concierge'— 'the more subservient you appear, the more you will hear.'

As I think about the things the prisoners on the island said and did, there is nothing about his statement that surprises me.

'I can do that,' I say. 'Anything ... in particular you need me to do?'

'Given where I last came across your ... associates, and what I know of their past, I'm assuming you will have your own priorities—likely overlapping with at least two of my own areas of interest.' He points a single finger skyward. 'How that has taken on a life of its own—or did—and the obscene interests of some of those who found their way there, like Aiten Gall?'

I stare at him. Coming here, I didn't know how Traelen would react. But knowing our exact priorities, the prison and breeding programs, was not even in the realm of what I'd expected. Slowly, I nod, and his shoulders release slightly. He doesn't mention the third priority, and so I say nothing on it either.

'There are documents I can't access,' he says, and I quirk a brow at him. Surely there is nothing here he can't access as a representative of the Prime Minister? 'Places in the House my profile doesn't allow me to get to without being noticed. You, though—and Teddy and Holland—blend in, stay nobodies, and you'll be able to go everywhere.'

I sit back in the chair and let my fingers scratch gently at the textured fabric on the arm as I spin the conversation around in my mind. Weigh up what to say out loud.

'Traelen, sir. You've told me who I can trust here, which I greatly appreciate, and how to make sure I hear things. But ... what exactly do *you* want me to do? Or listen for?'

He mimics my posture.

'For now, I'm content to align my interests with yours. I want the prison program exposed. I am too intimately involved with it to be able to do it myself—not yet. I want to pluck out and publicly burn the individuals who have been through the program.'

I frown, recalling snippets of conversations and modes of operating from my time on the island. 'Doesn't the Prime Minister manage it? You once called it his "ideal" even, I think?'

He makes a soft sound. 'I did. That was more keeping up appearances until I could be sure about you and Quillian. As for my access, it's managed out of his office. There have been ... challenges, but I've tried to maintain some semblance of control while I can.'

I nod, wondering if Quillian and Cortane realise they have this particular ally in the House. But, as clear as it seems to be that Traelen knows I am with them, I can't bring myself to confirm it out loud. Instead, I'm unable to shake the image of him ordering the Hunters to arrest Quillian, and I find myself biting back the question – why would he send Quillian to Vana? Would he do it again? What purpose did any of it serve if they are both fighting for the same thing?

'I also want to stop the trafficking of women and child soldiers from Tae, but there is a powerful sub-cohort in this government. It's an ... undercurrent I can almost feel, but I don't know who's leading it yet—it's most likely the Minister for Justice.' There's a certain tiredness that washes over Traelen's tightly composed anger. 'There are legally questionable policies being pushed through the House without due process, paving the way for atrocious "projects" bankrolled by Nuntainian taxpayers. This will be our downfall if they're allowed to continue, Luka. So, what do I want, and what do I want you to listen for? Everything.'

'Is the trafficking for the breeding program?' I ask, wanting to make sure we're talking about the same activity.

'It is. That ... team you know likely thought they'd shut it down, but it never actually stopped. It just became harder to find.'

My ears start to ring.

'And the child soldiers?' I ask.

Traelen runs his tongue over his top teeth, pushing out his lip – it's the most obviously uncomfortable I've seen him, and I try to brace myself for whatever he's about to share. We're having a dangerous conversation, that's clear. But there seems far less hesitation on his end than mine; I can only assume that's because he knows enough about where I am aligned, and how that in turn aligns with his agenda.

My mind wants to run away with this new knowledge, but I tamp down on where it could go. Make myself be present. To listen. Learn.

'Sir?' I prompt.

'The children who are left behind, and some who are just taken anyway, are sent to the front line between Coprath and Tae. Nuntainia would prefer to sacrifice the children of Tae than lose the access to the Gorge Tae gives them—or be outed as providing resources to Tae to hold Coprath back from the Rite Gorge.'

I frown. 'Why doesn't Tae just shut down access if they know Nuntainia is doing this?'

'Because both Nuntainia and Coprath are fundamentally stronger than Tae. Shutting our access and trade routes across the sea would see significant push back from Nuntainia and the obvious withdrawal of our support against Coprath. If Coprath have control of the Gorge, it's entirely possible neither Nuntainia *or* Tae could access external trade.'

I press the pad of my index finger hard between my brows. 'So we're helping them with one hand and destroying them with the other?'

Traelen nods and an unsettled quiet gathers around us. One filled with the enormity, and complexity, of these layered political decisions, and the fallout borne by everyday people.

My fear that Traelen was setting me up to go to Vana slowly melts away, along with the tension in my jaw – only to be replaced by the fierce reality that I will be walking straight into the poisonous pit that's behind it all.

I stare at Traelen. The man who had Quillian arrested is not only on the same side, but is now openly sharing information with me. Is that because it's now also clear where I stand? Was it not clear to Traelen where Quillian's allegiances lay? I can feel my brows furrow at that question – wasn't being a traitor exactly why Traelen arrested him?

'So,' I say, blowing out a breath, 'the Prime Minister's office?'

He steeples his fingers, his Chief of Staff expression coming back. 'Think of yourself as still on the island, Luka,' he says gently. 'You will see people here you served there as well. Your role is essentially the same—maintain that facade, and you will be fine.'

'Okay,' I say after a beat, 'I can do that.' It's essentially what I was already planning. 'Are there any prisoners—guests—shit—*politicians* who know ... how I got off the island?'

'No. All of the surviving guests were questioned, most of them outraged even at that, but, no. None of them gave anything on the breach. No one here knows you weren't actually "recovered".'

The rest of the day is spent getting a tour of the House, being provided with a security pass, and getting to know the other attendants, although

Teddy and I spend most of the time getting to know each other. I'm also assigned a duty phone that burns in my pocket – can they track me with it?

'Do you know why you're here?' I ask Teddy, as we make our way back out of the House and through the security station we came in. It's a bold question to ask, particularly here, but I need to test how much she will let me know. How much information she has, and what gaps we can fill for each other.

Without getting either of us caught.

She slides her gaze sideways at me. 'That's a big question. But, yes, I know.'

'Do you know why I'm here?'

'Yep,' she says, popping the 'p' and pushing the glass door open, the pleasantly warm air immediately caressing my face and neck. 'Damn,' she says, looking at her phone. 'One of the kids is vomiting, we'll have to take a rain check tonight.'

My stomach sinks. I'm exhausted from all the talking around of things I did today – something I might have thought I was good at on the island but, up there, I didn't realise death or Vana was a possible outcome for me. But, even with the tiredness pulling at my eyelids, I was seriously looking forward to seeing my best friends tonight.

'Does Zale know why you're here?'

Teddy freezes. 'She knows enough.'

There's the hint of a bite to her tone, and I immediately bristle at the thought of Zale's wife keeping secrets from her. Teddy softens a little as I stare at her.

'I have to keep her safe, Luka,' she says. 'I'm sure you can understand that.'

Holland flanks me by the time we're halfway down the front path, the first time I've seen him all day, and rubs his palms together.

'I am so ready to eat,' he says, and I can't help but laugh. Apparently, Holland and food are going to be a recurring theme. 'I'm going to order in.'

Despite my disappointment at missing Zale and Akira tonight, I'm quite looking forward to a night in with Holland and Finn. And it will be good not to be alone in my house that already feels like a stranger and I haven't even laid eyes on it again yet.

Teddy says her goodbyes and I silently hope she doesn't bring a vomiting bug back with her tomorrow as I turn and wave – my stomach is still uneasy after our exchange about Zale – only to find myself face to face with Finn at the bottom of the path.

'Where the fuck did you come from?' Holland says.

'I'm here to collect,' Finn says, looking at me, something dancing in his gaze. 'It's tattoo time.'

CHAPTER TEN

'I thought this portal was for emergency use only?' I ask, excitement to be going back rising in my voice. I only left in the early hours of this morning with no sure return date, and it already feels like too long away from Blossom, Quillian, and the brothers.

'They are normally,' Finn says quietly, despite us being the only two people in the deserted car park, Holland having gone to my townhouse so that someone is 'home'. 'But it's important we get you your tattoo.' He turns to me. 'I assume you're not having doubts?'

I laugh, but it's more out of surprise than humour as we walk further into the dark edges of the space. 'No, no doubts. I just hadn't expected to be going back so soon.' Placing a hand on his arm, I stop and he does the same. 'Are you having doubts about me?'

His answer feels as important as Quillian's would. But, while part of me doesn't feel like I need his endorsement to be doing this, I also want to give him an opportunity to raise any issues with me. He and Cortane are clearly very important to Quillian, and it's only Cortane's views I'm really sure of between the two of them. Does Finn see me as a distraction as well?

Finn places his other hand over mine which is still gently framing his forearm, his palm cupping the back of my knuckles.

'I have no doubts about where your loyalties or your values lie, Luka. I've spent a lot of time with manipulative people. You're not one of them.'

Cross-border negotiations, it comes to me quickly – that's what Traelen announced when Finn arrived in the prison. Perhaps that's what his undercover role was, the same as Quillian had a role in Nuntainia.

I smile at him, the confirmation of his belief in me bolstering my growing need to tell them about today and Traelen. How readily would they believe me about him? I'm not sure even I believe it yet. Not that I can tell Finn to gauge his reaction, my duty contract making the words stick in my throat.

'How do the tattoos work?' I ask. 'Beyond being a show of a personal commitment.'

Finn glances around again, scanning the stretch of pocked asphalt around us, before turning back to the far end and wordlessly, gently, encouraging me to walk with him. 'The ink is infused with a magic we came across in Tae, though it's from Coprath originally, that cuts the binds of your contract. It was an incredibly useful discovery. There are some who can read tattoos, like you,' he says with a quick but meaningful look at me, 'and make the connection. So it's a risk to have them anywhere public, particularly if we're in a group of any size—not everyone who can read them ultimately does good with that knowledge.'

'So the new ink allowed you to exchange better information without relying on the right person putting together the puzzle of the tattoo—or finding others who had them?'

Finn's boots crunch gently on the hard surface as we near the side we arrived. 'And it allowed us to expand with some organisation. It's difficult to scale when there were only a handful of us who knew, with certainty, who was committed.'

I think of Quillian's tattoo – an explosion of colour that runs up and around his ribs, around the front of his chest and up his neck, disappearing into his hairline. Like someone threw the most brilliant colour palette at him, the darkest bits dusting the top.

'So why is his so obvious?' I ask.

'Q's?'

I nod as we reach the far side of the gravel.

Finn is silent for a long moment, staring at the space I know he can tap into the portal Cortane has allowed us to access from this side. 'I guess ...

he has a big statement to make.' He smiles at me softly. 'You're good for him, you know?'

'Quillian?' I can feel myself blushing from my chest to my ears.

'Yes, Quillian. If there was anyone else, I'd have to dispatch them to save him from it.'

I chuckle, the image of a naked, colourful Quillian dancing behind my eyes. 'No killing required, promise.'

'Have you told him that?'

'Do I need to?'

He reaches out into the space in front of us, as if he is going to open an imaginary door. I suppose he is in a way.

'In my experience,' he sighs, 'I've found it's best not to miss the opportunities right in front of you.'

Finn twists his hand and the air before us starts to whirl gently.

'Ready?' he asks, taking my elbow and, without waiting for a response, we step through, my hair flying around my face.

'About fucking time,' Nix grumbles, crossing the short space between us after Finn and I appear in the camp square, and lifting me into a hug.

I laugh despite his tone, brushing the hair from my eyes and a feeling of home settling over me more quickly than it has in a long time. The air is hotter, drier, here, and the prickling of sweat begins under my arms. 'I literally haven't even been gone a whole day, and you've missed me already?'

'Luka,' he says seriously, 'we didn't see each other for five fucking years before this, did you forget? So, yes—after being with you on the island, and having you here doing this with me—I did miss you, smartass. And now I have to worry about you as well. I don't like it.'

'How was it?' Blossom asks as she joins Nix.

'Honestly? Mostly pretty tedious—tours, instructions, rules ... but ...' I search the space for Quillian, spotting him leaning against one of the dirty-cream buildings that circles the tiny town square, gaze focused on me.

Nix groans.

'Did you have to pick someone so ... Quillian?' he asks. The question is meant to be said in jest, I know. But there is still an edge of hurt to his tone, and I know he is trying to get beyond his difficulties with him for my sake.

I nudge Nix's arm with my shoulder, smiling at Quillian. 'I didn't really mean to pick him, it just ... kinda happened.'

'Quillian aside,' Blossom says, 'you look like you have an update.'

I open my mouth, but I can't form the words about Traelen and Teddy. Fucking contract. 'I need a tattoo.'

Cortane appears at Quillian's shoulder and, after a whispered conversation, he leaves the square with her, an intently focused look on his face. I swallow the small bite of disappointment that he's been called away before he even said hello.

'Can we do it now?' I ask Finn, who's watching Quillian and Cortane leave. But Blossom's right, despite the uneventful afternoon in Parliament House, my conversation with Traelen – the Chief of Staff who sent half the people I love to Vana – is still burning through my understanding of what unfolded on the island.

He looks at Nix. 'Find out what's happening and report back to me,' he instructs before returning his attention to me. 'Let me get my kit and I'll come to you,' he says, striding off towards the little streets of townhouses.

Their departures leave just Blossom and me in the square, the two of us together again in a swirl of activity that we're not completely across. But Finn is right, I don't want Quillian to miss any opportunities to make things better. Even if it means I can't be the first priority.

'Shall we?' I ask Bloss, brushing my hands down my sides as if I am dusting dirt off my clothes.

As we take the short steps to the house, I decide I'm not going to tell them about Traelen immediately. Other than knowing he's supportive, I don't actually have anything tangible yet. No understanding of who their contact may have been, and no evidence of either program. Traelen has confirmed the breeding program never stopped, but what good is that information without proof – or a way to stop it?

I fear they'd all just put themselves in danger without the full picture if I tell them now. And I need to give them more reason to be accepting of Traelen before I out him.

Blossom shuts the door behind us, and tiredness makes its way behind my eyes as I marvel at being on this side of the information. How, in a relatively short period of time, I have become one of the people withholding for the safety of those I love.

I lie as best I can on the small dining table in the house Blossom and I are staying in, my feet on one of the chairs while Finn looms over me.

'How about this?' he asks quietly, holding up a sketch. 'It's not quite what you said in the meeting room.'

I suck in a breath as I take in the line drawing. It's like a miniature of looking out of a window of the island prison. The columns, the balcony, and the sky beyond. And the words 'for those who prove' woven around the edges like a vine.

'Finn,' I whisper, 'it's remarkable. Will it be colourful?'

'If you want, yes.'

'Yes—I want that. But no jasmine, please.' After being in Parliament House today, knowing how suffocating it will be to once again be surrounded by people I can't give anything away to, people I have to hide my true self away from ... I don't want a reminder of that constriction on my skin. I want it to be a reminder of freedom. And of making choices. Of what it feels like to leap.

'Can I add something else, too?' I ask quietly, Finn waiting for me to continue. 'I'd like a heron.'

He nods once, picking up the vibrating pen. 'Ready?'

I swallow as my gaze runs over the instrument in his hand, heart thrumming loudly, and it occurs to me how pivotal my heart has been in getting me here. What it holds for the people I am doing this with – turning traitor for.

'I've changed my mind on where it goes.'

I undo the button-up shirt Blossom found me somewhere and hold it so my breasts are covered, but Finn can get access to the space in between. He shakes his head gently with a sly smile.

'Good thing Quillian's not here to see me do this,' he says.

'Too late for that,' a deep voice says from behind me, and I jump, warmth spreading through me as Finn assesses my chest. Manipulating my skin a little with his fingers, pressing and pulling gently as he seems to work out what will go where.

'You're going to free-hand it?' I ask, unable to keep the small tremor from my voice. In this moment, I don't know what feels scarier – the uncertainty about how much this will hurt, the possibility I'll hate how it looks branded on my chest, or the commitment it symbolises.

Finn just nods, concentration wrinkling the corners of his eyes.

Letting a long exhale leave me, and willing some of my tension to go with it, I drop my head back on the table and give myself to the process.

I can only hear the sound of my breath and the vibration of the pen. Blossom takes my hand and I squeeze, my stomach starting to somersault. Finn assured me it wouldn't bleed a lot, but it still makes me stupidly uneasy.

'Let's do this,' I say, and close my eyes.

A sharp sting, accompanied by a burning sensation, quickly travels the length of my sternum and snakes its way onto the base of my breasts, and I try not to press myself away from the source. Not that the table makes that easy. I focus on my breath, keeping it a steady rhythm for Finn to work with, the feel of Bloss's hand in mine, and what this means.

That I am no longer bound by any duty.

That I will be readily able to share what I find as I need.

With every moment that ticks by, the burning of Finn's work seems to sink itself further into my chest cavity and spins pain around my torso. Not enough for me to cry out, but I do clench my eyes closed a little harder. Bloss made this look so easy.

Every now and then Finn pauses, and I think I might finally be able to breathe again when he wipes at my skin before pressing the sharp tip back to me. I can't even tell if it's in the same place each time or somewhere new.

Eventually, my mind turns itself from the focus of the burn and into dark corners I haven't paid attention to in a long time – like the one where I keep my father. The disappointment in his face when I was unsuccessful for the Head role at the Academy, despite his refusal to recommend me for the role, is the first memory of him to find me. And it's as crushing as it was in real life, even after all this time. But I let myself wander past that hurt, and I imagine him sitting at his old, worn timber desk making notes upon notes on the history of magic. The different lines and how they came to be; of course, the line that occupied him the most – the Karaylia.

I can't help but think of what he might be doing now. What project is occupying his time, what he is recommending to those who commission his remarkable mind, and if he ever thinks of me. We haven't spoken since the day I told him I didn't get the job. I was ... wounded. I'd thought he'd seen so much more in me than just that role. He was my world, and I'd let him down. Let his legacy down ...

I left for my duty not long after, and I never wrote to him, nor he to me.

A sharp pang that has nothing to do with the tattoo strikes me – I never gave him a way to contact me, even if he wanted to. I had my phone then, sure, but he'd never really used one. Letters were his only way of communicating and ... I didn't give him anywhere to send one.

'Hey,' Blossom says, 'where'd you go?'

It takes me a moment to realise Finn has finished and isn't just taking another pause. I push any lingering sense of regret away as my stomach fills with nerves to see what he's done, what the permanent mark of the path I have chosen looks like.

I blink into the soft light, squinting slightly as I drag my consciousness forward.

'Just thinking,' I say, smiling at Bloss even as my eyes still water.

She gives me a slightly worried look but says nothing more. From the flicker in her face, I know she will want to pick this up again later, ask me what it is I'm not saying. And I find ... I might be ready to talk about him more.

'You did great,' Finn says, taking a cloth from somewhere at my side and wiping down my chest gently.

Quillian appears on the other side of where I still lie on the table, and I turn my head towards him, smiling at the warmth in his face.

'I can take it from here,' he says, holding out a hand for the cloth without looking away from me. 'Did River make the balm?'

'Here,' Bloss says, as she hands him a small, dark brown container.

'You need to see Cort,' Quillian says to Finn. 'Blossom, you're welcome to go too, it will impact you as well.'

A tiny seed of concern finds its way behind where I now have a dull heat pulsing through my chest. Cortane didn't look at me when she took Quillian from the square when I arrived, but the set of her jaw was clear.

'Clean her up gently,' Finn instructs, as he presses the cloth into Quillian's outstretched hand above me. 'Make sure it's clean and there are no broken lines. Then use River's balm and have her lie here for at least ten minutes. You need to make sure the markings are sealed, or we can't guarantee the contract will have been overridden, and her skin will be too raw for me to do it again quickly.'

Quillian just nods, and I watch Finn and Blossom turn away.

'Thank you,' I call after them.

'You were much more stoic than I thought you'd be,' Quillian says, a smirk on his face – clearly remembering how I passed out on him the first time I 'met' his wings.

'That's because, this time, I was expecting to be scarred for life. Perhaps I'm just not good with surprises?' I tease.

He makes a sound in the back of this throat that has my skin warming further than just under my new tattoo.

'Is everything okay?' I ask, moving aside the thickening in the air as he looks at me sprawled on the table, and making myself focus on what Bloss and Finn are about to find out. What I would like to know about the developments in my new world.

He sighs. 'Not really, and I would greatly prefer not to be talking about it while you're literally laid out on the table for me, but ...'

'It's important,' I offer.

'Yeah.' Quillian takes the cloth and wipes between my breasts softly as I study his face. There's a phenomenon about it that I hope never changes. The way it's so open and warm when he looks at me compared to when he's working. Or, at least, when he was Warden. Of course, I know now why he has such a hatred for those people – but I think he also shows me a little more vulnerability than the others here. Something I'm not even sure he realises.

But right now, there is a hardness, a worry behind the warmth as well.

I wait while he picks up the small, brown glass container and scoops balm onto his middle finger before slowly rubbing it over the patch of tender skin. Immediately, I'm flooded with a cooling, tingling sensation, and I can't help but sigh as my eyes close.

'You know we have outposts across the continent,' Quillian says, and I nod, eyes still closed as he smooths the wonderful healing balm into my tattoo. 'Two of them have been raided by Hunters.'

His finger stops as his voice hardens, and I open my eyes, catching the flash of something so much deeper than anger in his features.

'Oh, Quillian. What's happened?'

'We've lost some. Others ... have gone to Vana,' he says in a flat voice I know belies the emotion underneath.

'How many?' I ask, placing my hand over his at my chest.

'Too many, Luka.' He closes his eyes and his head drops forward a little. 'Too fucking many. I know it's to be expected, I know they understand what they're in for when they join, I know ... but they're still people who followed me into this. People I am responsible for.'

I move to sit up, but he flattens his palm and pushes me back down. 'Time's not up,' he says, opening his eyes again, searching mine.

'What are you planning?' I ask, thinking of the obvious conversations he's had with Cortane. The same topic Finn must be discussing now.

'I know where they're going next, and we're going to head them off.'

An icy, spiky sort of nausea rolls down my throat and deep into my gut, as if I've swallowed a poisoned thorn bush. 'Wha–what does that mean?' I ask.

He skims his hand over my front to lace his fingers in mine.

'I'm going to battle, Luka. It's what I do. It looks different sometimes, like it did when I wore the Warden's uniform, but ... it's what I do. Fight for what I believe in.'

My eyes sting with tears, but I know what he says is right, that he has a history here I am only just beginning to learn. I only met him because of this fight he is in.

'Okay,' I make myself breathe, unable to make it sound strong. 'What does that mean?'

He stares at me for a long moment, and I know he's weighing up what to tell me. But we both know my being here, this tattoo, my position in

Parliament House, those things mean I need the truth. And I don't doubt he will give it to me, even if it takes him a little to form the words.

'I'm going to lead a team that will include people you care about, like Nix and River, to assassinate the Hunters before they make the next outpost. It will probably look very much like the footage I showed you when you arrived. Then, I'm going to tell the House they've been killed on a mission they should have never been sent on. I'm going to make sure they know they can't wipe us out quietly. I'm going to protect the people in those outposts or ... die trying. And, if I survive, which I will, I will hope the Hunters' families find peace, eventually, without their loved ones.'

I stare at him as the weight of his words presses on my chest. The conflict of pain and violence in Quillian makes my heart race as I move to sit up again. This time he doesn't stop me as I slide from the table, my shirt still open, and hold him to me, my arms winding up and around the back of his neck and spearing through his hair. Our chests move against each other with our breaths, and I close my eyes. Not against this reality that I know must come, but at how ... immense it feels to try to comprehend.

'I will show no mercy, Luka, not to the ones who ...' he falters, 'and I fear you will judge me greatly.'

'I trust you, Quillian,' I say, drawing back to look at him.

I want to say I'm not so naive to expect there to be no casualties. But, despite what I know happened on the island, what I watched in Quillian's video, the truth is I wanted to believe that not only was there no more danger to Nix and River, but that there'd also be no more death by their hands. I got them off the island and away from Vana. Wasn't that supposed to be enough?

'Just ... remember they are following orders, too,' I say, and he gives me a long look.

'You are better than this world deserves, you know that, right?' he says, tipping my chin up and kissing me lightly. 'Better than what I deserve.'

CHAPTER ELEVEN

Cortane's command room, as I am coming to think of it, is thick with anticipation when Quillian and I enter, everyone paying close attention to Cortane as she delivers a briefing. The translucent, purple screen is lit up with a map showing a number of unnamed townships, black crosses, and red dots – none of which immediately means anything to me. But as I scan the image, the familiar geography starts to take shape; the body of water in the top-right corner could be the Klades river port, but I can't tell where the river disappears to on this map.

'—here,' Cortane is saying, not even a pause in her talking as we arrive, 'is where the most casualties were sustained—seventy people and counting. Then there are about a hundred and fifteen in the infirmary, and fifty still standing who are trying to run the camp and deal with the fallout. We're sending in teams from here'—she points to another part on the map with a quick glance at Quillian that tells me he already knows, or even developed this plan—'to do a staggered extraction.'

'Where are they taking them?' River asks, as my mind spins around the numbers Cortane is listing. The concierge team on the island was about fifty at any given time, and more than that have been wiped out or lie injured and possibly dying somewhere because ... what? They believe in something better? They were working to spill the secrets of this insidious government?

'Location number five on the list you and Nix worked up—it's got a balance of reasonable shelter for the wounded and a good chance of defence,' she says.

'Getting supplies in is harder,' Nix says, and River nods.

'Yes, but it's the best shot for now.'

'Janly has gone ahead to one of the other camps to coordinate the collection of any surplus supplies and begin rationing,' Quillian says, his tone hard. 'The loss of life and numbers is obviously a huge hit, but we also can't forgo the supplies that are in each camp. There is only so far we can stretch our resources, and I won't have people starving as well as coming under fire on my watch.'

His words 'my watch' snag on something in my chest. The loneliness of it.

'Emeris and Shiloh work well with Jan,' I suggest hesitantly, 'if you want to send them to her. Shiloh's Arkanan, too.'

'Yes, good idea,' Quillian says. 'I don't know Emeris that well, but I remember how Shiloh operates.' He locks eyes with me, leaving no doubt he's referring to the different healing sessions we both attended with Shiloh – mine and his and, of course, then Bloss and Freya.

Cortane gives a curt nod.

'What can I do?' Blossom asks from where she sits in a black chair. River's not far from her shoulder and goes very, very still as she asks her question, staring at Quillian.

Quillian looks between River and me before he finally looks back at Blossom. 'Can you help sort through the supplies we have here and work up some ration allocations? We'll need to tighten up across all the camps so we can spread it out.'

She nods.

'I'll need a list of how many you have here and how physical their roles are,' she says, shifting herself forward a little like she's ready to move now.

'I can get you that,' River replies.

'And then we're going in, I assume? Come from the north and cut them off?' Nix asks, as if he's just asked about dinner after a day on the water at the harbour, and not as if he's about to attack Hunters head on.

My breaths get shallower.

'What if the Hunters are like Casey and Holland, and not ...' I trail off, unsure how to further explain. But the thought of the people I care about charging in to take innocent lives makes me ill.

They're all quiet for a beat, as if thinking how to best answer my question. Cortane returns her attention to the map, her shoulders tight.

'We do our best,' Finn says gently. 'We try to keep casualties low and give some a choice. But, in the end, if we can't guarantee the safety of our network, there are people we can't leave living.'

'Being on this side of the fight isn't as pretty as the inside of the island, Princess,' Cortane says without turning around, the usual sharp edge to her voice slightly softened.

My head is beginning to feel like it's been stuffed with the inside of a cushion.

'And what if one of you is hurt?' I ask.

'Lu,' Nix says, taking my elbow and making me look at him, his champagne eyes crackling with emotion. 'We're the best of the best—we're not going to get hurt. Trust me when I tell you there was a very good reason the government wanted us on their covert missions, and why they were so keen to have us in Vana once they learned of our defection. The number of Hunters who ended up on the island to hunt us down wasn't just for show.'

I try to let that comfort me, I do, but it's like the words skim off my skin and fall to the floor.

'And what do I do?' I ask, more than a little panic rising up the back of my throat despite my effort to keep my voice steady. 'I can be helpful—I'm not going to ... sit here and wait.'

No one answers, but they don't need to. I already know what I'll be doing. I may not have found anything yet to stop this, but there is no chance I will be sitting in this empty camp while everyone else is helping the cause.

'You,' Cortane says, finally putting her back to the map again and facing us, 'need to find out what else they have planned. They seem to be only documenting one attack ahead at a time, which is why we missed the last one. That's either a strategy to lower the risk of their systems being compromised, or they are gathering further intel as they go. This is the first time we've suffered a direct attack. None of our locations have been so completely compromised before. We need to know what's coming next—if it was just a fucking lucky find for them, or if someone on our end is spilling secrets.'

Even though her calling me 'princess' still rankles, not once did she suggest just now that she thought I was 'almost' capable of getting the right information.

But the other issue she's so casually mentioned, about the spilling of secrets—

It feels like she's poured fuel over a fire that's been smouldering in the pit of my stomach. One I've never given much thought to. Or if I had, I didn't know why it was there or what to do with it.

My phone buzzes gently in my back pocket.

H: Change of plans. A group of us are heading to a new restaurant to the east of where we last ate. It was a knockout, but this one will be twice as good! Meet us there?

I stare at Holland's message for what feels like several minutes as the others talk about their next steps, but I have no idea what he's talking about, he'll have to wait until—

Plans.

He said 'change of plans' ... but we didn't have any.

'Wait,' I say, my phone halfway back to my pocket. 'Is there a camp east of where you were just attacked?'

Quillian's brow furrows in question, but he moves closer to the screen and points.

'Here,' he says. 'Why?'

'And you think the next target is where?' I respond.

'The comms said due-west, just here,' Cortane says, tapping the screen. 'Like Nix said, we'll go north first and then cut back.'

'What is it, Lu?' Nix asks. River and Blossom just watch me, waiting.

'Holland—he said there's been a change.' I hand my phone to Quillian, Holland's message still open. 'I think they're going to the camp east of the attack first.'

'Holland?' Cortane asks, a bite in her voice. 'Are we really going to trust a Hunter with this?'

Quillian lifts his head slowly and hands back my phone, his attention moving to Cortane, the hair on my arms standing up. There's something so ... intense about the movement. 'We're trusting him with Luka.'

A flush creeps up and over my collar bones and into my face, my heart racing a little faster at Quillian's low words.

Cortane waves him off, ignoring the rest of us. 'Because we also sent Finn to keep an eye on everything,' she says.

River is still staring at me, arms crossed over his broad chest, and I implore him with my eyes. I don't know how to articulate my trust in Holland, but the way he came through for me on the island ... with no hesitation that I was doing the right thing. It was like he was looking for a way to get here, to join us. And I believe it's for good intent only.

'I think we go east,' River says. 'Holland's good for this. Finn, you agree?'

Finn's black brows slowly lift to his hairline as if the question has taken him completely by surprise, but he's been intently following every word and expression of this conversation like normal.

He takes a step closer to the map and studies it for a moment.

'The camp due-west is closer, the road in wider,' he says. 'It seems a more likely place to attack. The one to the east is bigger and would cause us more casualties, but it's harder to access ... what did Holland say exactly?'

I read out the message and look back at Finn.

'Twice as good?' he asks, and I nod. 'I think ... they want to ensure they outnumber us, so initially the shorter, clearer route seemed the best choice for maximum boots on the ground. But this is a less obvious move that, if successful, would yield them better results and reinforce their initial statement.'

Cortane lets out a loud breath and Nix curses.

'That suggests they know all of our locations,' he says. 'That this one wasn't a lucky find.'

A cold slither of dread slips between my ribs with the knowledge that can mean only one thing – they're being fed information from the inside.

Blossom's gaze bounces around the room. 'So,' she says, 'we prepare to evacuate the original camp and set them up in the new location River said—number five?—and go to the east camp to head them off.'

Our gazes meet, and it feels like there's a current of electricity between us. Like we're both finally where we should be. But the thought of Bloss in the middle of all of whatever is going to go down at the eastern camp is like nails down the back of my throat.

'And I'll go back to the House and see if I can find out exactly how much more they know.'

Finn moves around the screen to stand by my side. 'We should go now before anyone has reason to wonder why you're not in the city.'

'No,' I say. 'I want you to stay with this team—they'll need you.'

'Lu—' Nix objects, but I hold up my hand and he clamps his mouth shut with a frown.

'You can't seriously tell me Finn is more useful babysitting me than being with you,' I say.

Cortane laughs. 'No, and I'm pleased I'm not the only one worried about where we're putting our resources.'

Quillian narrows his gaze at her and she rolls her eyes. 'Having him there is like a fucking beacon, Quill. If we're going to trust Holland, let's trust Holland.'

'Agreed,' I say before anyone else can add anything, the small fire Cortane poured fuel on burning a little brighter, hotter, at her agreement. 'And you can take Casey.'

Waking in my old bedroom, I'm gripped by a momentary panic. A sort of out-of-place feeling like I'm floating and desperately trying to anchor myself to something, anything, to bring my mind back into focus and my heart rate down.

It's the photo on the bedside table that does it – one of Zale, Akira, and me from long ago. Well before partners and children and duties. When my hair had a pale pink streak in the platinum blonde, and Akira was trying a new style of nose stud that was also chained to her left ear. Zale, as always, looked perfectly put together even then, a timeless vision of elegance. And while it brings a nostalgia with it, it also brings a heavy grounding.

Had it been Zale or Akira chosen for duty the first time instead of me, would their children still exist?

Automatically, I find myself looking out the window, but there's only the smallest sliver of sky to be seen from this angle. I now remember all too well that I could barely make out the night sky from bed, something I definitely grew used to on the island. But my thick, dark green velvet bedspread brings a warmth to my chest, and I curl a little deeper into it as I brace myself to face today.

But only for a moment. If I snuggle too deep, I might never get out. So I drag myself from the too-empty bed.

'Morning,' Holland says around a mouthful of something when I make my way downstairs in my white, knee-length skirt, and blue and white spotted shirt. One that buttons high enough to cover that I'm only wearing a sports crop underneath so no underwire rubs my tattoo.

'Your tipples were on the doorstep this morning,' he says after his swallow.

My footsteps falter slightly. Tipples.

Immunity and health with birth control would be good. But I don't know if I could physically make myself take the magic dampener again. There is still a vast silence in my veins where I imagine any magic might take hold, but I can't lock out the opportunity, just in case.

'You organised food?' I ask by way of answer, opening the pantry and ignoring the package the end of the bench, for now.

He makes a muffled sound and swallows loudly. 'Yeah, thought you might need fortifying to update me on last night. I'll cook.'

I sigh as I take a seat at the breakfast bar and watch Holland prepare me a breakfast of eggs, toast and grilled cheese. I don't hesitate to tell him what was agreed. In broad strokes, anyway, and he doesn't press me for any details I can't provide. He runs one hand down his auburn, slightly grey-flecked beard, assessing me with his light-brown eyes, which seem to hold a quiet understanding that he needs to earn the trust of the group – despite his tattoo and his promises.

But there's also something that looks how I imagine the fire in my belly might if I could show it to someone.

'I know this seems fast to you all,' he says, placing the eggflip on the counter and watching me. 'You only know me as the Hunter who coordinated the arrests on the island, only to turn around and freefall off the edge with you—and Casey as someone I dragged along for the ride.'

I don't tell him there's something about having them kill someone to get me to safety that trumps that. Not yet, anyway. He obviously wants to get this off his chest, and I can't say I'm not curious about his reasons.

'But Casey and me'—he grips the edge of the counter behind him as he leans back—'we've been talking, quietly, for a long time about the ... things we've seen. Things we've been ordered to do.' He draws a long inhale that whistles slightly between his teeth. 'I'll tell you over a drink one day, but suffice to say—working in Vana, learning some of those prisoners' stories—it was enough for us to be asking a lot of questions. And there were just never any answers.'

'At least you were asking questions,' I say, studying the thin layer of butter on the edge of the egg flip. 'I feel like I never asked enough—I just took everything I saw at face value.' The stone that never seems to leave my gut grows and shifts as I consider my own ignorance.

'I'm lucky you turned up before I asked the wrong one.'

I glance up at him. 'How so?'

'There was ... a determination in your face as you set fire to that office that was in such contrast to the last time I'd seen you leave it. I guess, somehow, I just *knew* you'd had the same epiphany as me: that all is not as we are taught to believe. More than that, we have to fight for the change we want to see.' The frying pan gives a particularly loud sizzle, and he turns away from me, picking up the eggflip and scooping my fried egg onto a plate. 'So following you gave me an opening to finally act, to grasp the bigger picture before I could be sent to Vana for being too inquisitive.'

The egg yolk wobbles slightly as Holland slides the plate towards me.

'They do that? Put people away just for asking too many questions?'

'If they're uncomfortable questions, absolutely.'

'I always thought Vana was full of the worst of the worst,' I say heavily.

'Oh, it is,' he says, 'I put some of those people there myself and, honestly, what they're subjected to in there is easy compared to what they actually deserve. It's just not true for everyone who ends up there, the same as the people in the other prison—your prison—committed a mix of crimes as well. I don't know all the details of the people they took out up there,' he says, and the look on his face tells me he's talking about the prisoner deaths, 'but we both know their serving on the Defence Committee wasn't a coincidence.'

I cut into my egg and toast, but I can't quite bring myself to actually put it in my mouth. Instead, words I have been too worried to form tumble out.

'I don't know how to be subservient to the people in the House now that I know what goes on. What if I get us all caught and sent to Vana?'

Holland laughs, and I stare at him, egg perched precariously on my fork.

'I don't think you give yourself enough credit. Think of it as putting on a dress you wore once and no longer like. If you focus on the fact it's a dress, and not what you don't like about it, it can still be clothing. Make sense?'

Letting the words roll around, I'm not entirely sure they do make sense, but I get what he's saying. I have been doing a duty for the last five years – I might know more now than before, but I still know how to do a duty. I have my own 'mask' I can don.

The thick paper bag that has arrived makes a crinkling sound when I finally reach out and drag it towards me on the bench. Pursing my lips, I pull out the three glass bottles with their brass lids and listen to them connect with the bench.

Holland leans back on the opposite counter and watches, arms crossed over his soft blue t-shirt, and I let my gaze flick up to him.

'Not so keen?' he asks.

I stand, magic dampener in hand, and walk around the breakfast bar and into the kitchen.

'Not so keen,' I confirm as I tip the dampener down the sink.

CHAPTER TWELVE

The Prime Minister's 'office' is actually a series of rooms. A reception type area – where it seems I will have a desk along the wall near Traelen's office, and a handful of other workstations. As well as a number of small meeting rooms, and a large boardroom.

My phone – the one that feels like a lifeline – buzzes, and I whip it out, palms sweating.

Q: About to leave, I'll message you when we're done.

I don't know what else I expect him to say, especially when we're not face to face, but the message feels laden with unsaid things. At the same time, he said he would survive. Perhaps there is nothing else he felt the need to say. On the other hand, I'm bursting with things I can't articulate.

Is it possible I have found my shot at love in the middle of this crazy situation? And, if so, what are the chances we would be able to see it through? Before I met Quillian, I would never have predicted I'd need to protect my heart from not only an individual, but the possibility of them dying in ... the act of non-duty?

L: talk to you soon x

There's so much I would like to say, even if it hasn't crossed his mind, but I know now is impossible timing. Whatever this is, wherever it's going to go, it's not what I want him thinking about when he's about to go into battle with some of the people I consider my family.

L: be safe, message me ASAP, I send to the group chat I have with Nix, River and Bloss.

N: always

B: you too - stay focused there, we'll be fine

River doesn't respond, but I can see he's read the messages as they've come in and I know all of his attention will be on keeping Nix and Blossom safe. He doesn't need to tell me in a message.

'Big day today, Luka,' Traelen says, as he strides through the office door to the reception area, the door swinging shut silently behind him as I slide my phone into my skirt pocket and out of sight. I smile like I would have on the island, even as all of my insides wobble. I *think* he's on our side, but telling him I'm nervous about the battle my team are about to be in, particularly here, feels like it would be very stupid. He dumps his dark-brown satchel on the desk next to mine, even though his name is in small letters on the door behind me.

'Defence Committee meeting. I want you to coordinate the support,' he says, and I suppress a sharp inhale. 'All the papers have been prepared and each of the members should have downloaded them to their own devices already—someone will say they didn't receive them though, there's always one. Direct them to me if that happens. You're in charge of catering and making sure the day runs smoothly. Every member needs ample fresh water, more pastries than they can possibly eat, and any other drinks of choice. You will also be a message runner if required. Got it?'

My mind flies through the instructions. It's a bit different to what I did on the island, but not so different to some of the board meetings I supported early in my career at the school. But 'Defence Committee'? Could it really be that Traelen has delivered me straight into the same committee the dead prisoners on the island had some involvement in?

He gives me a knowing look as I stare at him, mind whirling. He was, apparently, completely honest with me when I first arrived here. But the confirmation just stirs all the questions about his motives into an uncomfortable roil in my gut. Exactly how long has he been playing both sides? Where do his loyalties truly lie? Is he the contact Cortane spoke of?

'It's good to know who is on each committee,' he says, and I nod, trying to recall if I know when he took on his role of Chief of Staff. Does that align with when the contact went dark?

'Here is the number for catering,' he says, picking up his phone. My official one, currently sitting next to my keyboard, buzzes in response.

'And the rest of the time?'

He eyes me studiously before glancing around the empty reception area – our early start obviously not extended to the rest of whoever is on this team. Being on duty just before dawn is something I do by reflex - I hadn't given any thought to how the shift timing works here.

'Just be in the room. Listen. Take what you need to do your job,' he says, before taking his bag and disappearing into one of the small meeting rooms, door thudding shut behind him.

Traelen: log on details are under the keyboard

Under the keyboard? Because that's so secure for the Prime Minister's office.

Sliding the slip of paper out, the letters and numbers blur before me. Surely Traelen being the contact would be far too easy? Opening my computer and using the details on the pink note, I find nothing but an empty email inbox. My focus threatens to be absorbed by the phone in my pocket, desperately hoping to hear from the group. Any of them would suffice. But I know it's far too early. Holland told me this morning not to expect any news until nightfall.

The battle is one thing, the evacuation and cleanup is another, he said.

Giving myself a mental shake, I pop 'prison program' into the search function on my personal phone – Cortane having drilled me about not using the duty one for *anything* that could be traced to us – and am instantly shown numerous results. Scanning through them, most seem to be only vaguely relevant news articles from almost twenty years ago on Vanan prisoners, nothing that indicates anything about the program I want information on.

I pause when a more recent result catches my eye.

Aiten Gall arrested.

I open the article that uses a lot of words to not say much at all. It does tell me he was arrested as part of an investigation into fraud, but there is no mention at all of sex-trafficking, or anything that could remotely resemble unsavoury behaviour. Just a bland description of awarding a small procurement contract to the business of a family friend.

I search everything I can think of related to Aiten – his name, his title, more on the fraud allegations, but I get nothing back. Apart from historical notes that place him as Zenaton's assistant minister when they served in the Ministry of Communication at the same time. Their relationship went back some time, it seems. But does that mean the only information released was regarding this 'fraud', and then, as far as the public was concerned, he just disappeared? Or, worse, they assumed he'd been appropriately dealt with by the justice system? I probably would have assumed that, had I been on the mainland to see or pay attention to the article.

But it's clear, as expected, there was nothing published about his sex-trafficking offences and where he should have really ended up – Vana.

Not even an accusation from someone who would have been directly impacted.

'Hunters,' I type into the search instead. I know this general approach won't tell me their attack strategy but, until I work out how to do that, it will give me a better idea of how they work.

The first result is the Ministry of Justice, the overarching organisation responsible for the Hunters. That feels as good a place as any to start. I slide my finger over the result and enter a new page, navigating to the one dedicated to the Hunters.

... an elite number of squadrons whose sole goal is the safety of Nuntainia. Admission to the Hunters is exclusive and highly competitive. Applicants should be aware of invasive personal and psychological testing, as well as physical training and expectations ...

... Hunters are led by Commander Boulster, who reports directly to the Minister of Justice and Deputy Prime Minister. Given the nature of the organisation and the operations they may undertake for the country's national interests, the Integrity Commissioner is a secondary reporting line as required.

The dual reporting position is interesting. Normally, there would only be one minister for them to report to, and I don't recall the Deputy Prime Minister holding two roles before. But then, I have been on the island for a while - perhaps I missed the broadening of his role. Before I can dig further, my computer makes a soft chime and I stiffen as I glance up, seeing the little pink notification on my email.

FROM: Traelen Jardim

SUBJECT: Defence Committee meeting agenda

MESSAGE: For the catering timing, Traelen

I swipe the large screen in front of me to call up the attachment to his email, finding a list of people and attendees for the meeting today.

Among them is the Minister for Justice – and Deputy Prime Minister – Zenaton Blake.

The quiet of the office turns to a sharp ringing in my ears.

Zenaton Blake.

My vision swims as I'm sucked back to the night on the island. The way his face—

I grip the edge of my desk and will myself to stay present. To *think*. But my thoughts are overshadowed by *him*.

The way he reached for me. The sound of the rock Janly wielded as it knocked him to the ground.

You'll pay for that, he'd said – right before Casey stabbed him.

Zenaton Blake. Who knows exactly where my allegiance lies, and that I was not *recovered* from duty. Knows what a key role I played in bringing it all down. Who controls the Hunters *and* is Deputy Prime Minister.

I vaguely recall a news alert on the island about the previous Deputy Prime Minister retiring, but I'd never had cause to worry about who would replace her. Not up there.

Claudius would never send me somewhere I'd be compromised.

But he wasn't alive long enough to know what unfolded with Zenaton.

The hands of the elaborate gold clock hanging on one of the otherwise blank walls barely seem to move as I stare at them. When they do, they wind tighter the ball of tension I can't swallow around.

On shaking legs, I stand and make my way to Traelen's office, and knock.

'Come in.'

I push the door open, the blue and gold abstract painting on his wall a further reminder of just how much closer to everything I am here. There is no sky, no screen separating me from all of this. From all of them.

He does a double take as he processes what I can only imagine is a look of horror on my face. 'Shut the door.'

Numbly, I reach behind me and draw it shut.

'What is it?' he asks carefully.

'The agenda,' I whisper. 'It says Zenaton Blake is coming here. Now.'

'Yes ... he returned to duties upon his early recovery – is that a problem?' His question is slow. Assessing.

'A pretty big one,' I tell him honestly. 'He–he almost stopped me getting out.' I press my hand to my chest to calm my thundering heart. 'He tried to stop me, and one of the Hunters I was with stabbed him. I—left him. He knows about me.'

Traelen sits back in his chair and closes his eyes. It's as disturbed as I think I've ever seen him.

'Fuck,' he mutters. 'He will know you're here. As Deputy Prime Minister and Minister for Justice he will have been briefed on all new staff to this office. That includes you.'

'What do I do?' The room seems to get smaller as Traelen watches me, clearly thinking through the options.

'You'll have to face him. He won't harm you here—even he's not that stupid. I assume you came with some sort of protection?'

I nod.

'Use it if you need to. Do *not* travel anywhere outside this building on your own.'

He stands and paces the room, his peach-coloured suit contrasting the off-white walls.

'It will mean getting you close to the committee will be virtually impossible, and very risky. You need to do today, do your duty, and then the archives will be our only shot to get what we need.'

My skin cools as the claws of reality sink deeper. Zenaton already knows I'm here. And I have nothing. No plan, no weapon I can use without implicating Quillian, and no magic to save me.

I try to distract myself from the waiting by searching – this time on the work machine in front me – methodically going through every member on the meeting agenda. I can see different levels of information for each; there appears to be some vague protocol based on their level of seniority that dictates who has access to their diaries, for example. It's quickly apparent I can't see anyone's emails, which doesn't surprise me at all. Even at the school or on the island, I didn't have anyone else's email.

But I can see most people's diaries and details of their work history. Most of it seems sanitised enough for public viewing, but there might be something I use there another time, so I make a note where the information lives.

My gaze catches on what looks like a file system icon. It's unassuming, but something about pressing on the little blue folder with my finger feels ... significant. Before I've even taken my finger off the cool surface, my screen fills with folders that correspond to the different Ministries of Nuntainia and I quickly scan for, and press on, 'Justice'.

Here, hundreds of small blue folders run down my screen in an alphabetical list, my heart hammering as I scroll and scroll to 'p'.

Nothing.

But there is a 'research' one. Which probably means nothing, but it's an interesting title given what I am trying to do, what my life before duty entailed, and what my father did, or does, for a living. It's probably just that familiarity that tugs at me. Now I'm back, I should reach out and tell him. But I don't even know how to say hello after five years of nothing.

Male voices filter down the hall towards the open reception door, and I quickly exit the file directory and check for messages from the traitors.

Nothing.

I wipe my sweaty palms on my white skirt before standing, just as a group of three, middle-aged men enter the office. I smile in welcome, but not one of them looks my way as they move into the boardroom, engrossed in their conversation.

Another eight people filter in, only one woman and one man acknowledging my existence. Although I'm absolutely confident neither of them would recognise me on the street.

When they're all seated and taking out their letter-sized tablets, I quietly take coffee orders, biting the inside of my cheek as I wonder how I did this for so many years on Zanteera Island. But, then, my fingers weren't trembling as I waited for the arrival of a man who wants me dead. A man who knows I walked away and left him to die.

Three-quarter shot of darkest espresso.

Nausea swirls in my gut.

Room temperature milk with two ice cubes.

Bile presses up the back of my throat.

Blackberry tea with honey from Tae.

Tears burn in my eyes.

I tremble, blinking rapidly at what I'm writing. Focus. *Focus.* These orders are even more elaborate than those from the island, perhaps the prisoners there really did consider it a hardship. I stifle a mirthless laugh.

Messaging the order to the catering contact, Traelen appears at my side, peach suit perfectly pressed.

'Order is in,' I say, glancing up at him and his gold hair that's almost always perfectly in position. I remember what it would look like when he came in from the receiving platform and descended the stairs in the sky. None of the people in that boardroom were in the prison during my time there, and I can't help but wonder if that means they had no need to, or if they had already been through. How much is doing awful things and still being allowed to play a role in our government part of the 'natural order' of Nuntainia?

'Excellent,' he says. 'They'll bring them in when they arrive. Now, we go in and get ready to take notes.'

He walks ahead of me as if there is no doubt I will follow. Which, I suppose, there isn't. Traelen gestures for me to take a seat next to him at the edge of the room – neither of us sit at the actual table. There's a screen on the far right wall that takes up almost the entire space. Traelen taps his device a couple of times, and my breath all but stops as the agenda fills the space.

AGENDA

1. Updates on action items

2. Briefing on current status of Zanteera Island

3. Cross-border issues: resources from Tae

4. Discussion: location for Prison Program

5. Decision: rebel strategy

'Fucking rebels,' someone mutters from the other side of the room, dragging my gaze away from the screen. 'We should just wipe them all out.'

'And we may well,' another man says, 'but it's worth talking through the options—if they have any left after today.'

Traelen's knee sharply bumping mine tells me I'm staring, and I look at the notepad in my lap until the pale-grey lines blur into the white paper.

The door opens. His gaze sweeps the room, and the world freezes as a saccharine smile stretches his face when Zenaton Blake, Deputy Prime Minister and Minister for Justice, finds me. He takes his seat and places the reusable coffee cup he's brought with him on the desk.

'Shall we start?' he asks. 'This will be one of our most interesting meetings I'd wager, and I don't want to miss anything. I doubt any of you will, either.'

I sneak a glance at Traelen, but his face is impassive as he watches Zenaton.

The group go around the table, updating on the various action items they obviously had from the last meeting. They talk as if they all know what they are and it's hard for me to keep up – hopefully they're not anything I should know and need to report back to Cortane and Quillian.

'Excellent,' Zenaton says, 'and what of the island?'

The woman sitting two up from him looks down at her papers. 'The island has been scoured. All prisoners are now accounted for. There are still a handful of concierges missing, but I think we can all agree the loss of those from the committee—or those, like Davorous, who was going to join us upon his return to public life—has been hard.' She rests her palm on top of the agenda and looks around the table. 'Let's have a minute's silence for Kasera, Aiten, Miana, and Davorous.'

I press my teeth together and will my face to show nothing as Blossom fills my mind. The image of her bleeding on the hallway floor, Nix crouched over her. I can't believe I thought for even a *second* that he did that. That it wasn't completely because of Davorous. I can't even consider what Kasera, Aiten, and Miana did because the evil of it isn't something I can wrap my mind around even now, even if I knew all the details. I take great heart in the fact they're all dead—even if Zenaton is not.

'The prisoners are currently at a resort in Tae,' she says when the minute is up, and I want to be ill. 'But security there is difficult to maintain. We have a team working to restore the prison as quickly as possible.'

'Good—keep it on the agenda,' Zenaton says. 'I want those guests out of Tae as soon as you can. There's enough unrest across the border, they don't need to know we have some of our most prized members of government holed up over there.'

'Yes, speaking of,' another man says, looking at the screen and letting his sentence hang. He seems about the same age as Zenaton, if I go by the lines on his face, but his hair is dark-grey.

A burst of static fills the room and I flinch.

'Ah,' Zenaton says, looking straight at me, 'it's starting.'

Slowly, I turn to the large screen, fingernails digging into my palms. The words 'if they have any left after today' run in my mind on a loop.

'We're going in,' a voice says from somewhere beyond the screen, and the image starts to bounce as if I am watching the world from the chest of someone who's running.

Whoever it is, they're running straight towards what looks like a small township.

Then River, bladed wings out wide and high, and Nix with his swords, step out in front of them.

CHAPTER THIRTEEN

The entire room is dark around me, the pressure in my head and chest enough to pull the nausea from my gut into the back of my throat. My hands tremble on my lap, and I know I'm blinking more rapidly than normal. But it's all I can do not to scream.

Traelen clears his throat gently beside me, and the room creeps back in. I glance at the table. Only about half the people there are looking at the screen, while I feel like my world is about to implode. The others are either talking among themselves, or looking at their devices.

Zenaton sits back in his chair, fingers templed under his chin.

'Engage on my ready,' the screen voice says.

'Hold the line,' Zenaton murmurs.

Nix tosses his sword in his hand, looking as if he's about to play a harmless game of something that should involve a ball, not a blade.

'Engage,' comes the instruction, and the room fills with grunts and the sound of boots on packed dirt. Of metal clanging on metal, hard enough for my ears to ring even from here.

The visual is impossible to keep track of as the person – the Hunter – ducks and weaves and slams his body into others before they drop.

I can feel the blood drain from my face.

'One down,' he says, and the sound of a committee member dropping their device on the wooden table is loud for a moment.

A woman screams, but I can't see her in the wildly moving visual.

Not Blossom. It wasn't Blossom, I repeat as I desperately scan the image for anyone I recognise. But all I can make out is dark uniforms and bodies meeting in a fusion of blood and sweat. I can't even tell which side is which.

'Three down. Second unit—on my ready.'

Slowly, I turn my head to Traelen and catch the flash in his eyes. There's a second unit?

'Engage.'

Gunfire explodes through the room, cracking through the space, and I gasp.

Of course they have guns. But Nix had ... a sword.

I knew they were going to do this, but nothing about those conversations prepared me for what it would look like. And where the fuck are they? Where is Blossom? She can't fight. Surely River didn't take her there?

Why don't they have *guns?*

'Losing count, estimate twenty down.'

My mind starts to empty.

'How many have we lost?' one of the voices in the room asks, and a box opens up on the screen, partially obscuring the battle and showing a list of names and photos, some of which are bright white, and others pale-grey as if they have been deselected.

'About a third,' Traelen says, his voice level.

The person makes a sound that feels like he's talking about a shot of some mid-level drink – a commodity that's so easily replaceable. Like he could just pour himself another glass. Not like they're *people* up there. Dying and dead and ... for what?

A flash of something that looks like the blades of a wing crosses the top corner, but I can't tell who they belong to.

'Heads up—rebel wings out,' the screen-voice says.

And then nothing is distinguishable. All I can see is motion and dirt and blood, can only hear the thud of people hitting the ground as they scream or swear.

'Winged-bastards,' the woman in the room says.

Abruptly, the camera comes to a stop and lifts towards the sky, as if he's been yanked forward by the camera straps themselves.

'Pull back,' he says, his voice still full of authority. 'Pull back!'

The screen fills with a chest and I catch a glimpse of the colour on his neck before the ink disappears into his hairline. I freeze, my heartbeat stalling. Will anyone else notice it? Does it pass for blood?

'You have three minutes to have every *single* Hunter out of here,' Quillian's voice is like ice, 'or I lay waste to you all. And then I come for the House.'

The silence in the room compresses against me.

'We're done here,' the man on the screen says.

'Cowards,' mutters someone at the table. 'Freeze the vision.'

Cowards? Is he talking about the Hunters? The people they sent to kill and risk their lives while this room watches, and *they* are the cowards?

'Who is that?' the same person asks, but I can't bring myself to look away from the image of Quillian on the screen.

'We don't have a record of him, sir,' Traelen says beside, his voice steady. 'He's possibly new, or has recently risen through their ranks. They're probably testing him in this fight.'

The committee member makes a non-committal sound, as if Traelen's words don't ring true. But are they? Does he really not know the role Quillian has? Does Zenaton not recognise him, or at least his voice?

'Maybe,' he says. 'I want to know everything about him. If he's the illusive leader we keep hearing about—this Rebel fucking Prince—I want him eliminated.'

I can no longer make out the full sentences of the words being said – only snippets drift through my mind – still fixed on the partial image of Quillian.

There's no Nix. No River. Or Blossom.

Or even Cortane or Finn or ...

How many went? How many have died?

'... strategy?'

'... find their leader and take him out. Publicly.'

The soft sound of a chair sliding back on the carpet fills my ears. 'See you in chambers,' Zenaton says to the group, before shuffling the papers on the desk before him and pinning his attention on me.

'Traitors always pay,' he says.

I can only stare at him.

'Of course, sir,' Traelen says from beside me. 'As they should.'

The room empties as I remain seated; the realisation that my chair is so much smaller than the ones around the table pokes something sharp in my mind.

A scream that threatens not to remain silent winds its way up my throat, and I press a hand to my mouth.

As soon as the last person is out the door, Traelen presses on the back of my head, forcing it between my knees.

'In through your nose. Pause,' he murmurs. 'Out slow. Pause.'

He talks me through until I regain control of my shaking hands and feel a little less like vomiting.

But when I sit up, the phone in my pocket remains still. No buzzing of messages. While I am sitting in this nicely furnished room, some of those I care most deeply about are on the other side of that now blank screen, dealing with the aftermath.

'Did you know that was coming?' I sound strangled, even to myself.

'Yes.'

'And you didn't want to warn me?'

Traelen is quiet for a moment, like what we've just seen is still hanging on him too. 'It wouldn't have helped,' he says softly. 'I have seen that, and worse, from this room and others, and in person. Knowing in advance never helps.'

I sit forward, elbows on my knees.

'How long until you know something?' I ask.

He lets out a long breath. 'It's likely you'll hear before me. Either way, it shouldn't be too long now.'

'Fuck. This is bad.' I glance at the closed door. 'Do they know about you? That ... you're here?'

'Not them, no. And it needs to stay that way,' he says, eyeing me. 'I know too much, can access too much, for it to be jeopardised by the wrong person knowing. Zenaton is fucking with you—and he's going to enjoy every second of it. He has the upper hand right now, and he knows it.'

Whatever air I had left in my lungs whooshes out of me.

'You think there's someone in the traitors reporting back.'

'Of course there is,' he says, not missing a beat. 'Those locations have been tightly held for decades. Now we have a whole fucking list.'

I let the quiet settle around us, trying to think through the fog of not knowing who still lives. How they have the full list and, more worryingly, *when* did they get it?

'And now they're all on the back foot, scrambling to find shelter and safety, and the committee have a lead on the identity of ... the leader ...' I trail off, unsure if Traelen knows who Quillian is, whose face he looked into every time he went to Zanteera Island over the last few months, who he arrested in the end.

'I know who he is,' he says quietly in response to my hesitation, 'but you're right to be careful. He doesn't know, I know, but I do. Having me place him in Vana when I did was the only way to keep his identity protected until he was off the island.'

I gape at him, trying to place all of this together while my insides feel like they're being wrung out.

'You—protected him? By sending him to *Vana*? From what?'

'Do you really think the fact that former or current members of the Defence Committee started dying in quick succession almost *immediately* after the supposed *mistaken* arrival of two soldier brothers and a new Warden would not have raised suspicions? While those down here couldn't see what I could up there, the flow of information from that island was not something I could control in its entirety. We were *moments* away from having that island swarming with Hunters, who are *trained* to *see*.' He sighs heavily. 'I removed them from sight the fastest way I could, with unofficial charges in front of witnesses I knew wouldn't repeat what they saw.'

My mind whirls with the recollection of Quillian's arrest. Traelen giving orders to those two Hunters, what he charged him with, it all seemed so ... real. So real I can still feel the shadow of it in my gut.

My phone – the only one I care about – buzzes, and I drop it to the floor in my haste, cursing. A moment later, I hear Traelen's vibrate as well.

On mine, it's the group chat.

B: we're okay.

B: there have been a number lost but the circle is intact.

Circle is intact? Cortane drilled us about being careful in messages, and I think this is Blossom's way of telling me the core group is safe. Alive. I can feel how much it would have hurt her to write that 'but'. Losing anyone won't sit well with either of us.

I wonder how many of the rebels are also feeling a heavy weight at the death of the Hunters, too? Or is that just because I saw how expendable they are to their command?

B: the boys are a little busted—

My heart thumps harder in my chest.

—but fine. They'll be a little tender but are being seen to.

I swallow, blinking away the tears that press their way forward.

L: I'm so relieved to hear from you. Are you okay? What about the originals?

I can't think how else to describe Quillian, Cortane and Finn. But it raises another quiet question in my mind – who is the actual original? Who started the rebellion and why?

N: they're dealing with some shit but they're fine.

N: He's fine, L. We've got him.

The knowledge they're all looking after each other is a warm flood through my veins. Spiked with the tiniest bit of jealousy that I'm not there.

Traelen's phone buzzes in his hand, and his messages are open before it's even finished sounding. He straightens his spine, but I don't miss that his shoulders sink a little from his ears.

'Okay,' he says, mostly to himself. 'Definitely more losses than I'd like but ... they did well under the circumstances.' He looks at me. 'You need to tell him what happened here today and that he needs to keep a low profile. He mightn't like it, but he is the symbol all the traitors are rallying around, and that's just his reality. Nuntainia gave him that title of Rebel Prince, but it's one they will regret. They have no idea how quickly people are rallying behind his cause without even knowing him personally. But being dead, or exposed too soon, and he risks it all being for nothing. He is threat number one to this government, and they won't stand for it.'

I nod.

I don't know what else to do.

My mind swims with questions, like how is Quillian the symbol? If he's not Traelen's contact, who is? The only person I think that Traelen had some sort of relationship with on the island who is with us, is Janly. And why would Quillian not want to be the symbol of something which is clearly important to him?

But I have to silence them.

He's okay.

Everyone is okay.

The tips of my fingers still shake as my body's stress response to this meeting crawls away. Looking back to the empty screen, I know it will never truly leave me. No matter how safe they are now, the fleeting nature of that safety is overwhelming.

My ribs squeeze. If Quillian felt even a fraction of that with worry about me, instead of being wholly focused on what was happening in front of him, how much risk did I put him at without even knowing?

Cortane's warning about being a distraction thumps in the base of my skull.

That's all I can process while Zenaton Blake's chair feels like he still sits in it.

Watching.

CHAPTER FOURTEEN

'I think my nose might be clogged with vomit,' Teddy says, as she pours me a coffee in the attendants' room.

'Please tell me you did not bring a vomiting bug here with you.'

'Luka'—she hands me the coffee and I inhale deeply—'my unbroken rule of parenting is *never* catch the vomiting bug. I've taken three doses of immunity tipple this morning alone. Also, Zale is better at managing vomit than me, so I stay as far away as possible.'

I laugh a little. Zale always did have a stronger stomach than Akira or me. But it's hard to keep my mind from going straight back to the camp in Tae, my bone-deep need to be there. To see for myself how they are.

'Traelen,' Teddy murmurs, looking around the empty room quickly, 'wants to meet with us. Can you do it now?'

I blink, waiting for more information, but she just looks back at me. Checking my duty phone to find no new requests, I nod and silently follow her from the room as she furiously taps on her own phone.

Teddy leads me a short walk through the service halls of the House before ducking into a meeting room which looks much like the one Traelen and I met in on my first day here. Traelen stands with his back to the door when we enter, gazing out the window. Sandwiched between the sill and a large, navy wingback chair that forms part of a rich, but faded, velvet sofa set, he turns slowly as the door clicks shut behind us, gesturing to the seats.

'I'm due with the Integrity Commission in less than thirty mins, T,' Teddy says, as she smooths the back of her black pants and sits. 'Can we make this fast?'

I glance between them, still standing, as I try to process their familiarity. The fact Teddy just called him a nickname, something I *never* dare ...

'What is this?' I ask, willing any uncertainty from my tone. But it's clear I am out of my depth here, and being caught off guard in this House, in these times, does not make me feel in control.

'Please, sit, Luka,' Traelen says. 'We need to talk—and act—fast. We can speak freely here.'

Briefly pressing my palm against the feather that I place between my breasts each day, I sit. I don't envisage needing it here, but it brings me comfort all the same as I wait in silence for one of them to continue.

'We have a problem,' Traelen starts as he takes his seat in the wingback.

Okay ... not a good start. My breath quickens.

'Tell me,' Teddy demands, 'and skip the lecture, I don't have time.'

Traelen pales a little, but he still narrows his gaze at Teddy enough for me to know whatever 'lecture' she thinks is coming, he certainly doesn't think it's unnecessary.

'One, Luka thought Zenaton died on the island, so her team didn't know to confirm his whereabouts since leaving the island. This is a problem because Luka and her associates left him to die during their escape, so he can clearly identify her as an active traitor,' he says.

Teddy jerks her head in my direction. 'Oh shit.'

I ignore the burning at the base of my chest cavity at her reaction and focus on Traelen. 'You said "one"—there's something else?'

He looks up at the ceiling, pressing the back of his head into the wingback and pinching the bridge of his nose. 'I can't get in contact with the Prime Minister.'

The floor starts to fall away from me, but I don't know if this is good or bad news. Traelen's tight jaw says it's bad. Very bad.

The understanding of why slams into me with the same force as if I've just run into a wall.

Zenaton Blake is Deputy Prime Minister. Meaning he will be *acting* Prime Minister if the substantive Prime Minister is away for any reason.

I sit forward and cup my head in my hands, elbows on my knees. 'Let me get this straight,' I say. 'Zenaton, who—for reasons as yet unknown—has allowed me, knowing what he does about me and my allegiances, into the House. At the same time, he is actively wiping out the traitors from his position on the Defence Committee. *And,* as well as likely being at the very least complicit in the crimes of people like Kasera, Aiten, and Miana—not to mention Davorous—he's now *officially* running the country?'

The room is quiet for a beat. 'This is worse than we thought,' Teddy says, 'but we can manage. We've had worse.'

The statement snags as something I can grasp in the thoughts that are whirling through me right now.

'Worse?' I ask. 'Before or after Zale? You can't blindside her with this, Teddy, she deserves to know the risk you're putting yourself in. She's your *wife.*'

Traelen raises his brows at her but says nothing.

'Exactly, Luka,' Teddy snaps. 'She's *my* wife. And I will decide what she does and doesn't know. You cannot expect me to believe that after everything you've been through, you don't understand the importance of being judicious with information and doing whatever you can to protect those you love.'

'It can also be dangerous *not* to know,' I counter.

'And I think about that every fucking day, but it's not your call to make. Tell me, though, do you really think it would be *safe* for her to know our Prime Minister is currently missing and we're effectively in the middle of a silent fucking coup?'

I press out of my chair and pace the room. Fuck. She's right and, loathe as I am to admit it, there are some other pretty huge problems right now. Including why Zenaton is keeping me here and not shoving me straight into Vana. Or pressing me for information on where the others are.

Traelen clears his throat. 'Now we know Zenaton is clear on who you are, we've lost the advantage of you being able to pick up information just by being in the room. The only choice now is the archives—get evidence. That's what I need the two of you to do. I started the process for each of your access keys when I'd got your names confirmed on this duty intake, but they're still being worked through. I've got a meeting with Benita later today, so I'll get her to expedite them. In the meantime, try not to draw any unnecessary attention to yourselves. We know we're walking a tripwire with Zenaton already. He now essentially controls the entire government in the Prime Minister's absence, and the enforcement bodies like the Hunters already, plus he has Communication ties he could readily leverage outside official channels. We don't need to give him any reason to act rashly.'

The room feels more heavily decorated than when I first came in, like all the dark wood and patterned wallpaper is pressing in on me. 'Anything else?' I ask. 'Any more problems we should know about?'

Traelen stands, buttoning his jacket and checking his watch.

'You clearly have a leak in the camp and I can't get in front of it when it goes to Zenaton. Not like I used to.' Traelen's shoulders drop, just a fraction. 'Zenaton has the list of camps and there's nothing I can do.'

I suck in a breath. 'So you *were* their contact?'

He nods, not even surprised. 'For a time, until my role became too critical to jeopardise.'

'And now?'

He smooths his hair back, not that anything seemed out of place. 'Now, the whole country is in too precarious a position for me not to take more risks. Your people are where they need to be and, if I'm right, you'll be on the verge of making a wave we can't come back from. So I will do what I can to support that from here.'

'Fuck, Traelen,' I whisper, 'you realise what you've just admitted to me, right?'

He shares a look with Teddy.

'I think you'll find us not so different from your friends, Luka.'

***

Holland is waiting at the bottom of the grand walkway to the House when my shift ends. The sight of him, hands behind his back as he looks towards the river, sends a chill along my arms. Not just because it's like the contemplative stance Traelen had today, before he dropped so many pieces of information that have me tied in knots. I have no doubt about where Holland's loyalties lie, not after the island, but it still jangles my nerves to be in such close proximity to the Hunters. Knowing what I do – what I've seen – and knowing Zenaton directly controls where and what they do.

But worse than that is how close he is to Zenaton. There is no way that man won't recognise Holland.

'We need to move, now,' I whisper urgently, and Holland wordlessly falls into step with me.

'You'll need to be home for a while, and change,' he says quietly when we're out of earshot, and I get the strong impression he is managing my expectations, making sure I know I can't race straight to Tae. To camp. Not that I know how I would do that, but every part of me feels like I need to run as hard as I can to get there. The effort of keeping that contained is exhausting.

'I saw it,' I breathe, the words acidic. 'They streamed it.' My voice cracks and the nausea that still hasn't quite abated rolls through my stomach.

Holland mutters under his breath, but his steps slow.

After everything I learned from Traelen, and my tense conversation with Teddy, I'm just about vibrating to get to the camp in Tae. I need to see, hear, and touch every single one of my traitors.

But Holland makes me walk slowly to the pod station and climb in, going in the opposite direction to the carpark.

'Listen,' he says, leaning forward and placing a hand on my knee. 'I want to see those assholes as much as you do'—something flashes in his face—'but we can't be seen racing off somewhere after what you saw today. What you learned today. If anyone is watching, they need to see you going home. Under no circumstances can we lead anyone to that portal, understand?'

I nod. How do I tell them that person would likely be Zenaton? My mind is filled with the same static as my veins, with a desperate wish to know *more.* More about Quillian and the rebels and my *family's* wellbeing. More about why that room was watching, and how they knew where to find the traitors—did I enable that somehow? More about Zenaton and how he survived. What he wants with me there. More about how it all started, and *more* about myself and the magic I seem to have snuffed out.

'No,' I say in response to his question. 'There's not a lot I understand right now. But sure, let's go get changed.'

The rest of the ride is silent, and I watch Holland tap his knee with his middle and ring finger on his right hand. It's a nervous rhythm, and I wonder who he is so worried for – Casey? Because I'm pretty confident it's not just for him and me.

We disembark at my stop, another couple waiting patiently to get on. I don't know if the House think we are a couple, but I know we both gave the same address on our intake forms. So he's right about it making sense we'd go back together.

It also now feels very stupid.

I glance up at the small hill behind the station. Akira, Zale, and I rolled down that hill, before gorging ourselves on ice cream from the gourmet van to my left, on what might have been the silliest night of my life. The memory is bittersweet though, and I press a hand to my sternum. Part of me longs to go back, but the rest of me knows I could never do that. Never let all of this go, even if I wanted to.

Holland suggests I try to get some sleep when we arrive at my town-house, the dying plants on the stoop drawing a sharp pain from behind my ribs. But once I crawl under the comforter, all I can do is stare at the ceiling.

Dealing with some shit, keep your head down, Nix said in his last message, but I still haven't heard from Quillian.

Lying on my bed, I spin my phone in my hand. Blossom has messaged me on and off all afternoon, so I know they have gone back to the main camp and that she's been busy allocating survivors to rooms and houses and helping River and Shiloh with the healing. I know Nix has been working with Finn and Cortane on the hostages they now make of the remaining Hunters.

But Quillian? Not a clue.

I'm about to throw myself off the bed and demand Holland come with me to the carpark when my phone buzzes.

Q: hey

I write back, hands shaking, feeling completely inadequate.

L: hey. Are you okay?

Q: can I see you?

I don't even pause to respond. Instead, I run down the stairs and find Holland in the sitting room, still tapping his knee.

'Let's go,' I say,

He stands, drawing a deep breath. 'Agreed.'

The trip to the carpark feels like the longest trip I've ever taken. In my haste to get out of the pod on the street, I almost slip on a discarded flyer on the walkway. Instinctively, I pick it up and ready to throw it in the bin so no prisoners – people – find a mess. But there's none, so I pocket it instead and scurry across the dark carpark, Holland constantly checking behind to make sure we're not followed.

He reaches out the same way Finn did, and the air swirls around me as we step through. Bracing myself, I'm not sure I'm prepared for what I will find in traitor camp one.

CHAPTER FIFTEEN

Havoc.

That's what we find at the small township. The base of the ... Rebel Prince. But that thought can't find enough purchase in my mind to be a focus as people race about the square with all manner of things – mattresses, blankets, water, other people. It's dark out, a soft glow around the square that's bright enough to show me it's busier than I've seen it before, but not enough to make out anyone's faces from a distance. I don't even know how many of them noticed Holland and me step through from nothing. But the air here is very different to Klades. Here, there is a weighty sense of loss on the gentle breeze.

'Where should we start?' I ask, my gaze landing on what looks like a line forming before a table, perhaps where they are checking in the traitors from the now abandoned camp.

'I'm on my way to command.' I jump as Finn materialises out of the low light.

Holland looks him over. Slowly. I look between them as Finn watches Holland do his once over.

'You're not injured?' Holland asks, his shoulders tight.

'I'm fine,' Finn says quietly.

Holland grips one of Finn's upper arms, smiling gently. 'Well … I'm relieved,' he says, hand eventually sliding down Finn's arm and losing contact.

Finn shifts his gaze to me.

'Blossom's in the triage room with River and Shiloh; Nix and Quillian are in command. Where do you want to go first?'

Overwhelmed and unable to choose, I say, 'Whoever's closest.' Finn moves off, and most of the people we pass are either so focused on their task they pay us no attention, or seem to give Finn a respectful wide-berth. 'Are you really all okay?' I ask.

Finn's quiet for a while, and I can sense Holland's anticipation along with my own.

'Physically, yes,' he says. 'But … this is a difficult time. We've not only lost numbers and resources that were so important to our cause—a swell of support to make the government listen—but we knew these people. If we didn't recruit them directly, people we know did. At the same time, it's a brutal reminder why we're here in the first place. It's …'

'Hard,' I say, knowing that doesn't even begin to cover it.

Finn nods.

As we draw nearer to the main hall where the command centre is located, Finn slows.

'We still have a lot to do tonight,' he says gently, and I'm certain he is trying to manage my hopes of getting Quillian alone. However he might be dealing with all of this, I am absolutely certain he will not let his mask slip until much later, if he will at all. How much tension will he be carrying after today?

I tighten the ponytail I hastily shoved my hair into as we left, squashing down my longing to see him. It's absolutely fair that all of this come first. I just wish the truth that I'd hide away with him right now – just for a few moments – didn't make me feel so selfish.

'We're here to help,' I say, gesturing to Holland, who places a hand on Finn's shoulder.

'Anything,' he says.

Finn inclines his head, pushing open the door to the command centre. Nix's voice greets us.

'—still in range of camps four, seven and eight,' he's saying. 'I think we need to evacuate all those camps immediately—we don't know the strength of the Shaide with them, or if there's more than one to portal them all around. They came in on foot today, but that could just have been to keep us unaware of their full capabilities.'

'And put them where?' Cortane asks. 'They've been trained, Nix, they might have to defend on their own.'

'Against that group we saw today? Come on, Cort, you know as well I do they don't stand a fucking chance against them. Not on their own.'

I slip quietly into the room and stay standing near the wall with Finn and Holland. Nix and Quillian face away from me, looking at the screen with Cortane.

'We can't house them here,' she continues. 'Even if we had the space and supplies, we might as well be sending a fucking invitation to the Hunters to wipe us out entirely.'

Quillian's stance is woven with tension, but the sense of relief that washes over me as I see – for myself – that he and Nix are still standing, is warm enough to bring tears to my eyes.

The screen in the centre of the room is illuminated in that soft, purple glow and seems to be showing the same map it was the last time I was here. I have to blink several times to remove the vision of the attack that tries to overlay the image that's actually before me.

'We could send them to our allies in the Tae mountains—somewhere west of Villy,' Quillian says.

Nix drops his head back a little as he curses.

'Because those people haven't paid enough for the sins of Nuntainia?' he bites out, but I don't miss the wound underneath that his tone tries to hide.

His girlfriend was from the mountains in Tae. The one he lost.

On Quillian's orders.

My heart squeezes uncomfortably.

'They know where our camps are, Nix,' Quillian says. 'I know how you feel about Tae and what was done here, but our people also deserve a chance.'

'Not at their expense, Quillian, you know that. You fucking know it.'

Quillian sighs, and I get the distinct impression he agrees and has no intention of jeopardising the mountains of Tae. He looks down at the phone in his hand once before sliding it into his pocket, as if it didn't hold the answer he was hoping for, and I remember I didn't tell him I was coming.

I step forward, gently pushing myself between Nix and Quillian.

'Luka,' Nix breathes as he turns and takes me in, wrapping an arm around my shoulders and pulling me tight. 'What are you doing here? This isn't a safe place for you.'

My lip trembles as I look up at him, the memory of he and River stepping out onto that road filling my mind.

'I saw you. I—they—watched it, I couldn't not come.'

He closes his eyes and pulls me back into his chest. 'Fucking bastards.'

'What do you mean you watched us?' Cortane asks.

I pull myself free and turn to look at her, sliding my hand into Quillian's in the process. He squeezes.

Hard.

'One of the Hunters had a camera on.'

'Fuck,' she says. 'They'll be working around the clock to identify us, and anyone left to care about outside our camps.'

I look Quillian full in the face for the first time tonight, letting my gaze trace every part of it before dropping down to his tattoo.

'They're starting with you,' I say, willing the tremor in my chest not to be reflected in my voice.

No surprise registers on his face, just something more like ... regret.

He brushes a knuckle over my cheekbone.

'That's to be expected,' he says gently, before turning back to the map. 'So, we know our locations are compromised—we obviously have a mole. Finn, you're lead on getting to the bottom of that. In the meantime, relocating our people is the priority, and the mountains of Tae are out.'

Outwardly, Nix barely reacts, but I have known him long enough to know the relief that's eased the white-knuckled tension of his hands. 'Where does that leave us?' he asks, still looking at the screen, as if asking the map itself for answers.

I look at it too, and memories of time with my father seep in unbidden. Images from before I knew what it was to look at him and know what a disappointment I'd turned out to be.

As much as I often resent having to put my life on pause, I also can see the escape allowing myself to become absorbed in my duty provided. Not to mention everything that has come of it, everything I learned working with Claudius, who became almost a father figure to me. I wince a little, now, at what that says about my relationship with my actual father.

I refocus, studying the purple map before me, and the memory of my father's voice traces the shapes of the different regions and countries, like the scratch of the nib of his pen over parchment. Slowly, the maze of contested territories begins to unravel as my eyes trace the slightly darker lines of the current borders. The old stories my father told me supply the names of unlabelled landmarks, considered meaningless for military purposes, and the forgotten history behind the most sought after resources. The scar of the Rote Gorge that was formed in a war of the old gods; the curse that created Zanteera Island; and the inception of technology as we know it now on the far shores of Coprath. They're just myths, really, but they still played a role in the forming of our society.

I look harder at the Coprath border. Traelen said the Prime Minister was there, the last he'd heard from him. But, as I continue to scour the map in front of me, I can't see anything that gives me an idea of his movements from there. For all I know, he's voluntarily gone missing to make way for Zenaton. Although he could have just retired ...

A small marking on the bottom corner of the map, in an otherwise relatively unpopulated expanse, catches my eye. I've never been there, but I understand it to be a rocky outcrop with a long-ago abandoned fortress of sorts. What was once home to a people who served the gods of their time with sacrifices and self-flagellation. But also occupied a highly-prized piece of land known for its ability to be defended.

Food would be a challenge, I think, looking at the triangular markings on the map. But there must still be a way to transport goods in.

I look around the room, waiting a beat for anyone else to have a suggestion, my nerves fluttering a little, which seems silly. But this is exactly the knowledge that proved too limited before. What if it's not enough now, either?

I draw a lungful of air, giving yet another moment for someone else to have a solution I haven't thought of.

'What about here?' I ask, pointing to the little triangles.

Blossom is just about radiating when I find her in the triage room. Her sleeves are rolled up, her curly brown hair is tied in a haphazard bun high on her head, her focus fierce. I approach her quietly, keeping a polite distance as she talks softly with one of the injured.

The room is really the living room of one of the larger houses, all the doors open to the small backyard which is also filled with people. Everyone here looks to be in the middle of some form of healing, and I realise while there is a system to get people in and seen, there must also be a system to get them out again. Through the open door just behind Blossom, I find Emeris, Janly, and Shiloh moving through the injured, and a little portion of worry dissolves in my belly.

When her gaze finds mine, it's dark and pained but also ... exhilarated. I've never seen her so in her element before.

'Luka,' she says, pulling me tight, 'you have no idea how good it is to see you.'

I smile, pushing away the panic that threatened to rear its head when Nix and River stepped onto that road and I didn't know where she – or anyone else – was. 'I think I have a fair idea.'

She tugs me to the side of the room gently, glancing back to where I can now spot River leaning over someone lying on the floor.

'I have to tell you,' she whispers fiercely. 'Today—there—I think I felt it.'

'What?' I frown.

'My—it was like my blood was singing, and I couldn't get enough of it, couldn't make it go any louder.' She looks at me like I might say she's lost her mind, but I see the excitement – the hope – in her eyes, and my stomach sinks a little as I understand what she's saying.

'Your magic?' I ask.

'Yes! Well, I think so,' she says. 'What else could that be? It was not a day for that feeling to come on its own.'

I squeeze her hand and remind myself how happy I am for her. How much I'd want her to be happy for me if my magic was finally coming in after all that time on dampeners. 'That's incredible, Bloss. What do you think it is?'

'I don't know but ... something feels so right about being in here, about watching River ...'

I quirk a brow. '"Something" that's more than just about River?' I can't help the smile in my voice.

'What he *does,'* she says, but she does give a little grin in return that falls just as quickly. 'But now isn't the time for either of those things,' she says as if she's scolding herself. 'Are you free to help here? I promise not to send you any blood. Or much, anyway.'

I spend the next unknown number of hours helping Blossom and River in the triage room. She is true to her word on sparing me from too much blood; I mostly restock supplies and direct any visitors who come looking for the injured. The people who are injured are mostly men, but there is a solid number of women among them too. My chest releases a little when I don't find any children. But, despite how physically capable everyone here looks, minus their various injuries, I can't help but feel this is more like a community that's been badly battered. Not an armed, traitorous force.

And it makes me think of Nix's girlfriend and what she and her town must have endured. What they went through before nothing of them was left.

In what feels like my past life, I'd read about practices similar to what Nix described. But they were ancient. It never crossed my mind they might still be occurring under the surface. Not like I wish my magic was. Instead, it's following the orders from that fucking tipple to never manifest.

How is it possible to be so genuinely happy for Blossom and, at the same time, disappointed for myself? I collect some of the bloodied cloths they've dumped in a stainless-steel bin – there's something so much easier about blood when it's not visibly dripping from a person – and start sorting them into piles. Some that can be washed and saved, others that will need to be tossed. Not unlike the few occasions I helped Shiloh in the wellness centre on the island.

But the magic isn't the only thing that feels like it's cleaving me in two. The relief I feel that those I love are safe is palpable. And yet, there are so many that are not, who have paid with their lives or health for what they believe in. Their families and loved ones left in tatters. The last cloth hits the toss pile with a sickening, wet smack.

Traelen, Teddy, and I left our meeting confident that whatever was happening in the House was being spearheaded by the Deputy Prime Minister and Minister for Justice – Zenaton Blake. And I don't think we're wrong. What did Teddy call it ... a 'silent coup'. My stomach rolls on itself.

Zenaton took such pleasure in watching the confrontation today but, somehow, I think he would enjoy waltzing through here just as much. More, even. If we weren't people he could so readily arrest, I can easily imagine him in a broadcast talking about the atrocities of war, giving his love and sympathies to all involved. All the while, internally rejoicing that he brought this pain hailing down on us.

In my induction, Quillian told me the deaths on the island were almost an experiment to see if they could make the Defence Committee pay attention - put an end to the corruption on their own. If it was just the Defence Committee, I think I would agree with the traitors' plan of taking them out one by one. But Traelen said there is a powerful undercurrent of corruption in the government, and I agree with him that Zenaton must be the one leading the movement. The Minister for Justice is a key role in our government, even alone, but now Zenaton has also silently become the unopposed acting Prime Minister ... which can only mean his support is throughout the party like infectious tentacles. I almost sway on my feet at the enormity of that. That the entire party might have to be evicted, not just the initiator of the program, like Quillian thinks.

The last of the heavily blood-soaked cloths lands with a squelch as I toss it in the 'bin pile', a macabre metaphor for the sinking truth settling in me. If we're talking about getting rid of an entire government, how can I ever have thought I'd be able to contribute helpfully to that? The traitors have kept Quillian out of the spotlight, likely for this very reason – so he can rise with Tae when the time is right.

What have I added to that? Letting Zenaton live; possibly allowing a leak into the camp with my 'loose ends'; and, as Cortane predicted, being a distraction to Quillian. Who am I to stand at the side of a decorated war hero, the Rebel Prince, as he makes his move? A hindrance, not a help.

'You should head out,' River says, catching me between patients. Over his shoulder, Blossom and Shiloh are conferring about something as Emeris walks off into the corner of the backyard, stumbling as if in a stupor. 'We're about as done as we're going to get tonight,' River continues, 'and you need to be in Parliament tomorrow.'

I groan, glancing back to where Emeris stands with his hands on the back of his head, looking up to the sky. I'll have to check on him next time I'm here; today would have been difficult for everyone.

'I wish it felt like I was actually doing something,' I say quietly. 'All of you here—you're literally taking action. Defending yourselves while our government attempts to wipe you from existence. While I'm ... working for them.'

'It looks like that on the outside, sure,' he says, wiping his hands on a damp towel. 'But there are few people who can do what you're doing. The *only* place we will get the information we need to dig out the root of all of this is in that House.'

'No pressure, right?'

He laughs.

'None. You can do this, Lu. You forget I know how your mind works, how you gather information others might see as irrelevant, how you piece things together.'

I sigh. 'I think it's bigger than me just putting pieces together,' I say, and his chest falls. 'That's important, sure, but it won't stop ... the corruption.'

'One step at a time. That's why we need your brain in there.'

I try not to allow the little swell of pride in my chest to take hold. 'What you're saying is I'm more my father's daughter than I might like.'

'I always liked your Dad.' He looks thoughtful for a moment. 'He obviously thought Nix and I were a terrible influence on you, but—'

'That might be because you made me miss that exam.' I lift my brows at him, but I don't tell him how upset that really did make my father. How it was the beginning of my understanding that my academic performance really was the most important thing to him.

'*Nix* made you miss that exam, but I guess I'll have to take it for the team.' He winks at me, and some of the familiar warmth of our long-standing friendship creeps in between the worry and doubt about what's happening here, and what I need to do.

'How is he?' I shift on my feet to try to ease the ache from standing here half the night.

'Tonight will have been hard on him. We haven't engaged in direct combat like that since our duty in Tae. The last battle we didn't engage in—in the mountains—meant he lost the love of his life. So ... it's shit. Being camped here peacefully is enough of a challenge for him. But I'd leave him be for tonight—check in on him after duty tomorrow.'

'And you?' I ask. 'How are you holding up?'

He blows out a breath, and my eyes dampen watching him rally himself before he responds.

'I'm okay ... this is my focus now, and I'll start to process tomorrow.' He looks at me solemnly. 'This isn't our first go around this ride, Lu.'

'I just ... you seem so capable, but when I saw the two of you on that road—' a sob jerks my chest and I cover my mouth as if I can put back the unexpected sound. The spilling over of the trembling anxiety I've tried so hard to quell today.

'Hey,' he says, drawing me in against his chest. 'We're okay.'

I let him hold me there for long moments, letting his warmth soak into my bones, before pulling back and dabbing at my eyes.

'What about Quillian?' I ask, conscious of how shy I sound, but there's a little tremor underneath my ribs at just how much the thought of him makes me feel.

'He's probably the toughest of all of us.'

'More than Cortane?'

He laughs softly. 'No one is tougher than Cortane. No one gets madder, either. Seriously, though, you need to get some rest—you're the only one of us who can't look like they've been tending the battle weary all night.'

'I haven't—'

'He'll find you when he's done, trust me.'

CHAPTER SIXTEEN

I hear the door open from where I lie on the floral couch half asleep. I know it's him before his large, dark form appears at the end of the short hallway, and I watch him crouch down in front of me.

'You're awake,' he says, voice low.

'Mm hmm ...' I say, not sure it's quite true, but very aware of the tingle in my fingertips, of the need to touch him. To reassure myself that he's here. Not the Rebel Prince I glimpsed on that footage, but Quillian. The man behind the blank, stoic expression the rest of the world sees.

A gentle sensation runs along my scalp, and my hair feels like it prickles in the most delightful way as he brushes the mussed strands out of my face.

'You didn't have to stay up for me.'

I reach out and stroke his muscular thigh. 'I wanted to.'

I don't tell him it was more a *need* than a *want*. Or that the fear I could lose him to one of those battles is now etched in my bones, along with the images I can't run from. Nor do I tell him of the mounting worry about what happens even if we – he – does succeed, and what that means for us. There will be so much he will have to leave behind to take on the responsibility that seems earmarked for him, and him alone. How could I not be one of those things that just doesn't stand up to what he will need?

He drops towards me, knees quietly hitting the carpet as he drops his head to mine.

'Thank you … for waiting.' He presses a kiss to my temple and I turn my face into him, taking his next kiss on my mouth, clinging to the dedication in his tone like a prayer. A dedication that seems impossible in the face of what the future likely holds.

I sigh inwardly, pressing away the sting behind my eyelids as his soft lips meet mine, melting into the feel of them, the constant tremble of anxiety in my core abating for the first time since I left him last. His fingers slide into my hair and his kiss is suddenly harder, more desperate, and that tremble quickly starts to feel like a fire in the base of my belly. Groaning, I reach for his shirt and tug him towards me. I'm suddenly burning with the need to feel his weight on top of me.

He kisses me as if it's the last one he'll ever have, and I flush with an urgency to have him. To assure him, and myself, there will be more. That the mess of today doesn't mean any loss here, between us. At least not yet.

Leaning into me, but not yet taking my invitation to join me on the couch, Quillian runs open-mouthed kisses down my neck. Tugging the shoulder of my shirt away, he runs his lips over the exposed skin, and goosebumps explode across my flesh.

His breath is hot on my skin and I pull his face back to mine, sucking his bottom lip between my teeth and giving myself wholly to this moment. He groans into my mouth and I press my hips towards him, searching for friction against my throbbing body. My hands rove his torso, his slightly rough shirt bunching under my hands until I slip them underneath and trace the contours I find.

He pulls away, breathless, and circles my wrists in his hands, wrapping them with fingers I know could be doing something very different right now.

But he takes my hands from his body and holds them in front of him.

'You're exhausted,' he says roughly, taking my hand as he stands.

'I *was* exhausted.' I press my hands back to his body, sitting up and letting them find the edge of his shirt again. 'Now, I need you.'

His kisses are more gentle when I pull him down to kiss me again, and he pulls me in tighter, my hands going around his back and up into his hair. He bends into the crook of my neck and sucks on my earlobe, sending a bolt of lightning to my already wanting core.

I lift his shirt, exposing his stomach with its dark trail of hair that disappears into his pants, and then his chest, and gesture for him to take it the rest of the way as he stands above me. The explosion of colour along his right side fills my vision for a moment, but it's the line of dark hair that captures my attention again as he drops his shirt to the floor.

His pants sit low on his hips, just below a hard plane of abdomen, and the hair creates a teasing pathway to what lies just a little lower.

I lick my bottom lip, tugging it between my teeth as I think about what he tastes like. He watches me, as if he knows what runs through my mind, and is waiting to see what I decide. My pulse thrums in my veins.

Standing with him, I press my own kisses along his collar bones, before I make my way down, across his chest, and run my tongue between his pecs. He sucks in a quick breath as I pinch a nipple, and I smile into his skin. Moving my hands to the fastening of his pants, I look up at him and hold his gaze as I let them fall open and down, and free him from his fitted underwear.

His eyes flutter partially closed as I stroke him slowly, using one hand over the other, letting one at a time run over and off the top of his cock. Slowly, holding his gaze, I drop to my knees before him, and he inhales deeply.

A slightly sideways dip of his head is the only movement he makes. But it's not so dark that I can't see the way his pupils blow wide, or how he holds his arms more stiffly by his side, as if he's having to force himself not to touch me.

I grin.

And then I ease my mouth over his cock, feeling out the size of him as he curses. Briefly, I hold the head of him in my teeth. Just gently, but enough for him to know he's mine – this moment is mine. His gaze flashes, and then I take most of him again, fisting the lower length in time with the rhythm of my mouth.

His thigh tenses under the hand I brace myself with, and I reach up, guiding his hands into my hair. He immediately makes a fist on either side of my head in my loose strands, and it's my turn to groan around him as I slide my hands around to grip his ass. I press him towards me, encouraging him deeper as I draw long breaths in and out my nose. Tugging the hair at the back of my head, he makes me look up at him.

'Tell me if it gets too much,' he says. His voice is raw, and I have no doubt he will stop at any point if I want him to.

But that's the last thing I want.

I want this composed, chiselled man to lose his control.

Simply because of me. *With* me.

Quillian fucks my mouth, slowly at first, and then he moves faster, my nails digging into his ass cheeks.

More, I want to tell him, and I squeeze my hands tighter, rocking him into me as if I can convey that message. The throbbing between my legs is almost unbearable. I reach down and press my fingers to my wet core for some relief.

He makes a soft noise in the back of his throat and thrusts harder. Once, twice, three times, until there's a hot explosion in the back of my throat, and I swallow, dragging the last pulses from him hungrily.

I hold my position until his grip on my hair loosens, and I look up at him as I gently slide off him and place his slowly softening cock back in his underwear. He drags me up his body and claims my mouth with a clash of teeth and tongues and heady breaths.

Dropping his right hand between my legs, he strokes me over my pants, and I don't need a second invitation. Grinding myself against his fingers, and the fabric, I wind higher and higher. Waves of pleasure taunt me as the sensation mounts without crashing.

'Give it to me,' he says roughly into my hair, taking the circles he makes with the flat of his fingers wider, firmer.

His voice is pure command as I shiver from his breath in my hair. I have a flash of memory of him in his warden's uniform as I come, biting into his shoulder, the taste of him still on my tongue.

He holds me there for long moments, just the two of us, leaning into each other in the lounge room of this halfway house. My heart sings that it's never felt more at home. And I desperately push down on the truth that none of my homes have been based on as solid a foundation as I've believed.

'What are you thinking?' I ask as we lie in bed, night still in full force around us. The bedroom in this house is small, but I can see the moon through the window; between that, and Quillian, it just adds to my contentment. If I can put aside what else is happening in the world.

The skin on Quillian's torso puckers gently with bumps as I trail my fingers over him, feeling every inch of him. I'm tucked against his tattoo side, so I can't feel his scars beneath my fingers, but I know they're there. Know I still don't know how he got them.

He traces pensive shapes of his own on my arm. 'I'm thinking ... how did the most exquisite thing in this world end up here, with me?'

I smile into his ribs, kissing him there.

'I'm not sure what to say to that,' I say, still smiling.

He sighs gently. 'Don't say anything ... there's something we should talk about.'

My hand stills, and an icy drip runs down my spine. I've heard that tone enough times to know the 'almost' that's about to come out of his mouth. I make myself still, to not slowly climb from the bed and escape before he can say it. I've been there before, too – when it's implied, tip-toed around, but never said. Sometimes, that's the loudest way a person can say it.

I listen to the sound of his breath in what I now know is an in-between moment. How simple the rise and fall of his chest could have seemed only a moment ago. Now, his very next breath could hold the 'this is over' I can feel in the air around us. Words I can't bear to hear aloud.

'I know there's no forever here,' I say, and his fingers tighten on my elbow. 'You're the Rebel Prince and I respect that. I won't stand in the way.'

He doesn't say anything, and I try to breathe around the punch it feels like I've delivered straight into the softest part of my own stomach. Closing my eyes, I hold the tears back. Half an hour ago, I had him in my mouth, thinking of ... home. And yet, here we are – this inevitable fucking 'almost' that marks every chapter of my life.

'Okay?' I whisper.

I want my voice to be stronger, but what else do I say here? Do I lie and say that's exactly what I thought this was from the beginning, temporary? Or lay it all out and tell him I finally thought this might be my shot at ...

love? At a life that was mine? One filled with purpose, and opportunity, and ... a family?

No. I won't do any of that. I don't want to undermine what led me to this point. But nor will I flay myself now it's clear, between the two of us, that there is no future. I let the reality that he hasn't objected sink in. I knew it, really, but it doesn't mean I didn't hope he would push back, explain how we could do both – have this at the same time as bring down Nuntainia and ... whatever comes after for him.

Fuck, you're an idiot, Luka. He's the leader of a fucking band of traitors—that's not someone who can give you a family. Stability. Opportunity. How did I ever consider that could have been a possibility?

'No,' he says, voice tight. 'It's not okay. You deserve so much more than I can give you. If I were a better man, I would have never done this with you.'

'Do you regret it?' I ask quietly, cursing myself for asking such a stupid question. One in complete opposition to my desire not to tarnish what we've had. It's clear, now, there is no future. Why would I open up self-torture on what's already been?

'I regret *this,* yes,' he says, letting go of my arm, rolling away and out of the bed.

I sink into the mattress, the weight of what we're now doing – where we're not going – pressing down on me. I watch mutely as he dresses roughly in the darkened room.

'But you're right, I know what my future holds. Perhaps it's best you didn't fall for me.'

'I understand,' I whisper. Because I do. I understand what I am, and what I am not, and I'm not arrogant enough to think I could get in the way of what he is trying to achieve here. He's not alone in his wish for a better world.

As he walks away, a hole tears itself into my chest, and I wish I hadn't done exactly that – fallen for the man behind the Rebel Prince.

CHAPTER SEVENTEEN

The bedroom in my townhouse is still nice, I think as I stand in it, feeling quite adrift. This used to be my safe haven, and now ... it just feels lonely, even if it is still nice. I look at the picture of Akira and Zale on my bedside and my heart aches; I've been an 'almost' friend to them for too long. So focused on the other huge things happening in my life, and not giving enough thought to what might be happening in theirs. At the very least, Zale's wife is also risking a huge amount by being aligned with the rebels and walking into Parliament every day.

Carefully running a finger over the corner of the frame, I nudge it back a little on the table. With it, I imagine being able to package Quillian up in a frame of things that used to exist, and put him next to the boxes of other things I no longer know how to process. Like my father. My lack of magic. That everyone I love has someone and something that is meant for them, and I'm still searching for mine.

I pick up the phone I haven't been able to use to message them like I did on my old one – security reasons, Cortane had said. The hollowness in my chest pangs at the edges as I look again at Akira, Zale, and I in a different time. I ignore the warning from Cortane and open up my messages.

L: dinner?

A: yes! Yours at 7?

Z: We're in

L: see you then x

The sun is completely in the sky when I throw my phone on top of the green, velvet bedspread, groaning inwardly at the reality I have to report for duty on literally zero sleep, and one giant slice of heartache. Facing duty and Zenaton Blake on my best day would be hard enough. But today? *Fuck.*

A piece of paper falls gently from my pocket as I slip my jeans down my legs. I watch it as I step out and fold them, placing them in the dirty washing basket that sits just inside my wardrobe. Picking up the piece of paper, I remember it's the rubbish I almost slipped on when I exited the pod with Holland, but something stops me from immediately throwing it away.

Instead, I unfold it, wondering what sort of insignificant flyer stayed with me while I visited the traitors' camp, gave them an alternate location to extricate people too, and listened to Quillian tell me there's no future for us.

Plain on one side, the printed side of the flyer is cream with black lettering. It's almost vintage looking, but I know it's not actually old.

Struggling with understanding or finding your magic?

It's not always as straightforward as 'manifesting'. There are many of us who require some assistance to coax it into existence, particularly those who may have been magically medicated to delay their magic coming in.

If this is you, and you'd like a confidential consultation, please get in touch.

The flyer shakes a little in my hand as I stare at it, trying to comprehend that this is what was in my pocket as Blossom told me she thinks her magic is coming in. Without really knowing why I'm prepared to take this avenue, I find the online site they reference. The exact words from the flyer fill the screen.

Along with a 'book now' button.

Rolling my lips together, I check the availability. My stomach somersaults as the calendar tells me they can see me this morning ... and I lock it in before I can talk myself out of it. With my archive pass still coming, there's not a lot I can achieve today, anyway.

'You ready?' Holland calls up the stairs.

Shit.

I carefully place the flyer face down next to the photo of Akira and Zale, and scramble into my duty outfit. Holland is standing with Finn by the kitchen bench in dark, casual clothes when I race down the stairs. He grins and swipes a piece of toast off the board he's obviously using, and hands it to me.

'Pardon the fingers,' he says, 'but you need to run.'

'Just me?' I ask, Traelen's warning about not being on my own pulsing in my mind as I glance between them, wondering how long Finn has been here.

Holland laughs. 'Sweetheart, I've known you all a relatively short time, it's true. But I have heard of your fearless *Warden,* and I saw his face when you jumped off that fucking clump of dirt. So, no, not "just you". You—lucky Princess—get Finn.'

The grin that kicks up on his face is more than a little wicked, and Finn's neck seems to deepen in colour. But he doesn't comment, just gestures me towards the door. I raise a brow at Holland, both in response to his statement about Finn, and his use of Cortane's nickname for me.

'Oh,' I say, my hand on the door frame, 'I've invited some friends for dinner tonight, so let's do something easy. I can grab something on the way back? Pop it in the serving ware I never use?'

Holland waves us off. 'Sounds fun. I can sort it.'

We half-walk, half-jog to the pod station that will take us closest to the House, and I collapse into the next available one with a pant. Finn watches me as I take the last bite of my now cold, and very sad-looking toast, but I find it hard to meet his gaze. It feels like it sees too much, and me being sad and tired at the same time is making it harder to keep my defences up.

I still haven't told any of them about Traelen, or Teddy – or Zenaton. Not after how wrecked they all were yesterday, and then Quillian and I ...

But I remember what Nix said as soon as he saw me at camp yesterday. *It's not a safe place for you here.*

Imagine what he'd say if he knew I was trusting Traelen? Let alone that Zenaton is alive and knows exactly who I am. No, it's better they don't know for now. This is the one thing I can do. Holland's not on shift today so I know he's safe from the House for the moment. I just need a little more time.

'How are you managing?' Finn eventually asks.

I clear my throat. 'Fine,' I say. 'I believe all the documents we need are in the archives. Traelen is just—'

'I know Quillian very well, Luka.'

I frown, instantly on guard. 'What do you mean?'

He sits forward, elbows pressing into his legs just above his knees.

'I saw him this morning. I don't know exactly what happened between the two of you, but it's clear he's hurting.'

The blow – intended or otherwise – lands.

'And, so, I assume you are, too.' His voice is soft. Caring. I blink rapidly before tears ruin the makeup I've done for duty.

I trust Finn, but talking with anyone so soon after my ... our breakup – is that what it was? – feels heavy. But he's right. I am hurting. Even more so with the confirmation that Quillian is, as well. I lace my fingers in my lap and squeeze. I needed to get in front of where he was going. I've fallen far too deep to hear him say the words he was just about to last night.

'I think I ended it,' I whisper, and Finn sits back. A long breath leaving his lips.

'Can I ask why? You both seemed quite happy, given the circumstances.'

Dropping my head a little, I press my fingertips firmly into my forehead.

'I was happy,' I say, looking back up and out the window at the cityscape meandering by. 'But there is a stark reality here of who he is and what that means, a reality he can't be distracted from.' I square my shoulders a little, remind myself it was the right thing. 'Whatever we had is of secondary importance to the main goals here, and it was time to face that.'

Finn's quiet a long time, but I refuse to look at him, despite the weight of his stare.

'Respectfully, Luka, are you trying to convince me or yourself of the priorities?'

I can feel my face crumple, my shoulders sinking as the loss of Quillian hits me again.

'He had come to the same conclusion, Finn,' I say, swallowing the lump in my throat. 'I just said it first.'

The pod glides to a stop, and Finn helps me out onto the platform before we silently leave the station.

The pavement is busy as we walk towards the waterfront, where Finn will leave me to take the path to Parliament House alone. Finn briefly steps in closer to me as we pass a group of women in very high shoes.

'Sometimes he's his own worst enemy,' he says.

'How so?'

'He's spent his whole life fighting to get here—we all have. The three of us grew up together.'

'You mean you, Cortane, and Quillian?'

He nods. 'But we have few memories outside the events that led us on this path, the people that helped us, and then the path itself. So to be *here*—with a full complement of soldiers, despite our losses—to have had Quillian as Warden and a publicly decorated Nuntainian soldier, and now you—one of us—in the House to access the final pieces of information ... We've never been as close to pulling it all together before. It will devastate every single one of us if we don't succeed. But it's Quillian who will be the face of that defeat.'

I nod slowly, wondering if he realises he just made my point.

'But he deserves happiness as much as the rest of us,' he continues. 'He just doesn't believe that's the case. He sees himself as the vehicle for us to move beyond all of this, once and for all. To make those who did us wrong pay, and make sure there is a system in place that means it can never happen again. And ... the truth is, Luka, a lot of people see him that way.'

'So ... you're saying it's not because he doesn't care about me?' The question is empty, even to me. I don't doubt that he cares. We just both know there's something he has to care about over and above whatever we could be.

He laughs, and I almost stumble. I don't think I've ever heard Finn make that sound before, it's quite intoxicating.

'I am definitely not saying that. I'm saying he cares too much—he's scared of what it means, of the additional responsibility to keep you safe, too. He's very aware how he will feel if something happens to you, and he doesn't want you to feel the same way in the event of the real possibility something happens to him. He's worried he'll leave you hurting in the end, through no choice of his own. I'm saying ... as the closest thing he has to a brother, I really hope you won't give up on him.'

'Shit, Finn,' I mumble. 'What you're actually saying is that I proved him right. I took away the happiness he deserves.'

I look up at him and catch his sideways glance.

'That's one way to look at it, but it's not just about him.'

The words scramble for purchase in my mind, their hooks anchoring into my chest. I don't know if I can even let myself think it, in case it allows too much hope in. But ... what if he was scared of what might be open to him? What if he's more like me than I thought, thinking what he has to offer isn't enough? What if there's the possibility he might *like* the possibility of forever? What if ... maybe I was too hasty in jumping to conclusions about where he was going in our conversation last night?

'And what about you?' I ask, unable to sustain the building pressure that comes with what he's saying about Quillian. 'Would you give it a shot in the middle of all ... *this*, if someone came along?'

He smiles gently. 'In an ideal world, that person would wait until we were through *all this*, and if they couldn't—well, it would depend on the circumstances, but I wouldn't necessarily discourage it.'

Wait. That's exactly what Quillian asked me to do—but I bury the realisation for now, turning my attention back to Finn. The temptation to ask if someone has captured his interest is strong. Particularly when I think of that deepening colour of his skin whenever Holland opens his mouth. But this feels like the most significant conversation I have ever had with Finn, and I don't want to risk him retreating – or moving the topic back to where we started.

We're silent for a few paces before the waterfront comes into view, the smell of coffee wafting from the numerous little cafés that dot the street to my right.

I draw us to a stop before we come into full view of Parliament House, a hand on Finn's forearm.

'You should leave me here,' I say, hoping he can't see the half-lie on my face. 'Now they've got that video, we can't risk anyone in there seeing you here.'

His brows draw together.

'I'll text you when I'm inside, okay?'

Reluctantly, he nods, and I head towards the House on my own. Glancing back to check I'm not in line of sight, I sidestep into the garden a little, hoping the thin crowd of tourists and greenery gives me some cover. I watch the time on my phone tick over for two minutes before I send him a text, and another five minutes to give him time to move away. Then, I message Traelen from my duty phone to tell him I'm not feeling well.

I, of course, don't tell either of them I have an appointment with a magic finder.

Townhouses like my own line the footpaths, and wide, mossy green strips of garden and grass run down the middle of the streets of suburban Klades. The houses start to age a little the further I walk, but not in a way that makes it feel dilapidated. More like a sense of history lives imbued in these streets.

My heart skips a little in anticipation, despite my head telling me how unlikely it is that this alternative approach will deliver anything. Certainly not any magic. Apart from them telling me they can't *find* magic that doesn't exist.

Seven, the letterbox at the front of the house on my right reads. I know the number I'm looking for is sixteen, but I double-check the confirmation message, anyway. Just in case.

My steps slow as I reach the crisp, white picket fence, its black trim offsetting the pale grey of the house. There's a large weeping willow in the front yard that makes me suddenly nostalgic for my childhood and the tree my father built me a swing in.

My phone buzzes in the pocket of my black leggings.

H: hey, where are you? T said you haven't showed - wanted to check it's legit

Me:

I pause a moment, not sure what I should tell him, and a little taken aback that Traelen might have been concerned enough to risk reaching out to Holland directly.

Me: I have something I need to do.

H: Please tell me it's at the camp and you have a really good reason for leaving me - your security - out of the loop.

Damn. I hadn't thought how this could look for Holland, particularly from Cortane's perspective.

Me: Sorry, no. But I'll be back as soon as I can - no later than tonight.

My phone is quiet for a long moment before the little indicator comes back to tell me he's writing a message.

H: Half a day, Luka. That's as much as you get before I come find you. If I can't, I tell Q.

A chill snakes down my spine at the additional risk I have put us in. But I'm here now, so I pocket my phone and hasten the last few steps to the gate of number sixteen.

The house is quiet as I walk up the three stairs onto the expansive porch that lines the front of the house. Two white timber chairs sit on either side of the wide front door.

A black metal door knocker sits in the middle of the right-hand door.

Waiting for me.

Pausing, I steel my breath to find out, once and for all, if I have a spark of anything magical in me. If there is some hidden part of me that will erase the gap between who I am and who I could be.

The handle of the knocker is cold in my hand as I loop my fingers over it. I squeeze the metal, just for a beat, and then bang it twice against the polished-wood door. The sound seems to echo down the quiet, tree-lined street, but I feel it in my chest. The inevitability of the hard facts I will face, either here, or back at camp.

CHAPTER EIGHTEEN

'Welcome,' a woman in her mid-fifties says before the door is completely open. 'You must be our 10.30am.'

'Hi, I'm—'

'No names.'

When the door opens all the way, I can see how well dressed she is – black pants with free-flowing legs, a belt that cinches in her waist, and a crisp, white shirt. Large, black and gold earrings swing gently from her ear underneath the dark-brown hair that's swept back off her face.

A vague sense of familiarity tugs at me, but I can't place it before she ushers me into the foyer.

'It feels impersonal,' she says, I assume referring to the no-name rule, 'but it's for the best—harder to track anyone without names.'

'Ah, sure,' I say hesitantly, but relieved I don't have to think of a fake one to give her – or have the opportunity to stupidly give her my real one, which I very nearly did. Now it makes sense why they only required initials on the booking form.

The entrance hall is large, with ceilings the height of the full three storeys of the house. A carpeted staircase running up the centre loops around from the second floor to the third. Deep balconies overlook the shining black tiles, beyond which I assume are an assortment of rooms.

'This way,' she says, leading me beyond the stairs, down the right side of the entrance hall. The sunlight that was streaming into the foyer dims a little as we walk towards the back of the house, our footsteps that were loud on the tiles suddenly silent as we cross onto carpet.

She stops at the first door on the left and gestures me in.

'He'll be here in just a moment.'

'It's not you I'm meeting with?'

She laughs. 'No. I have many skills, but luring out latent magic is not one of them.'

'So what's your ... association with the magic finder?'

'Magic finder?' her brow crinkles. 'I guess that's one way to describe him.'

I smooth the hair back from my face. 'That's what he was called on the flyer.'

She rolls her eyes. 'Honestly, the least he could have done was show that to me before it went out. For someone who is supposed to be good at research and words, an *academic*, sometimes words are not his greatest strength.'

I smile at her, unsure exactly how I am meant to respond. But she's warm, and it appears there's a lot of affection between them, so I just let her words sit.

Muted footsteps stride down the carpeted hallway, sounding like they come from the opposite direction we did, and my heart rate quickens. Am I really about to do this?

My phone vibrates in my pocket. Presumably Holland wondering why I haven't responded again. But he said half a day. If that's literal, I only have until midday, and then they'll start looking. How long until he finds the flyer in my bedroom? Or Cortane traces my phone?

'Ah, here he is,' she says, as a man enters the room.

She might not have been going to give me his name, but I don't need an introduction.

Before me, stands Corvan Brideoake – my father.

My heart swoops towards the plush carpet.

His face pales as his mouth drops open, staring at me. I look wildly between him and the woman, trying to force it to make sense. But she just looks between us, a small crease between her brows.

'Well ... I was going to say this is your 10.30am, but something tells me that might be a bit superfluous,' she says.

My father gapes for another moment before snapping his mouth shut. I swallow, my hairline starting to prickle. He seems older, the passage of the last five years visible in the deepening of his frown lines, the slightly changed shape of the fingers on his writing hand. In the face of everything since Claudius's death, the attacks on the traitors' camps, his disappointment in my not getting the head position at the Academy seems so ... inconsequential. How did I ever think that was so important? So insurmountable I couldn't talk to him about it? The knowledge I am as much to blame as him for letting our relationship wane, settles uncomfortably among the other truths I'm not yet ready to process. What can I even say to him now, after five years of silence?

'Rosie,' he says, finding his voice. 'This is my daughter, Luka.'

So much for no names.

'Ah,' she says, completely unruffled. 'I'll leave you to it, then.'

My father waits for her to leave the room and then strides towards me.

'Luka,' he says, taking me into his arms, 'it's so good to see you.'

His voice is thick with an emotion that makes my eyes prick with tears. Tears that burn with an anger I have felt for so long whenever I thought of him – that acidic resentment of his disappointment in me. That he left me to be assigned to a duty and not take the Academy role. Never contacted me again.

Worse than that are the tears that push into the angry ones, filled instead with regret. Regret that I didn't dig into that further. Didn't try harder to understand his reasoning and fight for us. He was all the family I had, and I just let it wash away.

He squeezes me harder, as if he never wants to let go. I finally return his embrace, wondering how the cracking in my chest can be for so many things at one time.

Eventually, he releases me, and gestures to one of the off-white couches to my left. 'Please,' he says, 'have a seat. Your duty has finished, I take it? I'm so pleased you dropped by.'

I blink at him, realising I still haven't said a word, but there's something in his simple statement that catches in my mind. How would I have 'dropped by' when I had no idea he'd moved to this house? Heard nothing from him the whole time I've been away?

'I was hoping to collect you myself ...' he continues, his voice tentative, 'but when I didn't hear from you, I assumed you made other plans.' He puts on a smile that could only be described as brave when he looks at me. 'I'm so pleased you're back.'

For a moment, I feel like I'm back in that collection room, watching the portal disappear. Complete confusion left in its place.

'What do you mean ... didn't hear from me? Why would you hear from me when you'd decided to forget I exist?' After I left, I gave him nowhere to write to.

The bite in my tone carries every bit of hurt from our years apart. From our last conversation. And I find I'm not interested in hiding from that anymore. If we're to find a way forward, I have to let this go.

He stares at me for a moment before understanding crashes over his features. 'Ah, they didn't give you my letters.' A defeated laugh bubbles from his throat, and I shake my head a little. This morning is not going at all how I imagined. 'I suppose that's a relief, in a way. I know why you didn't reach out initially, of course, but I was struggling to understand why you would repeatedly ignore me over all these years.'

Long beats pass while we watch each other, neither of us seemingly knowing what to do or say from here. He wrote? *They* didn't give me his letters? Who is 'they'? The concierges who sorted the mail? I find that hard to believe. *No*, a voice in the back of my mind tells me. It wouldn't have been the concierges. It's something else. As I stare at him against the backdrop of this almost awe-inspiring home, I wonder how he ended up here, doing *this*, instead of sitting on review boards and advising government from the Academic Quarter. I watch him, his hazel eyes taking in every detail of me, as the pieces whirl around my mind like the flurries of leaves we'd sometimes get on the island.

Someone stopped his letters before they even made it to the island. Someone with easy access to contacts in the duty mail service on the mainland.

I open my mouth to speak, but no words come.

'Perhaps we should sit down,' he says.

His voice is resigned. Heavy. And it sends a shot of wariness through my limbs to join the overwhelming sense of not knowing where to start a conversation with him. That I missed him? That I'm still hurting from his disappointment?

A bitter taste creeps up the back of my throat as I perch on the edge of the couch he indicated earlier. He mirrors my action, gaze still running jerkily over my face, as if he's searching for something.

'Your magic didn't come in?' he asks with no surprise in his voice.

But it shocks me a little, in the face of everything else. That's not what I expected him to lead with. Although, given I didn't know where he was, he's obviously worked out that's the only reason I would be here.

Because I had no idea it was him I was coming to.

It pains me to think about answering him. Confirming how far short I've fallen from his expectations.

'No.'

'And you wanted help to see if you could get it to.'

'Yes,' I say woodenly. 'It's past time that it should have—if it's going to. But I was on dampeners for a long time, so I know it's unlikely at this point. What I don't know is how *you* can help with that.' *Among other things,* I don't say.

His silver hair is cut quite short, and it's striking against his tanned skin – more tanned than mine, at least. I let myself soak him in for a moment. He's kept himself fit, and he looks good. But ... sad. Not unlike the way Quillian, Nix, and Bloss have looked at me at different times over the last few months, and it tugs at something right in the middle of my sternum.

'Luka,' he says, more of that heaviness in his voice. 'There are things in my past that are hard to talk about for ... different reasons. Including my relationship with you. That's something I have lived without for a long time, and I am deeply sorry for that.'

I swallow, my blinking coming more rapidly.

'I've not ... shown you much vulnerability in the past, and now, having you here, within my grasp, that's something I know I need to rectify quickly. A rope I need to throw in the hope you will grasp the other end and we will find each other again.'

My bottom lip starts to tremble, but I find words still won't come as my buried need for my father tries to force its way to the surface.

His gaze softens a little as he continues. 'I can help people find their magic, particularly after taking dampeners, because I know how they work. Because I ... instigated their creation.'

My stomach bottoms out, and I recoil.

He scoots a little closer to me, barely sitting in his own couch as he angles his body towards me. Just how deeply involved with this government is he? *Was* he?

'You must understand, like so much of the work I did, they've been warped into something very different. Used so differently to how they were intended. What was supposed to be good and fair and'—his voice cracks—'*help* people, has been abused. And under my name.' Anger flashes across his face.

I shake my head. 'I don't understand. What do you mean?'

He sighs heavily. 'Before I can answer that, Luka, I need to know what you intend to do with the information I can give you. These are not conversations we've had before.'

'So much for vulnerability.'

He purses his lips. 'It's not that simple, Lu.'

Silence falls between us as we study each other. Torn between a battle of wills and a desperate attempt to connect with the other, quietly begging the trust to come between us instead of silence.

'My first duty was on Zanteera Island,' I say eventually, and he blanches. 'I'm in the city investigating some of the ... leads I discovered in my time there.'

My father's soft, green-hazel eyes close as he exhales gently, but I can't tell if it's in relief or not. When he opens them again, it appears he's made some kind of decision.

'Your magic hasn't disappeared because of the dampener. It's dormant because I stopped its manifestation before you could talk.'

CHAPTER NINETEEN

For a moment, I think I'm going to have to drop my head between my knees to stop the room spinning. Instead, I laugh – the sound verging on maniacal.

My phone vibrates again. I can almost feel it reverberate in the clenching of my teeth.

'*You* stopped my magic from manifesting? When I was a *baby*?' I suck in a breath. 'What the fuck, Dad?'

Tears well in his eyes, and I suddenly doubt everything I've ever thought. For so long I believed he was disappointed I hadn't manifested, along with my failure at the academy. But ... how could he be disappointed in me for something he caused? Something he'd made sure I'd never be able to do? If I've been wrong about that, then perhaps he had a deeper reason for withholding his recommendation to the academy ...

'Do you know what magic line runs in your veins?' he asks.

'Yours,' I reply automatically, a bit stupefied, thinking of his blended Clayti and Arkanan abilities that have just a touch of Shaide.

He hesitates, and I can tell we're about to venture into territory we so rarely visit. My mother. My palms start to itch, and I shift in my seat.

'And?' I ask. 'What was she?' A question I've never once asked him. Probably only wondered about once or twice. She left. There was only so much caring I wanted to send in her direction, wherever that was.

'Karaylia.'

I blink at him, still not putting this together. Karaylia are rare, strong. But not a cause for concern—

Sex trafficking.

Aiten Gall's numbers didn't add up.

Quillian's words float back to me. *Breeding program.*

I shake my head, staring incredulously at him, as if the connections will appear visually for me to follow – like an outline on the board from the prison concierge room.

'I still don't understand. Why would you take that from me? *How* did you take that from me?'

He leans forward, palms dropping between his thighs, where he rubs them together roughly.

Breeding program.

Acidity burns in my throat.

'Can you tell me what your plan is now you've finished your duty?' he counters. His face morphs into an expression I remember so clearly from my childhood. One I can never seem to defy. 'The actual plan, Luka.'

Blowing out a breath, I make myself move back in the chair, trying to appear more relaxed despite my heart hammering so hard I think I might crack a rib. This is my *father.* Someone whose approval I have strived for my entire life, even when I didn't directly allow him in it. Someone whose role I partially allowed Claudius to fill.

Perhaps someone who can read me more readily than I'd like to admit.

A stab of guilt lances just below my sternum. Because, while I will never regret my relationship with Claudius, I could have done much, *much* more to keep in contact with my Dad.

Looking at him now, seeing the small differences in his face, the colour of his hair, the way he moves, I know I have let too much time go by for something that now seems to pale in significance to the issues that are starting to take shape in my mind. The prison program, the breeding program, the loss of magic through dampeners – is that even legal? Is it *right?* The lists of casualties and missing persons from Tae. The way both Hunters and traitors died while I watched on a big screen, with morning tea on the table.

I was disappointed I didn't get the Head role of the Academy I'd worked so hard to create. But now that I'm faced with my father, armed with all the other knowledge I have gained, I can't help but wonder how much of his disappointment was in me…or *for* me?

He didn't give me a recommendation. But would I have managed to hold the role for long even with it? Would I have been undermined for nepotism at every turn if he'd given it?

But, more than that, if I'd gotten it, would I still be completely unaware of everything else happening around me? Would I have been a female Karaylia right under the nose of people like Zenaton?

A roll of nausea eddies through me.

And one thing about my father is true – he has never deceived me.

At the same time, I will never deceive Quillian and the others.

I clear my throat, dragging my mind back to his question of why I'm here. 'I … got to know some of the people I was assigned to on my duty. Knowing them, understanding how they got where they are was … eye-opening. The things I learned through those relationships—and others—do not line up with what I thought I knew about our government's motivations and actions.'

He's very quiet, still, after what is essentially my confession that I'm aligned with a way of thinking that is in opposition to our government.

'But we have a democracy, Luka,' he says carefully, in a way that reminds me of when he'd test me on different issues, or try to improve my debating skills. 'Our current government has ruled for a long time, it's true, but if you don't agree with the government, there are actions you can take, avenues you can use, to have your voice heard.'

I think of the Hunters and the way they swarmed the island, watching us all, the memory of seeing River, and then Quillian, through the bars of Vana. And I consider what I was told was happening up there compared to what I now know to be true. The faces of the people on the Defence Committee swim before me. There was no hesitation among them. No second guessing, or consideration, or concern, for the lives lost on either side. No discussion about what led to that point. And, for all I could see, they were the ones solely in charge of who would die that day – for reasons that were never shared.

Is it possible those things were considered before they went in? Yes.

But do I trust that they would have done their due diligence in working out right from wrong before they did? No.

Not when people like Kasera, who had child slaves, and Aiten, who bought and sold the less powerful for sex, were being completely excused for their actions. They were in no way being punished or receiving support to understand the grotesque nature of their actions.

No, they were simply removed from public view until the dust settled; then they were shipped back into the House, where they were handed another powerful role, their sins neatly brushed under the plush rugs of their offices. Any questions about their healthy return to the public sphere were either not asked, or simply swept away.

Not when individuals like that make up an entire government committing atrocious crimes against Tae. Crimes the average Nuntainian has no idea about.

And was I supposed to know any of that? Was I given an option to voice my opinion, or find a way to make it heard in a way that wouldn't land me on the wrong side of the law? Or was I contractually bound to never talk about what I saw and heard? What else has been occurring under this government over the last three decades that's meant they could never be bested by another party?

So, do we live in a democracy? No, not really.

'I think we need to do better, much better, than our current system,' I chance. 'But,' I continue before he can interject, 'what are you doing here? What happened to the Academic Quarter?' The memory of trying to see past the city skyline to that part of the city when I'd returned with Finn and Holland surfaces – those buildings, and my father, just out of reach. Only for him to be almost delivered to me. Or did I deliver myself to him?

He scans my face, the stiltedness between us rich with unsaid things. Words I think we both know we want to share – should be able to share – but there's more than just a personal risk in doing so. Certainly for me, knowing how connected he is. Would he turn me in? I don't think so. Not when it seems he has taken such extreme lengths to keep me safe.

But would he have the same qualms about exposing anyone I am working with?

'I believe I am here for much the same reasons you are,' he says, fingers lacing together, his words laden with meaning. 'To do better.'

The air races out of my lungs.

My father's a traitor.

And so am I.

My mind scrambles with questions, the one about my magic butting painfully against everything else.

'How is my magic related to all of this?'

The uncertainty that flickers across his features only adds fuel to my own. As one of Nuntainia's most esteemed academics, uncertainty is not something I've ever known him to encounter. A lack of knowledge, yes. More research required, yes. But uncertain in his views and decisions, no.

He draws a deep breath that expands his chest beneath his softly striped, button-up shirt. 'Rosie should join us for this,' he says before calling out to her, eyes never leaving my face.

We wait as her footsteps return, approaching softly up the carpeted hallway, and she appears in the sitting room. Her gaze flicks momentarily between us, but she's completely composed, a gentle, professional smile on her face, and recognition slams into me.

She's a political reporter.

One who interviewed my father multiple times throughout his career.

'Rosie,' he starts, as she takes a third armchair, face still impassive, 'has been researching the same things as me for almost as long—we just didn't always know it. I'm sure you'—he cuts a look to me—'can understand why that might be.'

'Because it's hard to declare, particularly to a journalist,' I confirm, and he nods.

Rosie doesn't move.

But she also doesn't interject. I've seen enough of her work to know she's whip-smart, and she would have to know where this conversation is going based on that statement alone. Which means she trusts my father implicitly – a thought I tuck away for later. What exactly is their relationship? And how long has it been going on?

'After the best part of twenty years working in siloed parallels, our paths began to intersect.' He pauses. 'That intersection brought us squarely to the attention of the government, who would have preferred we not shed light on different issues. The last five years have been ... interesting, Luka.'

Rosie sits back slowly, watching me. 'I suggest we talk plainly, Corvan. I do not think your daughter is here to betray us.'

Dad shoots her a grateful look, before nodding to himself, as if gathering his thoughts. Hopefully, this means no more tit-for-tat on the questions. My phone is now vibrating with incessant annoyance in my pocket, but I stay silent and hope to encourage him to share as much as he will before I have to go. Whatever may be happening between us, I am definitely not ready to have Cortane breaking down his door.

'About thirty years ago,' he says, 'I was approaching some key ... milestones in my career. More research meant more answers, and more access to information than the general person can find. Information the government only releases to trusted people. I found out a long time later that also means people they believe they can control. Often, they're not wrong.

'As part of that research, I discovered the Karaylia breeding program.'

A chill runs down my spine at the way his voice twists on the words. The same way Traelen's face did when we spoke of it. As did Nix and River's.

'Just the existence of the program was enough for me to want—to *need*—to take proactive action against any possibility of you being taken for—' he presses his lips closed for a moment. 'You were so young, but whether you grew into wings or not, having the Karaylia blood in your veins, and even a touch of magic, is imperative for successful ... breeding.' He spits the last word, fingers digging into the arms of his chair.

'I'd already been trying to understand why the Karaylia line was so rare, and yet so strong, in parts of the world. So much of my work was around what exactly triggers magic manifestation, how genetics play a part, and why certain bloodlines may be stronger with certain magic types.'

A memory of his home office flashes in my mind – in it, my father is hunched over the desk, flicking through book after book on Karaylia magic.

'It made sense, at the time, to not only focus on understanding what enabled our magic, but to also explore the potential of dampening one's magic, or even preventing it from manifesting at all.' He looks at me, sad but resolute. 'While the purpose of my research was always ensuring magic would continue to flourish, knowing what halted it went hand-in-hand—if I could pause it, I could perhaps learn to enable it in those with a strong magical bloodline, but no magic. But, it wasn't too much of a leap to ensure it *never* manifested either ... and so I did. Once I was sure it would work, I used my findings to permanently stop your magic.'

Nausea grips my stomach and twists.

'I, somewhat naively, failed to foresee the potential for harm in my magic dampening research until it was too late. When they discovered I'd found a way to nullify one's magic, they wanted me to adapt it to be used as a punishment issued in Vana. But I insisted that, criminals or not, it was still a breach of human rights, that it shouldn't be used on anyone—especially not those who *serve* our country. I tried to convince them that the purpose of the research project as a whole was to help people *enable* their bloodlines – to help ensure the survival of the Karaylia – not strip them of anything.' He sighs. 'Not long after, they seized my research and locked me out of the relevant communication channels, citing project closure. So, it's impossible for me to say with any confidence whether it was instigated in Vana or not—especially now there is virtually no appealing of any sentence there.'

I blow out a breath, my head spinning with everything he's shared. 'But *my* rights never came into it?'

My magic...

He spent so much of his time researching how to help others with their magic, fought to stop those in Vana from having it administered against their will, and yet—

'Your rights had everything to do with it,' he grinds out. 'But it was either take your magic so they never knew what you could have been, or let you be taken to breeding barracks to be held down and *used* in whatever way they saw fit. You would have been nothing but a vessel for making winged soldiers—child soldiers, at that.' He drags a hand over his face as if the thought still haunts him. 'As your father, I exercised my best judgement in keeping you safe. That was it.'

Now I do drop my head towards my knees, the room all but swirling around me.

'What does that mean really happened to my mother?'

'Nothing,' he says, a different kind of bite in his voice. 'She took the stopper as well, then left. Honestly, I think she was smart enough to know I'd find something like that eventually, and only held on until I did.'

I lift my head a little. 'So she knew about the program and left me, anyway?' It's a wound I've long grown past, even if this new knowledge stings a little. It's hard to keep hating someone I never really knew.

My father's eyes close briefly. 'Yes. And it remains true that I haven't heard from her since. Indirectly, I know she was fine for a long time, but I haven't heard anything more for a long while. I have no reason to believe she's in any danger.'

Mutely, I nod.

'With all due respect,' Rosie says after a moment, but I can't bring myself to look away from the floor. 'What happened to your magic—and your mother—isn't the right conversation for now.'

I do stare at her then but, composed as her expression is, there doesn't appear to be any judgement in it. It's almost ... soft. Firm, but soft.

'No,' I say, drawing myself up. 'You're right. I came here to see if I could get an answer to a question, and I found it. But ... if you two know so much—I can only assume much more than what we've covered here so far—why haven't you exposed any of it yet?' I ask. 'You must know the breeding practice still exists? Do you know why they're so desperate for winged soldiers?'

This time they look at each other for a long time, clearly weighing up what, or how much, to share. My father sighs heavily, as if he's weary of this battle and is ready to throw caution to wind.

'We're just two people from Nuntainia. Rosie has a profile, a strong one, but with only a supposedly 'retired' magic historian and social policy expert by her side, we fear our whistleblowing could too easily be drowned out or explained away. Goodness knows we've seen our fair share of erasure in the media to last a lifetime. There is a movement we've heard about, they're painted as a 'vigilante' group here, but we know better. They're led by the Rebel Prince, the whole of Tae is in support of them, and we've been trying to track him down. We got as far as a lead on the head of his intelligence, then it went cold. But we need his kind of weight behind the information we can make public. We need a face of our agenda—one with the backing he has—and we won't share our information with anyone but him.'

I stare at them, watching their stillness as elements of my world collide, the final destruction of my old beliefs in my government, my duty, or my magic. Their lead that went cold – an intelligence one – was surely Cortane? Then she ended up in Vana.

The continuing buzzing of my phone breaks the silence around us.

'Perhaps it's important,' Rosie says, and I sigh as I slide it out, turning the smooth device over in my hand.

11.55am.

13 missed calls.

19 messages.

I open the most recent one.

H: sorry sweetheart, time's up. F is outside. Move now or he comes in.

I stand, my head spinning with the collision of people and information and motivations. How is it real that my father is trying to get close to the very person I distanced myself from last night? How is it possible that he has known about this corruption for the best part of my lifetime?

F calling, the phone in my hand announces with yet another fucking vibration.

'Shit,' I mutter. 'I need to take this.' I look at my father, his hazel gaze latching on to mine. The sound of the vibrating phone echoes between us, my pulse ratcheting with every ring. I'm out of time.

'Pack a small bag each,' I say, already moving out of the room in a race to make sure Finn doesn't appear. 'I'll be back in a day or two. Stay close to home. You're going to want to come with me when I call.'

CHAPTER TWENTY

The looming dark shadow that is Finn waits at my Dad's front gate, watching every step I take towards him.

I can't tell if he's mad, but I feel like that's something he doesn't get very often. He seems more ... resigned? But he doesn't say a word as we walk away from the house and towards the pod station.

The silence makes my skin prickle. Between what seems like his quiet disapproval, and our earlier conversation about how much it would hurt Quillian if something happened to me – *and* the fact that I flat out lied to him this morning – it's not a great feeling. It's not like me to deceive those around me, at least those I care about.

'I'm sorry I lied to you,' I say, and he slowly stops walking.

He turns his head away, looking over his shoulder, and then tips it in that direction, towards a park bench in one of the small grassy areas I passed on my way here.

'Want to talk about it?' he asks when we're seated.

My phone is still blowing up. So much I vaguely wonder how much vibrating it can take before it falls to pieces.

Finn holds out his hand. 'Let me have it a moment. I've told Holland I've got you—he'll relay the message.'

The act of handing the device over feels freeing in itself, like I can think. Unfortunately, that also means the emotions I've been trying to keep at bay surge forward as well, and quiet tears wet my lashes.

'I feel divided,' I say, realising just how much it feels that way as the words leave my mouth. 'Between being where I know I'm supposed to be, in Parliament House and ... researching, and being with the rest of you where it feels like you're doing so much more. I am absolutely committed to helping, and I know you all say it's so important that I be here but, truly, I'm not doing anything but watch you go to battle.'

And holding information. At least while I try to process it.

Finn looks at me sideways. 'You feel ineffectual.'

'Well ... yes.' And *ineffectual* is not something that sits well.

'Have you made good contacts in the House outside of Holland?'

I think of Traelen and Teddy and that, because of the meeting, I now know all the Defence Committee and their support staff, even if it's not well. I also know how to access their diaries. And I know Zenaton Blake is leading the committee, and is both the Deputy Prime Minister *and* Minister for Justice now. There is no way he's not intimately connected. On top of that, I know Traelen was their contact, we have a leak, and there's a missing Prime Minister ...

'I guess so ... but what do I *do* with that?' I ask, realising I haven't even mentally got to the part about my Dad and Rosie.

'You have an academic background, is that right?'

My throat tightens a little.

'Sort of,' I say.

'So, start mapping it out with what you can find in there. When did the programs start? Who signed off on them? Who is still in the House? How do they work out who goes through the programs and who doesn't? Who might be on our side? They're the sort of questions we need the answers to.'

I blink at how simple that sounds. How silly I feel at not having crystallised it so succinctly myself. But then, my first proper day in the House began with watching the Hunters try to wipe out the people I love.

I nod. 'What are you going to do with the information?'

A gentle breeze rustles the short bushes next to us, and I have a sudden longing for the forest of the island.

'Quillian—one of Nuntainia's most celebrated war heroes and the Rebel Prince—is going to take it public.'

The way Finn says it, *celebrated war hero*, completes a part of the puzzle that had been staring me in the face. 'He held the line,' I breathe.

'Pardon?' Finn asks.

I shake my head, still thinking about Quillian bringing it all down. 'Nothing, just something Zenaton said.'

I huff a humourless laugh, marvelling at how the pieces of my life have not only collided, but now seem to be perfectly aligned in a way they haven't been before.

'Wow, I thought I was tired,' Holland says, eyeing me as Finn and I walk in the door of my townhouse. He's dressed casually in jeans and a bright red t-shirt that somehow goes well with his red beard, one of my tea towels slung over his shoulder.

Apparently, my days of bouncing back well after losing a night of sleep are long behind me.

He doesn't move as I make to go past him. He's not able to block me completely in the open space, but I know what he's doing, and I know I need to let him.

'Have a happy little adventure?' he asks, his voice deceptively calm.

'I'm sorry,' I say, and mean it. 'I didn't want to give you the slip, I just ... needed to do something.' I shrug my shoulders. 'And I ended up with a whole lot more.'

'What's that supposed to mean?' he asks. 'And was it worth Cortane tearing me another asshole?'

Finn makes a sound suspiciously like a snigger behind me, and Holland slowly pins him with a glare. 'Nice for you, who gets to play the hero. Anytime you want to play *my* hero, you just let me know.' He lets his scowl drop away before his gaze travels the full length of Finn, the intent in his look making my cheeks burn. Finn remains silent as he gestures me out of the doorway and locks the door behind us, raising a brow at Holland until he moves out of the way.

I make my way to the kitchen, consciously looking away from whatever other silent exchange they might have, and at the explosion of food on my countertop instead. Tins of things, spices, vegetables of all colours, and large bags of flour and rice, line the space around a clean chopping board and knife.

'What's all this?' I ask, aware of Finn coming up beside me and taking a seat at the breakfast bar. He studies Holland as if he's some curious sort of creature ... which I suppose he is a bit, but says nothing.

'We've got your guests tonight, right?' Holland asks, but it's not really a question.

I blink. Yes, we do. Something I'd forgotten in the whirlwind of today's events.

'You didn't like my idea of takeout in fancy kitchenware?'

He glances at Finn for a moment before fixing me with his gaze.

'No,' he says. 'This is me ... processing.'

He passes me a glass of sparkling silver, and I drop my gaze, awash with disappointment in myself at worrying him.

'Don't look like that—you're not the worst of it, don't worry.' He points at the drink. 'That will give you some pep back for tonight. Go wash up, I've got it down here.'

The pull of the quiet of my bedroom and a shower is infinitely tempting. Not least because I've given Nix long enough to do his own processing, and now I want to hear his voice. I cringe at how angry he's going to be with me after so many unreturned messages today – he will be far worse than Holland. But I also wonder if a shower and some space will help me do my own processing of the last twenty-four hours.

The ones that still sting.

'Are you sure?' I ask, guilt at Holland preparing all the food for my dinner keeping me in the kitchen.

'Please,' he says, 'I've got enough of an audience here already'—he winks at Finn—'I could do with one less.'

The deepening colour on Finn's prominent, dark cheekbones makes me laugh, and I leave them be, dragging myself upstairs with my silver sparkle.

Settling on my bed, I grab my personal phone and call Nix, studiously ignoring the unread messages from Quillian.

'So, you do live,' he says after the first ring.

I sigh. 'Yes, I live.'

'You realise I'm not going to stop any punishment Cortane might wish to impart, right?'

I splutter. 'Punishment?'

He makes a non-committal sound but otherwise doesn't respond, leaving that threat hanging over my head.

'How're you holding up?' I ask, changing the subject. 'What's happening there?'

There are voices around him that fade away in the background, and I imagine him moving through the traitors' camp to find a quiet spot.

'Okay,' he says. 'The location you gave us is great, Lu—I was out there this morning, and we've started moving those who can travel there already. Janly's gone with them to lead the set up and sort everyone out.'

I smile a little. 'She'll be good at that.'

He talks me through the different logistics, and who is doing what. I listen patiently as he tells me about River and Blossom, and how Cortane is interrogating every traitor before they go to the new camp. Whoever gave up the list of camps isn't going to remain unknown for long, and it makes the hair on the back of my neck stand up – like the feeling before an electrical storm rolls in. It's incredible what they're achieving over there, and a familiar twinge of envy that I'm not part of it – or doing more myself, other than following my own needs, at least today – makes itself known under my ribs.

Now I know the archives are going to be our only reliable option, thanks to the additional warping Zenaton could do to anything I see or hear, and I also know I need to get in there as soon as possible. I make a note to tell Traelen I'm feeling better and hope he has my access sorted by then. Despite the events of today being a bit ... off script ... after the discussion with my Dad and Rosie, I do feel a renewed sense of purpose of what I *can* find in there.

'And you?' I ask when he pauses.

'I'm alright, Lu,' he says after a moment. 'Honestly, it's nothing I haven't done before. But that was the first time I've been in an open confrontation as big as that since my active time in Tae ...'

Nix said there were no survivors from that attack. That his girlfriend was killed in the assault he wasn't there to stop.

'...imagine what they went through.'

The mix of sadness and anger in his voice is thick even through the phone, and my heart aches for him.

'I'm so sorry that happened to you,' I say softly, leaning back into my pillows.

'Yeah, me too,' he breathes. 'I'd never have not loved her, though, you know? As much as it hurts now ... at least I know what that felt like. We had that.'

I close my eyes and a quiet tear escapes. The loss both he and Blossom have had in their lives is hard to witness, and it presses on my chest. Even though it's not my pain, it still searches for a home in me somewhere. There's a pinch there too, though – one of envy, maybe, that I may never have what they did. That, as painful as it is for them now, they both had great loves.

'I wish it didn't end like that for you,' I say.

He laughs without humour. 'Yeah, me too. But let's talk about you and Quillian—'

'Or ... we could not? I know you hate him for what he did, and I don't really know if there is a "me and Quillian", not really.'

He draws a deep breath. 'It was easy to hate him when I needed a focus for my pain, Lu, but—the truth is, it's not his fault. I would have given the same order. Told us to get out. Saved what lives I could. I just didn't know what my personal cost would be for that. There is no time I wouldn't have spent in Vana—or dead—if it meant she got to live. But that's ... just not how it turned out.'

'I'm trying to find out who is giving those orders, Nix. The orders that make those impossible choices necessary.'

I can't bring myself to tell him about Zenaton and, as Minister for Justice, it's almost impossible that it would be anyone else. Not now, when it feels like we're having one of the most real conversations we've had in a while. Like we would have before he was hurt and even more overprotective.

'I know. Just like I know it's a huge risk for you to be in there—add that to the list of things I hate—but knowing we can bring down the entire corrupt government with what you could uncover ... that's pretty motivating.'

'Yeah, I'm working on it.'

He's quiet for a beat, and I know what's coming. Loathe as I am to go through it again, I don't want to cut Nix out now I have him properly in my life again.

'Tell me, Lu—whatever's happening with Quillian—was it your decision, or his?'

Running my fingers over my bedspread, and watching how the pressure changes the direction and colour of the velvet, I sigh.

'I don't really know anymore. I thought he was going to end it so ... I sort of did it first. Said I knew there wasn't a future for us, and he said it was good I hadn't fallen for him.'

'Ouch,' he half laughs, and I groan. 'Well, that might explain why he's only been half here today.'

'That doesn't exactly make me feel better, if that's what you're going for.'

'Far out,' he mutters to himself, 'how did I end up here?'

I frown. 'What are you talking about?'

'I can't believe I'm about to say this, but I think you're being stupid. Or short-sighted. Or something else River would be better at articulating. But anyone with half an eyeball can see the two of you are supposed to be. You've just found something that terrifies you both—possibly for slightly different reasons—and neither of you know how to work that through.'

I don't respond, a tightening in my chest like he's just grabbed all of my heartstrings in his fist, halting my breath for a moment. Perhaps ... he's right. And so is Finn. I certainly felt like my feelings for Quillian were reciprocated. I've been 'almost' long enough to know I don't want that role anymore. That allowing in too much hope of being something else ... something *more,* some*one* more, is only a road to more heartache. But I also know, when I revisit the conversation in my mind, I did jump in. I was so scared of what he was about to say, maybe he—

I shake my head. I'm so sick of the 'almost' – what it means and how I react to its possibility. I want to strike the word from my vocabulary.

My veins buzz as the time for dinner approaches, and I pace my bedroom, wondering what in the world to wear. What do I possibly choose from a wardrobe that belongs to past-Luka to see friends I haven't seen since I was her?

Rummaging through my drawers, I discard all the particularly fancy lingerie that occupies one side, and search for some of the comfiest underwear. If the smells drifting up from the kitchen are any indication, Holland is an excellent cook. While I wish to look put together, I do not wish to be uncomfortable in my own home.

Settling on a pair of wide leg jeans and a pale blue blouse with a deep v-neck that highlights both my collarbones and the colour of my eyes, I examine myself in the bathroom mirror.

My hair was only cut for maintenance on the island. There were no extreme hair changes allowed unless it was to conform with a more conservative look. So my hair is many inches longer than when I left, and I pull it over my shoulder where the platinum blonde strands drape and fall to below my right breast. I wonder, briefly, what it would look like if I cut it all off – would that better reflect who I feel like right now?

Pulling it into a high ponytail, I resign myself to this being the best I will be able to do.

Akira's squeal as she barrels into my open-plan living space is almost deafening. My face splits into a grin as she runs through the cosy space and envelopes me in a fierce hug. Before I even lay eyes on her, Zale is around us as well, and my eyes well with tears at the sense of being squeezed by warm, unconditional love from all sides.

They talk over each other for several minutes – how good it is to see me, how much they missed me, that they love my hair, that life has just been the same for them, and so many questions about my duty that I can't answer. Ones I probably could answer, now I have my tattoo, but the less details they know about all of that, the safer they will be. But I can't help the regret that stings my eyes when they tentatively ask how my new duty is going. Less now because of the duty itself – if I wasn't already all in. More because it's such a huge part of my life, of me, that I can't share with them.

I untangle myself so I can look at them properly.

Akira's thick, brown hair is a bit shorter now, the gentle waves just resting on her shoulders. Tiny creases around her eyes give her a boost of character, like she's growing into herself in a way I wouldn't have predicted. But her smile, and the warmth that radiates from her dark eyes is the same. And it presses on my chest. Zale is taller than Akira by a nudge, slighter too, but her hair seems a bit darker than when I last saw her. But, then, she has always experimented with her hair colour, so it could be anything on any given day. Her gaze is a little sparklier than Akira's – is that because her kids are slightly older and she's getting a bit more sleep?

But, no matter how they look, how they feel is the same – a thick, almost syrupy warmth that seeps into all of my corners.

'I can't believe you're here,' I say, staring at them and giving them my own once over.

'Don't worry, I'll bring the wine in,' Teddy says from the doorway, a bottle in each hand, clearly having been left behind as Akira and Zale rushed into my house.

Zale just about bounces in place. 'I am *so* excited the two of you are in the same place!' she squeals. 'You remember Teddy, right?' she asks, looking at me, and I flick my gaze back to her wife, smile stuck in place. Has Teddy told her nothing?

'I certainly remember you,' Teddy says, walking in and kicking the door closed behind her. She holds out the wine and I take both bottles, but she hangs on a moment longer, as if checking I will go with this version of events. 'Granted, it would be hard to forget given how often they talk about you.' Her smile is wide, but there's a hint of steel in her brown eyes.

'It's lovely to see you again, Teddy,' I make myself say, and her smile grows a little wider still.

'Teddy is actually on duty in Parliament House at the moment,' Zale says, cutting between us to take the wine and moving away. 'How crazy you can be in the same place and not get to see each other.'

I turn away from Teddy before I say something I will regret, Teddy's warning about keeping Zale safe ringing in my ears.

'Wild,' is the only reply I can manage.

Behind Zale and Akira, who is dumping her bag in the small lounge room on the left, Holland and Finn move around the kitchen together as if they're listening to the same music – gently weaving in and out of each other's space but never crossing over. Never touching. Finn pulls his phone from his pocket, before saying something to Holland that's too quiet for me to hear, and walking around us, disappearing out the front door.

Holland locks it behind him before joining Akira, Zale, Teddy, and me.

'Righto, are you ready to introduce me to your gorgeous friends?' Holland asks and Akira blushes.

Watching Holland and two of my oldest friends get to know each other is like watching a scene from a movie I feel like I could have written, and I can't help but smile at every word that comes from their mouths. On the surface, Teddy blends right in, exactly like I would have expected her to, but I'm very aware of her and what she says. Not because I don't trust her, but because willingly lying to Zale and Akira is unfamiliar territory for me, and it doesn't sit well.

Particularly since Teddy isn't the only one with secrets from them.

'Did you cook all this?' Zale asks Holland, looking towards the kitchen.

I laugh. 'What, you didn't think it was me?'

Akira's brows lift in mock surprise. 'I am very certain your duty did not make a cook out of you.'

'Don't get too excited until you taste it,' Holland says, 'but, yes, and it's time to eat.'

'We're not waiting for Finn?' I ask.

Holland's gaze flicks to mine momentarily. 'No, he could be caught up for a while.'

I catch the meaning in his look, but I keep my smile in place as I ferry dishes from the kitchen to the dining table, Akira and Zale set the table, and Teddy pours wine.

'Should I be worried?' I whisper to Holland when it's just the two of us in the kitchen briefly.

'I don't think so,' he says. 'He'll call if it's important.'

I nod, and force myself to exhale.

'Luka,' Zale calls, 'where's the salt?'

A knock at the door has Holland and I eyeing each other, but Akira is there before I can think, opening it.

'Ohhh—hi,' she says into the evening. 'Ummm, Luka?' she calls over her shoulder, but I can already see.

There's a tall, broad, dark-haired man in my doorway.

One that makes my stomach bottom out.

Akira stands aside, and a wave of emotion I don't know how to name shudders up my spine.

'Hello to Luka? Are you still in there?' she asks, cocking her head. 'I'm assuming I should invite him in?'

Quillian's gaze finds mine, but he doesn't cross the threshold.

'Oh—' I say, making myself step forward after a long, awkward pause. 'Of course. Akira, this is my, ah—my ...'

Boyfriend? Boss? Ex?

'Quillian,' I say thickly, looking back to him.

There is another beat of silence as Akira looks between us, and I can feel Zale drifting closer behind me.

'Your ... Quillian?' Akira asks, brows now just about reaching the ceiling.

Fuck. I fight the urge to close my eyes against the heat racing over my chest and up my neck. Why in the world did I choose a v-neck tonight? *My* Quillian? If only I had Shaide abilities, I'd portal straight out of here.

'Dinner!' Holland calls, and I could kiss him for breaking the moment.

Akira gives me a sly, sideways grin, making her way to the dining table, pretending – not at all well – to be oblivious to what is unfolding, or not unfolding, between Quillian and me.

'Come in,' I say quietly, and he slowly steps over the space that now puts him firmly in my house, Finn following behind.

Finn locks the door and slips around him, giving my arm a squeeze as he moves to properly introduce himself to Akira, Zale, and Teddy.

'Hi,' Quillian breathes when he's right in front of me.

'Hi,' I repeat.

'I—' he starts.

'Time to eat, people, it's going cold,' Holland calls.

CHAPTER TWENTY-ONE

By the time I turn away from Quillian's searing, green gaze, the table has filled with my other guests and left two places.

Side by side.

I try not to falter as I walk to the table, knowing he's following me, but completely unsure how to act now. There is the obvious issue of not telling Zale and Akira who any of these men really are, and the cause they are aligned to. Not to mention the forensic way Teddy is examining him – does she know him by appearance or only reputation? And then there's Quillian and me. We'd never had any discussion about officially being 'together', but did we need to? And now we're ... not whatever we were? Or have we both overcomplicated it, like Nix thinks?

The swirling thoughts haven't settled as I grip the back of my chair and take a seat, Quillian sliding in so close to me his knee brushes up against mine. He doesn't move it, and I sneak a look at his profile. His proud nose and full lips.

Zale is smirking at me when I look away.

Fuck. Keeping secrets from Akira and Zale was never something I enjoyed, even when my duty contract made it impossible not to. But now my tattoo means I can tell anyone anything I like, and having to *choose* not to say anything makes me feel a bit queasy. Particularly when it involves Zale's wife.

I glance up from my wine glass, only to find Quillian laughing and smiling with the others around the table, and I feel like I've been punched in the gut. Not because, outwardly, he seems unaffected by our conversation and my departure yesterday – there's too much charged tension between us for that to be the case. But because he seems so ... at home here.

In my home.

Sitting here, with me, his leg against mine, our fingers brushing as we both reach for the salad bowl, seems so ... intimate and natural I almost choke on it.

The whole table is engaged by him. He's quiet, although less so than Finn, but there's such a commanding presence about him, it's impossible not to be pulled in.

Akira catches me staring at him and winks, obviously enough for Quillian to glance between us, and I flush.

'So ...' she says, and I widen my eyes at her in a bid to silently beg her not to finish that sentence – which she studiously ignores. 'How did the two of you meet?'

I glance at Quillian, the memory of him in the meadow at Claudius's send-off flashing behind my eyes. The way he gave me that red flower which would now be burned to cinders. I try not to think of that as a parallel for Quillian and me.

'Ah, while on duty,' I say, standing abruptly, before taking the now empty plates to the kitchen.

Akira follows.

'I hope I didn't just put my foot in it, Lu,' she says quietly. 'I can almost snap the sexual tension between the two of you. I just assumed ...'

'No, it's fine,' I murmur back, eyes on the kitchen bench. 'It's just ... complicated.'

She sighs. 'I'm sorry it's complicated,' she says. 'For what it's worth, he seems lovely. And he's *hot.* Can we just acknowledge that for a moment?'

I stifle a laugh, but can't help looking at Quillian, and how his shoulders fill out the dark blue t-shirt he wears, and the burst of colour that graces his neck above it. Or how his cheekbones catch the light, and the side of his lips ...

I drag my attention back to Akira.

'Yes,' I say, 'he is definitely hot. And he is lovely ... I just—' I cut myself off as I catch Quillian looking over at me.

Holland glances between us and rolls his eyes before returning his attention to Finn and Zale.

'Just what?' she asks.

'I have no magic,' I blurt, surprising myself.

But as the words come out, I do wonder if that's part of it. I have no magic – is that what people are picking up on when they assess me as less-than, somehow? Am I holding *myself* back because of it?

'What's that got to do with Quillian?' she asks.

I stare at her.

The simplicity of her question is smarting. What *does* it have to do with Quillian?

'Luka,' she says gently. 'You're going through a pretty massive adjustment. You've just spent five years in a location you can't tell us about, doing who knows what, and now you're back and have been called up for another duty. It's okay to be a bit lost in that. Perhaps even a bit lost as to who you are—'

The back of my eyes sting with tears.

'—but we know who you are. Sure, we might not know all the ins and outs of your experiences on duty, or what's happening here with the three beautiful men in your house.' She nudges me in the ribs, and I laugh a little thickly. 'But we know *you,* and we know you're smart and capable and loving. So you will find your centre again, Lu, I know it.'

This time I hug her, hard.

'How is it you always know what to say?' I ask into her hair.

'Ha—that husband of mine sometimes wishes I did not have that particular skill.'

I smile. 'He knows how lucky he is.'

'That he does,' she says, 'and I make sure I remind him, particularly when he drew the short straw on having *all* the kids tonight. Maybe you need to remind Quillian, too.' She winks at me again and returns to clear more things from the table.

'Your friends are fabulous,' Holland says after Zale and Akira have both returned to their own homes, but left my house full of their warmth. Teddy gave me a firm squeeze when she left, whispering a 'thank you' in my ear.

I hadn't forgotten, exactly, the impact of Zale and Akira, but there's nothing quite like being in the same space as them. It reminds me how keen I am to introduce them to Blossom.

'I bet you were a wild trio at one point in your lives,' Holland says.

I give him a wicked grin. 'Maybe a little.' I don't tell them the stories that would bubble to the surface if River and Nix were here, too.

'But they don't know about your work in the House?' Finn says, the mood of the room suddenly serious.

'No,' I confirm. 'Not really, anyway. They know I am on another duty, and where I am, but not what I am doing there. And they certainly don't know about any of you, or what you're really doing here.' I don't look at Quillian as I say it.

'Good,' he says quietly. 'I think it would be best for them to be kept in the dark. Just in case.'

I don't want to think about what I might have to tell Zale one day if she doesn't know about Teddy soon.

'It's too early to say anything to them, Luka,' Quillian says from where he's swivelled on the dining chair, clearly somehow reading the direction of my thoughts on my face. 'If you don't think they're a risk to us, we will support you bringing them in when there's less risk to them.'

He stands to his full height and my stomach flops over itself as he walks towards me, both at the sight of him and the ease at which he just gave his support to my friends. 'I'll help clean up.'

Holland and Finn disappear into the small backyard, Holland muttering something about plants – not that I think I own any that still live.

Quillian and I work together to clean the kitchen, Quillian doing the washing up while I put everything away. The silence is thick with unsaid things, but still comfortable somehow.

When all trace of the dinner party has gone, Quillian dries his hands on a tea towel and slowly turns to face me. He leans against the bench, hands resting at his sides, and I brace myself for his reaction to my 'disappearing' today.

'Thank you for having me here,' he says, throwing me completely off. I don't know what I expected him to say, but it wasn't 'thank you'.

'Oh, sure,' I say hesitantly.

Long moments pass while I stand in my kitchen with this man who made me feel sparks of hope for all the possibilities of what we could be, and have no idea what to do with myself. His expression is about as lost as I feel, his mouth set in a straight line as he examines me. Part of me, a very large part, physically yearns for him to pull me tight and erase the conversation from last night.

He rubs the back of his head, running his palm over his short, dark hair, and I try to look away from the flex in his arms as he does so. But it's easier to look there than at his face that's marred with hurt.

'I—' he starts, before whatever he was going to say falls away, his hand dropping back to the bench, his eyes never leaving my face. 'You really scared me today.'

My bottom lip starts to wobble. 'I'm sorry,' I breathe. 'I just—I thought this was done, and I needed to do something for me.'

'Luka—' he moves towards me, but I hold up a hand and he halts.

'I've thought *a lot* about it, and I think I may have leapt ahead last night, but it raised something important, and I want to be clear. We need to be on the same page here, there is enough uncertainty around us already. We haven't made any commitments to each other, I know, but if this—regardless how you feel right now—isn't going anywhere, I'd prefer to stop now.'

His eyebrows shoot towards my ceiling the same as Akira's did, and I absently wonder how many more surprised faces this house will see.

'Stop?' he asks, voice rising a little.

I shrug a shoulder, desperately trying for some semblance of calm despite the caving of my insides. 'I want more,' I say, lifting my chin. 'And, while I don't need you to know right now if this is it for you—if I am it for you—I'm no longer at a stage of my life where I don't care if it's not even on the table.'

My fingers tremble at my sides as a rush runs through me. This might be an incredibly mortifying conversation, but at least I will know I was honest. That I took a stand for myself, whatever the outcome. Quillian remains looking at me, searching my face, but I make myself stay silent, to give him room to respond.

'Stop?' he asks again, looking a little dumbfounded. 'I think I'm really messing this up,' he says on an exhale, and I blink away the tears that threaten, but say nothing.

'I–I'm going to tell you something,' he says. 'Do you have anything to drink?'

'Top cupboard,' I say, moving to the lounge and waiting for him, heart thrumming in my ears as he unstoppers a bottle I haven't drunk from since my father would come visit.

Our fingers graze as he hands me a glass of dark, amber liquid and holds my gaze, something burning in his eyes that I'm not sure I've seen before. His 'warden mask' is so often in place, and then it's replaced by warmth when he's with me. But this looks much more like hurt. Or regret. Or something deeper than both of them which makes it feel like he's holding a very practiced composure over the top of a still raging flame.

I can almost see the memory of the prison fire reflected in his forest green pools, but I don't think this is about that.

'I'm from Tae,' he says and pauses, as if waiting for the pieces to come together in my mind. But, while Tae has been on my mind a lot recently for different reasons, I don't know why it's of particular significance that he's from there, or what he's trying to tell me, so I stay silent.

'When I was four,' he continues, 'Hunters came to my village'—my heart sinks as those lists loom in my mind again—'and took my mother, killing my father in the process. They took almost our entire population of adult women, by force, with no warning. No explanation. And certainly no remorse. Some of them didn't even make it out of the village and were slaughtered as they fought capture. I know now it was because she and many of the others descended from some of the strongest lines of Karaylia.'

He faces me on the couch, but he's no longer looking at me. As if the memories are too heavy to keep his gaze anywhere but down.

'My uncle, Ronan King, was the Chieftain at the time and took ... an offensive approach. Anyone, boy or girl, over the age of eight was enlisted into a duty of sorts—to learn the art of war. I was the exception to the age limit and started my training much earlier. So the children of my village began to fight – Cortane, Finn, and me alongside them. My uncle coordinated a joining of forces with other Tae villages who'd adopted his approach and, with the full grown warriors, we launched an offensive attack on squadron after squadron of Hunters. Coprath, too, when they tried to shift our borders, but mostly on Nuntainian forces that came into our villages.'

Quillian takes a sip before twisting the glass in his hand. 'But our losses were high, year after year—so many of us were kids, going up against adult Hunters and, worse, children from Tae we would have grown up with had they not been taken. And so I'—he gives me a heavy look—'along with Claudius, convinced my uncle there was a better way. A longer game, yes, but one more likely to succeed, and with significantly less loss of life for Tae. And, while I was taking a group to infiltrate the highest levels of government, he started to rebuild the villages of Tae. Together, we created the creed and ... our movement began.'

My stomach twists as I think about children facing what I've now seen footage of – Hunters who don't hold back. Of children fighting children.

'Cortane and Finn came with me, but it's me the country expects to topple the government.' He lifts his gaze to mine. 'It's me they expect to return to rule Tae in its independence from Nuntainia. Me, they expect to lead them out of this mess and into the next chapter as a country.'

I stare at him, the enormity of what he's saying pressing in on me from all sides. The sudden understanding why he has a mask in place so often. The Rebel Prince of Tae has been hiding in plain sight in Nuntainia for a long time.

'So,' I say quietly. 'You started your service in the Nuntainian military already a traitor?'

He nods. 'By uniform, yes. My heart's always been with Tae.'

Quillian takes my hand in his and threads his fingers in mine, although the processing my brain is trying to do means my hand lies limp in his. But as his face twists a little, a tumbling sensation fills my chest.

'The entirety of my life has been building to this point—the best part of thirty years of planning, manipulating—killing—to be here. With a contact in Parliament House who has committed to helping me bring them down.'

Nausea grips my gut for a moment; he tucks a stray strand of hair behind my ear.

'Before I left last night—and I shouldn't have left—I wanted to be upfront with you about what might come our way, *your* way, if you and I ...' he clears his throat. 'I can't let all of those people down. I can't let my uncle down. Or my mother. She was our most powerful Karaylia, and—'

My heart twists. 'She was your mum,' I say gently, swiping my thumb over his knuckles.

He nods and swallows before he continues. 'I can't offer you the forever you deserve because mine has been so clearly mapped out, and it doesn't include any ... space for anything else. But,' he whispers, 'trying to free you from that doesn't mean it's not happening for me, anyway. Because the truth is, I'm falling for you faster than your dive into the sky. But I don't have "forever", Luka. Not one that looks remotely like what your friends appear to have.

'I will always be wanted by Nuntainia, whether or not they know my identity yet. You deserve the best kind of forever and I just ... I don't know how to have that and do this at the same time. But I wanted to see what you thought about it all the same, particularly in light of what's coming. Because you're right, in an ideal world, we'd have time to figure it out. But here, now, in this reality, I don't want to be wondering every minute of every day if I pushed you away too hard.'

I don't know what to do other than watch him.

He's falling for me.

But he can't offer the forever he thinks I want.

Is he right? Do I still want the family and the security and the warm, glowing love? The way my chest suddenly feels immeasurably lighter says, *yes*, I most definitely want that. With zero doubt. But, as I think on the last couple of days with River and Nix, and Holland and Finn, and Akira and Zale – or even longer, back to when Blossom dove off the island with me – I understand that I do already have a family. Is my forever secure? No. But I made that choice for myself, too. What do I know of the future that's so certain that I could make him guarantees in the absence of his?

The only certainty in my own life is that I know I am taking a very real risk of ending up in Vana for being a traitor.

That being a traitor is now etched in fine, dark lines down the centre of my chest.

And I know now that Quillian has not only had his future determined by Tae and Nuntainia, but, between them, they took his childhood too.

I trace his fingers with the hand he's not holding. 'So …' I say quietly, 'you want to know if I will take a forever with you, even if it looks very different to what I've ever imagined? Even if it's filled with danger and risk and the possibility of losing everything I love?'

My voice feels like it's barely a breath, and he laughs, completely devoid of humour.

'I am definitely messing this up.' He squeezes my hand a little harder. 'It's a pretty shit deal, isn't it?'

'But you care enough about me to give it a shot, anyway?'

'Luka,' his voice is rough, and he pulls my hands into his lap. 'I *really* fucking care. I can barely breathe when you're in that House without me – doing the riskiest part of everything I have been working for. We could end up dead, that's true. Maybe in Vana if we're not dead before they get us there. But, if you get caught in that House, they won't kill you, Luka. You will be publicly destroyed along with everyone you've ever known, including Akira, Zale, and their children. Then, and only if you're lucky, they will take you to Vana. If not, depending on who catches you, they will do *whatever* they like to you—we may never even know where or what. I could—I could have no way to come for you.'

My veins run cold as I think on Zenaton's face when he saw me in the meeting room. The delight that I was there to watch. But I can't tell Quillian that now. He's so on edge right at the moment, if he knew, I think he'd try to make sure I never went back, and I'm not done.

'So, yes, if I had a forever I could offer, it would be yours. And if I were a better man, I'd walk away altogether so you could find that with someone else—someone who would never put you second to anything. But you have seen how feeble my attempts at that have been. Because I want you to be mine, Luka. Even if it's only for my version of forever. It's the most selfish thing I've ever done. I want you to be mine.'

CHAPTER TWENTY-TWO

I smile gently into the soft kiss I place on Quillian's mouth.

'I'm sorry,' I whisper against his lips. It's painfully clear now that I let my own history get in the way of us last night. Quillian wasn't going to end it, he wanted to find a way to make it work.

'Me too,' he says, pulling me into his lap. I straddle him, and he runs kisses down my neck. 'But we have the whole of our forever to figure it all out, right?'

I smile, pressing another firm kiss to his mouth, willing his uncertainty away. Because there is no remaining doubt in me. This is what I want, *who* I want. And I will do whatever it takes to keep it.

I take his face in my hands as I sit back and examine him.

He looks at me quizzically. 'What is it?'

My heart kicks a little at his curiosity, wondering what he would have been like as a child, before he was turned into a soldier.

'We're going out,' I tell him, standing as I catch his hand and gently tug him with me.

I call for Finn and Holland, who take a moment to reappear in my lounge room from where they'd excused themselves outside.

'Everything okay?' Holland asks, as Finn moves to assess the windows and doors.

'Yup,' I say, the gentle glow of happiness licking at the edges of my heart, 'but it's time for ice-cream. We're going out.'

Holland laughs. 'I'm in.'

Finn and Quillian exchange a look, one I know means they're weighing up the risks of what I'm suggesting.

'It's close,' I say. 'Near the pod station here, and it's likely to be quiet at this time of night—it's just about close time.'

Quillian slides his fingers between mine, dragging his gaze from Finn's. 'Let's go.'

The pod station is brightly lit at the end of the street, and my stomach skitters a little. Should I really have risked bringing them – him – here so blatantly? Quillian and I walk in front, Holland and Finn behind, flanking us slightly. Excitement flurries in my stomach, along with nerves, as we approach our destination. Right now, I want to give Quillian a memory so badly the risk is slightly muted. A silly, fun memory. Because he is sorely lacking in those. But as we approach, I wonder if he will get it – will this even be fun for him?

A few paces before we reach the little collection of shops at the edge of the station, I cut to the right towards the small picnic area that's partly a little hill. A very grassy, low-lit hill that has just the right angle for a roll ...

'This okay?' I whisper to Finn, but all three men are looking around.

'Yeah,' he says. 'But let's be quick.'

Grasping Quillian's hand, I pull him into a jog to the top, my breathing a little harder than his when we get there. We turn to look down at the pod station, Holland and Finn stalking up towards us, and Quillian pulls me in and places a kiss on my hair.

'What are we really doing here?' he asks.

'Yes,' Finn says when he arrives, 'the ice-cream is down there.' He points to the bottom of the little hill, where it eases out to street level, his face full of questions – and a little spark of mischief, as if he knows exactly what I'm trying to do. But he still sweeps his gaze behind me, checking our surroundings, and I swallow down the reminder we could be being watched. That *I* could be being watched.

'Yup,' I say, a gentle laugh bubbling up my throat at their confusion. We're here now, and I'm going to make it fun before we have to leave. 'Now, we go get ice-cream.'

Holland is the first, and only, to join me in the laughter. 'I'll race you?'

'You're on,' I say, dropping to my belly in the grass, Holland only a moment behind me as Quillian and Finn stand over us, watching.

'What are you—' Quillian starts, but I cut him off.

'One, two, three!' I shout at Holland and push myself off, arms outstretched and rolling sideways, over and over, down the hill. I squeal with laughter as I bump along, squeezing my eyes shut against the onslaught of grass before we collapse in our respective piles of limbs at the bottom. Me, a moment or two behind Holland.

Holland's laugh is deep and infectious, and soon tears are spilling from my eyes as we lie, breath heaving, in the grass.

'Come on already you two!' he calls out, and I turn to see the silhouettes of Finn and Quillian still standing at the top, Finn a little taller than Quillian.

They turn to each other and I wonder if they're not going to do it, before they each sink down and are immediately racing to the bottom.

Quillian somehow curses and laughs at the same time, where Finn is completely silent, even as Holland and I cheer them on from below. I squeal as Quillian comes racing – or rolling – towards me, and leap out of the way as he comes to a stop.

But not before Finn is already standing, a wicked grin stretching his whole face as Holland shakes his shoulders and whoops into the sky.

'Damn,' Quillian says, 'did I lose?' he asks as he looks up at us, a stick in his hair, and we collapse into giggles, Holland's hands dropping to his knees as he gasps for breath.

'Fuck,' he says, 'I haven't done that in a long time.'

Quillian draws himself to standing, grass covering his clothes, and my laugh goes a little breathless as he stands over me, mouth pulled into a half-smile.

'I've never done that,' he says, 'and it is strangely invigorating.' I laugh again as I fold myself into him, pressing up on my toes to give him a full mouth kiss. 'Now, we get ice-cream.'

Waking up next to Quillian has quickly become my favourite way to start the day. Particularly when the slow exploration of his hands along my stomach ... across my ribs ... cupping a breast ... rolling my nipple ... is what rouses me from sleep. When I can smile into his chest, my eyes still closed, and have him kiss my nose gently before taking my mouth with his, running his tongue along the seam of my lips until I open for him and his kisses become deeper. Hungrier.

Pressing him back, I straddle him, his hot erection pressing against my most sensitive places as I slowly move myself along his shaft. Opening my eyes, I take in his slightly sleep-mussed hair and half-closed eyes before glancing down at the tattoo on my chest. Seeing it there sparks a hotter fire in my chest – right where the tattoo sits – and between my legs.

We don't talk as I slide over him, making myself wetter and wetter, his hands on my hips but letting me lead. Until the ache in my centre demands I take him, and I shift my position to come down completely, stretching wide to accommodate him. I bite down on my bottom lip, trying to stifle the groan of pleasure that bubbles from me as he touches all the right places with the slow rocking of his hips.

'Don't do that,' he says, brushing my lips with his thumb. 'Let me hear you.'

'I have guests,' I whisper, shifting up and down and raising my face to the ceiling as the pressure starts to build.

Gripping me around the waist, Quillian rolls me onto my back so he fits between my legs, and I let them fall out wide. He leans down to whisper in my ear. 'If I wasn't so greedy, I'd say I didn't care who heard you.' He thrusts harder, sliding me slightly towards the pale bedhead. 'But you're right, those sounds are mine, too.' His voice takes on a rougher quality as he starts to pound into me, and I gasp quickly before he covers my mouth with his hand.

I stare at him as a ball of tension grips me from the inside out, breathing hard through my nose. I whimper.

'Scream for me, Luka,' he says, his voice barely there, changing the angle of his hips so he hits that exquisitely sensitive place deep inside.

I moan, pressing my head back into the pillow and meeting him stroke for stroke, taking him as far as I can. With his other hand, he digs his fingers into my left hip and lifts me fractionally from the bed. But it's enough, and there's nothing I can do to keep the hot waves of pleasure from dragging my scream into his palm, before I sink my teeth into the soft part of flesh at the base of his thumb.

'Oh, fuck,' he mutters, gritting his teeth as his own wave threatens to drown him.

Wouldn't that be a nice way to go, I think dimly.

As we lie tangled in each other after, watching the light grow outside, I push away the worry at just how short our version of 'forever' is. And what my life would look like with no Quillian, no duty, no traitors, and no purpose to serve. If it will look like anything other than being back on the prison island.

Instead, I close my eyes and breathe him in, and settle in the knowledge he's mine for as long as time will allow.

'I'll come by the compound tonight,' I tell Quillian and Finn as Holland clears away breakfast in my kitchen, the space still dark in the early morning. I could get used to having a live-in chef.

'Sounds good to me,' Holland says, slinging a tea towel over his shoulder and giving Finn and Quillian a pointed look. 'I'm assuming the two of you will be able to keep Cortane from kicking our asses for non-life threatening usage of that portal?'

Finn laughs, and it's impossible to miss how much wider it makes Holland's smile.

'Nobody has that power, my friend,' Finn says.

At the word 'friend', Holland's gaze narrows and Finn glances away. He doesn't catch the look on Holland's face that seems to say 'challenge accepted'.

I watch the three of them move around my kitchen like this is their home, too, and a sharp pang digs in the side of my ribs. Last night, in the end, was a balm to everything we have been doing and been through. But I know it can't happen again. My stomach turns as I think on Zenaton and his unrelenting desire to find Quillian while I watch – even if he doesn't exactly know yet that it's Quillian he's looking for. But given everything he *does* know, and that I was essentially complicit in his attempted murder, it's not a leap to think he will be watching me and my movements.

'Um,' I say to no one in particular. 'I need to tell you something. Well ... a few things.'

All three of them turn to me slowly with varying degrees of worry on their faces – Quillian the most, Finn the least, or maybe he's just best at holding a neutral expression.

'I don't think you can come here again.'

Quillian's brows quirk, but it's only a moment before he seems to catch on. 'What is it?'

'Zenaton Blake is alive and is the new Minister for Justice as well as Deputy Prime Minister. He's leading the Defence Committee and ... he knows who I am and is enjoying having me watch him hunt you. Literally. I'm worried he is, or will be, watching my house. I didn't—I should have thought of it before, but I ...'

I trail off at the dumbfounded, angry expressions they wear as they stare at me. The house is quiet a moment, before it explodes in a small chorus of swearing and questions.

'Pack your things, Luka,' Quillian grinds out. 'You are not going back in there.'

Holland shakes his head at me, as if he can't believe Zenaton survived that wound.

'You sound like Nix,' I say gently to Quillian.

'That's not always a bad thing. We need to move.'

I remain planted where I am, grounding myself by focusing on the feel of the carpet beneath my bare feet.

'No. I still haven't been into the archives. I know what I'm looking for, I just need some more time. And I have two excellent contacts in there—I've even found your previous one.'

'Who?' Finn asks immediately, and I look between them all.

'One is Teddy—she's with us and Zale doesn't know. The other ...' I think of how Traelen went dark and the particular risk he is in as Chief of Staff. One who can't locate the Prime Minister. 'It's best I share that later.'

'Luka, please,' Quillian's voice is strained as he takes the few steps towards me. 'You can't go back there.'

'I know this worries you, I do, and I'm sorry, but I *need* to do this. If he was going to get rid of me immediately, I'd already be dead or in Vana. But I'm still here, and I have to make the most of the opportunity. I didn't come face to face with him again only to run away now, before I can get us what we need.'

'But—'

'Can you replace me with someone else?'

Quillian tips his head back and looks at the ceiling. 'Fuck.'

'She's right, Q,' Finn says from where he stands near the dining table. 'This is the shot, she has to take it. And I need to get you out of here before day breaks. There is a *very* small chance he hasn't made the connection as to who you are by now, and with your connection to Luka—'

'I'm sorry,' I say, voice trembling. 'I didn't mean to endanger you anymore than—'

'Nothing would have stopped me from coming yesterday,' Quillian says as he draws me to him.

'What about Holland?' Finn asks.

'I was wondering when one of you was going to remember the fact I'm implicated as well.' Holland gives a weak smile, clearly trying to break some of the tension. 'I'll see if I can get some of my shifts reassigned—not go into the House. If I do ... I'll keep a lookout and avoid him. I'll also vary the routes Luka and I take to and from the House to make sure we're not followed. But I'm not leaving her here, and you'—he points at Quillian—'cannot be taken out before the cause gets to see you spearhead it. Too many have been lost for that to happen. So you two need to get out. Luka and I will make our way to the compound tonight, as we've agreed, providing we are absolutely sure no one is surveilling us. If there's doubt, we won't show.'

Finn turns on his heel to face Holland. 'And if Zenaton already knows you're here?'

'Then at least it will just be the two of us that are fucked, and not the rest of you,' Holland says grimly, and a wave of nausea washes over me.

'Not a fucking chance,' Quillian says.

I lift my face to Quillian's. 'I can do this.' At least, I hope I can.

He blows out a breath that fans my face. 'I know. But Zenaton—'

'I'll be done before he decides to act—he likes the audience too much,' I say, desperately hoping that's true.

Holland checks his watch and looks outside. 'We're close to having too much light,' he says, 'it's really best you go now.'

Quillian's jaw ticks. 'Keep my feather on you at *all* times—do not hesitate to use it. No negotiating.' Quillian kisses me goodbye, a kiss I'd very much prefer was hello instead. If I could forget the conversation we just had, and who I'm about to face, I almost feel like part of a normal couple. Just an ordinary pairing in Klades about to go about their days, minus the children. I feel my face flush at the direction of my thoughts.

But it also reminds me of my father, and that I will need to tell the others about him quickly if I am to connect them before Zenaton interferes.

Watching Quillian and Finn walk down my front steps and out the gate, I suppress a shudder at who else could see them. There is little about them that looks like they fit in here. Everything about them screams ... something else. Some extra. Something the average person would likely find dangerous.

I'm halfway back up my stairs, consumed by that, thoughts of seeing my father again, and the harsh truth that I do not have anything extra – other than Quillian's feather – to help me get out of danger, when a new, different, thought hits me. If I'm going to do this – get the information, stay ahead of Zenaton, connect my father with the traitors, and stand beside Quillian as it all comes crashing down – I need to stop believing that not having magic is an impediment. I've achieved a lot with no magic and very little information before. Now, I have more information, more access, and I still have me.

By the time I reach my shower, I've almost convinced myself.

CHAPTER TWENTY-THREE

The Prime Minister's office is quiet this morning, with only Traelen and me and one receptionist, Elias, who seems to be perpetually answering phone calls. My desk is sparse, as are the others that are in this space, like no one really sticks around too long. But I know Traelen has been Chief of Staff for at least five years – he was in that role when I started on Zanteera Island.

Squeezing my eyes tight for a moment, as if I can clear the exhaustion that's clinging to the underside of my lids, I start up my computer and try to let my brain find its way back to research mode.

'Luka,' Traelen says as he walks out of his office. He's looking at me expectantly when I glance up, his soft beige linen suit completely wrinkle free. 'How are you feeling?' he asks as if he knows full well I wasn't sick.

I nod. 'All good.' He gives me a long look but doesn't press. I think we've come far enough now for him to respect there are things I can't – won't – share.

'I've got a stack of old filing I need you to archive today, please. Teddy will bring the boxes along in a moment and take you to the archives. I expect it will take you some time to do it properly.'

I cock my head in question. 'Does that mean ...?'

He almost smiles, but it's tinged with too much worry to be real. 'Came in last night, it will be against your record now, so you really can't delay.'

He looks at me just a fraction longer than would be expected, but he doesn't have to worry that I don't understand. He told me himself that most of the records I will need are in the archives, and my heart does a little loop in my chest.

Finally, I might be able to make some traction of my own.

Teddy and I walk in silence as she pushes a large flatbed trolley stacked with boxes. The rhythmic squeak of its front wheel is oddly hypnotic as we trace numerous hallways and pass more office doors than I can count, Teddy steering the heavy trolley confidently through the opulent maze. It makes me wonder how Teddy knows the layout so well, when she was part of the same intake as me. But, then, I can only imagine the knowledge Traelen insisted she study when he realised she wasn't going to back down from being here.

Eventually, we enter what looks like a large, old service elevator and descend five floors. The lift lurches a little as it starts, but soon enough the doors drag themselves open onto a room half the size of a floor of the House. Boxes and folders are stacked upon rows and rows of metal shelving units that run away from us so far I can't see where they end. All of which is blocked from access by a mesh, metal wall.

'Can I help you?' a tall, reedy looking young man asks from a desk just on the other side of the mesh wall, talking through a cutout in the metal. Before I spent time on the island, I would have said he looks like a receptionist for a jail. But I know Vana didn't have any need for one, all their prisoners went straight into interrogation and there were no visitors; and Zanteera Prison was far too elite to have something as basic as a reception desk.

'We've just got some archiving to do,' Teddy says with a swish of her curtain of dark hair over her shoulder and a casual tap of the boxes on our trolley.

'Sign in here,' he says, sliding a rectangular device across his narrow desk. 'Please note the conditions of entry and penalty for misuse of documents, artefacts, and any other manner of product held in the archive.'

I glance down at the form illuminating the screen of the device.

... confidential ... bound by the terms ... remains property of the Government of Nuntainia ... misuse or misappropriation is punishable by incarceration ...

Incarceration? I suppress a shudder. That can only be a sentence to Vana. I knew my working with the traitors had high risks, but seeing the penalty in writing brings the reality of what's at stake into clear, stark relief. Zenaton, stealing information from the archives, and being so connected to the traitors, are all roads that lead to Vana. Or death. Maybe it's the same thing. Maybe dying would be the better option.

'You've got ninety minutes in there, no more,' the attendant says in a bored voice. 'And you will be subject to a search on your exit. Place all phones and devices in the box on your left before you enter.'

He nudges the form closer through the hole in the mesh before him. Teddy signs without missing a beat and, swallowing, I repeat the action.

Sliding my hand into my pocket, I go by feel to pull out my duty phone – it's slightly larger than the one the traitors gave me – and I place it in the box. I glance at the man in a nondescript suit as he checks our forms, his brows furrowing a little as he looks at my details.

'Luka Brideoake?' he asks, looking up.

'Yes.' I will my voice to be steady.

'Huh,' he says, eyes narrowed on me. He shrugs and waves us away as my heart pounds. The barred door to the archives creaks softly as the attendant presses a button somewhere on his side and allows us entry. He watches us walk past, Teddy still pushing the trolley, and I try not to let my skin crawl with his attention. 'You have ninety minutes,' he says as the door slams closed behind us.

The room is lit by long, high, bright white lights that illuminate each row of shelves, leaving dark corners where they don't quite overlap. I squint a little at the brightness as we assess the rows. Beside me, Teddy blows out a breath.

'Let's get this done,' she says.

We spend the next hour doing what we're officially down here to do – archiving the boxes on the trolley as quickly as possible. But as we move through the space, I search every label for something of interest. The labels themselves are easy enough to find, most of them being a cream or dirty-white rectangle with black font. So far, I haven't seen anywhere for electronic archives, but I imagine they must exist somewhere as well.

I try to absorb the meaning of each one, but so many are called the specific names of different pieces of legislation or policy, and I simply don't recognise them. Many I assume also must have had different names as the policies or programs were being worked through the system before being publicly known as something else.

A swirl of dust dances from the shelf as I drag down a box marked 'PM expenditure', and I stifle a sneeze.

'How is there so much dust in here?' I ask Teddy, who's still archiving in my row.

'The air ducts,' she says without looking my way, something in the file in her hands obviously capturing her attention as she flicks through it.

I file the relevant papers in the 'expenditure' box, but my gaze lands on one tucked behind where I am about to return my updated archive box.

There's nothing overtly different about it apart from its label – *Top Secret: Tae missions.*

Glancing down the archive row past Teddy – who is still examining files of her own – and determining we're still alone, I slide the box from the shelf. It's heavier than it appears, and I almost drop it to the floor. Crouching with its weight, I flick the lid off as a bell chimes.

My heart lurches.

'Ten minutes,' Teddy whispers.

I turn back to the box, palms starting to itch. The inside is packed with files, and my stomach sinks. I will never have enough time to go through them all right now. Still, I take out the first plain folder and open it, holding my breath.

Tae.

Apart from my father's teachings, I'd never given Tae a lot of thought until recently. Then I learned it's where Nix and River served their duty; where Nix fell in love and lost her; where the traitors' camp one, among others, is located; and where I was able to use my father's teachings to provide the team with a possible location for a new camp. Now, staring at the papers in front of me, I know it will never be far from my thoughts for reasons far beyond anything tied to me personally.

The pages swim with names, locations, and personnel reports dispassionately detailing how and when those places were 'neutralised' by Nuntainia. The clinical phrasing so neatly strips the humanity from the victims as I move through the files that I find myself simultaneously fighting the urge to be sick, and to burn the House I stand in, and all those in it, to the ground.

The towns of Goerd, Noston, and Villy all list survivors – people taken to something called The Ridge.

Arilon, Elitti, and Fragg do not.

Some of the names I recognise from my studies, others from my recent viewing of the map in Cortane's command room. But Villy catches in my thoughts for another reason, one just outside my grasp.

The bell chimes again.

'Luka,' Teddy whispers. 'Pack it up. We've got five minutes to be out of here.'

I jerk my head up at the sound of the footsteps of someone else moving through the archives.

Incarceration ... I shiver.

Scrambling to get the papers and their folders back into the box, I grunt as I heft the box back up onto the shelf.

'Time's up,' the reedy attendant says with a grunt. 'Whatever you didn't finish can wait in the bay behind my desk. No documents leave here—not with your level of clearance.'

I don't look at Teddy as we pack up the two boxes we hadn't finished, conscious of his watchful gaze, before we walk back to his desk. The only sound the slight squeak of one of the wheels on Teddy's trolley.

'Arms out,' he says when we've placed the boxes on the shelf he points out.

I can barely breathe as he pats Teddy down and then gives her permission to collect her phone and wait at the locked door.

He nods at me as he takes the single sidestep to be in front of me, and starts patting around my ribs.

Sweat prickles my forehead, and I imagine the second phone still in my pocket might burn a hole—

The phone on his desk rings. The sound cutting through the air is sharp enough to make me wince.

Teddy gives me a cautionary look and I still, focusing on steadying my breathing.

'Archives,' he says into the mouthpiece. 'Ah, yes sir.' He takes a seat and pulls out a notepad. He glances up at us distractedly, indecision in his features, before he presses the button and the door swings open.

But as the blood starts to circulate in my hands again, all I can think about is the names of the dead and relocated people from Tae. Is where the survivors were taken worse than the fate of their 'neutralised' communities?

'In here,' Teddy says as we reach a nondescript door in the bowels of Parliament House.

The now empty trolley still squeaks a little on one side as she ploughs it through the carpet of the hallway.

Opening the door for her, she slips into the darkened space, a light coming on automatically as she does, illuminating several other trolleys in what is clearly a storage room. She gives me a pointed look and I join her, letting the door fall shut behind us.

'Listen,' she says, one hand still on the metal handle of the trolley. 'I know the other night must have been tricky for you, and I really respect the fact you want to protect Zale's interests, but I know it's right not to tell her.' She gives me a sad, almost desperate look. 'She needs plausible deniability.'

I press my palm to my chest on reflex, closing my eyes against what she says. Because, whatever in her history that's compelled her to be here, she hasn't come face to face with Zenaton. Hasn't seen in his face that 'plausible deniability' is a dream – one he will destroy in a second if he wishes.

When I open my eyes, she's still staring at me, knowledge of my unvoiced concerns etched all over her face, her mouth set as if she's ready for any argument I might offer. And, in this moment, I understand what it is to allow someone with everything to lose to hope that, should the worst happen, their actions won't mean the downfall of their loved ones. I firmly believe Zale should have a choice, but the cause we fight for is bigger than any one individual, and it's not my decision to make. What right do I have to destroy the tiny fragment of hope keeping Teddy in this fight?

'I get it,' I whisper, dropping my arm by my side. 'I like it about as much as I like the fact I haven't reported what I've discovered here yet, among other things. But, I get it.'

She latches onto my hand, gripping it between hers.

'Thank you, Luka. I mean it.'

I pull her into a fierce hug. 'Let's just make sure we all make it to the other side of this, okay?'

She nods against my shoulder before I pull away and see the sorrowful look on her face that says the truth we both know – no one will get out of this unscathed.

Teddy clears her throat and blinks rapidly. 'Anyway, speaking of things we haven't shared—I haven't told T I'm pretty sure you're sleeping with the *actual* Rebel Prince. Am I right?' she exclaims, excitement creeping back into her features.

I laugh. 'I am,' I confirm, 'and it's about as complicated as you'd imagine.'

She frowns a little, her dark brows drawing together and creating a small crease between them. 'With the two of you?'

'No,' I smile. 'Just because of what we need to do.'

There's an urgency in the office when I return from lunch that almost makes my steps falter. I glance around for Zenaton, willing myself to have a calm outward appearance, but he's nowhere to be seen. His absence doesn't ease my nerves much; as acting Prime Minister, he could turn up here at any time. Conversations buzz from each of the workstations as people discuss whatever they are finding on their screens. Others come in and out of the boardroom with papers and clipboards and barked instructions.

'Luka,' Elias, calls. 'Can you take the tray of snacks in?' He points to the timber tray that's laden with biscuits and pastries on a buffet just outside the boardroom, before the phone rings and he answers.

Given how much that phone rings, it's about as much as he's said to me the whole time I've been here.

I place my small bag on my desk, wave my hand across the power key on the screen to start my electronic mail, pocket my phone, and collect the tray.

Loud voices meet me as I enter, and I recognise the members of the committee meeting I observed not so long ago. Minus Zenaton, and I let go a long exhale.

The screen is on again; displaying a smattering of photos and documents. The images are a mixture of colour and black and white – mostly a combination of uniforms and lists and what look like accounts of different attacks.

But it's a smaller, partial image on the bottom right that makes the tray in my hand start to tremble. It's been zoomed in on the part of Quillian's tattoo that's visible above his shirt. The shape it makes looks nothing like the words I know exist there. But even without that, I'd recognise his neck anywhere.

'For fuck's sake, you're making a mess,' one of the men snaps, jerking my attention back to the room and the scented sugar that's starting to sprinkle the table close to where I stand.

I know I should apologise, but I can't bring myself to respond as I lower the tray, catching some of their documents underneath as I look back to the screen.

Just next to the photo of the tattoo are multiple photos of what appear to be different military teams.

'... there is no way Tae have units as elite as that without us knowing,' someone says. 'They're just not that sophisticated.'

'Agree. We're systematically going through our own specialist teams and our intel on Coprath agents for anyone with a matching mark,' another says, and I freeze, their voices spinning around me.

'How long?'

'We've got the full team out there looking now, and Blake has his best investigators involved as well. We'll find them.'

'Not fucking fast enough.'

'Faster than he'd like, though.'

They don't know that they're talking about Quillian – yet. But the moment they take this to Zenaton, if they haven't already, he will know. How could he not?

Forcing myself to leave the room before they can see on my face that I know far more than I should, I keep my steps slow towards Traelen's office.

He looks up before I knock, and a beat passes as we look at each other before he waves me in.

'How long?' I ask.

He glances behind me before handing me a folded piece of paper.

'I want you back in the archives,' he says. 'Find everything you can on the prison, Teddy will get the breeding information. We need it by the end of the day, Luka. If anyone asks, you're researching old records of known Tae rebels—use the name King if you have to.'

There's the tiniest crease in his brow, and I know he's just answered my question.

One day.

Fuck.

At the same time, I'm sure he's aware that using the surname of Quillian's uncle might give me credibility if I'm questioned, it would also be dangerously close to exposing us all.

Taking his note in my trembling hand, I all but race to the archives, not caring what looks I attract on the way.

If this is my last day here, I need every second I can get.

CHAPTER TWENTY-FOUR

The archives are just as quiet this afternoon as they were this morning, but this time the attendant narrows his gaze at me. Looks me over more closely. I've slid my phone in the front of my underwear, where it's as hidden under my full skirt as I'm going to get it. I drop my duty phone in the basket before holding my arms wide, and he gives me a pat down that feels much harder than the last. But he doesn't touch me inappropriately.

'Back so soon?' he asks, and I feel my throat closing over.

Perhaps the whole House knows there's an urgent task happening in the Prime Minister's office. Or perhaps, I think, my scalp prickling, he knows I shouldn't really be here ... that the business I am on is nothing the House would approve of.

'Yes,' I choke. 'I need to finish those boxes we left last time,' I say, 'and get some information for the Prime Minister's Chief of Staff. There's a ... priority project unfolding.'

It's bridging the gap of truth and lie so finely, and I desperately hope he thinks it's in assistance of the office.

'I've heard rumours,' he says, and then laughs a little. 'But that shit is above my pay grade—I just get to read about things after the fact, if at all.' He nods in the direction of the shelves. 'Make it fast. Access is being restricted down here from the end of the day.'

'Of course,' I respond automatically, my voice covering the panic that's starting to fire through my veins.

Pushing the barred door open, I all but run into the archives, leaving the other boxes where they are.

My thoughts seem to stall as I look down the rows and rows of box after box. Quickly, I unfold the paper from Traelen, expecting the list of things he talked about.

Take Teddy with you.

My heart skips a beat. What the fuck does that mean? And what does it mean *now*?

As I give the room another scan, the number of bays and aisles seem to double, and I curse myself for not thinking that we would work faster together. But I'm here now, and I can't waste the opportunity.

Heart pumping, I scan the rest of the space. I just need to focus on the task at hand – find information on the prison program and leave the breeding program to Teddy – maybe she'll get more time, and we'll be faster taking an issue each. *Also the massacres in Tae,* I add to myself. I'm not leaving without more on those. As the aisles start to blur before me, it's clear the only approach I can take is a methodical one. The same one I used to take when doing my own research or project scoping – understand what I'm dealing with.

Shoving the note back in my skirt pocket, I start with the row on the far left and make my way down that side, scanning each and every box as thoroughly, but quickly, as I can before coming back up the other side. I hold my hand out, first two fingers spread, and I can almost imagine the air shifting between them as I focus on the titles.

Heritage Buildings of Klades.

Amendments to the Building Code of Nuntainia.

Builder Licensing Requirements.

The second row seems just as inane and I curse whoever hasn't put anything into alphabetical order. How Teddy knew how to navigate it so readily last time must have been thanks to Traelen. But as I start the third row of labels – knowing there isn't enough time in the world for me to go row by row – which seems to be family-focused, as opposed to building or upkeep of the capital, I wonder if they have, at least somewhat, categorised them by what each Smaller House manages.

Casting my mind back, I think on the different Small Houses and their respective portfolios. Heritage and Restoration; Regulation and Licensing ... The files I found about Tae and the list of names of the affected individuals were towards the middle. If my emerging theory is correct, the files for the superior Small Houses are stored in the middle section of this vast room.

The less influential, both in money and resources – like building and national gardens – are on one side ...

I race to the other side of the room, the distance so far my breath is heaving after the few minutes it takes to cross. I scan the boxes in this row.

Regional Populations.

Funding for Regional Sport.

So there's minor Small Houses on each of the far sides.

The Tae projects were in the middle. Given their secrecy, the level of clearance that would have been required to undertake them, and the money it would cost ...

Their placement can't have been an accident.

Running back towards the centre, ducking into the first row that seems close to the middle, I scan box after box.

So many my vision starts to blur even with the assistance of my fingers to focus.

Zanteera Island.

My heart skips as I skid to a halt, slide the box from the shelf and drop it on the floor. Slipping the lid off, I flick through the files, and a list of names falls out.

Traelen's voice as he announced their arrival on the island echoes in my head as I run my finger down the columns.

Using my phone, I attempt to keep my hand steady as I record a video of page after page, no time to stop to take photos of every one – I just have to hope Cortane can make this work.

Hastily placing that box back on the shelf when I'm finished, I search for any references to how the prison program started, but there's nothing. I keep scanning, heading towards the centre, each minute feeling longer than the one before. *Finally*, the labels begin to reference the laws, policies, and amendments fundamental to our system.

Prison Program.

I stare at the faded label that looks exactly like the others, stuck to a box just sitting on the shelf. As if cycling corrupt, or worse, politicians and other high-profile people through a luxury resort, instead of the prison sentences they deserve, is perfectly acceptable. As ordinary as funding sport centres for regional areas.

Reading through the evolution of the program isn't as sickening as I thought it would be. Perhaps because I've already learned the truth myself, the knowledge now settled like a rotting piece of food in the corner of my stomach.

But as I read the initial proposal, I think I might actually be sick. The earliest entry is dated about thirty years ago – a policy outline proposing the design of the program and arguing the case for its creation. Skimming the headings as I flick through the pages, it's clearly presenting the advantages of the program and how it would be beneficial to Nuntainia. It's signed by the designer of the program, a bold and complex signature I know so well I can almost hear the scrape of the pen over the page.

Printed below ... is my father's name.

Shoving everything away – including the surging in my gut – with shaking hands, I replace the box and check the time on my phone. I've got less than fifteen minutes before my time is up.

Retracing my steps, I find the row I first came to with Teddy, and the box on Tae. I record all I can of the attacks, the survivors, and anything I can see referring to what happened to them and their families. The village of Villy appears again in the files, the same or similar sort of entry that I noticed last time, and I know I'm not imagining it. Villy is the last village Nix fought in – where Quillian ordered them out and Nix lost his girlfriend – and it has survivors listed when Nix said there were none.

It might be the tiniest possibility, but if Nix's girlfriend's name is on there, I intend to find it.

The ten-minute bell sounds through the space, echoing through the aisles.

Shit. I *will* find out if her name is here.

I just can't do it now.

'I remember your name, now,' the attendant says as he opens the access door for me to leave. 'Brideoake—I've filed more papers from Corvan Brideoake in here than I could count.'

He hands me my duty phone but doesn't let go. 'You know, it was the strangest thing,' he says. 'He kind of just stopped appearing here one day. Are you related? Do you know what happened to him?'

I try to stem the shake in my fingers lest he feel it. 'I heard he retired,' I say, 'I guess when you're done, you're done.' I smile and look at the phone we're both still holding awkwardly. 'But otherwise I don't know much about him. May I?'

He blinks as if coming out of a small trance. 'Yeah, I guess so. Still ... interesting connection.'

I feel his stare at my back the whole walk out of the archives, the information I have both freeing and a weight around my throat. But it's incomplete without the breeding program, we need—

Traelen said leave it to Teddy but, as the ringing in my ears starts to fade the further I get from the archives, the more I know I can't leave here today without knowing she's got what we need. So, instead of returning straight to Traelen, I make my way to the Office of the Integrity Commissioner where Teddy is based, one phone tingling in my palm, the other burning in the front of my skirt. My mind turns itself over at my father's name on those documents, and the fact the attendant made the connection between us. Who will he tell about that, and when? Who else has already made the connection? Is that part of why Zenaton has kept me alive?

But another thought pushes through as well – why didn't I record anything that will confirm his involvement in the creation of the prison program?

The halls of Parliament House stretch out before me as I force myself not to run, the rooms spinning in my mind as I try to find my way without drawing too much attention to myself.

My mind keeps circling back to the archives check-in form. *Incarceration.* The thought lodges in my throat so tight I might choke. While I've always known being sentenced to Vana is a very real possibility, given what I now possess, if I am arrested the opportunity to do anything about the programs will be lost. I don't know when that became a more terrifying thought than what I know happens in Vana, but somehow it is.

Not to mention I will lose any opportunity to find out how, and why, my father had anything to do with that island at all. The magic dampeners were one thing, but this ...

A small group of men speak quietly just ahead, clustered under a sign that tells me the adjacent hallway will take me to the Office of the Integrity Commissioner. But they pay me no attention as I duck my head and I slow my steps to walk past, turning the sharp corner without even a glance from them.

My pulse races as the number of people around starts to increase the further I walk along this hall. All of them dressed in suits of some kind, far more professional looking than me. It could be more about the way they hold themselves – or the fact that they're not blatantly walking around the House with a device, and recordings, they shouldn't have.

I make myself look straight ahead as I walk, not at the high gloss floors where I can almost see my guilt. A woman in a red pantsuit catches my eye when she looks up from her papers, and I give her a thin smile.

She doesn't return it.

My fingers start to burn.

This area of the House is familiar in terms of its decorations and furnishings, but otherwise completely foreign. I spin back to see if I can find any further sign that I am going the right way. The feather at my chest is heavier than ever and—

I need to get out. Do I finish my shift first? I need to get to Traelen. But if I stay—

Take Teddy with you, Traelen's note said. What if he didn't mean the archives at all, but that I needed to get Teddy out of the House – and Klades – too?

A roll goes through my stomach so strong it all but freezes my bones, as Zenaton steps out of one of the many offices and into my path, gaze flicking up and holding mine.

I bite down on the insides of my cheeks as we walk towards each other.

What would he do if I turned and ran? How fast would he have Hunters after me?

I glance over my shoulder, scrambling to remember the closest exit that way.

Zenaton's smile is cold when I look back, and my heart slams in my chest as I try to ignore him and prepare to walk past. He nudges closer to me, the view of him sucking every other detail of the space away. Like only the two of us and this moment exist.

I don't dare look at him as we draw side by side, gaze focused straight ahead as he steps past me. I hold my breath and take another two steps beyond him, the sounds of the House slowly edging back in as I do.

Slowly, I release my breath and swallow, still striding towards the place I really fucking hope Teddy is. The need for us to get out is like a force shoving me from behind.

'Oh,' a male voice calls down the hall, and I run cold. 'Luka.' There is nothing inquiring about Zenaton's tone. Nothing but complete authority in the command that's far too loud for where we are.

I stop short, numerous people looking between us, and I turn back to him, pasting on my best concierge smile. 'Yes, sir?'

He gestures to the space beside him and says nothing.

Gritting my teeth, I retrace my steps, very aware I can't ignore him here – not with all these witnesses. My pulse flutters in my neck as I close the final gap between us and stand within talking distance.

'Yes, sir?' I ask again, willing some steel into my words.

'Are you enjoying your time here?' he asks, and I stare at him.

'Yes, sir.'

His cold eyes sparkle with something that makes me feel ill. I glance between the people who mill around the hallway, perhaps waiting for him, and those who stride purposefully to their next destination. One woman looks sideways at me but quickly puts more distance between us, and I feel more isolated than I did facing him on the island. Then, there were fewer people around – just Holland and Casey. But they backed me in a way I know no one here will.

The faces of the men behind him blur as Zenaton and I disappear into a vacuum, Quillian's feather pressing against my skin. Surely, he won't give me reason to use it here? Even if he did, I'd be signing my own arrest.

'Good. Good,' he says. His rigid, broad stance as he continues to study me screams military. 'And it's a short commute. Very lovely neighbourhood to entertain in, yours, I think. It's good to see you making friends in your duty cohort.'

His words ring in my ears. My neighbourhood. I knew he, or least the administration, would know where I live. But the confirmation *he* knows it is like swallowing thorns. And 'entertaining'... I push back on the growing sense of nausea in my gut. Was his team watching us last night? Has he already seen Quillian?

Worse, he's let me know in soft, measured words that land like a punch to the throat that he knows Teddy was there.

'I'm sure it's not as lovely as yours,' I say finally, voice thin. 'You've certainly stayed in some nice places.'

He draws his head back a little, as if he's surprised I've openly made the connection to him, me, and the island. But it's not concern that licks his features, it's satisfaction. As if I've just stepped into a game he was hoping I would play. One he is sure he's going to win.

He makes a noncommittal sound in the back of his throat.

'Yes ... I do find it's always good to know how *the people* live. To watch them in their everyday lives. They don't always know what's good for them, see.' A grin spreads across his face slowly. 'And I love to watch the self-righteous shits burn.'

I stumble back a step and he laughs. Pure, uninhibited laughter. A sound I think might never leave me.

One of the men behind him smiles, but it's more like he's baring his teeth at me.

'Get back to work,' Zenaton spits, half turning away. 'I hope you didn't lose anything while you *researched*.'

My mind spins, searching for a response. Anything.

Nothing but screeching silence fills my ears as Zenaton leans forward. Just a fraction.

'Nuntainia *will* hold the line, Luka.'

CHAPTER TWENTY-FIVE

My head is still ringing with Zenaton's words as I stumble towards the Office of the Integrity Commission.

Take Teddy with you.

Take Teddy with you.

I repeat Traelen's note over and over, drowning out my interaction with Zenaton. I just need to focus on my very next step. I have information, good information, from the archives. Now, I need to get it out. The files are too big to send from here. I just have to hope Teddy and Traelen have enough on the breeding program.

The Office of the Integrity Commissioner is quiet when I arrive, my breath sawing in my ears. The suite is similar to the Prime Minister's, with rooms branching off the reception, but just far less of them. The lone receptionist glances up and smiles.

'Can I help you?' she asks. 'We don't often get visitors when the Commissioner's not in.'

'Ah, yes.' I swallow, forcing my breathing to even out. 'I'm looking for Teddy.'

She pulls a face. 'She's not in—poor dear came down with a tummy bug at lunch, apparently. I don't envy her. Can I leave her a message?'

The floor seems to tilt beneath me.

Luka, she'd said, *my unbroken rule of parenting is* never *catch the vomiting bug ...*

My mouth dries. On the surface, the connection seems tenuous – of course she can't guarantee not getting sick. But, after my conversation with Zenaton ... did he arrange to have her taken while I was in the archives? Is that what he meant by 'lose something'?

'You okay, dear?' the receptionist asks.

I nod. Smile woodenly. 'I hope she feels better soon. I'll come back later—could you direct me to the Prime Minister's office from here? It's still my first week.'

Part of me screams to run while I can, but I need to get to Traelen. Make sure he's still here. Tell him ...

Shit. What about Zale and the kids?

I break into a jog, holding my duty phone against my tummy, where it in turn steadies the one hidden in my skirt so I don't lose it, and enter the mayhem of the Prime Minister's office. There's no sign of the Ministers, just the support staff scouring every known record to identify Quillian.

Military, I hear someone say, and the hairs on the back of my neck stand up.

'Luka,' Traelen says from the door to his internal office, 'a word.'

Images of units of soldiers are on almost every screen I walk past. One has a picture of a village. Another of an older man.

'King.' Someone says, but I don't have time to see if I think there is any resemblance to Quillian. I block them out, ice in my veins. Ronan King. Quillian's uncle. A man instrumental in where we are today. Do they know that? Do they know the link to Quillian yet? Do they know Quillian is the Rebel Prince?

'Where's Teddy? Did you get what you need?' Traelen asks, closing the door behind me, face tight.

Mutely, I shake my head. How do I tell him—

'She's not feeling unwell?' I ask.

Traelen's chin lifts ever so slightly. 'I know she *was* well. What are you telling me, Luka?'

I press my palm to my lips. *Don't panic. Just tell him the facts.* 'The receptionist for the Commissioner said she's gone home sick.'

'Teddy?'

'Yes. But I saw Zenaton in the hallway on my way there, and he said—nothing in a way, but I think—and your note ...'

Traelen loops the room, hands behind his head.

'Traelen,' I whisper, 'I'm so—'

'Did you get what you need?' he asks again.

'I think so, yes. But there's so much more down there, Traelen. I found—' I blow out a hard exhale as the reality of the Tae file starts to form in my mind. 'I found a whole box of files on Tae, on the conflict there, and I think ...' I don't know what I think. 'I don't know what Teddy has on the breeding program, if there's enough, or if ... she even got in there again today.'

Traelen's face hardens.

'I'll go back,' he says. 'I know where she was looking last. You need to leave—they've already worked out Quillian has been in the service somewhere. It won't be long until they work out who he is and track his career. Then they'll link him to you, and everyone you know will be implicated.'

'Zenaton's had my house watched,' I say, the words turning sour as I realise they will have seen Akira and Zale, too.

'Where's Teddy, Traelen?' I ask, voice trembling. 'Please tell me she's safe.'

Traelen looks at me carefully, as if he's trying not to let it crack. 'I asked her not to go to your house for dinner, but she knew Zale would think that very unusual.'

I stare at him as the biting concern crystallises. Something has happened to Teddy ... something orchestrated by Zenaton because, thanks to me, he knows she is connected to me outside the house. That's what glinted in his eyes as he talked to me in that hallway – the knowledge he'd already won, already inflicted damage I was yet to discover. He wanted me to know he had the upper hand, how easily it could have been me instead. As I think of Zale's face, bright with happiness as she laughed with Teddy at dinner, I wish it was.

A chill snakes its way across the back of my shoulders as Traelen's face falls, the most vulnerable expression I think I've ever seen him make, and it cracks something in my chest.

'You need to go,' he says, his voice thin. 'Please—ask your team to find her.'

My palms start to feel clammy.

'Aren't you coming?' I whisper. 'All of our names will be connected, now.' I think of where I signed Traelen's name as the authorising officer for my archives access. How long did he really think he'd have before all of this came crashing down?

'I need one more thing on the breeding program,' he scans the semi-frosted glass behind me, as if he's monitoring the movements of the people on the other side. 'If Teddy didn't go in there today, I know she doesn't have enough—we'll need something more. I'm going to have to get into Zenaton's office.'

'Wait, what? If he catches you—'

'What, Luka? If he catches me I'll end up in Vana? No. If he catches me, my options will likely be death or to be consumed into his Karaylia program along with Teddy.'

I stare at him, his words slicing into me, what they mean about him and Teddy ...

'You think that's where she's been taken?'

'I don't know for sure, but what I do know is wherever they've taken her isn't going to be good—and I can't find her on my own.'

We watch each other for a moment, our worlds clearly starting to come down around us. The busy sounds of the office outside his door are a chilling reminder that we are literally standing on the other side of Nuntainia's largest manhunt.

'Traelen, your name is—'

'No. I need to find the last known location of the breeding facility, and then I'll leave, providing I can take the evidence with me. But Teddy, I really need—'

'Of course,' I say, blinking at him.

'And Zale and the kids—get them out. The only way we can protect some part of her right now is to get them somewhere safe.'

My stomach rolls over itself, knotting painfully as I nod mutely, despite a complete lack of understanding.

'Who is she to—'

'My sister,' he bites out.

The room eddies around us. Shit.

'The abandoned carpark, past the last pod station on the blue line,' I whisper, knowing Cortane will probably make good on her word to kill me for this. But I can't leave Traelen here with nothing. I ignore the whispered reminder that I may have caused a leak of the camp locations – I can't do anything about that right now. I am also now the reason Teddy is missing. The more I think it over, the more I am sure it's Zenaton emphasising his message from today. That the only reason he has Teddy and not me is because he's the one calling the shots.

Despite the things that will, understandably, give Cortane more reason to doubt me, I know in my bones I can trust Teddy and Traelen. Not to mention they have information the traitors need as well. 'Go to the far end,' I continue, 'there's an ... exit there that will get you to me.'

His eyes shutter. 'Thank you, Luka. You'd better prepare them for that possibility. If you don't hear from me by this time tomorrow, destroy the portal on your way through.'

Fifteen minutes.

The amount of time Holland told me I had to pack up my life and leave my home, with no guarantee I will ever return.

But as Holland contacts the camp about Teddy and to organise Akira and Zale's extraction, I stand in my bedroom, looking at the soft linen I was last cocooned in with Quillian. I find my only craving is to be back with him and the others I love at that camp, to confirm they're safe myself. See them with my own eyes.

Quickly packing some underwear, comfortable pants and tops, and my skincare, I take one last look around. My gaze lands on the picture of Akira, Zale, and me, and a stone turns over in my chest. I haven't been able to talk to any of them since leaving the House, and I can only imagine how stressed they are. How panicked their children must be. And how much harder it will be for them to condense their whole lives into a few bags.

To convince Zale to go without Teddy.

Sliding the frame into my small bag, I close the door behind me and walk out of my house with Holland.

It feels very much like diving off Nix's island once more.

Except, this time, the impact feels much closer, so close I can almost feel it reverberating already. And, alongside that suffocating sense of dread, is the burn of just how much my own choices have led us here.

We travel in so many pods I can't even guess at how many rides we've taken, crisscrossing all over the city, walking between different stations, and even backtracking to the one closest to my house.

Finally, Holland decides we've done enough traipsing around, and we would have lost anyone who may have been following us. If I'd been with Cortane or River instead, I wonder if they would have just portalled or flown me to Quillian.

I gently pull him to a stop, hand on his arm, and look up into his inquiring face, bracing myself.

'I can't go yet,' I say, and watch as his brows raise. 'There's something we need to do first.'

He watches me for a long moment. 'I'm waiting for it to make sense,' he says finally, and then smiles thinly. 'Although I guess I should be happy you're not leaving me clueless about an upcoming ass-whooping from Cortane.' He crosses his arms over his chest, widening his stance like he's settling into our spot on this unknown street. 'Give it to me, then.'

I run my hands over my hair, as if I can smooth my thoughts at the same time.

'That first time I snuck away,' I smother a wince at the things I have done to endanger those around me, 'I met someone. But it turned out I already knew them and ... while I got what I went there for, it opened a raft of different questions and issues that need addressing and ...'

Holland's frown is deep. 'What's the short version?' he asks.

'It's my father. I thought he could help us and was going to bring him to camp. Now, I have information that means I don't know if we can trust him. But we still need him.'

He nods, his beard gently tapping towards the top of his chest as he does.

'So we need to assure ourselves of his integrity and, one way or the other, get his ass to camp?'

I blow out a breath, glancing around us. 'Yeah, I think so.'

'Tell me everything you know about what we're walking into.'

After giving him the address so he can work out the convoluted route he wants to take, I tell him as much as I think is relevant for today. My father's role in government, the state of our relationship, that there is Rosie to consider, how they had seemed so aligned to us. But also that now I have found his name on the prison program documents, and how they are insistent that the Rebel Prince is the one they need. I also tell him what they don't know. How intimately involved I am with the traitors, that I have been in Parliament House, anything about my links to Zenaton, or that I am returning today, despite telling them to be ready once I called them with advance warning. Finally, I tell him about Traelen and why Teddy is really missing.

Holland stays quiet, scanning our surroundings as I talk, and then turns to the practical things. Grilling me on the security I noticed at the house, had I seen any neighbours, how physically capable are my dad and Rosie, what magic do they have ... On and on until my mind is dry of things left to tell him, and my heart is full of all the reasons I am putting more and more people in difficult positions with every step I take.

If I could go back, I'd change so many things. If I'd been more judicious about who I brought with us off Zanteera, we wouldn't have lost so many in the camp raids. It's a thought that forces itself into my mind further and further, like each footfall is hammering it home, and I just want to close my eyes and make it go away. But, the truth is, someone I brought with us on instinct alone betrayed us and cost lives. Holland has beyond proven himself to me. Which leaves Casey, Shiloh, Emeris, or Blossom. I know Janly was already involved with the traitors, so it's unlikely to have been her. My chest aches at the thought of it being Blossom, but she's also done more than enough for me to know it's not her.

Casey, Shiloh, or Emeris.

All people I trust, but one I really don't know – Casey. The one who apparently failed to kill Zenaton.

I wring my hands thinking about what is, or will be, happening to him. But he also caused so much pain.

Traelen's face when I told him Teddy is missing flashes in my mind. Someone else who I've caused immense pain. If I wasn't so focused on Quillian and me instead of the bigger picture, would we have even fought? Would I have gone against Cortane's express instructions and invited my friends for dinner because *I* needed comfort? Did I give any thought to how dangerous that would have been for them? Did I think about how compromising Quillian in any way would mean ramifications for literally every one who follows him?

A fist turns deep in my gut, pressure rising into the back of my throat. I gasp for air.

'I think I might be sick,' I blurt, and Holland practically shoves me towards the grass a foot to my right.

'Take a sec,' he says, rubbing my back where I'm now bent over, elbows on my knees. 'You're not sick, you're freaking out—I can see it a mile off.'

My breaths get shorter, my vision darkening at the edges. 'But you don't know what I've done,' I choke out.

His hand stills. 'Is it more than what I already know?'

I shake my head, still turned towards the ground, and Holland returns to running his hand up and down my spine.

'Then we're fine,' he says. 'You're fine, and everyone is going to be fine.'

'You don't know that.'

He laughs. 'No, I don't. But I know you throwing your guts up in the street isn't going to help us. So, take a beat, and let's do this.'

Fuck. He's right. I imagine what Cortane would think if she saw me now. But I do need a moment, and so I take deep breaths, counting my exhales to ten, before drawing myself back to standing.

Holland takes my shoulders in his hand and locks his eyes with mine. 'We all do the best with the information we have at the time, okay? You think any one of us doesn't have regrets? No. This is the path, Luka. This is what it means to be a traitor. You learn, and you act, and you fucking hope like hell the cost is worth the gain in the end. Because there will always be a cost. But the possibility of living without change? That's worse.'

I roll my lips together to hold back the tears that threaten and nod, giving him a weak smile that I hope conveys how appreciated his words, and understanding, are.

We resume walking, and I take stock of where we are – my father's neighbourhood. I have to watch my feet in case I trip over the uneven pavement in the growing dark, the sun now sinking behind the tall buildings of the Academic Quarter lining the western city skyline. After a few quiet minutes, I glance sideways at Holland.

'What?' he asks, looking everywhere but at me.

'Do you have magic?'

'I don't need it,' he says with a shrug.

'Really?'

He seems so sure of himself, so confident in his every ability, I'd never even questioned before that he must have manifested something.

'Luka,' he says. 'I promise you, you do not *need* magic. Would it be nice? Sure. But is it *necessary*? No. Have you not managed every single moment in your life so far without magic?'

I can only look at him as he throws me a quick wink before returning his attention to our path.

'Exactly,' he says, turning us towards the address I gave him.

The magic finder's house.

My father's house.

A traitor's house.

But who is he a traitor to? Nuntainia, or me?

CHAPTER TWENTY-SIX

'Who is it?' My Dad's voice comes from the other side of the front door.

'Me,' I say, hoping he will recognise my voice. 'I've got a friend with me.'

It's quiet for some time before he opens the door and looks between Holland and me.

'It's time, I take it,' he says, ushering us in. 'We're ready, I'll grab—'

'Not yet,' I say as he closes and bolts the front door. He turns towards us, wariness written all over him. 'First, you both need to convince us we're not endangering people by taking you with us.'

Understanding clears his features as he flicks his gaze to Holland, who remains silent. 'Of course, this way.'

We follow my father to the same sitting room I met him in before, and I marvel at how much the sting of finding out about my magic has lessened in all that's happened since. Or perhaps that's just because everything else is so much worse.

But we don't have time for that now.

'I need to know how deeply embedded you are in all of this,' I say, 'and you *both* need to convince Holland and me that you're on the right side now.' I press my palms together between my knees where I sit on the settee. 'I'll be upfront—we don't have a lot of time and I think you could be valuable. But I won't risk the safety of anyone else by being wrong, and it's on you to convince me.'

My tone is firm and surprises me a little, but I take heart in the steel I've managed to infuse into the sentiment.

'Anyone else?' he asks gently. 'Are you okay?'

'Not particularly,' I say, and swallow. 'But here we are.'

He clearly reads in my expression that I'm not going to share any more – not yet – and he shares a look with Rosie, who sits next to Holland, and she nods.

'We *were* deeply embedded—me particularly,' he starts. 'You know I worked in government for the entirety of my career. Rosie was always looking at it from the outside, always objective, but she was as close to these people as I was, just in a different way.

'But,' he continues, 'when I eventually found out how my work was being twisted, despite my every effort to stop it, I had to draw a line. The system clearly could not be fixed from the inside, as I had once hoped.'

'How does that apply to the prison program?'

'That's a good example,' he says, the words soaked in a deep-seated rage.

'Explain it to me.' I demand, jaw tight.

He sighs heavily. 'Before I can do that, Luka, I need to know what you intend to do with the information if you decide not to take us with you.'

'You don't trust me?' I ask, but the sentiment doesn't sting. It is, after all, exactly what I am trying to ascertain as well. It's been a long time since we've been in each other's lives.

His gaze is loaded when it finds mine. 'I've spent a lifetime trying to protect you from all of this. Under no circumstances will I dump you straight in it. Not unless I can gauge how much you already know. Not until ... I can understand if it's too late for you to retreat or not.' His eyes beg me to understand his position, what he's done as a father to keep me safe until now. How hard it might be to give that up. 'It has nothing to do with *trust,*' he says fervently.

'The people I ... work with,' I hedge, 'are looking to dismantle the Karaylia breeding program, expose the prison program ... and its creator,' I say, and Rosie glances at my father. 'I know you designed the prison program. I found your signature on the policy documents in the House.'

My father nods, and I see his understanding of what I've been doing come together. 'I did,' he says simply. 'You want to know if I did it intentionally, if I knew what the program would become.'

It's not a question, and I let my silence answer for me. Something inside me settles at his open demeanour, his lack of any attempt at denial. The man I once knew never lied to me, whether I agreed with him or not. I hold tight to the hope he won't start now.

'No, Luka, it was not my intention—none of my work has been intended to do harm.' He sighs, a quiet sense of defeat infusing his voice. 'Do you know what it's like to make decisions you think will *help*, only to find they've become a poison your government willingly wields?'

I look at Holland, thinking of our conversation about doing the best you can with the information you have at the time, and I let myself soften towards my dad a bit. I *do* know harm was never his intention in anything he said or did – his life's work has been dedicated to the reduction of harm and injustice. I just don't think he realised how painful only 'lack of harm' could be to a daughter who needed more. But I quash that thought. It's irrelevant now.

'Look,' I say, 'I have my own views, but Holland will have his, and your actual *lives* will depend on how you answer these, and more, questions if we take you to meet the others.'

'You said you found my name on the original policy outline—did you read it?'

I'm taken aback slightly by the question, and shake my head mutely.

He laughs, completely without humour. 'I can see how finding my name would raise these questions, then.' He looks almost helplessly at Rosie. 'Just like they intended, right?' he asks her quietly, and I don't think he's talking about Holland and me.

'Luka,' Rosie says, 'you need to understand that the prison and breeding programs are linked. The prison program—not its original name, by the way—was your father's attempt at providing a safe place for rehabilitation of children and families affected by war and unrest. Particularly those in Tae, who are under siege by Coprath in one moment and Nuntainia in the next. In Corvan's original proposal, that island'—she gestures towards the sky—'was supposed to be a sanctuary for the refugees. But, unknown to him at the time, the Nuntainian government had already discovered how valuable those misplaced in Tae could be in other ways.

'Some of the strongest Karaylia come from Tae—the magic runs strongest in the female line. So they began the breeding program to strengthen our forces, the details hidden under the cover of the conflict between Tae and Coprath. But, as you know, these crimes never go completely unnoticed, and the minds behind the breeding program were looking for a way to scrub clean the records of those involved. This is when they began to take an interest in Corvan's research and—well, you know how that went. Eventually, they developed what became the prison program, and much more, for their own warped means. The island became a place where those critical to that program's success could go to be out of the spotlight if needed, to take "refuge" if you will,' she says, her tone coloured with disgust, 'and then return to continue their work.

'Since then, it's evolved to cover all manner of crimes and corruption of those in power, but it's the same principle: remove those that come under fire from public view for a time, let the population believe they are serving in Vana and forget about them, then quietly bring them back to leverage their ... expertise.'

I let it settle over me. Five years ago – *two* years ago, probably – I would have denied anything like this could happen here. Especially on this scale. I would have said Nuntainia is too ordered, too structured, and too ... evolved compared to the countries around us, who constantly descend into chaos fighting each other.

How fucking wrong I was. So sheltered and naive – exactly like I was supposed to be.

'So you're not responsible for covering up what goes on up there—what those people do?' I ask. They each shake their heads without so much as a glance at each other.

'No, Luka,' my Dad says. 'I have only ever wanted to better our world for everyone in it. Creating a two-speed society, where those with power are so far ahead we can't even see them, was not on my wish-list.'

His statement reverberates through my limbs. It's so ... him. The confirmation that he hasn't changed, isn't different at his core, makes me feel almost weightless.

'Do you still want to stop it?' I ask. 'You will not get a warm welcome where we're going. Things are moving quickly and—' I stop short of telling them about Teddy, that knowledge won't help them here.

'Luka,' Rosie says, standing. 'We packed our bags the moment you left last time.'

My Dad joins her. 'We might not have yet engaged in open conflict like your colleagues,' he says with a glance to Holland, 'but we've been scarred by these practices in our own ways. Even if we hadn't, it's still the right thing to do—no one should walk by something they can help make better.'

Holland looks between my dad and Rosie as they stand before us, and then shifts his gaze to me. 'I think he just put my thoughts better than I can.'

I search his face for any doubt. Any sense that I am letting my biases cloud my judgement. I don't find any.

'And why the Rebel Prince?' I ask, turning back to them. 'What can he do that you can't?'

Rosie smiles. 'He's already inspired a nation to follow him—that's not something we can do. But we can help solidify the Prince's foundation of knowledge, make it harder for the government or media to pick holes in. We can help make sure he's not discredited straight out of the gate or, worse, never even gets the chance to make his case publicly.'

'How?' Holland asks, and they shift their attention to him.

'I have the inside knowledge of how it all came together, since much of it is based on my stolen research,' Dad says, then gestures to Rosie, 'and she knows these stories from more angles than I can count, as well as how to navigate the media. They are almost always an extension of the government's thinking. It takes skill and knowledge to get any real messages out. Have you not wondered why there's never even been a whisper of any of this, at least not that's gained traction?'

My eyes meet Rosie's, their intensity tugging at the flame ignited in me that night on the island.

'They take the people you care about,' my father continues while I still look at Rosie, 'and if you have skills or knowledge that they need, they use them to control you—keep you silent, make you talk, or coerce you into doing things you would never do, to betray yourself.'

Rosie holds my gaze, and I wonder who she lost in her quest to expose this government. Yet she's still here, trying again, no matter the cost. But there's something else in the silence, a message in her look that I'm not quite ... then she flicks her eyes to my dad, and his words from my last visit slam into me.

'The government would have preferred we not shed light on different issues. The last five years have been ... interesting, Luka.'

I tear my eyes from Rosie as it hits home and look at my dad, the new lines around his mouth, the intelligent shine in his eyes as sharp as ever. He is looking at me the way he would during one of his many lectures, waiting for me to formulate my own thesis on which to build an argument. I was summoned for my duty – on Zanteera Island, a place originally proposed by my father – five years ago. They stopped his letters.

They take the people you care about. To control you, keep you silent.

The last five years have been interesting, Luka.

'I think it's time for you to meet the Rebel Prince,' I say.

I'm flooded with a cool relief that I haven't told the others of my dad's involvement as we leave his new house with he and Rosie in tow, each of them holding an overnight bag stuffed to the brim. Intellectually, I know I am taking a huge gamble here. How will they be received? What will their immediate reaction be to having my Dad delivered to them?

I have Holland with me – he might not yet have totally won Cortane over, but his support will count for something. At least, I hope it helps smooth the introduction.

But what will my Dad think of Quillian? Not as the Rebel Prince, but as ... mine? And then when he puts those two things together? I shake off the feeling, trying instead to focus on the gentle warmth of the sun on my skin.

For what could easily be the thousandth time, my phone buzzes in my pocket. Though I studiously ignored it while talking with Dad and Rosie for most of the day, I know I can't put it off any longer. There are numerous missed calls and messages from Quillian, Nix, River, and Bloss – they have Zale and Akira, but no updates on Teddy.

And two missed calls from Traelen.

My fingers shake as I call him straight back.

'Anything?' he asks, picking up in less than one ring, the tremor in his voice telling me everything. There's no sign of Teddy for him either. Zale will be beside herself, I think, guilt weighing on me.

'Not yet,' I reply gently. 'Did you get what you needed?'

There's a long pause, and Holland looks at me expectantly before returning his attention to Dad and Rosie. Though it's clear he's still listening.

'I don't think it's enough and I just—this can't have all been for nothing.' Traelen's broken vulnerability would have probably frightened me a few days ago, but it steadies me somehow in the face of everything we've uncovered between us.

'It won't be,' I reassure him, watching my father and Rosie walk ahead of me. 'Can you meet me where I said? I'm not sure there's anything more you can do from where you are. Not if ...' I let my words trail off, but I'm sure he knows I can only mean if he's found out.

'I can't leave Klades,' he chokes out.

'I know it feels that way,' I say gently. 'But you can be there for her family while we're still looking.'

He's quiet again for a long time, and I'm reminded of the only other phone conversation we've had, when I told him Claudius had died. I glance again at my father, talking quietly to Rosie by his side, and I'm filled with a sense of purpose. Perhaps Claudius didn't know exactly who I was going to bring together – or perhaps he did. I'll never know now. But the knowledge that I have brought all these people together, when they have been fighting the same battle separately for so long, builds like a heat source through my middle. I use it to keep the little voice in the back of my mind at bay. The one that worries what the others will do, particularly Cortane, when I turn up with more 'loose ends' – at least one of which is on their most-wanted list.

My phone vibrates against my head.

'You'll come?' I ask Traelen. 'Please, I think you'll want to know what I've got.'

My father glances back at me this time, and I don't avoid meeting his eyes. I could swear he almost nods before he turns forward again.

'I'll come,' Traelen says eventually.

The pod station is busy as we make our way through, the humming of the overhead lights somehow still audible over the din of passengers.

'It needs to be now,' I say gently, pointing to the pod waiting on the right-hand platform. Holland watches our backs as my father nods, gesturing for Rosie and me to go in front of him. He places his hand gently on my elbow as I step in behind Rosie, and my chest warms in response to the familiarity of his cool, dry touch.

Traelen exhales. 'I'll be as quick as I can.'

'Be safe.' The words are heavy as I listen to the line go dead.

Gripping my phone, I settle into the hard bench seat across from Rosie and my dad in the pod.

Rosie pins me with her soft green eyes. 'Is this safe?'

'Not entirely, no,' I say honestly.

She nods sharply. 'Probably means you're taking us where we need to go,' she says, before looking out the window as if she's mentally saying goodbye to the city.

Scrolling through message after message of an increasingly worried Nix, I find the group chat with him, River, and Blossom.

L: how are A & Z? Where?

N: Shaken but safe. In the spot you suggested. What's your ETA? I want you back here.

L: On my way. Please tell C to stand down.

The sound of a gun cocking is the first thing I hear as we step out of the portal and into camp one.

My father curses, placing himself between Cortane and Rosie.

'I asked you to stand down,' I say, looking desperately at Nix and River, who flank her.

'This is me *standing down*, Princess. And you don't give any fucking orders here.' The black handgun is pointed directly at my father's face, and my pulse thrums in my ears as the air is choked from my lungs.

'Cort,' Quillian says, approaching me by walking directly into her line of shot, with the confidence perhaps only he and Finn could have that she won't shoot him. 'Put it away.'

My breath doesn't completely release until he has his arms around me and presses a firm, almost desperate, kiss to my mouth.

'You had me really fucking worried,' he says quietly, paying no attention at all to the tense scene in which we stand.

I kiss him back briefly, then pull away. 'Is it too soon for you to meet my dad?' I ask, looking up at him between my lashes, our conversation about futures tight in my gut. But he wanted me to be his and this is who—

'Professor *Brideoake*?' Nix gasps, stepping away from Cortane.

River just watches me, his mind clearly whirling behind his eyes.

'Boys,' my father says from over my shoulder. 'Why am I not surprised to see you here?' He says it with a touch of disdain in his voice, just like he used to when he thought they were getting me mixed up in something I shouldn't be, but underneath that, clear enough for River's composed expression to flicker, is pride.

Cortane lowers her gun the merest fraction. 'You know each other?' she says, disbelief dripping from her tone, cocking her head to the side in a way that makes her look younger – just for a moment.

Quillian stays looking at me, wide eyes boring into mine, as if he can't quite face what's unfolding.

'You'll be great,' I whisper, pressing a soft kiss to his frozen mouth and turning him around to face the group. I could swear a ghost of a smile dusts Finn's face.

'This is—ah, quite the welcoming committee,' my father says, taking everyone in.

I wait a beat, but it seems no one else will take the lead.

'Dad,' I say, gesturing to Nix and River, 'you know "the boys", the one holding the gun is Cortane, then we have Finn, and ... this is Quillian.'

Cortane glares at me, as if giving their real names is an offence. It probably should be, to be fair; it would definitely be risky if it were anyone other than my father. But he and Rosie have taken the greatest risk of those here by blindly following me to a location they have no way of tracking – straight into Cortane's waiting pistol.

'This is my father, Esteemed Professor Corvan Brideoake, and Rosie Ellerson.' I look at her as I purposefully omit what she does for now. That, along with the information they can share, is key to what I think they can do for our common cause. But it's for them to share.

Quillian steps forward, holding out his hand to shake my dad's.

'Sir, I'm Quillian O'Daire.'

I don't know if my dad has any idea who Quillian is yet or not but, despite the height and overall size difference, he still manages to look Quillian up and down with a coolly assessing gaze. I glance to Nix, who can barely control his smirk. I want to tell him to cut it out, but Finn and Holland are the same.

'You may call me Professor,' my dad responds, taking Quillian's outstretched hand, and I cringe. Could he sound any more condescending?

'Of course, Professor,' Quillian says, not missing a beat. I think of him in his Warden's role, how obvious it was he wouldn't take any shit from anyone. Is he being deferential to my father because of his relationship with me, or has this hint of superiority come so often in his life, the subservience slips in faster than he can hold it back?

'Rosie,' Quillian shakes her hand next. 'Lovely to meet you. Welcome.'

'I've heard of you,' Cortane says, body now completely turned towards Rosie. 'Both of you.' She inclines her head to include my father. 'A fact that is *entirely* lucky for our resident Princess,' she says without looking at me. 'I do *not* take kindly to accepting strays—something she seems to struggle with.'

I ignore the obvious jab, opting to leverage my slim advantage instead. 'Then you have an idea of why they're here, Cortane—I think you need to hear what they know. And Rosie will be able to help us take the fight public.'

Cortane remains still for a long moment, before she completely lowers her gun by her side.

My dad, who has been standing quietly during this exchange, focus pinned entirely on Quillian, finally speaks. 'You, I assume, are the Rebel Prince.'

As Finn leads us to the main meeting hall, Quillian hangs back, hand on my elbow as he gently tugs me to keep pace with him.

'Your *father?*' he asks, voice low.

I nudge into him with my side. 'I'm sorry I couldn't warn you. I didn't want to put it in a message, and I know there are so many other things going on—'

Quillian stops short, my arm still in his hand as he pulls me towards him while the others continue on.

His green eyes are bright when he looks down at me, his hand shifting up and around to my shoulder. 'Luka, I am *honoured* to meet your father. Is this'—he gestures around to the slightly dilapidated village around us—'how I envisaged that? No. I would have much preferred all of this was behind us and I could have welcomed him into our little, but spacious, cabin in the woods of Tae with you in my arms and not a *gun* in his face.' He sighs. 'But this is my—our—life for now. I will never regret meeting anyone who is clearly important to you. You're right, there's a lot going on right now.' He rubs his forehead. 'But I meant what I said.'

My whole body feels warm, and I don't resist the urge to step into him, his hands slipping easily around my sides. *Princess*, Cortane calls me. That's something I can almost imagine myself being of that little cabin Quillian talks of.

'You've thought about that,' I say, lifting my brows, and the tops of his ears appear to darken as he looks down at me. 'The cabin.'

'Luka, I'm always thinking about how I can keep you in my life,' he says, and I can't help but laugh.

'I think you'll find me particularly hard to get rid of. Especially now you've put forever on the table.'

He pulls me into him at that, pressing our bodies together, his palm on the back of my head as my forehead comes to his shoulder.

'Thank fuck for that,' he says. 'Whatever stupid things I have said and done in the past in an attempt to save you from all of *this*, I am desperate for you, Luka. I am yours for as long as you'll have me.'

I stand on my tiptoes and push up to his face, gripping his cheeks.

'The feeling is mutual, Quillian O'Daire, Rebel Prince.'

He claims my mouth so fiercely I can barely breathe. There is only him, and me, and the fact we're fighting together for whatever comes next.

'They're so close to knowing who you are,' I whisper.

'I know. That's how it needs to go,' he says into my hair. 'I'm just so fucking relieved you're out of there.'

We turn back to the main hall without either of us mentioning my father's role in 'all of this'.

CHAPTER TWENTY-SEVEN

Cortane's handgun is still unholstered when Quillian and I enter the hall behind my father and Rosie. She taps the length of it against her muscled thigh as she watches us all.

'You have thirty minutes to convince me you're useful and not a complete breach of security,' she says, before any of us have even sat down.

Holland and Finn collect chairs from around the room and place them in a haphazard circle, but there's not enough for all of us and no one takes one. Nix and River stand to the side, River on his phone, and I hope he's telling Blossom what's going on. I assume she's still looking after her patients with her new magic. In the space where jealousy about Bloss's magic might have taken root before, I find myself recalling what Holland said, along with what I *have* done without magic.

I stay mostly quiet as my father and Rosie answer every question thrown their way. There's a slight sense of reservation about my father – more so with Rosie – but I don't get the impression either of them are holding back on anything vital.

Nix shifts on his feet, and I register the ache in my own. By contrast, Cortane's stance seems to soften – just slightly. As if having people as knowledgeable as her – or more – about the wrong-doings of our government has eased some of the fight in her, almost as if the information she's been grilling from them is finding its way home in her. The longer I watch her, the more I understand that's probably exactly what it is, what makes her so hard all the time. Constantly fighting to make people see beyond the shiny surface our government portrays, to what's hiding underneath, has meant she can never be anything but vigilant.

I think on my interaction with Zenaton today. The immediate, blood-stopping sense of fight or flight as I tried to work out the direction he was going to take, how I would need to respond to keep myself and the people I love safe. While, at the same time, both preserve and escape with some of the most valuable information the movement has ever had. Information that could allow us to bring everything that our government continues to allow to an end.

What sort of person would I have turned out to be, if that had been my whole life – constantly trying to work out who to trust, and who to kill? Kill, or be killed.

I certainly wouldn't be the woman who leapt off that island in blind faith.

'We have been quietly working towards this for a long time,' Rosie says, without looking at my dad. 'Gathering information, working right in the thick of it, and then retreating—avoiding attention so we could get here. I want to be clear—we came with Luka because we believe we need to align what we know, our expertise, with you, Quillian, as not only the Rebel Prince, but the Prince of your people.'

My skin tingles. Prince. *Princess.*

I knew he was the Rebel Prince, of course, but I thought that was more a figure of speech. Tae doesn't have a monarchy, but perhaps that's irrelevant to them now. Quillian told me how this all began with violence, driven by his uncle, until they rallied around Quillian and Claudius's alternative strategy. Perhaps he doesn't need to be a blood prince to have a title that's become legitimate in Tae. How ironic that the very government that gave him that moniker, likely in dismissive arrogance, may have sparked the fire that clearly burns behind the lore of the Rebel Prince.

Cortane started calling me 'princess' as, I thought, an insult to the woman who wore pretty dresses in a castle in the sky, hiding from the horrors unfolding under her nose. I'd moved through the motions of my duty without ever questioning the absurdity – or purpose – of a gilded prison. It took Nix failing to collect me, and everything that followed, for me to finally pay attention, to ask the right questions.

But, as I consider the weary faces before me, what they've all been through, what they know, and where they've come from, a part of me feels like this was inevitable. Perhaps that's the sense of rightness beginning to envelop my chest.

Not only are the people I care most about on this side of the fight, but many of them are in this camp fighting for a better world. As I look around the room, knowing Traelen is also on his way, a little thread of warmth takes hold. One that starts to feel akin to a tiny swell of pride.

For the first time, I consider that Cortane's nickname might not have come from a place of disdain. Perhaps Quillian had told her about me somehow and, knowing him as she does, she just ... knew. Or maybe there was something about me, without Quillian needing to say anything. Whatever the case, with knowledge now that I didn't have then, the nickname no longer rankles quite as much.

Quillian's knuckles brush the back of my forearm, and I welcome the contact.

'But,' Rosie is saying, 'you need to understand that we don't come here as ignorant citizens in need of a cause. Nor are we wounded souls, displaced due to the actions of the government and seeking a soft place to land—or revenge.'

Cortane's chin rises a fraction. But Rosie is right. Each of us here fit into one or the other of those categories.

'We come as highly educated individuals who do not go along with anything for the ride. We will want a voice in how things that involve us and our expertise are executed, particularly in the exposing of the government. Because, without our help, you will lose this fight, becoming nothing more than a nuisance vigilante group, your cause just another they inevitably sweep under the rug.'

The hall falls silent as Rosie's words sink in. I'm once again struck by the level of trust between my father and Rosie, that he's willing to let her speak for them both. Even if it wasn't already clear to me, there's now no way anyone could have any doubt that having his words and work manipulated by others is never going to happen again.

Nix and River look between Finn, Cortane, and Quillian, but neither of them seem surprised by this approach. Corvan Brideoake might not have been the one that proclaimed it, but the sentiment matches what the Kilroy brothers know of him after a lifetime of lectures.

'Look,' my father finally looks Quillian full in the face. 'You've rallied people far beyond what either of us could ever hope to, but they are primarily from Tae, or those who have been victimised by Nuntainia. They make a resourceful and effective vigilante force, determined foot soldiers, if you like, in a skirmish.

'But this next bit—it needs something other than brute force, more than picking people who have offended you off one by one, more than just leaking all the information you have and hoping it's enough to turn the tide. You need a strategy to get the people of Nuntainia behind you, and you do not hold the power in that arena—the Prime Minister and his government do.'

I catch Nix's gaze and think we're wondering the same thing – how does he know people, prisoners, were killed off one by one?

More than that, I have to swallow my discomfort at not having told any of them about the Prime Minister yet. But now, I want Traelen to be able to share that information – to use it as a way of building, if not trust, then credibility with this group.

'You need us,' my father continues. 'We have between us the knowledge, expertise, and connections to help you turn the tide. All we're asking for in exchange is the right to autonomy, to decide for ourselves whether our own knowledge is put to use, and how.'

'You're right,' Cortane says, slowly, as if she can't quite believe what she's saying. 'We can't fail at this point in the game. We've come so far, and we need to be smart.' She looks at Quillian, whose hand is still pressed against my arm.

Cortane turns to me. 'Did you get what we need? Anything we can use to substantiate any claims we make in a public campaign?'

'Mostly.' I can't help my gaze flicking to Nix, but I won't raise anything that I found on Tae yet. Not until I know more about what it is I actually found – and if it will help or hurt him. 'I've got the records on who's been through the program, including their actual crimes.'

Cortane claps her hands together, and I flinch.

Nix exhales loudly. 'Shit's about to get real.'

I lift my brows at him. What is not 'real' already?

'Show me,' Cortane says.

I look at my father, hoping I'm not about to blow this thin understanding between us all to pieces. Dad lowers his chin a little, and I know he understands what I need to do. Is ready.

'First,' I say, 'perhaps you should ask if I found who created the prison program.'

Rosie goes still.

Cortane's gaze flares.

I don't look at Quillian or anyone else. I just watch as she turns her head like a predator back to my father and Rosie.

'Who created the program?' she asks, voice level. Cold.

Quillian nudges in front of me, pressing me back with his elbow and gently placing himself closer to Cortane. Closer to my father.

Tears prick my eyes as my dad meets her gaze front on.

'I did.'

All the air seems to suck out of the room as the knowledge sinks in. They wanted the creator of the program to kill them. I delivered.

But, for at least Nix, River, Quillian, and me, it's far more complicated than that.

'Did she tell you that means you're on our list?' Cortane asks, gripping her pistol tighter.

'She didn't,' my dad says without missing a beat. 'Probably because she knew what we can contribute is far more valuable than just ticking another name off your *list.*'

I exhale.

I know she won't harm him. Not now. She's too smart to not see what more we can do with him alongside us.

Cortane laughs, putting the gun in her belt at her back and turning to me. 'I don't exactly know what to call this trait of yours,' she says, 'but clearly it runs in the fucking family. Let's have a look at what you got.'

She moves away, towards the command room, and the others filter after her, only Quillian remaining with me.

'I'll just be a sec,' I say, and he gives my fingers a squeeze before leaving me with my dad and Rosie. 'You two okay?' I ask, and Rosie lifts her brows.

'Well,' she says, 'I guess that's probably warmer than I would have expected.'

Dad stays silent, watching me.

'I'm sorry I threw you under the bus,' I say. 'We needed—'

'To gain their trust, I understand,' he says, his shoulders dropping. 'I'm proud of you, you know?'

The clenching in my chest is hard enough for me to worry my ribs might crack, and I fight back an audible inhale.

The door to the command room opens. 'You coming?' Cortane barks.

Once I've joined the others in the command room, Dad and Rosie following close behind me, Cortane doesn't waste any time. 'Let's see it.'

I bring up the file on my phone, careful not to enter the one from the Tae box, and hand it to Cortane. 'It's just the one.'

Within seconds, she has it on the screen, pausing and taking still images of the video that scrolls past. Record after record of the people who have been through, or are currently in, the program, as well as their crimes. Sex trafficking, child slavery, extortion, embezzlement, sexual assault, and the list goes on.

Quillian presses a kiss to my temple. 'You're incredible.'

I swallow back all the things I want to talk to him about – the list of survivors from Tae, Traelen, and the fact I don't yet have anything on the breeding program. 'Has anyone located Teddy?' I ask, dreading the response.

'Not as yet,' Finn responds. 'But we're looking.'

'Who is looking?' I ask, glancing around the room and not caring about the bite in my tone.

Finn glances at Holland briefly, before turning back to me. 'Casey.'

Holland's eyes go wide. 'Well, shit—about time you worked out he's one of the good guys.'

Lead fills my gut. That means they've either cleared him to be part of this, and know he's not the leak—or are putting someone well below par on finding Teddy.

'I'm not sure any of us are "good",' Finn says quietly.

The image of Kasera, lying in a pool of silk skirts and her own blood, comes to me first; then Miana, already cold, still tangled in her sheets as if she'd just slept in. I never saw Aiten ... after. Even though I know they were awful people, I still find myself wondering if they really deserved that end. Who was it that killed them in the end? Does it matter if everyone here was complicit? How does that make us better than them?

'Can we get the list up?' Quillian asks, ignoring Finn's comment.

We all watch as Cortane exits my video and pulls up her captured stills, selecting the latest one and zooming in on a series of names I recognise, a list that includes Kasera, Aiten, and Miana.

Then, she puts a strike through their names. 'Dealt with,' she mutters to herself.

Cortane turns back to the rest of us, the list of struck out names still visible. 'This is good,' she says, looking at my father and me. 'We can use this. Use you.'

Quillian links his hand in mine as he also turns to face Rosie and my dad. 'Every decision is still ultimately mine,' he says. 'I will take ... significant, if I must, advisement, but I have been responsible for this group and my people for the best part of my life and I remain responsible for the actions we take.'

Finn seems to let go of a long, slow breath as he gives Quillian a shallow nod.

'Right,' Cortane says, looking around our circle. 'This is us, then. You survived the House, and your latest strays have proven useful, Luka, but this is where we draw the line. We can't afford any further compromises to our position when we're so close.'

I don't miss the unsaid implication in 'further compromises', but my phone buzzes and I dig it out, heart pumping.

T: coming.

'About that,' I venture. 'I may have asked one more person to meet us here.'

'Shit, Luka,' Nix says. 'Why? You know he arrested us?'

River runs his hands through his hair. It's the most agitated I've seen him since he arrived on the island. His eyes keep flicking to the door, and I don't know if he's looking for Blossom or waiting for my 'guest' to arrive.

My chest burns a little at the thought of Blossom. She should be here. With me. But she's stepping into her own power – literally – and I don't want to hold her back from that.

The same as I didn't want to hold Akira and Zale back. And now Zale is in her own personal hell as well.

'Secure the square,' Cortane barks into her phone. 'River—get to the other side of the portal. That man does not set foot in this camp.'

River looks at me, a certain begging in his eyes. But it's Nix and then Quillian that steal most of my focus. Quillian's hand is still against mine, but now it's like it's frozen in place, as opposed to being a comfort, and I slip my fingers into his and squeeze. He returns the pressure.

'Hold, Cort,' he says, and I let my breath go. I cannot leave Traelen stranded in Klades. Standing at a portal that won't allow him through.

'Traelen Jardim?' my father asks and I nod.

'He's—' I start.

'The asshole that got the best of us landed in Vana,' Cortane snaps.

'Yes,' I say more forcefully. 'He is.'

Dumbfounded looks stare back at me and, one by one, I steadily meet the eyes of all the people whose lives it now feels like are in my hands. But it's really only Cortane who has significant doubt in her expression. My father doesn't know any of this history; Nix, River, and Quillian know there is no way I would take any chances that get them sent back to Vana; I told Holland about Traelen on our way to collect Dad and Rosie, and Finn is stoic as ever.

'You need to trust me on this. I saw what Traelen did—I was in that room when Quillian was arrested.' My grip on his hand gets tighter, and he nudges into me. 'But we worked together in the House—'

'What?' Nix cuts in, his face twisting at the information I haven't shared before now.

Quillian stills before turning to look down at me, but he doesn't speak.

'We knew him being there was a possibility when I went in, but Traelen's an ally. He's more than an ally,' I correct myself. 'You wanted me to find your old contact. I did—Traelen. He went dark when he took on the Chief of Staff role and his position became too precarious.'

'Are you sure?' Nix asks.

'Yes. He helped me get the records from the archives – I couldn't have done it so quickly without him. I'm telling you, he's an ally.'

Cortane's attention flies to the command room entrance. 'What he is, is almost here.' She heads towards the door. 'You already gave him permission to use the portal, didn't you? Told him where it is?'

My palms start to sweat, but I shout—'Stand *down*, Cortane'—my free hand slapping my thigh.

She slowly spins on her heel. Everyone simply watches, like they knew this moment was coming and need to see how it plays out before they decide their next move.

Quillian remains holding my hand, but says nothing.

'He's an *ally*, Cortane,' I say again, projecting my voice across the space. 'I saw, every day, what he is and isn't doing in that House. I know who he cares for, where he comes from—information I will not give up here until you prove that you will keep him safe. He deserves to be part of this as much as anyone here. He's been fighting just as long as you. For just as valid reasons as you.'

'Holy shit,' she says. 'You're actually defending him.'

'I am.' I lift my chin.

She stalks towards me. 'Let me understand this—you're happy to protect the man who put people you supposedly *love,'* she spits the word, 'in Vana, *and* you're comfortable bringing in a leak that literally made us bleed? Is that where you stand, *Luka?'*

The lack of the 'princess' hurts more than I would have expected.

'No, that's not where I stand,' I say, voice steady despite the pounding in my ears that's so loud I can barely think. 'I made a mistake somewhere, I know. But I won't apologise for doing the very best I could. It was all of you that kept so much from me, left me to work out what the fuck was happening on my own. Did I know or fully understand all the risks? No. But did I act out of love bringing everyone here? Yes. Have my eyes now been opened to what mistakes truly cost in this movement? Also yes.'

I drop Quillian's hand and take a step closer to Cortane, needing to do this on my own. 'But where do I stand? Right here.' I shove a finger towards the ground. 'And, yes, I will protect the person who has protected me in that House. Who has helped me find that damn list. Who has been risking his life to feed you information without you even knowing who he was, knowing he'd likely be a target for you, particularly after the events on the island.'

Cortane lifts a brow, but I plough on.'And no, I am *not* comfortable that my trust in people created a leak. But I have also—'

'It's Emeris,' she says.

My breath comes to an abrupt halt. I can't tell if I'm spinning. Or falling. If it didn't feel so different to when I dived off Nix's island, I'd say both. But the truth is, everything is quiet. Waiting. The world isn't doing anything, it's me. My thoughts, feelings, are spinning so fast I think I might be sick.

All of the injured I helped in the infirmary, the grief etched into their faces, presses into my temples. The trauma I am sure they will live with for a long time. Then there are those who didn't survive—

The memory of watching Nix and River step out onto that road on the bodycam drags under my skin. The blood that dripped from Quillian's wings.

All because Emeris gave us up. Gave our locations to someone in the House Traelen couldn't intercept. Did he give the list directly to Zenaton?

I clench my teeth, knowing I am taking too long to outwardly react to the bombshell Cortane has dropped.

Why did it have to be *Emeris*? His face when he came to tell me about Claudius's death crowds everything else in my mind. His ... sadness. Confusion. His hope that I would tell him something different. Make it alright. Quickly followed by the faith he had in me when he joined us on that breakaway island.

Cortane's grey eyes are narrow as she assesses me. 'And what is your judgement on Traelen?' She's still looking at me, but it's clear she doesn't expect me to respond. Wants me to sit with the knowledge of Emeris for now. Her question is for the core group, perhaps only Finn and Quillian. I send up a desperate wish that I'm right about Traelen, that we are not about to get played in the worst possible way.

'We trust Luka,' River says.

'And we watch Traelen very fucking closely,' Nix adds, 'but he's not executed.'

A beat of silence washes over us. Quillian's lack of response feels like it scratches on my skin, my palm burning where it once sat against his.

Executed? My vision swims. But what else did I really expect her response to be?

'We trust Luka,' Finn says quietly.

Finally, Cortane takes her gaze from mine and looks to Quillian. Long moments pass between them, and I almost feel like I'm watching the final straw with Cortane play out. The minute softening after talking with Dad and Rosie has gone. She's back in fight-to-the-death mode, and there's a very real risk that she'll kill Traelen on sight.

'He knew the Hunters were coming,' I say, straightening my spine and taking another step towards her. 'Traelen knew the body count of Defence Committee members was starting to attract attention, and they were about to step in. Which they *did*. So he ordered the arrests to get Quillian, Nix, and River out of where there were about to be too many eyes he couldn't guarantee the loyalty of. He sent them to Vana, with no official charges filed, to *save* them.'

Cortane scoffs, but I plough on. 'Who do you think so quickly and conveniently marked you all as dead on the scene or unaccounted for, except me? The only one of us with a ready recommendation for a place at the House. We thought having the record show you died rather than escaped was to save bureaucratic face, but what if it was to throw them off your scent? So you—all of you—could continue what you're doing here.'

She watches me take the last few steps to her, and I'm struck by the feeling I'm approaching something – someone – almost wild. Someone so used to running on hair triggers to keep those she loves safe, it's perhaps become almost impossible for her to think any other way.

'And he was going to conveniently get us all out of Vana again?' she asks, the bite in her tone sharp.

I don't answer. The truth is, I don't know how he would have got everyone out again. But if he had enough Hunters prepared to follow his lead to get them in there, surely he could get them out had we not orchestrated it. Right now, though, that's not the issue.

'I know what it will cost if I'm wrong,' I whisper. Her eyes flash. 'I know I haven't always gotten it right. But I'm right now, Cortane, I know I am.'

'Do you?' she asks, but her tone has lost some of its edge. 'You love him, I know,' she says with a sigh and a vague gesture to Quillian, but we both know she's no longer talking about Traelen. 'But imagine you've fought alongside River and Nix since you were a child—literally. No playing. No pretend. No imagining a battle. But knowing, with every breath, that you either saved them or killed for them, or they were the next ones you'd lose. Imagine having that. Doing that. *Being* that. And then being asked to trust the man that put them in one of the worst places imaginable. *I* went there, Luka. I know what happens there. I went there to keep them out.' Her breath shudders, as if she's tearing the words from her chest. 'We've been in a hell every day of our lives so far. I do not intend for them to spend the rest of it in another. If we lose this fight, we die. It's as simple as that.'

For a moment, I can see the little girl she could have been. Wild, of that I'm sure. Pale blonde hair cut just below her ears, clear eyes missing nothing. I can imagine what she would have looked like playing. Laughing. And my heart aches for her that she never had that.

'Hear what he has to say,' I plead gently, 'and then you decide if he stays or goes. But you can't kill him, Cort. I understand what you're saying, but he can't die.'

Stillness occupies Cortane's entire body, but, behind it, she seems to pulse with an energy she's almost physically restraining. It's obvious bringing Traelen here goes against all her instincts. At the same time, she's trying to have faith in me, or in Quillian's faith in me, and a little bit of gratitude for that seeps into my skin.

The force of her attention on me thickens my throat, but I refuse to look away. I need to hear her say it – Traelen won't die.

She levels me with a look overflowing with contradictory energies.

'I give you a short-term pass on Traelen. I won't shoot on sight.'

The inhale I suck deep into my lungs is audible.

'But,' she continues, 'you do not get the same for Emeris.'

CHAPTER TWENTY-EIGHT

Quietly, we file into the courtyard to stand in front of Cortane's portal. The silence is thick, and my hands start to shake a little. My heart hurts for Cortane, but that glimpse into who she is underneath hasn't completely eased my worry she might kill Traelen on sight.

Just Emeris, I think, my stomach turning. My mind crowds with thoughts on that, but they're so loud I can't make sense of them. Right now, I need to make sure I'm focused on how she responds to Traelen – he's too vital to lose. Emeris ... he's proven the danger he poses.

There's a steady rhythm in my chest that tells me bringing Traelen here was the right thing to do. Quillian, Finn and Cortane started this fight a long, long time ago, but it's now clear they can't win without help. And I've brought them my father, Rosie, and now Traelen, to sway the odds in their favour. It's a shift, an alliance, that might make them a bit wary, but they weren't in that meeting as the Hunters tried to pick them off, while the committee members had morning tea.

As my father said, this is a fight that won't be won in a skirmish, no matter how many they have. It's a fight that needs to go straight into the heart of the government.

And it's a fight I want to be over.

Quillian's confession about 'our' cabin is like my secret balm, his vision of it so clear. I ache to give it to us, though I can't imagine where that would be right now. Perhaps Tae, if he is so revered here they call him Prince. But it won't be Klades. My townhouse will have to go, if they don't strip it from me and freeze my accounts first. If they do, I will have no money, no assets, nothing to help us start a new life—

For a beat, I wish I could disappear there now. Have Traelen and Teddy be okay, not have to face Emeris's betrayal—

'Hey,' Blossom says a moment before drawing me into a hard hug. I grip her hard, my eyes burning at her sudden appearance. 'You've been making waves for someone who was worried about having no impact,' she jokes into my hair, likely not realising she's just told me how much she's talking with River.

'If I'm wrong about any of this, those waves might drown me. Are you okay?'

'Yeah,' she says, pulling back and glancing around quickly, her gaze landing on River. 'But Traelen?' she whispers.

'I know. But I trust him.' Coming out as a traitor will be a huge step for Traelen who has been fighting on his own. I'm not even sure he planned to tell anyone else except me. I can only assume the disappearance of Teddy forced his hand.

No government, new or otherwise, is likely to take in someone who spilled secrets. No matter how important it is that those secrets be shared, and I'm sure that truth won't be lost on Traelen. Unless he were to completely chance it on his own, he will never work in politics again – and I don't know how he will feel about that.

'He's invested in helping us,' I say, giving her hand a squeeze in a way I hope conveys that I'm not keeping her out.

She nods and looks towards the portal as Traelen steps out.

For a moment, I'm taken straight back to the prison. When he'd arrive in the announcement hall, all cool and crisp with his gold hair and pale suits – the picture of icy containment. At the time, I thought it was because he thought the concierges were beneath him.

Now, I wonder if it was a coping mechanism, a way of operating that helped him rise to his position in the House undetected.

He takes in the group before him and immediately raises his hands to show he's unarmed, but shows no surprise at who he finds here.

'Traelen,' I say, and his gaze catches, and holds, mine. 'Thank you for coming—put those down,' I say, indicating his arms. 'There's ... at least a temporary truce here.'

I don't look at Cortane. Instead, I watch his shoulders inch a little away from his ears as he slowly lowers his arms, looking over my left shoulder.

To where I know Quillian is standing.

Quillian brushes a hand down my shoulder blade as he steps up to Traelen.

'This is not where I expected to see you again,' Quillian says by way of greeting.

Traelen gives half a smile, but it's clear to me that he is still churning with worry about Teddy.

'I knew you were involved when you were appointed,' he says, 'but coming face to face with the Rebel Prince himself did surprise me.'

'As did my abrupt ... invitation to Vana,' Quillian says coolly.

'Stepping in to arrest a decorated war hero turned Warden of the Defence Committee's favourite prison on the eve of a full-scale investigation was ... a challenge and a risk,' Traelen confirms, 'but a calculated one. Having you in plain sight of a full cohort of Hunters wasn't acceptable.' Traelen straightens further, gaze firmly on Quillian as he ducks his chin, just a little. 'I feel a deep obligation for keeping your identity safe for as long as possible, as do a number of people I care about—my family and I voted for our village to join your cause, Prince of Tae.'

Quillian's brows shoot to his hairline but, darting my focus to Cortane, I find her mouth dropped open a fraction before she crosses her arms over her chest.

'Well,' she says, 'I'll be fucking damned.'

The band around my chest loosens as Quillian shakes his head in disbelief and holds out a hand for Traelen to shake.

'Welcome to camp one,' he says, the shock still etched on his face.

We end up at the house Blossom and I are sharing here instead of the meeting hall again. Nix, River, Finn, Cortane, and Holland line the space, standing practically shoulder to shoulder – a wall of traitorous muscle. My father, Rosie, Blossom, Traelen, Quillian, and I take the couches. It's a bit overcrowded with everyone in here, but it keeps us out of the way as the camp is evacuated. They are prioritising the injured and families first, so, for now, we remain despite knowing our location is compromised.

With the introductions and greetings over, there is a long discussion about where exactly in Tae Traelen is from, and working through the connections to Quillian's village, followed by a similar conversation between Traelen, Rosie, and my dad. Though, establishing where they had come across each other before in their different lines of work and interactions in the House over their respective careers quickly becomes difficult to follow. Then, we all look at each other.

'Where should we start?' I ask.

My father waits a beat before responding. 'I suggest we talk about where we want to finish, and work back from there.'

A cabin in the middle of nowhere flashes in my mind.

With regular visits with Blossom.

And, of course, Quillian. One look at his face tells me he's warring within himself between his future, and everyone else's.

The room is silent. What I thought was a straightforward suggestion from my father has the group either unprepared to share what they want, or unable to find the words.

I hear Traelen draw breath before he speaks. 'I want to find the Prime Minister.'

Given how Traelen was able to so quickly establish his credibility with the traitors after coming through the portal, I now feel bad I didn't share this piece of information with them.

'Wait, what?' River asks. 'What do you mean, *find* him?'

'He means he lost him,' Cortane chimes in. 'Surely that's hardly a loss.'

Traelen pins her with a cold stare. 'The Prime Minister has nothing to do with the rot that's taken hold in government—he is a victim of trying to stand against it as much as the rest of us.'

I let that settle for a moment, the supreme confidence – arrogance – in Zenaton's face when I met him in that hallway burning in my mind. The man who is now acting Prime Minister.

My father nods. 'So reinstate the Prime Minister, should he prove innocent and willing. I will add that we need to expel the militant approach that has held our government in its grip for so long. It's time to find different solutions to the Tae-Coprath conflict and Nuntainia's covert involvement. Anything else?'

'The breeding program,' Nix says, voice low. 'It needs to be ended. Completely. And I think people should know what's been happening. The victims are going to need a fuck load of support if they get out.'

Blossom looks softly at Nix, a look so different to when they first met. 'I agree.'

'The crimes of those who have been through the prison program should also be known,' I say, my mind going to the families of the children Kasera held captive. 'I know we're already working towards that, but anyone directly impacted by their actions should be compensated.'

'Compensation takes time,' Rosie says, 'but I agree, when we're through the heat of it all, this needs to be included in the plans to deal with in the aftermath.'

River clears his throat. 'I want to know what the aftermath looks like for us.'

A dull ache expands in my chest. He has so much to give, having it all come to a crashing halt once we go public would—

'I want us all to live,' I say, looking at my dad and painfully hoping he and Rosie can help us with a strategy that achieves that. 'And live freely,' I add, thinking of Vana.

Dad gives everyone a moment, waits to see if anything else is added. 'I'd suggest that's key to our approach—no self-sabotage or sacrifice.' This last part seems to be directed at Quillian, who sits next to me on the couch, and I couldn't agree more.

He shifts his hand to rest on my thigh.

'We live freely,' he says, and my cheeks heat.

My stomach turns over, the lists of potential survivors burning in my mind. How free are any of them? 'I want to search for survivors in Tae.'

Nix's gaze slides to mine, but he says nothing.

Dad blows out a breath. 'It's a solid list,' he says without jest. 'And you can see how much comes after we go public. That—and everyone remaining onboard with the 'living' option—will determine exactly how we approach getting the information out there.'

'I think we also need to be clear with people – citizens – what has happened and how,' I add. 'This situation can never be repeated, and we're going to need the people of Nuntainia to understand that.'

Blossom nods. 'To really do that, we'd need to give them another choice. The government has served for a long, long time. You'd have to give them confidence in what else they could vote for.'

A little flurry of tingles starts in my limbs as I look around the room. At this group filled with soldiers and academics and politically minded people and a journalist. A combination of people that have witnessed all of this corruption through a different lens. Experiences and learnings that, when shared, will add up to the most robust representation of what we're fighting for as we could have hoped. Taking us all in, I imagine just how it might feel to be on the other side – when we are liberating and compensating and *living* – and a small smile dances at the corner of my mouth.

Dad runs his palms down his thighs. 'This sounds like the moment you've been waiting for, Quillian?' There's a lightness in his voice that mirrors the little sliver of excitement in my chest.

Quillian turns to me, his fingers pressing into my thigh with a reassuring grip. 'Yeah,' he breathes. 'This is the moment.'

The room stills, as if readying itself for a collective inhale—

'I have a different view,' Traelen says, and looks between Quillian and me. 'Luka has probably told you how close they are to figuring out exactly who you are, despite my misdirection with the records from the fire. From there, it's not a long leap to work out who is with you, to track your career and your history. Not to mention, they have the list of camps, so it's only a matter of time through a simple process of elimination alone.'

'They were always going to find me eventually,' Quillian says. 'This way, we get to control the narrative.'

'Yes, but right now, Zenaton thinks he has the upper hand and he's letting himself enjoy it. Your going public will bruise his ego, so he'll ensure their efforts to find you will double, if not triple, what they are already. If you're lucky, you'll get one piece of information out before they find you. No matter how truthful or revealing, that will barely create a ripple in Nuntainia, let alone a wave. By contrast, they get their hands on you, and the whole of Tae will suffer. They will have nothing to rally behind, no hope. No.' Traelen shakes his head. 'It can't be you—not yet. Your personal safety is too tenuous right now if we want ourselves—and the citizens of Tae—to survive the fallout.'

Quillian looks like he's about to object, but when I turn to Cortane she's giving him a warning look that tells me she agrees with Traelen. Finn also gives Quillian a single shake of his head. Clearly, he agrees as well.

'Luka?' Quillian asks me quietly.

'I want you to live,' I whisper, and he closes his eyes gently and nods.

But the room is now silent. Clearly they haven't a solution either.

I sit back in the couch, slumping a little into the cushions and Quillian's side. It's almost like we've been silenced before even attempting to speak. The nagging feeling I had when I read articles about Aiten Gall returns to me. The knowledge that there didn't seem to be a single note from one of the affected women or their families. Like they never existed. Never had a chance to have their voices heard. Did they try, only to be met with ... nothing?

A small but incessant burn starts low in my belly, fanning up behind my breastbone.

'I can do it,' I say. 'I worked in the prison for five years, I've served in the House, and I'm the daughter of Nuntainia's most prominent magic historian and social policy expert.' I meet my father's eyes. 'I'll do it.'

Dad's chest rises and falls as he breathes deeply, a sign I know he's digesting a piece of information.

'Ah—' Nix starts, 'exactly what will that mean? We can't save Quillian just to lose Luka.'

Quillian gives him a lethal stare that seems to say 'no shit'.

Rosie clears her throat. 'Most likely, it will mean Luka is subjected to a smear campaign in an attempt to discredit her.' She turns and speaks directly to me. 'It would be messy and ugly, and it would invade every part of your life—if we can keep pushing—and you will often wonder if you did the right thing.'

I swallow, staring at Rosie, willing her to have a better outcome to offer.

'But,' she continues, although I don't let relief in yet, 'we can be persistent and get ahead of them with exclusives and interviews that air time and time again before they can start any slander. Use the channels that target women audiences, wives and mothers, parents, and also students, young people. They're not the only ones affected, of course, but they are more likely to be sympathetic, which will help to quickly build the swell of support.'

When she's finished, I ask, 'Dad?'

He rubs his forehead, brows furrowed. 'Rosie is right about the smear campaign and—no matter how well you've lived—they'll find something to twist or just make something up,' he says. 'It will hurt, and I don't want that for you. At the same time ... we need the Nuntainian public—not only to understand, but to inspire them to take action. We need to empower people, not just overwhelm them with awfulness they can't do anything about. I just—' He cuts himself off, the logical academic at war with the protective father in his expression.

The burning in my gut starts to take shape, its edges becoming clear, and I understand *this* is what I am supposed to do – use my naivety, my trust, my willingness to serve my country. What once made me an upstanding citizen of Nuntainia will no longer serve as something I feel a sense of guilt about, but as the vehicle to show other people they can have the same journey. That it's okay to open your eyes later than you may have liked, as long as you open them and face what you see.

'I understand,' I say. 'And I'm doing it.'

The room quietly erupts into multiple conversations. My father and Rosie as she tries to comfort him that she will guide me through as best she can; Nix, River, and Blossom softly asking if any one of them could do it instead; and Cortane and Finn discussing Quillian's safety and what they need to change in light of Traelen's news.

'Are you sure about this?' Traelen asks me, Quillian still at my side.

'I'm not,' Quillian says. 'I didn't bring her into this to be torn apart by people who have no idea what's happening, sending comments and spreading lies from the comfort of their homes.' His voice is level, but the anger is clear behind it.

'No,' Traelen says, 'I can see that and, unfortunately, Zenaton is very aware of the link between you. But I think this is the best compromise. If you're sure, Luka? You know Zenaton will make this very personal.'

I blow out a breath. Even hearing his name sends a shudder through me. 'I know,' I say. 'But he tried to kill me, and he took Teddy to prove how easily he could have come for me again ... it's already personal.'

Rosie and my dad turn towards us, joining our conversation wherever theirs has ended, and she nods at the last of what I said.

'It needs to be you, Luka,' Rosie says. 'We have a shot at positioning you well in front of the media—you're passionate about the cause, you've been in key positions to access information, and you're not the leader. As a Nuntainian citizen, you're also less likely to be executed, should you be captured.' My heart drops into my stomach. 'But there's not a chance they will let the Rebel Prince live should they get their hands on him.' She gives him a long look, which Quillian returns with a steely glare. 'Quillian—if you want to live, the Rebel Prince needs to take a back seat on this one.'

'I'm sorry about Emeris,' Quillian says when everyone has dissipated from the house and we're lying in bed. 'I know he was your friend.'

I nod gently, my head on the pillow, wishing it didn't hurt so much. 'I don't really want to think about how to manage that right now, is that awful?'

He takes my fingers and kisses them. 'One thing at a time,' he says. 'It won't be different in the morning.'

'Tell me about the cabin,' I tell him, gladly taking the opportunity to put at least one difficult thing aside, just for tonight.

The night is more than half over, and it feels like the world is at rest. It also feels like that rest is going to be short, even beyond the morning that's coming.

It needs to be you, Luka.

I roll into Quillian's naked side and tuck myself against his chest, his hand automatically curling around my body and fingers gently stroking my ribs.

He closes his eyes and smiles towards the ceiling as if he's really seeing it. 'There is nothing but space, green grass, trees, the blue sky, and us in the middle of it. Nothing but the freedom to make our own choices.'

'Oh, so there isn't actually a cottage?'

He laughs. 'There is ... somewhere. But mostly I think about the space, and the freedom, and having you there. I just assumed there'd be some sort of dwelling, I guess.'

'Hmmm,' I sound, running my hand over his torso, skimming the sides of his tattoo. 'Whatever would we do with so much space and freedom?'

He turns to face me, our bodies flush under the cool sheet, and I wrap my hand around the back of his neck. Dropping his head to my ear, he takes the lobe gently in his teeth before softly kissing the most fragile part of my neck.

'Well ...' he says in a whisper, 'in my version, you—we—get to do whatever we like. No government to answer to, no duty or service, no people dying on our watch.' His breath gets deeper. 'And I'd take every possible opportunity to explore you, take advantage of every moment we have together, make it ours.' He runs the flat of his palm down my back and cups my ass before dragging my leg over his hip and trailing his fingers gently between my ass cheeks.

My brows shoot up at the same time as a liquid heat races between my legs.

'Oh?' is the only response I can muster.

'You'd say that with a different intonation, but, yes, "oh",' he says between kisses over my collarbones, as his fingers slip lower between my legs and softly stroke my centre.

I press my hips into him, lifting my knee to give him more space and bite back a moan as his fingers slip inside, just a fraction. Slowly, he teases my entrance, running the pads of his fingers between my lips and upwards, teasing my clit.

'What does it look like in your version?' he asks, breath in my hair.

I grapple for words as my body starts to throb. What would I want it to be? I gasp as he applies a little more pressure.

'Well, Luka?'

'I'd make us memories,' my voice is almost all air. 'So many fun, playful memories we won't know what to do with them all.'

'Like this one?'

I shake my head where it rests on his chest. 'No, this is ... a different kind of memory.'

He makes a guttural sound in the back of his throat as he drags his fingers between my legs.

'Is all that wetness for me?' he asks against my ear. A shiver runs down my spine as I pull his head to mine and kiss him deeply.

'I want to hear you say it, Luka,' he says, lips moving against mine.

'Yes,' I breathe, 'it's all for you.'

He sucks my bottom lip into his mouth and sinks his teeth into my flesh, gradually building the speed of his fingers on the hot centre of my body.

'Always only for me?' he asks, releasing my mouth lazily.

I bear down on his hand, pressing his fingers further into my entrance on their downward stroke, gasping as they start to stretch me. The anticipation of feeling him deep inside me building a heat that expands out to my hips and into my lower belly.

'You know that already,' I say, starting to pant, grinding myself against his hard abdomen, but doing so means I lose his fingers and I whimper into his mouth.

'Say it,' he repeats.

'Only you,' I say, my voice ragged.

He notches his cock at my entrance, cupping my face in his hands.

'Open your eyes, Luka,' he whispers, piercing me with his dark green ones when I do. 'You're it for me. Only you for me.'

I take a second, before I let the feel of him consume me, for his words to sink in. And I smile, my whole body flushing with the warm surety that Quillian is mine, and I'm his, and we will never let each other go.

He curses as he sheaths himself in one, strong thrust, burying himself in me and I cry out. We move together, Quillian's fingers digging into my thigh as he pulls me against him to take him deeper and deeper, and I give it all up. Any semblance of control, all my worries about never finding my purpose or my person, and I pour it all into Quillian. Because, if I have learned anything since I met him, it's that life is too short not to.

As he drags me over the edge so fast I feel like I'm diving from the island once more, he gives me everything, too.

This is what I want. This expanding sense of fulfilment – contentment – that's bursting behind my rib cage. This tingling sense of warmth that's running through my veins and out my fingertips. This person who gives me all the choices.

But as I listen to his breathing settle, tucked back into his side where I can feel the ridges of his scars, I can't help but feel like it's all going to be ripped away.

It needs to be you, Luka.

Me.

The one who needs to speak up, who becomes the face of the call for justice.

CHAPTER TWENTY-NINE

Blossom grips me hard when I emerge downstairs, Quillian having left earlier for meetings with Cortane and Finn.

'I've missed you,' she says. 'It's not the same without you.'

I smile at her. My own heart feels lighter in her presence, but there's still a painful shadow. 'Well, I'll be here for a while now. If they haven't by now, the committee is about to identify Quillian. Once that happens, it will only be a matter of time before they link the rest of us. Zenaton already knows I am very involved.'

Blossom takes my hand where we sit side by side on the couch, her hot drink in her other hand. 'I still don't regret it,' she says. 'Not now you're away from that asshole who should have stayed dead.'

Closing my eyes against the knot that's growing behind my ribs, I try to push away how acute my regret will be if any of us get caught. What it means now that Emeris has been caught in a different way.

'I don't regret jumping,' I say, bracing myself. 'But I do wish—did you know Emeris is the leak? He gave the camp locations that informed the raids?'

She sucks her teeth and blinks like she's holding back tears. 'River told me,' she whispers. 'I just ... I can't believe it.'

I press my head back on the couch and look at the paint peeling on the ceiling. 'We can't take the risk he shares anything else and ... others will need to know how seriously this kind of thing is taken,' I say, unable to voice the fact he's going to be executed.

Blossom stays silent, and I can barely believe the words that are coming from my mouth – about *Emeris.*

'What if he—'

'Could you ever trust him again, Bloss? You literally helped save the people that could be saved from those attacks. Could you entrust all those lives to him again? Our lives to him?'

She presses her other hand to her mouth and shakes her head.

'I need to see him,' I say, my tongue thick in my mouth. 'Do you want to come? I've texted Nix.'

She shakes her head again, and we sit in the silence, gently holding space for each other.

'Do we have a plan for when they formally identify Quillian?' she asks a long time later.

I sigh. 'No. The plan is that we can expose Zenaton and those who follow him before that.'

She nods again.

'How is your magic feeling?' I ask, not wanting to colour this one exciting thing for her with what I now know about mine.

Her deep, teal eyes sparkle when she looks at me.

'Amazing. I feel like ... my chest is full of Koko's crackling chocolates.' She laughs. 'Okay, that's a terrible way to explain it—but it's good. River's been helping me learn the nuances of it. Much of the basic healing comes naturally - some innate ability to use what I've got, I think. But there is so much to learn about the human body and, without that, I don't always know what to do. River's knowledge is ... incredible, actually.'

Her cheeks flush softly in the lamplight coming from the side table, and I decide I've been quiet on the idea of her and River long enough.

'Anything else you want to talk about on that front?'

'Healing?'

I lift a brow at her. 'River.'

The rose pink on her cheeks quickly turns to crimson, and I wait.

'Nothing's happened,' she says quietly, 'if that's what you mean. But ...'

'But ...' I prompt, 'could he have anything to do with the chocolate crackles in your chest?'

She ducks her head into her hands, but I can see the smile crinkling into her cheeks.

'Maybe,' she confesses, gently lifting her head again and resting it on the back of the couch. 'He's so patient, Lu, and I ... think I want to go there but ... I feel so conflicted. I–I made a vow, Lu. Like we did here. A promise I meant to last forever.'

I let that sentiment sit for a while. Intellectually, I get it, but I haven't had my heart broken in the same way she has.

'Bloss ... was there anything in those vows that asked you not to be happy?'

'Well, no, of course not, but I was supposed to be happy with Frank.'

'And you were.'

Her eyes line with tears. 'I was.'

'That happiness won't disappear if you explore something with River. But ... perhaps you have an opportunity to have another sort of happiness live alongside it.'

She turns her head to me, her brown curls swishing a little. 'Do you think so?'

'Yeah, I do. I didn't know Frank, so I can't speak for him, but I just can't imagine anyone deserving of your love who wouldn't want you to be happy.'

'Thank you,' she says, squeezing my hand and clearing her throat. 'Anyway, what about you? Any magic coming in?'

I purse my lips as I wait for the lingering sense of disappointment. It comes like stale breath in the back of my throat – not pleasant, but something I know will pass. Something I can get rid of. I'd be lying to say it didn't impact me at all. I've spent my whole life researching, wondering what I would manifest, and watching the people I love growing so completely into themselves. Now, though, I find my focus has shifted, and my purpose has become clear. One that doesn't need magic.

'No, nothing,' I say, turning to look at her. 'But I know why now, and I also know for certain it won't come.'

Blossom frowns as she draws her mug to her mouth with both hands and takes a sip. 'What do you mean?'

'It's kind of a long story, and I assume you will need to go back to the infirmary?'

She nods and I let out a breath.

'Okay, so, short version: there was a fairly strong possibility I'd be Karaylia given my genetics and, because of this breeding program that's been around since I was young, my dad used his research to ensure I'd never manifest. His position was it was better to have me be magicless and safe, than have magic and risk being taken for the program.'

I let the silence fall between us as Blossom stares at me over her gently steaming mug, mouth dropped open. Blossom loves me enough for me to know this will be a shock that she will also need to work through a little. Particularly around how she can support me.

'I'm okay,' I say, placing a hand on her thigh. 'Truly. It was a shock but, honestly, there have been other things to focus on. And I feel good about where we landed last night. What I'm going to do and how I can contribute.'

She lowers her mug towards her lap. 'It's not that you don't have magic. It's ... that it was taken from you.'

'Yep,' I agree, popping the 'p'.

'I also can't imagine what it would be like for a parent to have to make that decision.'

A beat of pain cuts into my chest at the truth in words – I don't either. I hope I never know.

She cocks her head a little. 'You know, though ... Karaylia would have made sense given how you leapt off that island.' She gives me a little smile and I laugh.

'I can definitely think of times it would have come in handy.'

A sharp knock at the door accompanies Nix's voice before he strides down the hallway.

'Do you know,' I say by way of greeting when his broad form appears in the living space, 'I'm struggling to recall any occasions you've knocked before.'

He runs a hand up the back of his neck and pulls a face. 'Yeah, well, with the situation with you and Quillian, one can never be too careful.'

I laugh as Bloss stands from the couch and takes her mug to the kitchen, Nix immediately sliding into her spot.

'Okay,' she says, turning back to us, 'I'm off, River is expecting me.'

'You know River is completely gone for Bloss, don't you?' Nix whispers.

I glance up at him, his champagne eyes tinged in sadness.

'They'd be so good for each other,' I whisper back.

Her eyes narrow when she sees us talking as she comes back around the short bench.

'What are you two talking about?'

'That you should stop messing around with my brother and come out and tell him you love him already,' Nix says.

I choke, sitting upright. 'Shit, Nix, you can't say that.'

'Pretty sure he just did,' Bloss says, her whole face and neck a little flushed. There's a hint of amusement in the sparkle of her ocean-coloured eyes, but a bite in her tone. A contrast that probably reflects how she's feeling about her husband and River. 'And I will pay you no more attention on matters that don't concern you, Nix Kilroy.'

'You're wrong, though,' he says, 'it does concern me, and you know it.'

She sighs. 'I know, and you're right. But I just—not today, Nix, okay?'

Nix purses his lips a little but nods, and I give Bloss a small smile in farewell, watching her leave, wondering if she's aware of what she just confessed.

Beside me, Nix glances down at his phone, his demeanour changing immediately, all rough edges returning. 'If you want to see Emeris, then we had better go now.'

They're holding Emeris on the far side of the camp, away from the meeting hall. I haven't ventured this far across the camp before, and the unfamiliarity smacks at me as Nix leads me onward.

The building where I will see Emeris for what I know will be the last time looks almost like a repurposed barn. Traitors line each of the walls that I can see, staggered at intervals along the space. My skin prickles. I know Emeris isn't a physical threat to anyone here, so I can only assume this level of security is standard for where I am about to enter. Too bad they can't protect me from how any of this is going to feel.

I rub the heel of my hand into my sternum, willing the sharp pain there to abate.

The two armed women on either side of the door give Nix a nod as we approach, subtly standing aside.

'Sure you want to do this?' Nix asks quietly as we take the last few steps. 'This will be ...'

'Not something I can come back from, I know,' I say, knowing my words sound empty. I have no idea how I'm going to cope with seeing my friend face to face, knowing he is both the reason so many people are dead, and that he, too, is going to die.

What could he have been thinking? Do I really want to know?

Nix sighs heavily, coming to a stop at the large, sliding door and turning to me.

'We're a long way from tree climbing in Klades.'

The weight of that acknowledgement is clear in his posture. It's not an admonishment of me, nor an indication that he doesn't think I can do this, but almost a wish our lives hadn't come to this.

I cup his slightly bristly face, stinging tears pooling in my eyes. 'At least we're in it together,' I say just as quietly. 'And we're going to leave the world a better place.'

He nods against my palm, and I swallow against the unspoken words that hang in the air. The ones that sound a lot like 'leave the world a better place, or die trying'.

He pulls away and slides the door open, revealing a long walkway down the middle that's dotted with doors on either side.

Janly stands with her back to the third door on the right, staring at the high ceiling. She turns and watches us approach, but doesn't say anything. When she's within reach, I pull her into a hard embrace. We stay like that, silently, for what feels like a long, in-between moment. Like we both know what will come when we part, and neither of us know if we're strong enough to face it.

I pull away first. 'Have you seen him?' I ask.

She nods, quietly. Heavily. 'I've tried to understand his reasoning,' she says, her voice thick, like she's spent a long time crying or a long time not talking. 'Claudius and I, we—' she shakes her head with a grim smile. 'I guess we just didn't get this one right, or I lost him after Claudius. But it's a hard lesson.'

I take her hand in mine. 'It's not your fault, Jan,' I say, with a squeeze to her fingers that mimics the one in my chest. 'I brought him here, too. I vouched for him to the others. I was wrong, too.'

Gentle tears fall over the apples of her cheeks as she looks at me.

'I know you love him,' I whisper, tears now blurring my vision too.

She gives a rueful huff of a laugh. 'He's as close to a son as I've got.'

I have to cover my mouth with my hand and bite back a sob. 'I'm so sorry, Jan. We can talk to—'

Janly shakes her head, her short brown hair moving along her jawline. 'No,' she sniffs. 'You know as well as I do we only have one way forward. There can't be rules for us and rules for everyone else. Emeris didn't make a mistake. He knowingly endangered hundreds of people, put targets on all of our backs, and so many of us paid the ultimate price for that.'

I blow out a breath. 'Even loving him as you do, you think he should pay with his life?'

'Don't you?'

My chest seizes. Do I? I came in here knowing I was saying goodbye but, now that I am feet away from doing so, is it really what I think is right? Do I not even want to *try* to push the others on it?

The images from watching the confrontation from the House are etched into my mind so deep I know their paths by heart, and I wasn't even there. I didn't have to smell the death, the blood, or taste the fear.

But I knew, in that moment, I would choose my loved ones' lives over any of the Hunters Zenaton had sent there.

It's the same choice I'm making now.

I nod, and Janly closes her eyes and cries, head held in her hands as I watch.

Nix shifts beside me and clears his throat.

'Want me to go in with you?' he asks roughly.

'No.' I sniff and clear my throat. 'Stay with Janly.'

Emeris is lying on a single bed, curled into a ball when I enter. His clothes are dirtier than I know he would like them, but he looks well – physically, at least. There's colour in his skin, and he's got food and water on a table in the corner. There is a pile of books on a little shelf next to an armchair on the other side of the room, but it's the vest lying crumpled on the seat that makes me turn my attention to the books and count their spines as I compose myself.

'Hey,' I say, walking further into the room. 'Can I sit?'

'Sure,' he says almost automatically.

I run my tongue over my teeth as I sit, searching myself for words that seem appropriate in this moment. Instead, I grip the arms of the chair and focus on the fabric under my palms.

'Do you understand what's happening?' I ask.

Emeris pushes himself to sitting, legs over the edge of the bed and feet on the floor. He presses his hands into the mattress and leans forward a bit so he's facing the floor, dark hair going in the same direction.

'I do, yeah,' he says. 'Are you going to ask me why?'

I lace my fingers in my lap. 'Do you want to tell me?'

He rubs his face. 'I don't think it will make any difference.'

I let that sit for a moment. 'Do you think it should?'

He lifts his head and holds my gaze. I'm immediately taken back to the day in the Warden's office when we found Claudius. Pain and panic scored in Emeris's face.

'No,' he says finally. 'I don't. All the things that led me here ... despite them all, I value Janly and Claudius above all others. I want ... I want to accept this fate for them.'

It's my turn to cover my face with my hands, but I bite my tongue – hard – forcing myself not to cry, until I've got a tiny grasp of control, and lower my hands again.

'I really wish you hadn't put us here,' I whisper. 'I wish we could take it back.'

He nods, gaze returned to the floor again. 'Me too. I thought there'd be arrests, but ... they came in hard.'

I can only stare at the top of his head. Part of me yearns to give him comfort, but it's small compared to the part that rages at him for making such a horrible decision. One that none of us, living or dead, haven't felt the ramifications of.

Staring at my friend who may as well have murdered innocent people with his own hands creates a void that burns around the edges.

'I think I need to know,' I say quietly. 'Why are we here?' My voice is thick and my nose burns, but I refuse to look away.

The soft sound of his exhale fills the room. 'I've been thinking about that a lot and ... I now understand Claudius dying was a crossroads for me. One I was lucky to have been presented.'

I frown. 'How so?'

'Because it saved me from becoming like you.'

I pull back, unable to comprehend what he's saying.

'But you loved Claudius,' I say, 'you just said—'

'I did. I do. But it doesn't mean he was right. Claudius opened my eyes to so many things, it's true. But then, I had my eyes opened to him, too, the dangerous potential of what he was starting. He told me people were coming. I thought they were going to help us—then I was cleaning up after dead bodies. Cleaning up his office after the new Warden was brawling with a prisoner, one you value above so many others.'

My mind spins back to the day Nix launched himself at Quillian after catching us in the hallway. The day I'd asked Emeris to clean up any disturbance.

'But—' I start.

'Mr Blake had told me what to look for,' he says, and my stomach sinks, filling with icy dread.

'Mr Blake?'

He nods. 'He's former military, I don't know his rank. But he helped me after I lost Claudius. Told me what to watch for and that I could help him make sure the rot didn't spread further. That I could help Nuntainia hold the line.'

Slowly, he raises his head and searches my face.

'I can help you, Luka,' he whispers. 'I can put you in touch with Mr Blake and you don't have to live this life anymore.'

Mutely, I shake my head. 'Emeris—'

He smiles sadly. 'I can see I don't have time to change your mind,' he says. 'I'm sorry I didn't try harder to save you.'

I'm not sure how to respond, the wrongness of it—

'I'm not going to ask you to try to stop it,' he says quietly. 'But will you come?'

My face crumples. Hot tears spilling from between my lashes as the gap between the Emeris I thought I knew and the one sitting before me creates a burning fissure in my chest not even River could mend. One I should have seen coming. Should have protected him from creating.

'I'll come,' I choke out.

CHAPTER THIRTY

Quillian, Cortane and Finn are talking with a small crowd of traitors, including Holland, on the edge of the field that runs behind the camp as Nix, Janly, Emeris, and I arrive.

Cortane sees us approach and holds up a hand to halt us before we're in earshot of what they're discussing. My whole body feels like it's vibrating as we wait for her.

'Luka,' she says, without looking at anyone else, 'a word.'

I glance at Nix as I follow Cortane off to the side, but nothing about her frightens me anymore.

'You don't want to be here for this,' she says.

I frown at her. Is that concern? *Now?*

'Thank you,' I say hesitantly. 'But I'm going to stay.'

She glances over her shoulder to where Quillian and Finn are addressing the group, their backs to us.

'Princess, I really think you should reconsider. He was your friend.'

'Which is why I'm staying, Cortane. Please,' I say, 'let's just do this.'

I don't want to watch her kill Emeris – or anyone. But I understand why we're here, what has to be done.

She mutters under her breath and glares at Nix. 'Over to you,' she says, gripping Emeris by the elbow and dragging him off towards the main group.

Nix steps in front of me, blocking my path, hands on my shoulders. I peer around him to see Emeris almost at the group, a small gun in the back of Quillian's pants.

'Lu, let's go back,' he insists, pulling me back so he fills my line of sight. 'Jan doesn't need to be here for this, either.'

'Nix,' I snap. 'I told Emeris I'd be here, I'm fucking staying. I know what she's going to—'

I cut myself off as I finally understand.

It's not Emeris dying they're worried about me seeing.

It's that it's not Cortane who will be seeing it through.

My lips tremble and I roll them in.

'I can do this, Nix. I made a vow—multiple vows. I can do this.'

Closing his eyes in regret, Nix lets his hands slide down my shoulders and moves to stand beside me.

'I'm going to be right here, okay?'

Cortane guides Emeris to stand in front of the field, an inaudible conversation between them where Emeris shakes his head, and Cortane steps away. I reach out and take Janly's hand in my own. Over my shoulder, I see Bloss standing not far behind us, staring straight ahead, River several paces beyond her. Quillian takes the gun from his pants.

He lifts it to about shoulder height and aims straight at Emeris, who just stares at Janly, his hands clasped loosely before him. I can feel the tremors in my legs as I make myself stay rooted to the spot.

Memories of Emeris on the island assault me like blows. His smile. The way he danced. The late nights he would join Blossom and me for tea, then crash on our couch. His face the first time he had one of Koko's fizzing chocolate balls. That one time I made him laugh so hard he snorted his drink from his nose.

But those moments are no longer our reality.

My chest starts to crack and I no longer even try to hold back the tears. Despite the damage he's caused, the awful decision he made, the person he decided to trust, I still want him to know he was loved. Wherever he goes from here, maybe he will have a chance to make different choices.

Quillian's back deflates a little, like he's exhaled, and a crack splits the air.

The world is still.

Except for the tall grass. It sways gently, little drops of red blood sliding down the stems.

Emeris lies crumpled in the dust, a dark pool extending into the dirt around his head.

Janly squeezes my hand. 'Go well, my boy. Look after him, Claudius, my love,' she whispers, before releasing me and walking away.

Cortane approaches Quillian and says something that has him freezing in place. Slowly, he turns to face us, his warden's mask almost completely in place except for one fast flash in his eyes.

Cortane continues towards us, Blossom now taking the place Janly left at my side. A roll of nausea grips me as Quillian hands the gun to Finn, the other traitors around me fading into insignificance.

A breeze picks up, as if it could wipe away what's happened here.

But no bout of nature, however powerful she might be, can blow away the stain of an execution.

The silver hair of Cortane's short style is blurry before me as she gets right up close to Blossom and me. I always knew she was capable of killing people. But Quillian?

'Whatever you do from here,' Cortane says in a low voice, one I struggle to hear over the noise in my head. 'Be careful what you say. No one struggles with this more than him.' She pins me with a stare, and my shallow breaths are sucked from my lungs. 'Do *not* break him.'

Blinking at her is my only response.

'Fuck this up, and I kill you,' she says, before walking away.

Somewhere in the recesses of my mind, I wonder what happened to the semblance of understanding she and I had. But all I can see is Quillian's face.

The one with the mask still in place.

I remind myself he doesn't show that to me. Not when we're alone. Not when it's important.

But this *is* fucking important.

Emeris is dead. Emeris is ... *was* my friend. Emeris betrayed us.

Do not break him.

Fuck.

The enormity of what's happening here is dragging at my shoulders, as if my weight could drive me into the ground.

I look at Bloss, whose gaze is locked on Emeris. She slowly turns to me and we both move forward, hands still joined, towards Emeris. I ignore Quillian for the moment, focusing instead on the encroaching twilight and the messy way Emeris has fallen – something he would have despised. So, as I kneel in front of him, avoiding the pooling blood that makes my stomach churn, and gently close his eyes, I imagine him in his white concierge vest. Imagine the broad grin on his face that I will now never see again.

And I can't breathe beneath the knowledge of how much of this is my fault. The assumptions I made that brought him here. How I could have included him better, even as I was flailing to understand myself. Because, no matter the choices he has made since, the truth is Claudius and Jan had him and then ... I let him go. Without even knowing, I left him ripe for Zenaton to prey on.

Blossom and I sit with Emeris for a long time.

Long enough that night falls and someone starts a large fire to my right.

Nix says something to me about taking Bloss away, and I nod absently, dimly aware it was Nix and not River who took her.

I close my eyes. It seems the only response I have left. My friend is dead. But so are so many more because of his actions. My actions. All because I brought him here. Vouched for him.

Whatever else was happening in his life, he gave us up.

He gave me up, too.

In the end, it's Holland and Finn who sit with me the longest. One on either side. Until eventually, Holland runs a hand down my back.

'We're going to give him a farewell now, okay?' Holland asks and I nod, again, and watch him start to arrange Emeris's limbs.

'He didn't want you to see this part,' Finn says quietly, and I know he means Quillian. 'None of them did. But this is real. I'm sorry, Luka. This is what he does, so the rest of us don't have to.'

Maybe being the Rebel Prince isn't all it's cracked up to be. Once I am the face of all of this, will I have to be part of these decisions? Even more so than I already am? Who am I to decide if someone lives or dies? Isn't that what I did today – decide not to take up a fight for Emeris's life?

I watch, sitting alone in the dirt now, as Holland and Finn carry Emeris between them and throw him on the large fire, sparks flying in wild, high circles. The stench of burning flesh that fills the air is one I will never forget. But it dissipates after a while, leaving just the raging flames in its wake, and I wonder how they are covering the fire or if, somewhere, Hunters are marking its location.

The moon traverses the sky and the chill of night sets in, but the fire still burns.

And one figure watches, his dark silhouette framed by the slowly diminishing glow.

One I don't know exactly how to approach, but one that hasn't left me alone since Emeris was killed. Since he killed Emeris.

I drag myself from the ground, without bothering to brush the dust off my pants, and make my way to Quillian. I'm sure he's heard me, but he doesn't turn around. If he were to ask me if I was okay right now, I don't know how I'd respond. Emeris was my friend, he was trying to join us. But he gave us up. People died because of him. The Defence Committee will know Quillian's identity because of him. Because of me.

When I reach him, I wind my arms around his middle and drop my head between his shoulder blades.

Then I cry.

For long moments, Quillian remains still, hands in his pockets as I let my tears soak the back of his shirt. Part of me yearns for him to turn around, tell me it was a mistake. That I didn't see what I saw, and he can take it all away.

But we both know he won't lie. Not now. And I wouldn't accept it if he tried.

Another part of me recalls Nix's story of Quillian ordering them out, and leaving the civilians behind. Civilians I intend to find – if any survive. I wasn't able to fully comprehend it then, but the memory of Nix's anger towards Quillian is clear. Now, perhaps, I understand that a little better.

More than that though, more than the bubbling hurt and anger at Quillian's actions, is the pain that he was driven into this life at all. That I'm the reason he had to make that choice with Emeris – because I brought Emeris in.

I sniff, drawing my forehead away from his heat a little.

'Are you okay?' I ask, having no idea what I want the answer to be, but hoping with everything I have that he doesn't ask me the same thing.

As soon as the words leave my mouth, Quillian takes his hands from his pockets and runs them over my forearms that are still around his chest. As if he was waiting for me, giving me the time I needed before I addressed him. As if he knew looking and talking to him right now would be hard.

'I'm not sure how to answer that,' he says, his voice hollow. 'That was everything I wanted to keep from you, and knew I couldn't. The pinnacle of what I do, what I stand for, is who I protect. And I had to do it, despite knowing it will likely cost me you. That there is no world in which someone as good as you loves ... what I've become.'

He bows his head, drawing my hands up his chest to kiss my fingers. His gentleness such a jarring contrast to the executioner he also is.

'Just ...' his voice is a breaking whisper, and I feel like it's taking pieces of my heart with it, 'please don't make me watch you walk away.'

The people of Villy are not lives I really believe lie at his feet, not when he had a team to save. But Davorous. And Kasera, Miana, and Aiten – how many of those did he have a direct hand in? All those lives I thought Cortane, or Nix, maybe River, had taken – was allowed to believe they'd taken.

I know he's killed Hunters, too, but I was relieved about those because it meant it wasn't him, or anyone else I care about, losing their lives that day. And, while it initially sat uncomfortably, I was ... *pleased* about those on the island who didn't get away with atrocious things.

But this is ... this just hits so much closer to home and I don't know how to process it. There is no simplicity in the death of Emeris. He did a terrible thing, sharing that list, but I can only hope he thought he was doing something right. Something good. He *was* good. Not like those others. But maybe we're not all one thing?

'How many?' I ask, my lips brushing against his shirt.

His shoulders drop a little. 'Too many.'

'Is it always you?'

'The executing? Yes. I will never ask someone else to carry that burden.'

I think of Nix and River, and a rush of gratitude swims through me. At the same time, my stomach churns that I'm currently embracing an executioner. But then I think of Cortane's cold eyes.

'Why?'

He sighs. 'Because I led us here. Because so many people have followed me here, have given up any semblance of a normal life because they shared my vision for a better world. They fight enough beside me to never be the same, I won't ask them to take the lives of people we thought we could trust.'

I press my forehead into his back.

'You're not leaving.' He says it over his shoulder a little, I can feel the muscles in his chest and shoulders move as he turns his head.

The statement should surprise me. Once upon a time I would have run a long way from someone who murdered one of my friends. But, then, I would have gone straight to the Hunters. And, right now, despite knowing Holland and Casey, I know they are the last place that would be safe to go.

Where I feel safest, like I am *doing* something, is right here.

'I'm not leaving.'

Without breaking my hold on him, I shuffle around to his front, pushing myself underneath his arms and looking up into his face. His arms encircle me, but he remains looking over my head to the flames now warming my spine.

His Adam's apple bobs as he swallows, then slowly tips his chin to meet my gaze.

'I'm sorry,' he whispers, pain lancing through his green eyes that look so dark in the shadows of the fire.

And it's not just his words that seep through my skin, but the look on his face. The one that is so thoroughly Quillian; the one I get to see every night, and every morning, as if he puts armour over it during the day for everyone else.

'Me too,' I say, pain ripping deep in the crevices of my body. 'But I'm not leaving. Our forever isn't done yet.'

CHAPTER THIRTY-ONE

The weight of yesterday, of Emeris's death, hangs on me like a fever. A sickness making its way into my bones. Neither Quillian nor I slept last night but, at some point, there wasn't anything more we could say. So we lay, tangled in each other, listening to our breaths.

Bloss moves slowly around the small, beige kitchen, a jarring reminder of how far we've come since the days she would prepare our tipples. Then, I would have been preparing to serve the prisoners. Today, I'll be helping to prepare an article that will expose them all and, hopefully, tip the scales in our favour.

My phone buzzes with a message from River.

R: We'll have a celebration for those who have fallen tonight, can you let B know too?

I frown, wondering why he wouldn't tell her himself, and remembering the distance between them last night.

'Do you really love River?' I ask, and her shoulders tighten.

She closes her eyes briefly and groans. 'I think so, and I did *not* intend to blurt it out to Nix. I just—you haven't been here, and I didn't want to text it to you, and I–I think I just bubbled over. Shit. How likely is Nix to tell River? He can't tell him, Luka.'

I consider that a moment as I shift to ease the dull ache in my hips where I've been leaning on the edge of the benchtop.

'He'll give you a bit of grace, given your past, but ... did something happen between you and River?'

She looks at me, filled with emotion, but says nothing. My heart sinks. Whatever was the cause of their distance last night, that look tells me more than enough to know it was Blossom who pushed him away.

'If River's hurting,' I say gently, 'he will come first for Nix. Nix might not completely give you up, but he's not going to let River suffer, either.'

'So ... possibly not long?' Her voice cracks. 'I don't want to—'

I look sideways at her, a pang of protectiveness for River ricocheting in my chest. 'What happened, Bloss? How pained do you think River is currently?'

'This is impossible to manage, Lu,' she says, her voice cracking. 'I don't know, maybe a lot? I think he ... I think he was going to tell me how he felt, and I may have asked him to please bury whatever he wanted to say and never share it. That I couldn't—wouldn't accept whatever it was. If Nix says something now, I ...'

I stare at her, willing the protective pang not to turn into a searing heat beneath my skin.

'Shit, Bloss.'

A lot is well and truly understating where River's head is going to be at right now. In the whole time I've known him, I have *never* heard of him giving up his feelings to someone first. I'm not even sure he's ever loved anyone before. Not outside of Nix and me.

'Did I wreck it?' she whispers.

Sighing deeply, I step forward and take her hand. 'Honestly? I can't imagine his feelings for you changing in a long, long time. But you asked him to bury them, and that will be exactly what he's doing now—trying to bury them so deep that it also buries the hurt. If you didn't feel the same, I'd tell you that was his burden to bear and help him through the other side. But ... you do?'

Bloss sniffs as she nods. 'I think I do. But I also feel like the world's worst person, and if Nix says anything, it will just make it all the more confusing.'

'Then you need to tell him that,' I say. 'You know I think you deserve another shot at love, something no one is going to judge you for. But River deserves love, too. Don't take that away from him, Bloss. Not unless you have a very good reason.'

My phone vibrates where I left it on the low coffee table.

'That will be them ready to do this news piece,' I say, tucking a curl behind Bloss's ear. 'Maybe we both need to say the things that scare us.'

'Yeah, maybe,' she breathes, before huffing a sigh and seeming to mentally shake off her mood. 'But your sharing is more important today. Have you thought through what you're going to tell them?'

I nod. 'I spent a good portion of last night running over everything I can remember from the island, so, yes. I'm sure Rosie will have lots of questions, too. It's the reaction I'm most nervous about. It's one thing to say I can survive being picked apart by complete strangers, but I've never been in the public eye, you know? I can't help but feel like I'm about to be stripped bare.'

Bloss steps away from the counter, where she was also leaning. 'Rosie is smart. Professional. There is always pushback on anything political parties don't like, but she is the best person to position you well. You're going to smash this, Lu, I know you will.'

***

For what feels like the next several days, but is only a matter of hours, I talk. Then talk some more. There is nothing Rosie sees as off-limits. From the island, to my schooling, to my past relationships, my mother, the academy.

I tell her everything. So much, my voice feels hoarse by the end.

Cortane, Quillian, and Finn have popped in and out, but Rosie and my Dad have stayed with me the whole day. It's been nice to watch them work together, the mutual respect they have for each other. Something he obviously didn't have with my mother.

'I think we're clear,' Rosie says when the six of us are back together to decide the final strategy. 'We'll do it in serialised form, so we don't give them everything at once to dispute. We start with the prison program – they will expect that to be the extent of it, given your experience there, and that's what they will focus on covering up. They don't know about Traelen, or how far your connections here run, so hitting them with the breeding program, the abduction of Teddy, and the issue of the missing

Prime Minister later, will catch them off guard. It will also come after we've planted the seed of doubt in the minds of the people.'

Dad clucks his tongue. 'That's the hope.'

The others nod. We've been around and around the different options, but this still feels like the best strategy. It will go in article form in episodic releases, with photos of me on every news platform and social media Rosie can get it to. Then we hope others – people, individuals, influencers – will pick it up as well.

Rosie reads the first one out loud for the umpteenth time today, and the room stays silent.

No changes.

'Right,' Rosie says, sliding the computer Cortane gave her closer and not looking up. 'I'm going to send this out. You should all get ready for the evening.'

'It's done,' my father says when we gather in the meeting hall. It's a celebration. An acknowledgment of their sacrifice for the cause, and recognition of those who still stand with them.

A long breath leaves me as I watch the people gather, most of them carrying drinks or a plate of food of some sort which are placed on the tables that line the room. There's nothing particularly pretty about the event, certainly not compared to those I'd organise on the island, but there is a strong undercurrent of unity that feels a lot like family.

'How long until we know if it's had any impact?' I ask.

'Hard to say much beyond the first flush of interest and outrage – which has been plentiful, particularly on the social channels. It's been live for about three hours now, long enough for it to have run on most major platforms in their "breaking" sections, and garner online interest. Probably not long enough for the government to have issued a response. But the number of people it's reaching is encouraging so far. The more every day

Nuntainians we get to start questioning things, big and small, the better our shot at getting their real support in turning against Zenaton.'

A quickening of my pulse makes my stomach turn. 'I'm not sure I want to know the details of the reactions—just if it makes an impact or not.'

He smiles a little. 'A little self-preservation never hurt anyone.'

'You mentioned the wish for an election today,' I say, 'and it reminded me of something Bloss said about choices. Do you really think calling for an election will help? How would we know they wouldn't just get back in?'

My father nods, his silvering hair moving slightly with the action. Our positioning like this, side by side as we watch the events unfold around us, reminds me of working with Claudius, and I'm suddenly swallowed by an immense wave of grief. I grit my teeth as I wait for it to wash over me and the sting in my nose and eyes to dissipate.

I wonder how different this would all be if we still had him. How he and my father would have gotten along. If Emeris—

'Luka?'

I blink. 'Sorry, what?'

'You asked me about an election,' Dad says, his brow furrowed, and I nod so he can continue. 'It will help, yes. By reminding the people they have some say here. At the very least, it will make them uncertain, create a challenge for the government to get them back on side. In the meantime, we go to work to raise other political parties and give people options. As we expose this government, we need to also give them the options—a desperate community doesn't make good decisions.'

The noise in the hall starts to rise as more and more people fill the space, and I seek out Blossom – something that seems so natural, particularly in this sort of environment. She's standing close to, but not touching, River. From here, it looks like she's quietly imploring him to talk to her, and he's staring resolutely into the crowd.

'You don't think it will take too long?' I ask.

'Well,' he says, 'I think that's relative. In comparison to your Quillian blazing in and cutting them all down to prove our point, it's much longer. But the chances of him—and the rest of us—surviving beyond that point are rather slim. So, yes, this will take longer, but it means our lives will be longer because of it. And, in the meantime, the prison is still out of action and the government will have much more scrutiny on what they do with ... unsavoury members of parliament and its workers, thanks to your articles. That's if they're not completely overturned or the poisonous members replaced.'

I continue searching the room, but I can't see Traelen anywhere. There's still no word from Casey on Teddy, so he's probably with Zale or on his own somewhere.

'You've done exceptionally well, Luka. We've taken the first huge step,' he says, turning to me. 'I made some very hard choices because of that program—I will not let them go unanswered.'

He and Traelen could make a formidable pair.

A shadow moves out of the window to my left, and I let my attention wander to the door to watch the next group come in. My stomach turns a little in hunger. Maybe I should get some food—

A crack so loud it feels like it splits my head in half. Followed by another. And another.

Too many to count as the hall fills with screams, my whole body freezing to the spot. Hunters take over everything I can see. People falling. Bleeding.

As Dad drags me to the ground, the only thing to properly register is Blossom's panicked face before River wrestles her out the side door.

Nix charges after them, blood leaking past his temple.

CHAPTER THIRTY-TWO

The world implodes around me.

Screaming – organised, coordinated shouts mingling with the cries of terror and confusion – the smell of blood, and what I can only assume is gunfire, overwhelm my senses. Covering my head with my arms, I hold on to the knowledge that Nix, River, and Bloss got out. I hold to it so tightly I think my chest might burst. It occurs to me that might be a preferable way to die than by a bullet tearing me through. The thought brings a certain sense of peace.

The Hunters are here, and I have nowhere to hide.

I peek between my elbows and try to take quick stock of the room as the frequency of the gunshots seems to diminish. At least in here. I can hear them outside in the street as well. Unless it's an echo in my broken ears.

The room is full of Hunters, at least thirty of them, all stalking the room, rifles held high as they creep around, searching through the bodies of countless traitors on the floor, poking guns in backs, rolling people over, shooting anyone that isn't who they're looking for.

Quillian.

My father shifts beside me, and another thought grips me like a vice. What if this is their reaction to the article? To learning about me and that I went on duty to the island to serve the prison program?

What if they're looking for *me*?

Both of us?

They'll come for me, a tiny voice says.

I ran from Zenaton. I exposed him.

Just stay alive.

My heart quickens, and I send a desperate plea to him to stay away. He'd needed an extra moment before joining the celebration and asked if I could go ahead of him. The unspoken worry that my absence, along with his, would make it more obvious just how much he was struggling with the execution.

'Get the fuck down!' The shouting in the room becomes more comprehensible, and I realise they've probably been yelling instructions the whole time.

Another gunshot goes off and I flinch. How many people is that now? People that will never get to see the end of this conflict, or know what it's like to return to their families peacefully. I'm very confident they won't make any list in the bowels of Parliament. And, as I think of that list of people from Tae, of the children Kasera held, the room around me snaps into sharp focus.

I can't die here. Not on this floor, with dead and dying rebels around me. These people who have given everything to make the world right. They all know about the article, know it's my face, my story, that's become the vehicle for their goals.

They need me to not roll over and take this. Quillian and the rest of the main group don't seem to be here. They're probably outside defending the camp and anyone not in this room with everything they have. Protecting Blossom.

'I'm sorry, Dad,' I whisper, 'for not trying to reach out sooner, for ever doubting you—for everything.'

'Luie, no.' He shifts on his stomach towards me, his voice panicked. 'Please—'

Keeping my hands behind my head, I awkwardly rise, slowly turning so all the Hunters can see me. So all the traitors that are looking can see me.

One of the Hunters speaks into a talking piece clipped to his shirt. 'Eyes on the target.'

The Hunter closest to me edges forward. 'Luka Brideoake, you're under arrest for the violation of your National Duty contract and dissemination of confidential information.'

My stomach dips into the floor, but I don't resist when she roughly grips my wrists and shoves them behind my back, securing them with a barbed vine that cuts into my skin. Pain snakes up my arms and into my shoulders, which protest against being twisted backwards. A second Hunter appears, rifle raised, as the first steps around to face me front on. Right where the bodycam she wears captures everything.

It strikes me how I must look, blown up on that screen in front of the committee – and Zenaton – and I lift my chin.

'You'll be transferred to Vana immediately to await your sentence,' the Hunter says.

My fingers tremble behind me and I grip them tightly, the skin on my wrists tearing on the binds. Just for a moment, I think I should be grateful for the pain, that maybe it will help prepare me for whatever is coming.

Or maybe it's the least amount of pain I'll ever feel again.

Either way, it's nothing compared to the look on Quillian's face as he bursts through the door I last saw Nix exit out of, deadly wings raised, as every rifle in the room turns to him. Only the woman with the bodycam stays trained on me.

'Iona,' I say. 'Briarly, Tymothy, Helena.' I look around the room at who else I can see limp on the floor before I look back into the bodycam and start to name our dead. 'Andrena, Milo, Clayton, Yvonne. These are the people the Nuntainian government has sanctioned the murder of today. Briarly was a mother, Tymothy a baker. Milo was a violinist celebrating his 43rd birthday. Yvonne was—'

'Quiet!' the Hunter says, eyes flashing as she whips her knuckles across my cheek.

My teeth rattle in my head as I swallow blood and look back at her. To her camera.

'There are too many of us who know the truth, and we will not stay silent,' I say, head spinning. 'Too many of us who know that child slavery, the trafficking of women and children for sex, the—'

The Hunter keeps her eyes trained on me as she obviously receives a message in her earpiece, and I shove away the thought it's an order to kill us all.

Quillian stays silent at the door, his body vibrating and the tips of his wings elongating into the sharpest blades I've ever seen. The anguish on his face chips into my chest. But he would know he's far outnumbered here, that these people, *his* people, need him.

I stare into the bodycam. 'Zenaton Blake, you cannot hide from us.'

A searing pain fires through the back of my head, and I crumple against the Hunter in front of me. Quillian roars, the familiar scream of portal magic growing louder as the Hunter grips me and the world goes black.

A deep clicking sounds once – somehow it's both immensely loud, yet far away. My head is thick and ... abrasive, almost like it's been stuffed with steel wool. There's a sharp throb in the back that makes me wince as I draw myself up, gingerly opening my eyes to find I'm alone in a cold, white-tiled cell, sat on a bench built into the far wall. The single door is narrow and reinforced with dark, metal bars.

Not that I really expected otherwise. Even if the others were with me, there's no way the Hunters would put us together. But I clearly remember being arrested alone. What further destruction happened after, I don't know. The realisation I am being punished both for speaking out, and to hurt Quillian, is sharp. Looking up, I find a small camera with a blinking red light in the corner.

Zenaton.

Or at least someone who reports to him, I'm sure of it. He knew who I was associated with – has since the island. He was watching my home, had the locations of the camps this whole time, yet only struck now. His desire to know I was watching as he destroyed the traitors seemed completely genuine.

An opportunity I've now taken from him.

Asshole.

I glare at the camera and clench my fist, which makes me flinch with unexpected pain.

The inside of my elbow aches a little, and I rub my thumb against the sore point. Glancing down, I find a purple bruise about the size of a coin, and my insides churn.

It can only have been magic dampener – and they weren't gentle about it.

The invasion burns. Though, clearly they don't know I don't need a magic dampener – that was done for me a long time ago. A laugh bubbles from my throat, even as tears sting my eyes. The sound echoes strangely in the small space, but as it fades away, I hear something else outside my cell. From down the corridor, maybe. A slightly monotone voice is talking uninterrupted, and I strain to hear.

'... recently reported a story of a woman claiming to know sickening secrets about our government—'

I suck in a breath. *Is that it?*

'—it has come to our attention that the woman making these claims is not the selfless, duty-serving citizen she claims to be. Not only did she steal confidential records, we now know Luka Brideoake was having an inappropriate relationship with her superior. Following a rigorous investigation into the claims, the Defence Committee have determined that the misinformation spread by Ms Brideoake was just that—misinformation spread by a disgruntled lover. The committee have asked us to assure you the claims Ms Brideoake made were false, and she is now receiving care for her mental wellbeing.'

The room seems to spiral away from me as I let the broadcast fade back into the background.

Tears slip from the corners of my eyes. Dropping my head between my knees, I let them fall. But they don't stem the sick feeling crawling up my insides.

I knew this is how they'd retaliate – completely undermine my claims by attacking me as a person. The fact they are already so obviously working to discredit me gives life to a little flare of hope. We struck a chord.

But to hear what's being said. How easily everything I have worked for, all the time I have dutifully given to this country, my desperate hope to make us a better country, to liberate the people of Tae ... *everything* has been lost to the falsehood that I am an unstable woman ... it still stings.

Once, I held so tight to the fact I had my reputation. That I could use that to do good. I don't have magic, I can't literally fight people, but I had my mind, my experience, the knowledge people thought well of me, and now ... I have a future in Vana. One I am headed towards while leaving the traitors with nothing but a handful of other articles to publish that will only be dismissed as wild, unfounded claims. If they see any airtime at all. Will my arrest make the news? That's if Zenaton doesn't have the rest of the traitors wiped out before anything more can be published. How many people died after I was taken away?

My breaths get tight.

My first article, my truth, didn't even last a day before they attacked.

Wiped us off the playing field before we'd even really begun.

Does anyone still live to release the rest?

I don't even bother to try to make it to a corner as the nausea climbs up my throat and vomit splashes onto the white tiles beneath my feet.

'Time to find your new home,' a bored voice says what feels like hours later.

I lift my head slowly, my neck aching, and find an older Hunter at the door. Older, but no less deadly. I wonder what got him assigned here, instead of out in the field. Not that it matters much to me now, I suppose.

The door creaks on its hinges as he opens it wide enough for me to know what he's asking, and I drag myself to standing, stepping over the now mostly dried puddle of vomit, and leave the cell.

He sniffs as he escorts me down the short, pale corridor. 'That sick is going to be hard to get out of your hair where you're going.'

'I'm pretty sure that's going to be the least of my concerns,' I mutter.

He grunts in response and clasps the door handle as we reach the end of the corridor. 'You're not wrong about that.'

The door swings towards us, revealing a portal twice as large as Cortane's. I desperately hope that, wherever I am in that prison, that I can see some part of the island. Or the sky.

Please just let me know the island is there.

Perhaps its red flowers will be blooming.

The trip through the portal is fast, and I stumble into what is obviously Vana's version of the receiving plane. But, instead of a marble platform in the sky, this one feels like it's in a dungeon – complete with a moaning man strapped to the stone wall to my right. The leather binds that hold his arms above his head cut into his skin, but the one around his chest is completely soaked in blood.

His head lolls to the side, blood dripping from the corner of his mouth.

'Welcome to the end of the world, goldie,' he splutters. 'You should have taken your life while you had the chance.'

CHAPTER THIRTY-THREE

Vana is everything the other prison wasn't. Stark, damp, and seemingly all of its ugly on full display. Escorted by a Hunter on either side, I'm struck by an almost blinding light when we exit the receiving room – or whatever they call it here. And I remember the stories of what really eventually drives prisoners here mad. The never-ending flood of light.

In a strange way, the layout doesn't feel that different to the other prison, with hallways bordering a courtyard below. But that's where any familiarity ends. The nameless prison I did my first duty in was overflowing with golden sunshine, greenery, the scent of jasmine, gold-framed paintings on the walls, and people wearing the most beautiful clothes. Vana's courtyard is bare, the sky hidden by a roof painted white to reflect the glare of the floodlights bolted at regular intervals. We pass countless barred doors – some open, some closed – so close together I can't imagine the people in each cell have room to even turn around. Almost all the staff I can see lining the halls appear to be Hunters, but there is a smattering of attendants – I hadn't realised how few of them there really are.

Then there are the prisoners.

There's no uniform to speak of, as if the government couldn't even be bothered to pay for those, and their clothes are in varying degrees of disrepair.

Perhaps that's a sign of one of two things: how wealthy they were before they came, and that the clothes were of good quality, or how long they've been here. Looking around, everyone here was either very poor, or they've been here a long, long time.

'This is you,' the Hunter on my left says, stopping us outside a cell on the top floor. It's so bright my head starts to pound, and I note for the first time that the Hunters and attendants are wearing sunglasses.

Sunglasses for the light that's nothing like the sun.

'You'll be here until dinner,' the Hunter explains, his uniform making me ache for Holland. Did he make it out of that confrontation?

Numbly, I walk into the cell and stand rigid as I listen to the barred door clang shut behind me.

What feels like a lifetime ago, I could almost imagine Vana was nothing but an urban myth as my life stretched out before me, even if I felt constrained by my place on the island, frustrated by the loss of time in my own life. Now, I desperately miss the opportunity that was ahead of me. The ending of my duty, the opening of my eyes to what was really unfolding in our world, Quillian's unguarded face in the mornings. Reconnecting with my father.

A sharp pain lances through my chest, and I close my eyes against the sting. Logically, I know the sooner I accept my new reality, the better. Emotionally, I know I will never be able to let that life go. Not what it was, and not what it promised.

The narrow cot groans as I lower myself down to wait until dinner.

Now, it seems I have nothing left to do but wait for whatever scheduled item comes next – and hope I can withstand whatever torture is coming.

Because I know it is.

Zenaton has a debt to settle, and now I'm in his grasp he doesn't even have to lay eyes on me for me to feel his grip.

A loud horn sounds and the door to my cell opens. A quick glance into the hallway tells me all the others are now also open, and prisoners start to file past. No one says a word as they pass by, I'm not even sure they realise I'm new here. Standing, I move to my doorway; joining the strangely quiet line of people seems like the right thing to do. I pick a small gap in the line, and I step in.

There's a fast gasp from behind me, and the man in front looks over his shoulder at me quickly before returning his gaze forward.

In single file, we make our way along the narrow hall, the inner courtyard three storeys below on my right, the row of cells on my left. As we walk past cell after cell, I become increasingly aware of the smell. It was less evident in my own cell. Perhaps there is some basic cleaning done between prisoners – not that I could ever call that cell clean. But, out here, the stink of sweat and urine mingles with blood and dirt, and it lodges itself in my nose and the back of my throat so deep I might choke.

As we walk along the top floor and down the stairs, I realise the prisoners aren't wholly quiet. There are whispers that feel like they are being passed up and down the line, but I can't make out their words.

On the ground floor, I follow the line into a large, still brightly lit room. The size of it seems to magnify the light even more, and I squint as I look around.

Rows and rows of metal tables and chairs fill the room, places slowly being filled as the line of prisoners pass by what must be a food station on the left wall and then freely into the space.

The smell of the food as I draw closer seems a marginal improvement on the stench of the cells, but not a single person complains. I almost want to laugh. Knowing the impeccable food we served in the other prison compared to what's here, it's just ... incomprehensible.

I shake my head, taking a tray as I reach the food bench.

The whispering around me seems to increase, and a sense of foreboding takes flight in my stomach.

These are not people I should be feeling sorry for about what they get to eat. Not all of them, anyway. I know more than enough now to know there are innocent people here, but I still remember my conversation with Holland when he told me not to feel bad for everyone in Vana. The tray starts to tremble in my hands, the back of my neck prickling as I think about what they could be in here for.

Perhaps whatever torture I will experience here will be nothing compared to what the other prisoners could do to me.

An attendant piles something grey and lumpy straight onto my tray, complete with rust spots, and what looks like a brown rock.

I swallow a gag. A metallic bang sounds at the same time the grey sludge flies into my face, my tray hitting my chest and the brown rock rolling along the floor.

Gasping, I flick the grey food from my face to find the woman behind me staring coldly. A chill snakes down my spine at the fierce look in her eye, a look that suggests she's intent on one thing only – taking me down.

I say nothing – no words come to mind anyway as I stare at her.

'You wait 'til the end like all the new shit-kickers, pretty one,' she says, eyes narrowed. 'You sure as fuck ain't going to eat before me.'

She shoves past me, her shoulder driving into my chest, and it's all I can do not to cry out. But I know I can't give her the satisfaction.

'Hold your chin high,' the man behind her whispers to me. 'It's all you can do right now. Hold your chin up and wait your turn. Honestly, you're not missing much.'

I look up into his face. It's weathered and bruised, and it cracks something deep inside of me. What could this man have possibly done to end up here?

My heart beats a little too fast as I realise I have no way of telling if he's here for a legitimate reason or a made up one.

'Thank you,' I whisper, hoping he can't tell how shaky my voice is. His deep brown eyes are kind as he gives me half a smile – it seems one side of his face doesn't move very well.

'Not all of us are like that,' he says quietly, 'but best you watch out for the ones that are.'

Nodding briefly, I make my way to the door to wait for the seemingly endless stream of prisoners to make their way into the food hall. Six Hunters flank the entrance, three on each side, their faces almost entirely obscured by dark-olive masks that sit underneath their rounded helmets.

The one nearest me looks down to where I stand next to him, his rifle pointing towards my toes where he holds it across his body.

He says nothing.

The grey sludge they're serving for food feels like it's drying into cement on my skin and clothes, but I don't dare move it. I'm not game enough to try to seek out where the woman went, but my skin prickles with what feels like the judging gaze of everyone in this room.

Marking me out as the new one, perhaps.

Sizing me up.

The line of people feels never-ending, but when it finally does reach the end, I take a deep breath and join the queue. A large part of me doesn't know why, I'm certainly not hungry – the nausea swirling in my gut from the smell, the altercation, and being in *Vana* has taken care of that. Not to mention that even if I was hungry, I don't think I could bring myself to eat whatever it is that's currently sticking to my skin.

Quietly shuffling forward, I focus on the back of the person in front of me. They seem old, but not like someone on the mainland would appear old. The shape of this man's back and the colour of his hair makes me guess his age at about the same as my father's, but the broken way he moves screams that he's done.

I can't even see his face, just the nape of his neck framed by dark, greying hair, as it bows towards the floor, and it feels like he has no more fight left.

How long until I am the same?

Reaching the food counter, I once again take a tray and, with trembling hands, hold it out for another smattering of inedible gunk to land on.

'No one gets seconds,' a voice to my right spits, and I flinch. I try not to lower my chin as I turn to look at the woman from before. She gestures to my front, a mocking grin on her face. 'You already had yours, remember?'

The people around us go quiet as the air seems to thicken with anticipation. My heart hammers behind my chest and I can only think this woman is intending to hit me. I've never been hit before, and tears threaten to prick the back of my eyes.

A half ring of prisoners now hems me in between the woman and the food counter, all clearly wondering what is happening. Some of them quietly cheering for it.

My ears ring in the near silence as she spits on my chest.

'You ain't no better than any of us – why should you get two servings when we all go hungry?'

She shoves into my chest as I continue to blink at her, willing words to come to my mind, but I have no idea how to manage this situation. I stumble a step but stay upright.

'You're right,' I stammer, 'I'm just ... working this all out.'

She laughs out loud. A full-bodied laugh, like she hasn't done it in a long, long time, and it echoes around the otherwise still strangely quiet room. When I glance around, every person is now turned towards us. Even the man that was in front of me in the queue.

The woman straightens. She's shorter than me, but her shirt sleeves are torn off at the shoulder, providing clear evidence that she is somehow still strong in this cesspit. She cracks her knuckles.

'That's alright, new kid. I'll help you work it out.'

I cover my face with arms and close my eyes just as she starts to swing—

'What the fuck's happening here?' a voice behind me says. It sounds so familiar my chest aches, and I can't turn around. Can't face the disappointment when I see it's just one of the Hunters from the doorway and not Holland.

The woman cocks her head as I let my arms fall back to my side.

'This little bitch thought she could get seconds.' There's no question in her voice. No defensiveness. Like maybe the Hunters would disagree with this, too.

The Hunter sighs, as if he does this exact intervention several times a day. Maybe he does.

'Go back to your dinner, Slay,' he says. 'It will be getting cold.'

Slay scoffs as she starts to back away, still facing me and the Hunter, a promise in her eyes that this isn't finished.

The Hunter grips my arm, jerking me towards him, and she smirks. 'You'll get no favours here, Rebel fucking Princess,' he grinds out.

I choke at the same time Slay's face falls, the blood draining from her cheeks.

This time, the faces looking back seem to have lost a little of their harshness. Those looks replaced with almost a ... curiosity.

The room goes quiet, Slay still staring at me mutely. Someone else digs their fingers into my arm and I wince. Glancing over my shoulder, a Hunter stands so close to me, I can barely make any space between us. But he's a second one. I pull my arm away, facing the original Hunter, as if I can fool myself into the thought I could take either of them if I can just address one at a time. This one is staring at me intensely, like he's trying to convey a message – like he's trying to make me remember I am the unofficial, untitled, Rebel Princess. Like I should know who he is behind the uniform.

A little bit of fire starts to lick in my veins—

'Zenaton has a message for you,' the second one says, grabbing me again and muttering against my ear. There's nothing familiar about him at all. 'He will hold the line.'

All traces of heat leave my body.

CHAPTER THIRTY-FOUR

The second Hunter, who's face I can barely see between his helmet, glasses and mask, drags me out of the food hall and into the even quieter hallway.

'Let go of me,' I demand, jerking my arm from his grasp. Very aware that he could force me if he wanted to.

He shoves me ahead of him. 'Keep walking.'

When we reach the stairs, I slow my pace a little to navigate the narrow, stone stairwell. The Hunter sighs behind me and I try to go a little faster, anything to avoid his irritation.

About a third of the way from the bottom, he shoves me again – hard – and I go down, tumbling the last several stairs. The jagged edges catch in more places than I can count.

On my knees at the bottom, I gasp for breath as the walls spin around me, head aching. A dull throb radiates from the back of my right hip, and a drop of bright red blood falls from somewhere on my face.

'You wanted me to let you go—now, get up,' he spits from behind me.

My hands and knees tremble as I awkwardly draw myself to standing, pain lancing through my right knee – right on the top, where it took most of the impact. Limping forward, with no idea where I'm supposed to be going, the Hunter's presence is like a menacing shadow at my back.

I press my palms against my stomach to try and stem the tremor in my fingers, to stop him from seeing how hurt and vulnerable I feel right now – something I haven't felt so acutely since I escaped from the island the first time. Except, this time, I don't have Holland and Casey with me to cut down anyone who would try to hurt me – and I certainly don't have Quillian, Nix, and River waiting for me.

Or Quillian's feather, still beside my bed at camp.

The reality sits heavily in my chest and seems to weigh my limbs down with longing, as well as pain.

'Here,' he says as we approach a small door on the left of the hallway.

As I turn to face it, I realise I'm now lost, my focus having drifted to my loss instead of my direction.

The Hunter shoves me through the door, the pain in my knee burning as I struggle to stay upright. Dragging me towards the centre of the room, he roughly drops me onto a wooden chair and swiftly binds my hands behind the backrest, my shoulders pinching with the force of the angle.

I twist against the rope that wraps around my front, but it's wound so tight I can barely move. The room seems to compress around me and a scream tears its way from my throat, fuelled by an anger I've never felt before.

'Let me go!'

The Hunter barely blinks. 'Zenaton wants to know where the other locations are.'

I stare at him. *What fucking locations*?

Then it dawns on me. Emeris leaked the list of the camps. But I moved them. Or at least, told Quillian where else they could go. Where the survivors might be able to find some safety to recover, to recoup, before making a stand.

The Hunter's face is completely unknowable behind his uniform, and I wonder if he knows what he's really asking. If he knows that I will die before I give up the locations of the rebel survivors. So his question is not 'where are the other locations?', it's 'are you ready to die?'

It's both chilling and terrifying ... and somehow freeing. I have spent so long walking a fine line between dutiful citizen and traitor, never really able to be one or the other. But, here, with that question, he has opened the door for me to be wholly, completely, what I believe in. And that is never going to be that the government of Nuntainia has acted appropriately with the prison program. It will never be that the forcible *breeding* of Karaylia is okay – even the terminology around it makes me sick. And it will certainly never be that it's acceptable to imprison and torture people like me for simply stating my truth, or using my relationship with my supervisor as a tool to undermine everything I have said and done. Never.

So I draw my chin up – and spit in his face.

He kicks my feet out from under me so quickly I can't help but cry out as my legs are jerked to the side, my right knee screaming in protest. Despite the pain, I kick out at him as he collects my legs. Thrashing my weight around so hard, the chair rocks precariously – the only thing holding me in a semblance of an upright position is the grip he has where his arm wraps around the top of my thighs. Working with sickening calm and efficiency, he binds my legs together above the knee and at the ankle.

Dropping my feet back to the ground, he stalks to the corner of the room and drags over a low bench. The scraping sound of the timber on the rough, tiled floor skitters down my spine and sets my jaw on edge. He drags it opposite me and, for a moment, I think he's going to sit down – right in spitting range, should I do it again. Not that I think that will get me out of here, but the anger boiling in my veins feels like enough to spit at him every time he touches me.

But, instead of sitting, he picks up my legs again and drops them on top of the bench. In another time, I could be sitting on a couch with my legs on the coffee table. Here, though, he rips off my shoes and pulls out what looks like a thin strip of hard plastic from a little drawer in the bench.

I watch him as he moves silently around the room. He hasn't uttered a single sound since he asked me about the locations.

He stares at me, not that I can see his eyes behind the dark glasses, but it's clear in his stance he's staring as he looks down at me.

And then he whips the soles of my feet with the plastic stick.

I cry out again, wishing I could give him no reaction, but the whiplike sting in my feet is a pain like I haven't felt before. Because, with it, comes the knowledge that this is just the beginning. Even if I thought one of the traitors could get in here to save me, the chances of us ever getting back out are zero. If they gave themselves up, their chances of being killed before coming here are very high. And the Hunters found us this time, even without being marked by the wards. How would we ever outrun them indefinitely with the mark?

So, yes, I think as I draw a steeling breath. This is just the beginning.

'Zenaton wants to know the other locations,' he says again.

'And I gave you my answer,' I grind out, my feet still radiating with the aftermath of his strike.

He raises the stick and toys with the end of it with his opposite hand. As if he's considering his next move.

Faster than I can track, the stick whips across the soles of my feet.

Again.

And again.

And again.

The sound of the stick smacking on my flesh echoing in the room. Until it sounds wet as well.

So many times until I can only whimper in response, tears streaming down my face as my feet are ripped raw.

His breathing is a fraction laboured by the time he stops.

'Know where they are now?' he asks.

I close my eyes against the drops of red I can see gathering on the tiles below my heels. The pain is a living, breathing thing as it wraps around my lower limbs and snakes its way towards my thighs. But, somewhere in the recesses of my mind, I know it will likely feel worse when I'm done.

'You can tell Zenaton I wish he'd died a long, slow death,' I say between wracking breaths. 'I will never give him anything.'

There's a dark, smattering stain on the ceiling of my cell. Depending how long I look at it, how I squint my eyes or let my vision glaze over, it makes different shapes. Different memories. Right now, it's Blossom's curls. And I try to hold on to the image of her laughing, curls bouncing around her face. Whatever it is, it's a small solace from the otherwise overwhelming brightness of the room.

How long will it be until I forget their faces? Will this strange mark be all I have to find them in?

Quillian's wings take shape before my eyes and I focus on them, resolutely trying to ignore the painful throbbing in my feet. The soles have been torn to shreds and the tops are now grazed from where the Hunter dragged me back, facedown, to my cell and dumped me where I now lie – though I must have somehow turned myself over at some point.

I don't know how long I look at the rotating images before me, but I know I don't sleep while I do. The only slight reprieve comes when I roll onto my side and make myself close my eyes.

It's a reprieve from the memories, until I start to think on all the things I could have done differently – should have done differently.

I should have shared the list of Tae survivors. I should have given more locations that could be safe havens. I should have told Nix, every day, that I love him even with his broken heart. I should have gone to the beach. I should have taken so much more from the archives. I should have never stopped communicating with my father. I should have kept Quillian's feather with me at all times, even in camp.

I press my palm to the place I'd normally carry the feather. I'd rather die here than give anyone up.

I should have made sure Zenaton was dead.

A shift in the almost oppressive silence of the prison tells me it's morning. At least, I assume that's what's happening – the night has stayed blindingly bright since I got here. I knew that to be true about this prison but, as I try to blink open my gritty eyes after just one night, I understand how quickly it really could send people mad.

There's a loud creak and my cell door swings open at the same time as all the others, something I am gathering might only happen at meal times. A gentle shuffling of feet starts down the hall, and now, I know not to even think about joining that line until it's well and truly ended. But just the thought of my feet touching anything makes me want to whimper. I will never make it down there. I don't care about missing the food, or what passes as food here, despite the growing pit in my stomach. I'm still not hungry enough to put it anywhere near my mouth.

That will change, a small voice says in the back of my mind, and I push it away.

No, I don't want food. But I do want water.

I consider it for a long moment as the footsteps get closer to my cell door, weighing up my options. And I decide the pain in my feet is too much to bear for water.

So I lie here. Waiting for what comes first – my feet to hurt less, or for hunger and thirst to drive me to walk on them.

I'm about to lie my head back down and curl into a ball when I realise no one is passing my door like they did yesterday. Carefully, I peek at it, a sudden rush of nervousness taking my limbs. What if the threat and humiliation of yesterday isn't enough for that woman – Slay? What if she's not satisfied with my removal by the Hunter? Maybe she knows that seems to have had nothing to do with her, and everything to do with me. Maybe she still wants to ensure I learned my lesson.

I swallow, imagining her face looming in the cell doorway.

'Princess?'

I start, both at the title and the voice that is clearly not Slay's. No, it belongs to the kind man who told me to wait by the door yesterday. The one who tried to help me navigate the unwritten rules of Vana.

'You ready for breakfast?'

His face is dirty and weathered, like he's seen too much pain, but the generosity of his spirit lights a little spark of hope in me. I tuck it in beside the anger Zenaton and his Hunter have ignited.

'I ... was waiting,' I say, a little haltingly. 'But'—I gesture to my feet—'I'm not sure I'll make it down today.'

He frowns, but he's not surprised. Given that my feet face the door, I know he has seen them already. He nods solemnly, the deep-set lines in his face telling me they are perhaps even worse than I thought.

'I'm sorry they did that to you.' His voice is soft, genuine, and it forces tears to my eyes. Such a simple statement, and an apology that doesn't belong to him, but it makes me so grateful to not be completely alone up here.

Because, otherwise, this is the most alone I have ever been. The thought opens a fissure in my chest. Growing up, I had my Dad, and Nix and River, then Akira and Zale. Then I added Blossom and Claudius. Quillian and everyone he brought with him. I added Holland. My breath gets tight when I think about them – the people I pulled around me and never wanted to let go.

And here I am.

In Vana, with busted feet that are probably just the start of what I'm to experience here.

A stranger staring at me.

And I haven't even seen the sky. Or the island.

A tear slips down my cheek.

I'm sorry they did that to you, he said. I wonder now if he knows that could mean so many more things than just the soles of my feet.

Me too, I think, wishing I could voice an apology for him, too. I just feel so ... raw.

The man turns away, but he doesn't move past my door towards the stairwell that will take him to breakfast, instead turning back the way he came. A moment later, he appears in my doorway once more, a person I can't make out the details of hovering behind him.

'We're going to help you, okay?' he asks.

Carefully, I nod. While he doesn't seem the type to hurt me, offending someone – two someones – two days in a row here doesn't seem sensible. I swing my legs over the side of the narrow cot, making sure not to put any weight on my feet and rolling them outwards, so only the outside edges come into contact with the floor. They're not wound free, but they are the most intact portions of my feet. Apart from maybe the pads of my toes.

They come round to place themselves on either side of me and hoist me up, one under each shoulder, arms wrapping around my waist. Neither of them even grunt as they help pull me to stand, and I can't help but wonder how many times they have had to do this to make sure their fellow prisoners can access food and water. As they walk me out of my cell, the barest parts of my toes touching the floor, I wince. I can't stay off the balls of my feet entirely and, open wounds aside, they feel more bruised than anything I've ever experienced.

As we reach the door, I suddenly understand why no one has been going past.

They're all waiting in line for me.

The two men, who virtually carry me, turn us to the left before I can really get a grasp on how many are silently lining up to the right of my door. My skin prickles with some just out of reach understanding of what's happening, why it's so different to yesterday.

We make our way to the food hall, the rest of the prison slowly, quietly, following in our wake. The men help me sit on one of the metal benches at a table closest to the door, right at the front of the room. Somehow, though I'm not sure why, I feel like I have been placed here for maximum visibility. But my feet breathe a small sigh of relief once they're no longer bearing my weight, and being the centre of attention seems a small price to pay in exchange. Right now, I can't imagine ever standing on my own or wearing shoes ever again. A hot sting rushes across my chest. If River were here, he'd be able to—

I cut myself off.

I do not want River here. Never again. I will do this for all of us.

'Please, eat,' the man from yesterday says to the line, and they start to make their way forward.

A tray of slop is placed on the table for me as prisoner after prisoner gathers their meal and finds a seat. Gradually, after many, many long looks at me, they turn to their food and begin eating – with their fingers. There are no utensils in sight. My stomach turns over itself as they each scoop the mess into their fingers and mouths, sucking the remnants off before taking the next scoop.

As they finish, people begin to line up to talk to me. To tell me their stories. To thank me. Their words simultaneously chip away at me, deepening the wounds inside, yet fill those same wounds with a warmth I've not felt before. They almost look at me the way I have seen people look at Quillian, or Cortane, and my throat tightens at the thought that these people could see me like that.

It's only because they haven't met the others.

But I don't tell them I'm a poor substitute, relay parts of my own story, or try to offer words of solace – there are none. All I can do is listen. But as a man tells me about the abduction of his sister – the pattern so like at least ten other stories I've heard just now – the weight of all that these people have experienced seems to press my chest to the table. The pain in his face is physically reflected behind my sternum.

I look away, just for a second so I can breathe, then give him my polite, concierge-turned-rebel-princess mask again. But when I turn back, I look right up into the face of a different man, the first one now retreating back to his place. I make a note to start asking people their names.

'Princess,' he says, now the second person today to call me that.

'I'm not—' I cut myself off from the almost automatic response in the face of so much suffering. How much bolstering has my presence brought them?

He waves me off as the room falls completely silent, his somewhat frail body seems to exude authority. But also a brokenness.

'Perhaps, before you tell me what you are not, you will allow me to introduce myself?'

His tone isn't rude, but there is something underneath it that makes my heart race a little faster. I nod slowly, eyeing him carefully, and he holds out his hand.

'Rebel Princess,' he says as I wrap my palm around his and shake it, 'it is a pleasure to meet you. I am Tomas Millyn, Prime Minister of Nuntainia.'

CHAPTER THIRTY-FIVE

A quiet *tap-tap* starts to fill the space around me as I stare up at the Prime Minister, his hand still in mine.

Tap-tap.

Like a heart-beat.

Tap-tap.

Tap-tap.

His eyes are so dark brown they could almost be black. He flicks his gaze around the room at the building *tap-tap*. Heart starting to race, I follow suit. The prisoners – so many of whom have just been speaking with me – some silent agreement passing among them as they each use two fingers, the heels of their palms resting on the table. They watch us, the noise gathering in intensity and speed until it reverberates in time with the beating in my chest.

Tap-tap. Tap-tap. Tap-tap.

The Hunters on duty seem to stand a little straighter, as if the noise is creating something electric in the room, and they're not sure if it's going to strike.

'Quiet!' one of them bellows, and the sound starts to die away.

But not one prisoner stops watching us.

The Prime Minister lets go of my hand as I grapple with what is unfolding. Something I instinctively know I am right in the middle of.

Princess.

Even the Prime Minister is intent on calling me that, when I have old vomit caked in my hair and food-turned-cement on my clothes. The Prime Minister Quillian once said he would welcome a discussion with. But Quillian isn't here.

'Traelen has been looking for you,' I say.

The Prime Minister sighs gently and clasps his hands behind his back, as if he's practiced in trying to hide such responses.

'Yes. It is clear now I was too slow to understand the things Traelen has been trying to warn me of for some time.'

'Anything in particular?'

'May I sit?' he asks, gesturing to the space beside me. 'I fear some won't finish their meals while I'm standing over you.'

A quick scan of the room confirms everyone still watches us closely.

'Of course.'

The room seems to relax, at least a little, as the Prime Minister lowers himself to sit on the bench.

'I assume they're correct?' he asks. 'You are, in fact, the Rebel Princess?'

I give him a long look, a ringing in my ears at how dangerous this could be. Everything points to him not being aligned with Zenaton – but that doesn't mean he's automatically aligned with us.

'I don't think that would be wise of me to confirm or deny,' I say. 'Do you know these people we sit with?'

'I can tell you quite a lot about why people are here. That man,' the Prime Minister says, pointing at the man who was kind to me yesterday and who helped me this morning. 'He is here because he tried to let me know of an abhorrent program to augment our military.'

I swallow. The Karaylia breeding program.

'And the woman who accosted you yesterday—she's here because her son was sent into a war he was too young to fight. She ... disagreed with that decision. She knows, I believe, while her life may have been hard before then, it was her actions after the removal of her son that condemned her to be here. But on some level she's also a victim, is she not?'

My chest pounds. The things he's saying ...

'Is every person here because they disagreed with the decisions your government has made?'

He cocks his head just slightly in what I hope is an expression of sad acceptance and not challenge. Then he bobs his head in a slow, shallow nod.

'Too many are,' he says sadly. 'But it's not true for everyone.' He inclines his head to a table at the back. One full of people engaged in their own sullen interactions, and not – at least that I can tell – the slightest bit interested in the two of us. 'The man on the end there—with the bald head—he's here because he trapped his children in a car and lit it alight.'

The breath rushes out of me, leaving a hole in its wake.

'The one next to him is here because he slit his boss's throat when a woman was promoted over him. On the other side—the woman with grey hair and her back to us—is here for the abuse she inflicted on her ageing mother.'

Fuck.

I knew Vana housed people who have done things so awful I couldn't even imagine, and Holland assured me of that, too. But hearing it out loud is worse than I expected. My blood chills as a weight takes hold of my chest I don't know if I will ever now remove. How is it possible such people exist? At the same time, is any of what he's said worse than what the 'guests' I served on my duty were sent to the island for? They just happened to be in positions of greater power and influence, or have connections to those with the ability to cover up their crimes.

'Do you know why I'm here?' he asks, and I shake my head. 'No. And I'm willing to bet that, aside from Traelen, no one even really knows I'm gone.'

I narrow my gaze at him, unsure if he's bitter no one has missed him, or that it was possible to remove him so easily.

He laughs a little. 'I'm not sure I would have believed it had I not ended up here. Such is the power of being able to show people what they want to see, what they think they know.'

'So ... why *are* you here?' I ask, wishing I'd started asking this question of prisoners so very long ago.

His brows lift a little – reminding me sharply of my father, and I smother a pang. 'I'm here,' he says, 'because Zenaton Blake needed me out of the way. My ... awareness of the severe corruption taken root in my own government—my own party—took far too long. Something I will regret until the day I die, and probably beyond.' He rubs his palms together for a moment. 'I didn't see what was really at play when the Defence Committee effectively took control of the government finances through one of its members. Or when the committee members were gradually replaced only with those who had been through the prison program multiple times. When it became commonplace for committee members to hold multiple ministries. By the time I realised the balance of power had shifted far more than what the 'efficiencies' should have called for, it was too late. Zenaton was securing his support within the party to take it over—sometimes it's easier to take what already exists than start again. Unfortunately, I trusted Zenaton implicitly. I simply saw a strong, former military leader creating efficiencies in our government.'

I frown. 'That sounds like everyday politics, not a reason you end up in Vana.'

His shoulders sag a little. 'I can see why you'd say that. But when it's your whole life, and the leadership responsibilities increase, it can get harder and harder to walk the line between what's real and what's required for the party to remain in government, to hold on to that power.' He laces his fingers. 'The party's agenda becomes the sole goal. But as Prime Minister, I thought myself above that, thought I had risen high enough to see it all from a greater perspective. Instead, I allowed myself to become a passive bystander in my own party, part of an audience being fed carefully curated messaging to distract from what was real, from the machinations of my Deputy.'

My collarbones crawl for a moment as I think of my own passivity during my first duty, the things I saw as simply enabling the efficient and fair decisions of my government because that was what I'd been told. Only to find, once I stopped accepting such messaging at face value, that the government itself was, *is*, so flawed.

'And which are you most upset about? Being here, or the missteps that led you here?'

He laughs, but it's hollow. Brittle. 'I'm upset I've put so many at risk and enabled so many dangerous players. I'm ... upset I didn't see what was happening when talented people—advisors—were no longer able to access me properly, unable to provide the robust advice they'd been employed to give. I'm ... upset that the system has been taken out from under me, and it's harming the people I became Prime Minister to help.'

I blow out a breath. 'Careful, Prime Minister, you almost sound like a traitor.'

'Well, I don't know how happy that side would be with me now,' he says, looking sideways at me. 'I have much to answer for, and there is a lot of righting that needs to be done. That said, I can't see any way to move forward without exposing Zenaton and forcing the government to call for an election. An election unswayed by political misdirection, that people can vote in with the full knowledge of everything that has occurred.'

I blow out a breath. If I had ever thought of meeting the Prime Minister, this is not the direction I would have imagined the conversation would take – the Nuntainian Prime Minister giving voice to the same priorities as the traitors in Tae. But, then, I never would have imagined meeting him in Vana, either.

It's impossible not to feel like the room is holding its breath. Like everyone here – apart, perhaps, from that back table – is waiting to see what I will do. I'm still struggling to wrap my mind around the enormity of it, my thoughts spinning with the stories of the prisoners who approached me, what the Prime Minister has told me – the fact that I'm sitting with our Prime Minister, in *Vana*, discussing calling an election.

'So many of these people have been considered traitors,' I say.

'Yes,' he says, a weary sort of confidence in his tone. 'When I got here—when I had a reprieve from the early ... t-time—'

'Time?'

He swallows.

'The Hunters here specialise in torture—a most purposeful decision on my government's behalf, unfortunately. When they can't for any reason, the attendants step in.'

I think of the haunted faces of the Vana attendants at the occasional gatherings in the forest on the island, and a chill snakes down my spine.

They didn't hide that they did horrendous things on their duties, but perhaps those nights were so much more of an escape for them than I ever realised.

At the very least, they could see the night – the stars, and the trees, and feel the breeze on their skin. Something I find myself longing for more and more. I thought I would hate this island when I first arrived, but I've never been able to. It feels like she has also been a prisoner – forced to create a space for some of Nuntainia's worst secrets. What if she wanted to be used for our best?

'In the first weeks of a prisoner's arrival,' the Prime Minister is saying, 'the Hunters take particular care to break the prisoner's spirit, with day after day of whatever they can think up at the time. Some plan it out in advance, others just follow whatever sick whim strikes them on the day.'

And the Hunters all report through their Commander to the Ministry for Justice, and therefore Zenaton, who chairs it.

'Time,' I say slowly, my feet throbbing in protest as an acidic pit churns in the depths of my empty stomach. How much time can I really withstand any of this?

'So mine has only just begun?'

'I'm afraid so, Princess,' he says, gaze lowering towards the hands he presses between his thighs. 'But your being here can either fortify the traitors here with you, or destroy them. Only you can now decide how far you all bend to Zenaton.' He shifts in the seat so he's almost completely facing me, knees just about touching mine, and a soft expression seems to take over his whole face. 'Know this, though,' he says gently, 'not one person here will blame you if you break.'

The Hunter roughly grips my arms, jerking them behind my back and binding them with rough rope as I push the Prime Minister's words from my mind. I don't have a choice.

I will not break.

I walked out of the food hall with my head held high, biting the inside of my cheek until I tasted blood to distract from the burning pain in my lacerated feet. At least now, I know why the Hunter chose to hit them first – it's a very effective way of making someone feel powerless.

Unfortunately, I now also know that was just the warm-up – an assessment, probably, of how I'd react, how much I'd fight back. The thought of Quillian's feather grips my chest. If only I had—

I cut that thought off.

It's just me.

And the Hunter.

The skin on my wrists burns a little with the scrape of the rope as he tightens it, and I breathe around the sting.

I will survive whatever he brings.

Zenaton doesn't want me dead.

The feeling is not mutual.

My shoulders bark as the Hunter pulls me backwards by my bound arms, and I stumble towards the wall. Bending them at the elbow behind me, he almost carefully lifts, and then lowers, my arms over something I can't see. Something cold and hard on my biceps.

A bar.

All my weight is precariously balanced between the ruined balls of my feet and my arms over the bar at my back, shoulders pulled tight at the uncomfortable angle. My knuckles scratch against the brick wall and my knees begin to tremble, but I don't dare move my feet, the raw flesh fighting to keep me upright.

'Where are the other locations?' the Hunter asks as he comes back around to where I can see him in the small room. Not that it means anything – I can't make out any of his features behind his uniform. He could be anyone. If he didn't move with the strength and ... expertise of someone who has done this a long time, it could even be Zenaton.

I want to smash his sunglasses into his eyes.

Silence is my only answer. I told him yesterday I'd never tell him, I don't need to say it again.

He nods, no hint of surprise or annoyance in his stance. He just moves to the corner of the room, towards the end where I'm partially suspended, and almost completely outside my field of vision. But I think he starts to turn something. A soft creak fills the room a moment before pain radiates across my shoulders and down my chest and arms as the bar starts to lift.

The balls of my feet are peeled from the ground as I slowly go higher until just the pads of my big toes are bearing any of my weight. But any relief for my feet is totally drowned in the agony shooting through my torso. I forget about trying to see what the Hunter is doing and let my head drop towards the floor, biting back a cry.

'Know where they are yet? Those shits you've hidden?'

When I don't answer, there's a slight movement in the corner as he turns away from me again. My eyes sting from the pain that tries to steal the breath from my lungs. But I won't cry, I tell myself. Don't break. Don't cry. I let my mind go back to the stain on the ceiling of my cell and all the faces I found in it.

To the traitors I spoke to in the food hall. The stories they shared with me, the weight of their stares as they watched me limp from the room.

I will *not* break.

But my shoulders give way under my weight as the bar lifts me totally off the ground.

A scream tears from my throat.

Then all I know is darkness, and I'm momentarily grateful someone has turned out the lights.

CHAPTER THIRTY-SIX

I'm jolted from the serenity of the blackness by another blast of searing pain through the entire top half of my body, and I whimper. I don't know if I feel sick or have already been sick as the waves of pain beat down on me from above, narrowing my whole world to a blurred view of the floor. The Hunter has lowered the bar, and I'm now kneeling, arms still suspended behind my back.

'I'll leave you here for a bit,' he says, standing over me, his voice far away. 'Might help you remember.'

I don't know how long he leaves me; my legs have long since gone dead, my feet a strange combination of numb and throbbing, but nothing compares to the searing hot pain in my shoulders. Every now and then, it recedes a little, only for the movement of my next breath to send the waves crashing over me again.

As I hang my head, desperately trying to keep as much weight from my shoulders as possible, I almost wish I was someone who could give them the details. Could tell them where I told Quillian to send the recovering traitors and where to set up new camps for the rest.

But, while I have been searching for direction for a long part of my life, this is a purpose I will never walk away from. What Zenaton doesn't know is that this very action – having me tortured in Vana – coupled with the knowledge that other traitors have been subjected to this same treatment for no reason other than believing in something better, is only strengthening my resolve. He talks about 'holding the line', something I can only imagine comes from his military days, but I will hold mine, too.

'Luka,' a voice breaks into the bright silence of the room, but it's too familiar and I can't bear to look.

Can't bear to see that my mind is already warping to show me what I want.

'Luka,' they say again, and heavy footfalls stride across the room before a Hunter crouches in front of me.

I flinch when they reach for my chin, then whimper at the pain the movement causes in my shoulders, arms, and back. The Hunter drags his mask down and removes his glasses, revealing kind, light-brown eyes that blink back at me.

Holland.

A hope so wild it rips the breath from my lungs whips through me.

'What–what are you doing here?' I stammer.

'Helping. What else would a handsome rogue like me be doing up here?' He winks.

'It's really you,' I say, unable to direct any energy into schooling my features or the disbelief in my tone.

'Lucky for you, yes. And we're going to get you out of here.'

I bite my lips together against the sob that threatens to break free.

'I'm going to get you off the bar, okay?' He doesn't show any sign of surprise or pity for my current situation, and I wonder how many times he had to do this to others when he worked here.

A series of noises I've never made before are all I can summon as Holland gently unbinds my hands and guides my arms to the front of my body. They hang before me, heavy and useless and radiating pain.

'We don't have a lot of time—'

'Wait, I need to do something before we go.'

Holland stares at me like I've lost my mind. And maybe I have. But the Prime Minister ... if we could ...

My thoughts are sluggish, but I know I have to talk to him – to ask him outright if he would support us if we can get him out, how we can trigger an election Zenaton can't refuse. Give people the choice. The weight of how much work that could be is almost crippling, but I focus on what I can do now – find the Prime Minister. We can work out how to make sure Zenaton loses an election later.

Walking through the prison on busted feet with two arms I can't move is so much slower than I could have ever anticipated, and my heart gallops with the need to be faster, better. To be *out.* Holland helps where he can, but being touched in any way that shifts my weight is almost worse, and it's safer he keeps a distance and maintains his cover as an active Vanan Hunter.

I ask several prisoners if they've seen the Prime Minister, none of whom have any idea where he is, before I stumble on the kind man from my first day and a small trickle of relief runs down my spine.

'You need to sit down,' he says quietly, throwing a wary look over my shoulder to where Holland stalks a few paces behind.

'Yes,' I whisper, 'but I need the Prime Minister first, do you know where he is?'

He glances around. 'I'll bring him to you. Go back to your cell and rest—and don't move those shoulders until I bring someone who can put them back properly.'

He starts to walk away, but I move to grab him – a cry dying in my throat as I try to rein in the pain. The kind stranger looks back at me questioningly, even as he eyes Holland warily.

'Are you ... are you really here because you tried to make the Prime Minister see?'

He studies me a long moment. 'Yes.'

I close my eyes. 'If I can get you out of here, would you let me tell your story—stand with me?'

His touch is warm and light where he places two fingers on my forearm. 'Princess, I already do.'

'I don't like this,' Holland whispers, when he delivers me to my cell. 'We should be well clear of here by now, Luka.'

I can't face lying down on my back, unsure where the weight of my shoulders would go if I did, and willing to do anything to avoid any fresh waves of pain. So I perch on the edge of the cot, back straight, and try to lessen the contact my feet have with the floor as much as possible.

My eyes sting and I blink in the brightness. If my body wasn't hurting like this, I think I'd be running through the halls to get out – Hunters be damned. I've done it once; I could do it again. But then, I'm not naive enough to think I could fluke that again.

'Please hurry,' I whisper, ignoring Holland's statement.

The Prime Minister arrives what feels like an eternity later, stopping short when he sees Holland in my cramped cell. I urgently usher him closer.

'If I can trigger an election, would you support us? And how do I do that?'

He looks incredulously at Holland for a moment before a knowing smile graces his face – a smile I've never seen in person before, but seems so familiar from seeing his different presentations and speeches broadcast.

'Not a princess indeed,' he says, mostly to himself, before answering me. 'You will need to have a public declaration of no confidence passed—more than public discontent, and different to waiting for it to happen from the inside. The fastest way to do this will be to expose Zenaton by making public what you know, and call the people to demand action—Traelen will know how to handle the rest, including the declaration.'

My heart sinks a little, but I look at Holland. If he's here, hopefully that means there are others left who are releasing the stories as planned. I push away the sharpness of the not knowing who remains after the breach, and return my focus to the Prime Minister.

'We've started that. It got me slandered and sent here. But there are others continuing the fight to spread the information.' I don't look at Holland, in case I see a contradiction in his stance.

The Prime Minister runs a hand up the back of his head. 'Yes ... I can imagine. We are good at that, I'm sorry.' He paces for a moment. 'But it's good you didn't go for a "one and done" approach. Ideally, I would go with you to help with the election, but that would destroy any chance before you even begin. Zenaton watches me closely, as he does you—speaking of,' he says, gaze going slightly distant for a moment, 'we might need to get someone to pose as you for a while ... let me work that out and buy you time. It won't be a lot, though. They'll see through any guise quickly.'

He stops in his tracks and looks intently at me. 'In the meantime, at my holiday house, in a locked box in a space under my desk, there is a notepad. It details all the decisions I wasn't sure of once I finally started to become aware—a process I used to look back and see if things were really going wrong, or if I was doubting myself and my government too much. Unfortunately, the picture it builds is the correct one, but I caught on too late and ended up here before I could do anything about it. Take that, take it public along with what you've already got, and ... tell the people I'm sorry.'

'Will it be enough?' I ask, thinking of everything we've found and shared so far, only to have it explained away by me supposedly being a harlot. But we're not finished yet, and having the Prime Minister's support for an election could bring about change so much faster.

'My voice behind it should be, yes. But you have seen Zenaton in action. I can't guarantee he hasn't already undermined my credibility to the point that the book will be meaningless, or predict what he will do to defend himself from it.' He pauses, as if weighing up if he should continue. 'If you can't get any traction that way, he will need to be assassinated—that will then trigger an election as a matter of course. I assume you don't have an issue with making that order?'

I hold his gaze, the question about how far I will go to right our world hanging between us.

'I can make the order.'

My arms are heavy, on the verge of numb. I brace them awkwardly against my body to try to stop them moving as Holland shadows me down the hall. Whoever the kind man was going to send to reset my shoulders didn't show, at least not before Holland decided we couldn't wait anymore.

But whether I'd be in more or less pain right now if my shoulders were back in place, I don't know. Hitting the stairwell at the end, I can't help but cry out softly as the impact of my steps downwards send shock waves of pain through my feet, back, and shoulders. My vision blurs, sweat beading on my forehead and slipping down my spine.

'Not long now,' Holland mutters.

But a pair of Hunters block my path as we reach the bottom, and I draw up short.

'Ah, we've been looking for you,' one of them says, as if they're talking about some casual meeting we're due to have.

My heart hammers in my chest as Holland takes the last step behind me at the same time the second Hunter notices my arms.

'Well, they're out good and proper, aren't they?' Pressure builds behind my eyes, but I refuse to cry here. 'You're due for your next session.'

A caving sensation grips the centre of my chest.

'She is,' Holland says from behind me. 'We're on our way.'

The two Hunters before me exchange a look, their expressions completely unreadable behind their glasses and masks.

'We were—'

'Zenaton's changed the schedule,' Holland says, 'and we're late. Never seen someone move so slow. We're headed for room two.' He pushes me sharply in the back of my right shoulder. I cry out and stumble forward, nausea surging in my gut.

The two Hunters step swiftly aside as I lurch towards them, but I manage to catch my footing between them—one now on either side. The edges of my vision grow foggy, dark, and I barely manage to hold my forearms tight against my front.

'On your way then,' one of them says, and I don't look at them again. 'We'll see you if you survive room two.'

'Move,' Holland says sharply, and I wince at his tone. I know it's not him. Not the him I know. But between the uniform and the shove and his demand, my mind is muddled.

Cortane, I think desperately. Please just get me to Cortane.

I want that portal.

Shuffling forward, I move as quickly as I can. As far away as possible from anywhere Holland might have to touch me roughly again.

He's quiet as we walk, pointing me towards the plain entrance of Vana. I don't know what I expected, but a small, empty room with a plastic window into an office of some sort probably wasn't it. Although I guess they don't need anywhere for visitors to come, and this isn't where I was brought in.

We move through the tiny foyer from a door next to what almost looks like a ceiling-high box. As we move further forward, I can see its small window and, inside, the empty office. Like a ticketing booth. A ticket to the worst part of the world.

Six more steps.

Then we'll be out the door.

Cortane is probably in the treeline.

I take a step.

Two.

Three.

Four.

An alarm screeches so loud it almost splits my head in half and I flinch, arms jolting in pain.

'Run,' Holland appears to say, but his voice is lost in the noise.

Drawing a deep breath, I run – stumble – my useless arms making me so much slower than I ever could have imagined.

Heavy footfalls fill the tiny gaps between each pulse of the alarm, and I don't know if they're real, or it's just my head filling with fear so fast I can taste it. Feel it beating in my blood.

If Zenaton knows I have tried to escape, he will never let me live.

Nor will Holland survive.

So I keep running.

Harder.

Feet burning. Bleeding. Chest heaving.

Sweat stinging my eyes as my fingers tremble with cold.

Holland keeps pace with me, even though I know he can go so much faster. And I'm slammed with a memory of us doing almost exactly this from the other prison.

Except then, I thought I'd killed Zenaton.

Now, I wish, with a fury I didn't know possible, that I had.

The trees loom in my vision, but I don't have the breath to ask Holland where to go. He just keeps running, gently nudging me towards our goal, never looking back. So neither do I.

I never thought I'd be so desperate to see Cortane.

Another thought pushes into my mind – even if she isn't here, I will keep running. I will run right off the island if it means I never go back to Vana.

We're not quiet as we crash through the forest, but the alarm is still so loud, I can't imagine anyone could hear us.

But when we break a tiny clearing right near the edge, there is no Cortane. The tide of emotion that's been building since the Hunters raided our camp starts to erupt, and I can no longer suppress the sobs that make my body heave.

Quillian waits for us, bladed wings out, the sun catching on the points.

CHAPTER THIRTY-SEVEN

A desperate sound rips from my throat at the sight of him, and my knees feel like they will give out. In two strides, he's before me.

'Careful,' Holland blurts quickly. 'She's busted.'

Quillian assesses me briskly, his cold mask – the one I know means he's ready for anything – slips as he looks at my shoulders, arms, and feet, a hot rage taking its place, mingled with pain, or perhaps its regret.

For a moment, the only sound is of me trying to catch my breath. It's almost peaceful. I look over Quillian's shoulder at the sky, the immeasurable blue expanse before us as the edge of the island falls away. I can't help but draw a little closer, stepping slightly to the side of Quillian so I can still feel the warmth of his presence.

I just want one more look at this view. Want to remember my time as somehow hopeful. Strong. Resilient.

Zenaton didn't break me.

No. He didn't break me. Instead, he delivered me straight to one of our most powerful – and completely unexpected – allies. A connection I will use to end him.

It takes me a moment to notice Quillian and Holland are talking over my head – quietly, urgently – and a coldness settles into my gut at the realisation there are two of us and only one Karaylia.

There is no portal to take us both off the island.

'This is going to hurt, Luka, but we need to go—I'll get you straight to River,' Quillian says, arranging what looks like a harness strapped to his waist. 'You this side. H, you're on the other.'

Holland steps up and lifts a foot to step into the harness Quillian holds out to him. Can he really take the two of us? My chest floods with relief, tinged with bitterness at the knowledge his strength is just one of the things that meant his bloodline has been one coveted for elite forces.

'Here!' a voice filters through the trees. 'They've been through here.'

A flash of the path of destruction we must have left in the undergrowth makes me freeze.

'Go,' Holland orders quietly, stepping out of the harness and turning his back to us. He draws a pistol from the side of his Hunter's belt.

'Take this,' Quillian says, drawing the sword from his back and handing it to Holland, who barely glances back as he accepts it, his focus on the treeline.

The Hunters crash through the forest even louder than we did.

'Ruins,' Quillian murmurs. 'Finn will be here in less than thirty minutes. Survive it.'

Surely we can't leave him here. Aren't the ruins of my old prison an obvious place to go?

'Hol—' I cry.

A gunshot cracks the air and I close my eyes against the shock. By the time I look up, Holland has gone, melting into the trees.

'It will keep them busy trying to find him,' Quillian says gently. 'We need to get you out of here. Finn will come, Luka. Turn.'

His voice is short as he instructs me, his arms quickly coming around my back and over my ribs, under my own injured limbs. I bite back on the aftermath of the movement as Quillian grips me tightly before launching us up into the air.

Our descent is sharp and hard. I can tell by feel alone that his wings are tucked in tight as we arrow towards the blue dome of wards.

He groans angrily as we go through. The wards stay in place, leaving their mark on him, so different to when I went through the barrier with Blossom – the contrast of magic versus no magic now clear.

The wind tears at my face and my stomach rolls over as we plummet towards the ground. The pressure forces my arms backwards, my mind starts to go fuzzy, and I feel clammy all over.

I close my eyes, wishing away the rest of the descent.

Our landing is smoother than I'd expected. Quillian scoops an arm under my legs, sweeping me up and into his chest. Letting my head rest against him, I drag in breath after breath. *I'm okay. I'm okay. I'm okay,* I chant to myself.

This pain is nothing to what Holland could be experiencing, and I want to be sick.

'Finn!' Quillian barks out, chest vibrating under my cheek. 'Prison ruins. Holland. Go.'

All I see of Finn is a dark shape in the sky as he comes into my line of sight over Quillian's head. Wings so black they almost seem blue, beating hard and fast towards Zanteera island.

'Luka?' Blossom's voice is like a magic balm. I turn to try and find her, but Quillian grips me tighter, striding towards wherever I assume he thinks River is.

'Luka.' The word is a flood of relief as she appears, jogging next to Quillian.

'Quillian, stop,' I say quietly. 'Please.'

It takes him a second, but he blinks down at me, steps slowing. 'What's happening?' he asks, scanning me from head to toe – at least as much as he can see.

'I'm okay,' I say, knowing it's a lie, 'just–just, please, put me down.'

'You need River,' he says, like it's a question and he can't work out what I'm really asking.

'I do. And Bloss will take me—I can walk. But Holland—Finn—they need you.'

He glances to the sky, and I can tell he's just as worried as I am.

'Are there others you can take?' I ask, thinking of the footfalls that I can still feel in my bones.

Carefully, he sets me down. 'Cort!' he shouts, voice echoing off the buildings of the square, and she appears beside us from a portal in almost less than a blink.

'Get a team,' he says, every bit the commanding officer. 'Finn and Holland need an extraction. I'm marked, so will Finn be, and I don't give a fuck if we all are now. I'm not leaving them up there. Secure the borders.'

She's gone again without even saying a word.

Around us, a make-shift camp I don't recognise bubbles into activity – word obviously spreading quickly.

'This way,' Blossom says, gently taking my elbow from underneath. There's pain when she does it, but mostly relief that she's taken the weight of that arm. Quillian does the same on the other side, and I feel like I could take a deep breath for the first time.

'I'll set her up on one of the beds here,' Bloss says, 'then I'll find River.'

'You sure?' Quillian asks, stepping in front of me and holding my chin carefully. His dark green eyes flick between my own, as if he's convincing himself I'm okay and really requesting he go. If I could squeeze him like I so desperately want, I would.

Part of me physically recoils at him leaving. At going back to that island where Holland is literally being hunted by Hunters right now. There is not a chance he'll be able to rely on his cover now. But this is him. It's what he needs to do. And neither of us would ever leave Holland.

'I'm sure, Quillian. I'm here. I'm safe. I have access to help. They do not. It's not even a decision.'

'Ready,' Cortane says as she appears again, Nix at her side.

Quillian crashes his mouth to mine, hands slipping to the back of my head, fingers in my hair as he breathes life into my veins.

'I love you, Rebel Princess,' he whispers against my lips, before striding to Cortane and Nix, gripping each of their upper arms where they stand either side of him. In a flash, they're above the buildings, Quillian flying hard, dragging Nix and Cortane along without bothering with a harness, as Cortane appears to portal jump them in bursts through the sky at the same time.

I remember Cortane saying she wouldn't be strong enough to portal anyone off the island before our last escape. Clearly, her magic – or maybe her – hasn't recovered enough from her time in Vana even now. Not to mention how many of us she had to portal when we'd arrived on the mainland when she was already so compromised. As I watch them part fly, part portal out of view, I wonder how much of me will now never be the same, either.

'Come on,' Blossom says, gently guiding me forward. 'We really missed you. I was ... I was fucking terrified, Lu.'

I look at her properly then, this staunch friend of mine who has been thrown into this world just as much as me. Her hair is tied off her face in a knot on the top of her head, the rest of her curls falling down the back of her neck. There's a tiredness in her features, but also a glow underneath. Something I don't think has anything to do with magic, but being right where she's supposed to be.

'Bloss, when I can move my arms without wanting to pass out, I'm going to give you the biggest fucking hug.'

River and Blossom tend to me in a triage room, having washed, healed and wrapped my feet, before beginning on my shoulders. Blossom has her hand on my face, her Arkanan magic relieving so much of the pain. It gently runs down my skin before joining with River's in my shoulder, providing further pain relief while he heals what's torn and damaged. He's already set my left arm, and now slowly moves my right arm this way and back, before straightening it right out in front of me and gently manipulating the shoulder joint as I sit on a bed.

There's a quiet look of concentration on his face while he works on me, and I can feel his magic like a warm, guiding hand inside my shoulder. Once upon a time, he would help Nix and I with small ailments – headaches, tummy upsets – and that felt a bit like being awash in a warm bath. Now, there's incredible precision in how his magic moves inside my body. A swell of pride rises in my chest and I blink up at him.

'What is it?' he asks distractedly.

'You're very good at this.'

'Hmmm,' he says noncommittally, and I smile. His gaze flicks to Blossom quickly before returning to my shoulder, and her fingers tighten a little on my cheek. I don't know if she's holding me there because it's best for her magic, or because she's my friend. But I lean into her touch, even though the flexing of her fingers is a dead giveaway her feelings for River are only growing.

'How's Nix?' I ask. 'The others?'

'We're managing. We had a scramble to get to this spot after the attack – we lost a lot that night.'

The memory of the bodies strewn around me as the Hunters took me away is one that burns. A groan escapes me as my right shoulder sinks back into position, now matching my left.

'I'm not sure the Hunters up there will be quite expecting the full force of Quillian and Nix coming down on them for hurting you,' he says, carefully placing my right arm back alongside my body, palm resting on the bed.

I shudder, still acutely aware of my clammy skin and racing heart that won't seem to still.

'If Holland—'

'Lu,' River cuts me off, squeezing my thighs just above my knees. 'You can't think like that. I can't promise you he will be okay. But I do know what this group is capable of—he has the best possible chance to make it out.'

I nod numbly as a wave of nausea grips me. If Holland doesn't make it because he got me out ...

'Quillian's marked,' I say, but my lips feel thicker than normal, and I glance at River to see if he understood.

'Marked?' he asks, frowning at me like my words were as mumbled as I thought.

He curses as I nod, my head heavy, and I wonder if this is what being torn between relief and terror feels like.

'We don't have long, then—'

'She's quite warm,' Blossom says from beside me. Her voice is low, almost curious, but there's something in it I can't quite place.

River's gaze locks on hers for a moment, and they seem to have a silent conversation. He places two fingers high up under my jaw and closes his eyes, his magic gently beating in time with my pulse.

It's fast.

His blue eyes remind me of the sky on the island. They should almost be full of soft, white clouds.

And maybe a heron.

I'd so love to see a grey heron again. Anything that could mean a sign from Claudius that everything will turn out okay.

I smile at the thought of a heron diving through River's eyes of sky. I blink as those eyes narrow at me.

'How are you feeling right now, Luka?'

Right now? Kind of floaty.

'Luka?' he asks again, and I frown. Did I not say that out loud?

'Ummm,' I croak, trying to pull my brain into focus. 'Kind of ... far away, I think.'

'I'm just going to lay you down a moment ...'

River's voice fades away as I lay down and close my eyes, vaguely aware of Blossom removing her hands.

'Luka?' Dad's voice echoes around me. Something in it pulls at the centre of my chest. Is that worry? Or maybe he's touching me—

'—infection,' I think I hear one of them say.

'Or poison?'

River's magic does wash over me then, and I sigh. They were good days.

'—in her bloodstream, check her feet for—'

A similar sort of darkness that came for me in Vana creeps in at the edges. But this time, I don't want to not see River's sky eyes or Blossom's ocean ones. Maybe that's why I know they'd be good together – each so capable of such vast love. Not that I've seen the ocean ... But there's something sinister about the darkness that doesn't feel like the relief I want.

Tears wet cheeks that no longer feel like mine. Were they ever?

'Luka, sweetheart,' my Dad says. 'Stay—'

I try to force my eyes open, a dim part of me aware that I should be thinking about things other than River and Bloss right now. But there's a tiredness dragging on me that's so heavy, I just ... can't.

There's a rush of activity around me as I'm cocooned tighter in River's magic, like it's sitting just underneath my skin and pulling tight. Then it pulls me under.

'Where are the other locations?' the Hunter asks me, the brightly lit room in Vana blurring around me.

My mouth opens. I can feel the words there, feel what it would be like to form them. The names of the places I told Quillian's team to send the displaced traitors. To hide them. To keep them safe.

They're so close, those words, they could almost slip right off my tongue – like ice cubes down a slide. Then I'd be powerless to bring them back.

I squeeze my eyes shut, something warm running under my skin. I can't tell them. I won't.

Something whips my feet—

'—put them there,' someone orders – River, I think.

Instead, I think of the list of survivors of Tae.

A different kind of sound fills my ears as my mind shifts away from Vana.

The quiet groaning of someone else's pain.

The shuffling of heavy boots.

The striding footsteps and urgent talking of others I can't make out.

River's magic stays with me in the darkness, grounding me out of my distorted memory of Vana.

'Where are the other locations?'

Whip. The sound of my skin splitting.

I whimper.

'—going on?' a deep voice demands, one that sends a rush of impossible warmth straight through the centre of my chest.

The darkness starts to recede a little at the corners as River's magic turns to a burn where it sinks into my veins.

'Hey,' Quillian says, voice laced with worry, and I moan as his hands slide over my shoulders, all the still tender parts. 'Luka?'

'Working theory,' River says from somewhere far away, 'is that they coated whatever they tore her feet up with in some kind of drug—likely to prep her to talk—but she seems to be having some kind of reaction to whatever it was. Find as much gauze as you can,' he barks – an instruction I don't think is directed at Quillian.

There's a gentle light behind my eyelids and I try to peel them open, but they're gritty. Sticky.

'I can't see,' I whisper, the sound scraping up my now dry throat.

What the fuck is happening to me?

'Is she stable?' Quillian asks.

River curses under his breath. 'As stable as I can get her. He's bleeding out.'

My chest starts to heave with a cry that hasn't yet made it to my throat. Not Holland, please not Holland.

The anger I felt in the prison rises through my centre and I want to scream, but it has nowhere to go.

'I need to see,' I beg into the space. 'Please, help me see.'

Quillian covers my eyes with the palms of his hands, and I breathe in his scent. It's like the darkest parts of the forest, hidden under the smell of dirt and sweat and the unmistakable stench of blood. But his gentle Arkanan abilities brush my eyes and start to clear my head. I know he's not as powerful as River, not in this, but this small action creates such relief. Enough that I can drag my mind from the fog and blink open my eyes, my lashes catching on his skin.

His face fills my vision as he takes his hands away, his dark skin covered in black marks and fresh and drying blood.

'I'm okay,' he says, to my unasked question, my falling face probably asking it clearly enough.

Carefully, I grip the front of his shirt, absently noting I can move my arms again, even if it's an effort.

'Is everyone?' I choke out.

His eyes, the same colour as the island forest, shutter.

'Not yet,' he says gently, stepping away a little, his eyes telling me what I do not want to hear out loud. 'We got Holland, but...'

I let my head fall sideways on the bed beneath me, looking past Quillian.

To where Nix lies, surrounded by River, Blossom, and a team of healers. Quillian's team hover at the edges in various degrees of injured, bloodied, and dirty. Their dark uniforms wet in places.

Nix, whose dark auburn hair is haphazardly spread out on the metal table. His left arm hangs lifelessly off the side of the trolley, blood dripping from his fingertips.

CHAPTER THIRTY-EIGHT

The room falls away as I stare, uncomprehendingly, at Nix's lifeless form. What I can see of it. Dragging myself to a sitting position, Quillian helps me off the bed and guides me to Nix's side, pressing us through a small gap between two of the team. I don't notice who.

'River?' I ask shakily, without taking my attention from Nix. The paleness of his face. The hollowed look of his cheeks. Did he look like that before? Is that his grief? Or his death?

Oh, fuck.

'Concentrating, Lu,' River says absently, his hands buried in the other side of Nix's torso.

Blossom stands at one of Nix's shoulders, another healer at his other, another two at his feet. They all have their eyes closed, palms on his torso and shins, while a fourth healer stands next to River providing a steady stream of gauze, mopping up what they can of Nix's blood. There's a sheen of sweat on Bloss's brow, and I wonder how many times she's done this in my absence – or are Nix and I the first?

'Please, Nix,' I whisper, kneeling next to him and dropping my head on the cold metal. 'Please.'

Quillian stands behind me, his legs bracing my sides just like he did on the island Nix created to get us off Zanteera Island the first time.

But I refuse to believe I am about to fall.

Lifting my head, I find Nix's limp and bloody hand and loop my fingers in his, staring at him – his face, his chest – watching for any sign of life.

Every now and then, I look up at River, Blossom, and the other healers.

River wipes his forehead awkwardly on his bicep without looking up.

'I just need to find ...' he mutters.

The room is so quiet, I can hear Quillian breathing behind me. He puts a hand in my hair, his palm making my scalp warm. So warm compared to the hand I hold in mine.

Please, Nix. I'm begging you.

'Fuck—where—I just—' River is saying, but no one responds.

Then Blossom gasps and I flinch.

'Here,' she says urgently, eyes closed. 'The bleed. River, help me.'

My heart pounds in my ears.

'Lead me,' River says, his voice brittle.

Blossom frowns, a crease forming between her eyes.

'Got you,' River says, 'go slow.'

I imagine their magic joining inside Nix's body, Blossom gently guiding River's to where it needs to plug whatever hole Nix has torn inside.

It's quiet for several more, long, long moments.

River makes a cracking, sob-like noise that cleaves me through the middle.

'Got it,' he says, and the whole room exhales. 'Fuck.' He exhales loudly before ordering the healers to send as much as they can to the location of the bleed. Now, he tells them, they can give as much as they like. Now, he's used precision to fix the worst issue. Nix shouldn't bleed again.

Slowly, the team of traitors around us start to filter away, and eventually so do the additional healers – probably to tend to the various injuries of the others.

Holland squeezes my shoulder as he leaves.

I give him a watery smile I'm not sure he sees because I can't take my eyes off Nix. Can't stop watching him breathe. Watching the rise and fall of the chest that was so inhumanly still before.

'Thank you,' I whisper, squeezing his hand. 'I know it took a lot for you to fight your way back.'

Thank you, I think as I press my face to the back of his hand.

And he squeezes my fingers in return.

Quillian passes me a glass of water, and I take it gratefully from where I sit in a chair beside Nix. For all the world, he looks like he's having the deepest, most restorative sleep of his life. Maybe he is.

'You should get some rest, too, Luka,' River says, pulling up a chair next to mine. He's washed and the colour has returned to his face. But the haunted worry hasn't quite left his eyes yet, the knowledge he could have lost Nix despite his very best efforts obviously still weighing on him.

I nod slowly and give him a long look, but words that feel adequate don't come. I can't even acknowledge out loud our unspoken shift arrangement of staying with Nix.

'I'll stay, too,' Dad says, before helping me out of my chair and pulling me into him, hugging me hard. 'I'll watch him, okay.'

My eyes burn as my chest shudders against him. He draws me tighter, and I drop my head into his shoulder, clinging to him. As we stand together, I can feel things between us shift and rearrange. Like the process of finding him and bringing him here were the intellectual pieces of our puzzle, and now our feelings are following that lead.

'Thank you,' I whisper, unsure if either of us really grasp the enormity of everything that could mean. 'Call me,' I say, finally pulling away and vaguely aware I'm back to having no phone since Vana, but knowing River will be able to get me through Quillian.

Standing, Quillian slides his hand into mine and guides me from the triage room and its scattered medical beds and chairs and into the darkness. He leads me down a narrow path, but I stop him after a few steps and look up at the night sky. Just for one breath, I take in the inky blackness and the stars that sparkle so brightly, like they never seem to do in Klades. One breath in which my heart aches to be in the sky again, but in a way that is peaceful and whole, not used as part of some hideous cover up. Then I exhale, grateful I am here and the people I love are safe. For tonight.

Quillian waits until I walk again, gently leading me towards a small, cabin-like building.

From the beige front step, I study what I can see of Quillian's back beneath his wings as he opens the front door. When he turns to let me into the open space, I catch the way he's slightly more careful with the left side of his body. We're still quiet, a comfortable if sad silence, as we stand in the sparse living room and look at each other.

'You got him,' I say, knowing those words are so inadequate for what clearly happened on that island.

'We did.'

'And you're marked.'

'Yes.' His face shadows as he reaches out and tugs me closer. 'So we don't have long. Cortane is working on scrambling the tracking signal, but that is temporary at best.'

There's a pressure in the depths of my gut that wants to break free, slowly pressing its way up into my chest, and I swallow against the tide.

'Hey,' Quillian says softly, pressing me against his chest. 'I've got you, you're here, Nix and Holland are okay, and we have right now.'

I drop my forehead to his body and feel into the movement of his breathing, the gentle force of it. We have right now and he's injured. Small steps Luka.

Slowly, I look up and take the rest of him in. He seems mostly intact, if not dirty, but the wings that frame him are almost completely covered in dark red blood.

There's a pinch in my chest at the wish we really did have a cabin that was ours. Something, some*where,* to call home. Somewhere to actually *feel* like home. Even if it was as simple as this one. But that's something people can only have if they're part of the system. A functioning, but unquestioning, member of the way Nuntainia runs.

Something neither Quillian nor I are. Something I don't think he's ever been.

We look at each other for a moment, and a warmth passes through me at having him. That somehow in this busted system, we found each other. And, despite everything, he's standing here with me. Has stood with me since we met.

I push myself onto my toes so I can pull him into a kiss. He inhales sharply, kissing me back with a possession that ignites everything from my scalp to my toes with a crackling fire.

'Let's get you in the shower,' I say, pulling back to meet his dark gaze. 'And I want to look at your left side.'

He drops a swift, firm kiss to my lips. 'Yes, ma'am,' he says, before walking ahead of me into the bathroom just off the bedroom that's far bigger than I would have guessed.

I watch the graceful, powerful way he moves, even beneath the layers of pain and fatigue I know he only lets me see. My heart warms and that heat gently starts to move lower through my body.

He tucks his wings in tight, and they disappear with a soft 'whoosh' as he removes his layers of black – jacket, then tight, long sleeve shirt, and finally, a sleeveless vest. Leaving his torso naked, black pants slung low on his hips, boots still on. He braces himself against the sink for a moment, and my gaze lands on the bleeding gash in his left side.

It's about as long as my hand, and fresh blood slowly leaks between dried, crusty patches of almost black blood. As if the blood stuck to his vest, tearing his wound further when he removed the fabric.

'Boots,' I say, and his gaze flicks up to mine in the mirror.

Wordlessly, he perches on the edge of the bath and takes one boot off at a time, tossing them into the far corner of the pale bathroom where they land with a thud. I reach my hands out and gently tug him to standing, watching his thighs flex under his pants as he does, before undoing them and wriggling them down his legs. He steps out and loses his tight, dark shorts.

I can feel his gaze on me, but I don't want to look away from his body and I don't try. Instead, I drink in his dark skin, the light dusting of hair that trails the base of his stomach, up and over his chest and down. All the way down. The cut of his hips, how the curve of his thighs presses outwards slightly. The rise and fall of his chest as he lets me watch him.

My fingers start to tremble and my eyes burn, even as heat continues to build within me.

I clear my throat. 'I need a wash cloth and a first aid kit.'

'Both should be under the sink. Washer in the bottom drawer, kit in the cupboard.'

He waits while I gather what I want from the bathroom vanity, patiently standing outside the shower. Reaching past him, I turn the water on and keep my hand under the running water until it's hot enough.

All the while watching Quillian watch me. Some deep, unspoken feeling passing between us.

'In,' I say, and he obeys immediately.

I'm momentarily breathless as he steps under the water in the middle of the huge shower and closes his eyes, the water beating down, over the top of his head and down his chest. He turns, brushing the water out of his face, and I follow the water's path down his shoulders and over his muscular ass.

As he stands there, I take my own position on the edge of the bath and remove the dressings from my feet. Breathing a sigh at how good they feel, and taking a moment to marvel at the slightly pink, healing skin.

The ruined clothes I wore in Vana come away like a layer of myself. I relish the soft light of the room and the cool of the air on my skin as I place them in a pile at the far end of the bathroom. I imagine that burning them will bring me the most peace. The thought is more liberating than I expected, and I almost smile as I retrieve the wash cloth and turn to join Quillian in the shower.

Where the air is cool on my skin, Quillian's gaze is scorching. The gentle throbbing between my legs intensifies, warmth tingling my cheeks as he starts to grow hard, the lids of his eyes lowering a fraction as I step towards the shower.

I suck in a breath as the hot water envelops me and Quillian wraps his hands around my waist.

'Wash,' I tell him, thinking particularly about that cut that needs cleaning, and he steps back under the water.

I start with his face, gently dragging the soft fabric over his closed eyes, his cheek bones, strong nose and sharp jaw, his full lips that part slightly as I brush them with my fingers. I follow the line of his neck and move across his chest, down his ribs, and the pattern of the tattoo on his side.

For those who prove the colour of their souls.

His erection stands tall before me, but I ignore it, for now, in favour of the cut on his side. It's not deep, and I can see immediately why he didn't have River or one of the others look at it. But it's still good for it to be flushed with water, and I'll dress it after to keep it clean.

Placing my hands on his shoulders, I turn him to face away from me and wash his back.

'Wings,' I say when I'm done.

A slight, cool breeze brushes my face as his wings come out, the water in the bottom of the shower turning pink as parts of them get wet. My chest tightens.

'Is any—'

'No,' he says quietly, 'it's not mine.'

I blow out a breath and start washing. Carefully brushing in the direction of the feathers from top to bottom.

Quillian drops his head to the tiles with a groan as I move over his spine, to where the wings start near his shoulder blades and up, over, and down the wings themselves. I wash every feather of each wing until the water runs clear and goosebumps have broken out over Quillian's skin.

Dropping the washer to the floor of the shower, where it lands with a wet smack, I place my hands on Quillian instead, palms running up either side of his spine and over the top ridges of his wings. The feathers are wet and silky soft under my touch as I trace the outer edges all the way to the tips of the feathers at the bottom. The ones that form the spiked edges of a sea of blades.

Quillian sucks in a deep, quivering breath.

I take a step closer, pressing into his back with my naked body until I can feel him trembling against me.

Snaking my hands around his front, I rest my forehead between his wings as I fist his length. He bucks into me, his hard cock slipping through my wet fist, and he releases a guttural sound that reverberates through his chest, vibrating against my breasts.

The ache between my legs grows as I pump him, his arms now braced on the wall. With my free hand, I reach further around and down, cupping and gently squeezing his balls as I work him harder, faster. His breath grows ragged in time with mine, and I lean into the rise and fall of his breathing where I embrace him from behind.

'Fu—' he groans, unable to form the word as I pump faster.

His ass cheeks tense against my lower stomach and I press myself into the back of his leg, getting just the smallest amount of pressure.

He groans loudly as I trace the place where his skin turns into wings with my tongue, and then he explodes, his cock kicking in my fist while I gently, slowly, continue to stroke him as he rides it out.

After several long, peaceful moments, he turns to face me, his breathing still returning to normal as he pulls me into him, pressing a soft, soft kiss against my mouth. And I savour the sensation of something feeling so right in a world that's so wrong. So busted. A world in which none of us traitors fit, yet we still have each other.

CHAPTER THIRTY-NINE

Slipping the shirt Quillian gave me over my head, I switch off the bathroom light before stepping back into the bedroom. Quillian releases a soft laugh from where he sits, leaning against the headboard.

'If I could choose one thing for you to wear every day, for the rest of our lives ... it would be that,' he says, face alight with cheek and desire.

I cock my head. 'Why this?'

'It's the hint of ass. That little glimpse of what I know is under there, but can't quite see. And ...' his voice softens, 'the fact I know what's under there is the best thing that's ever happened to me.'

I crawl up the bed towards him, feeling suddenly powerful, sexy – emboldened – by the depth beneath his words.

'Quillian,' I whisper, heart hammering as I straddle him, taking his face in my hands and searching his dark green eyes as I come to rest on his hips. 'I will spend every day of my life trying to live up to that.'

He strokes my still-wet hair back from my face, his fingers gentle, before a thought appears to occur to him. He drops his hand to my thigh, holding me in place as he bends to the side, reaching into one of the pockets of his pants on the floor and pulls out his – my – feather.

'You need this,' he says, handing it to me with a catch in his voice.

I watch the velvety edges slide through his fingers as I take it from him, and pressure builds behind my eyes.

'I have—' I cut myself off with a sigh. There's so much I want to tell him about Vana, but thinking about it compresses my chest so hard I can barely breathe.

'We have time,' he says. 'Take your time.'

It's a lie, I know, but my heart swells at the time I know he would buy for me all the same, the choices he would carve for me out of the impossible – if it were only him to pay the price. But the truth is, there is no time. He and Finn are marked, it doesn't even matter now if anyone else is. Zenaton will already know that I escaped, know there is only one person who could have coordinated that. And he now has a direct, if temporarily hijacked, tracking mechanism to find us.

I can tell part of Quillian wants to tell me I don't have to say anything at all. But we both know that if there's anything I can tell him that will help the rest of the traitors, and the people of Nuntainia, he needs to know. I can also sense his desperation to know how badly I've been hurt. Needs to soothe his own worry from while I was gone and know what traumas we will all carry forward.

'Do you want to see how it's been going?' he asks gently, and I know he means the reaction to my article.

I almost laugh, but I can't make the sound.

'I heard the initial response in the holding cell.'

He closes his eyes briefly, but doesn't ask anything more.

'Then you would have seen what the government and the media they influence tried to undermine you with – nothing less than what we expected. But you won't have seen the online reaction.'

The *tap-tap* sound of the Vanan traitors echoes in my ears as Quillian reaches for his phone, also on the floor beside the bed.

He swipes up and hands it to me. 'You should scroll through some of these.'

Quillian curves his hands around my hips as I sit back on his thighs, my first article open on the screen in my hand. I briefly scan the text as I scroll to the comment section. Rosie has cleverly used the headings and strategically placed bolded quotes to draw the eye so that, even if someone just skims, my words form both a scathing exposé and a moving call to action.

Then there are the comments – more comments than I can truly comprehend. Some sound like Zenaton could have written them himself; they echo the sentiment of the news I heard after my arrest. The others, though ... my nose burns with suppressed emotion.

Myriads of people express outrage, demand answers, defend me, condemn the secrecy surrounding the prison program, and speculate on who has evaded punishment through it. I cover my mouth with my hand as more are posted before my eyes.

Seeing – in black and white – that people are listening is more heartening than I imagined. I'd hoped they'd see the facts, would believe enough to question. But the fact they are enraged, begging for more details, fills me with hope for the reaction to all we are yet to share. The details of the prisoners, including Aiten, Kasera, Miana, Davorous, and Zenaton; leading to who Zenaton is under the surface; the political and physical destruction of Tae through the creation of the breeding program; and, finally, an introduction to the Rebel Prince of Tae – and Nuntainian war hero. The last one I didn't see, it wasn't written before I was taken, but that was our plan.

'This is ... really good,' I say. 'I worried—'

He nods. 'I know. But the wave is building. The comments follow the same pattern on the second piece we released while you were in Vana, and the remaining three are scheduled.' He takes his phone and drops it back down on the pile of clothes before replacing his hands on my thighs. 'We're expecting a similar response to those.'

I blow out a breath and slide off Quillian to lie beside him.

It's working. Slowly.

Buoyed a little by the article and its comments, I tell Quillian everything that happened on Vana. As the anger, horror, and then surprise roll across his face, I think about the system. The government that has so blatantly abused its power and not just turned a blind eye to, but enabled, celebrated, and rewarded, the heinous crimes of some of the worst people to exist. I know now that it wasn't Prime Minister Millyn. His desire for an election, his willingness to give up his long-held power for the possibility of making Nuntainia – and Tae – better, safer, are proof of that. But is a system where all of this can happen under the Prime Minister's nose the right one?

And if that system has failed us so badly, can we really risk Zenaton taking over officially?

What if an election is triggered and those same people vote Zenaton back in? What if he changes the rules so another election can *never* be triggered? What if the choices we present them after we expose it all aren't enough?

At the same time, don't the people deserve to know? Deserve a chance to form the Nuntainia we should be?

I think on the Prime Minister's comments about it being easier to take over something that already exists than start again. Which is essentially how Zenaton was able to rise to his current position of acting Prime Minister. Now, in the absence of Prime Minister Millyn, Zenaton is *the* Prime Minister for all intents and purposes.

'Prime Minister Millyn will support an election—he was keeping a record of things from his side too,' I say.

'What record?'

'When he started to have doubts, he wrote them down. Recorded the decisions so he could reflect back on them. It came together for him too late, but it's still something we can use going forward, I suppose. More evidence.'

Just thinking about the mission to retrieve the notebook, let alone the subsequent battle to have people take its contents seriously, makes me tired. But it's the risk we could – even after all of this – still end up with Zenaton, or someone aligned to him, that fills my stomach with acid.

Quillian blows out a breath.

'It's a good lead,' he says slowly, 'and an incredible, unexpected ally.'

'It is,' I say, turning to look at him. 'But the reality is, Zenaton already controls their party, and he has effectively made himself Prime Minister regardless of the 'acting' bit—we cannot risk him *officially* being elected Prime Minister.' The thought burns the back of my throat. The memory of Zenaton's enjoyment while watching the traitors die on screen, his toying with me that resulted in Teddy's abduction and ended with Nix bleeding out on a cold table. How many others will he treat like that before he's done? 'I don't think the original plan, even with Prime Minister Millyn's added support, is the right one anymore.'

Quillian takes my hand and laces our fingers, giving them a little squeeze as if to say 'go on'.

'At best, finding the notebook, drip-feeding the information to prevent it being buried, and then jumping through all the hoops needed to force the government to call an election could take months—years, even.' Quillian's expression shutters. 'It might work as a follow-up plan, maybe, but we need to act faster than that now. You and Finn are marked, most likely Nix and Cortane as well. We didn't have the luxury of time before, but now we've run out of time.'

My heart races as Quillian's forest green gaze shifts to mine. Expectant.

I swallow, thinking of how many could have been taken to Vana, or into the breeding program, or killed in Tae in that time. Sickness snakes through my gut as I think of Zenaton's long-standing approach to bolstering Karaylia numbers in Nuntainia's forces. How readily I could have been part of it, had Dad not stopped my magic. The Prime Minister asked me if I could give the order to have Zenaton assassinated, and I didn't hesitate in my response. Was that just how I was in Vana, or is it still me?

'What happened to the children?' I ask quietly, knowing I'll never really be able to understand the answer.

Quillian presses his head back into the timber and closes his eyes for a moment, as if trying to anchor himself enough to talk about it. He doesn't have to ask which ones.

'Mixed things,' he says, 'few of them good. We got some of them out—managed to find foster homes in different remote parts of Tae. But they're never the same. Many were lost in assaults against Coprath, like others from Tae. Coprath is so much stronger than Tae in size and resources, but really, all they've done is hold firm on their borders. It's been Tae, under coercion from Nuntainia, that's instigated most of the fighting.'

I think about some of the comments Nix and River have made about what led them to join the traitors, the catalyst for them abandoning their duty in the middle of the Tae and Coprath conflict.

'That's why they're here,' I whisper. 'They were asked, or ordered, or ...' I trail off, searching for the words. 'They were supposed to *help* with the breeding program.'

'Nix and River?'

The acidic wave crashes through me and I cover my mouth, breathing through my nose as I nod. Quillian doesn't say anything more, he doesn't have to. The short nod he gives feels like enough to bring any last doubt in my mind crashing down. Nuntainia, driven by Zenaton, has sheltered the political elite; let at least some of them personally 'benefit' from the breeding program. Aiten Gall's activities were surely connected here somehow, perhaps even the children Kasera had were from Tae – I'll never know for sure. But I am sure my home country continues to perpetuate a war using children as soldiers and civilians contracted to a National Duty as unaware participants.

Quillian's grip on my hand tightens. 'You can say it'

I consider my words carefully, closing my eyes to give myself a moment to reconsider. Take a different course. Quillian is studying me intently when I open my eyes again and place a hand on his chest.

'I want Zenaton to die.'

Quillian sits up straighter against the bedhead, not letting me go. He tilts his head at me, and I'm sure he's about to weigh in on my statement when his phone sounds, and he grabs it immediately. 'Yes,' he says, his gaze fixed on mine.

Would killing Zenaton even be enough, when the entire system has been built to enable people like him?

'We'll be right there. Have the team pack whatever last things they can or need, we're going to need to move after this—we've been here long enough.'

My heart hammers in my chest as I wait for him to hang up and place the phone down.

'Casey's found Teddy.'

As we stride back through the darkness, towards another small cabin, I take in more of our surroundings. It looks like a camping ground of some sort – a reasonably large, open space, a utilitarian concrete block with low lighting to the left that looks like it might house bathroom facilities, and a tiny scattering of four cabins. Including the one we've left. But in comparison to when Quillian led me to his cabin earlier, when the sky absorbed so much of me, the buildings scattered in the softly lit dark feel ... small. Foreboding. Like the world is closing in on us, and we're running out of resources to hold it at bay.

People rush around us, some nodding at Quillian, some giving him short greetings. Two stop me and tell me how nice it is to have me back.

The spark in their eyes reminds me of the people in Vana once they heard the term 'Rebel Princess'.

I smile at a woman as she stands before me, but my face feels like it's cracking.

'Thank you,' I say quietly, 'I would have ...'

I trail off. How do I convey how I feel about how it's all unfolding? That me taking on the face of the campaign was supposed to give confidence to the public that I was right. Me, born and raised in Nuntainia, served National Duty for my country, someone who followed *every* rule. As opposed to the battle-hardened traitors around me, *I* was supposed to bridge that gap in the public's understanding and inspire them to take a stand against Zenaton and the government.

Instead, the media focused only on my sex life, portrayed a scorned, unstable woman, and brushed me aside as a public nuisance. Until I ended up personally targeted because I took a stand – knew too much – and my being a woman made it so much easier.

The woman is about my age, with kind but haunted eyes and a tentative smile. As I look into her face, I find I can't bring myself to ask what atrocities brought her to this side of the fight. Nor can I articulate my experiences in Vana. But I make myself remember the comments Quillian showed me – the gentle swell of support, and questions, and how my story is being shared in corners of the online world I couldn't have predicted, despite the media's response.

I clear my throat as Quillian looks between us and the activity around the camp.

'I'm looking forward to what's next,' I say, and she takes my hands in hers. 'Because we *are* going to stop them.'

'We will,' she says. 'I can almost feel it. There is more support for us than you might realise—people who are too nervous to directly approach us as a group, or you, the Prince,' she says with a quick, almost nervous, look at Quillian. 'But it's there. It takes time, but once they start to see, it's hard for people to look away. You've given us courage with that article, Luka. There's a lot of people who wish to see justice done, not just in light of what you've revealed, not only because you're our Princess, but for a woman who used her voice, even after they tried to silence her.'

She smiles quickly before dropping my hands and continuing her work.

I look up at Quillian, who's waiting expectantly.

'This title thing is just figurative, right?'

He runs his thumb along my cheekbone.

'My uncle was Chieftain, remember? Ronan King? And I am his heir. So, yes and no. But'—he tips my chin—'at what point does the figurative become lore?'

'How is she?' I ask Blossom as we arrive in the makeshift infirmary I assume I was treated in not so long ago. Not that I remember a lot of the space itself. Just the confusion and then the gut-wrenching thought that Nix might not walk out.

Traelen and Zale hold Teddy between them on one of the far beds. Zale cries into Teddy's dark hair as silent tears fall down Teddy's face. Traelen stares at the ceiling, jaw clenched. The warring of emotions between the three of them makes my heart twist painfully. Quillian's grip on my hand tightens, and when I turn and see the haunted look on Blossom's face, my chest constricts, making it even harder to breathe.

'Physically, she'll heal,' Blossom says quietly, 'but ...'

None of us can truly know exactly what Teddy must have experienced, how long the road of healing she likely has in front of her – this is just the tiniest flicker. Yet even that seems to be catching fire around the room. As if Quillian is also remembering his mother being taken for the same purpose, and Blossom thinking how close Davorous got to her. Outside, I can hear Nix and River playing quietly with Zale and Teddy's children, but there is a flatness to their tones. How much of this is triggering for them, too? On top of the obvious grief and anger for Teddy and Zale.

Spotting us, Traelen stands silently, presses a kiss to the top of Teddy's head, then slowly approaches us, his shoulders dipped low and his shirt smeared with what looks like blood. As if someone with bloody hands gripped the front of his clothes.

He swallows when he reaches us, but says nothing.

'Traelen,' Quillian begins, his voice rough, 'I'm so fucking sorry. This—it was supposed to be done. I thought we'd got the last one. The last location.'

Traelen nods, his gold hair a little greasy and roughly swept off his face, like he's been running his hands through it.

'I know,' he says. 'And I knew they'd started again. I was trying to find the details, I should have'—he lets out a harsh exhale—'I should have reached out to you for help.'

Quillian grips his shoulder. 'We'll look after her.'

'There are still women and young children there,' Traelen says. 'Teddy thinks about fifteen women, but she's unsure on the kids. She only ... heard them. She wasn't where she could see them.'

'We'll send a team,' Quillian says, 'get them somewhere safe.'

I touch his arm. 'You're marked, you can't let them know you're coming. Zenaton will be acting to have them moved as we speak. You'll be effectively walking into an ambush if you go.'

'Yes,' he says thoughtfully and turning to me. 'I'll send Casey as lead. Cort will help him put the team together so it includes none of us who are being tracked.'

Leaving Quillian and Traelen, I make my way to the bed Teddy lies in, Zale still hunched over her, face buried in Teddy's shoulder. I reach out and stroke Zale's hair.

'Hey,' I say gently, when she lifts her tear-stained face.

Teddy just turns her head silently on the pillow and stares at me with now dry eyes. The almost vacant expression strikes me hard in the chest.

'I'm just one,' Teddy says, her voice hoarse. 'I was just one.'

I bite the inside of my mouth as the room tilts a little around me. 'I know,' I say, unsure what anyone can say. 'We're going to stop it.'

'I deserved to know, Luka,' Zale says, the bite in her tone cutting my skin. 'How could you not tell me? Keep her from this? I didn't—we didn't—I—I didn't *want* this.'

Tears spill down my cheeks now, too, and all I can do is nod. How can I convey how sorry I am that I didn't tell Zale, but also ... that I understand Teddy's deep desire not to tell her, to keep her safe.

But as I look at each of them, two things become very clear. There are more people's experiences that need to be shared as a warning of what keeping our current government in power will do. And, I am now even more steadfast in my view that Zenaton needs to be removed, one way or the other.

CHAPTER FORTY

'You're finally starting to live up to your title, Princess,' Cortane says, grinning at me in the new meeting hall.

The core group stands around a collection of empty chairs, none of us relaxed enough to sit. Quillian is a steadying force next to me as we tell them what I learned in Vana, and what we think should come next. It was a relief that Quillian and Holland filled in pieces when it was clear I wasn't going to fill the space. I couldn't voice it all – too ... tired, to cover it again in detail. Not that I mind them knowing.

I look around at them, including my father, who gives me a small smile, and Rosie. To have Nix here, blinking back at me as he processes what's being said, is both a balm and added fuel to the fire. Zenaton, through the Hunters he now controls from his position as head of the Defence Committee and Minister for Justice, tried to take him from me.

I will not allow him to take anyone else. Never again will he take anything from me, or anyone.

The room is quiet for a beat, but then the murmurs of agreement break through. My throat thickens at what we're deciding. If it will be enough. Traelen assesses me for a moment, letting the questions of the others filter around him before he lifts his voice. 'Prime Minister Millyn is right, we can invoke the citizens' right to vote on a declaration of no confidence in the current government. If the vote wins a majority, then an urgent election would be triggered. It would mean no more hiding, being clear with the people of Nuntainia on everything we know and who we all are, and it could fail. The hold our current government has on Nuntainia is strong, and well-established. There is a good chance even the truth won't be enough for the people to risk a change in what they know.'

I take Quillian's hand and lace our fingers. 'How do you feel about us going public together?' I ask him in a whisper.

He studies me. I don't know what he covered in his discussion with Rosie, or how detailed it was even able to be, with Quillian focused on getting me out. He lifts my hand and kisses the back of my fingers. 'I'd be grateful, you know that. But anyone else you want to check with?'

I shake my head.

'I want to change our final piece,' I say, addressing the group. 'I want there to be actual footage of the two of us as the Rebel Prince and Princess, and I want to tell the people the stories of the traitors we've met and know, including Prime Minister Millyn.'

Everyone just stares at me, but it's the slight kicking up of Cortane's mouth that assures me this is the right path. Quillian pulls me into him and kisses the top of my head as Nix laughs bitterly.

'Fuck, yes,' he says. 'Let's show the world our wounds, what can be worse than having them, anyway?'

'How should we do this?' Quillian asks.

Bloss catches my eye. 'I'd suggest we force Zenaton to give a public response, gain so much attention it's impossible for him to ignore—then use that public platform to openly call for the vote of no confidence and give him a chance to refute our claims,' she says. 'It's highly unlikely he will participate in any live debate, but that should play in our favour.'

All the air leaves my lungs and I shift my weight on my feet.

Does it say something fundamental about my character that I am ready for him to die, but am scared to see him again in the flesh?

'Yes,' Dad says, excitement creeping into his voice. 'That could work. He won't want to do it, but if we can generate enough public support and curiosity about what happens next, he won't be able to deny them without essentially admitting guilt.'

Cortane smiles. 'We can air your account of the stories at the same time. If we release a recording immediately before he makes his address, followed by the call to support a vote of no confidence, he won't be able to escape our claims or the public's reaction.'

'Would that be safe?' River asks. 'For Luka?'

'We'll be there,' Quillian says. 'We can tell our own stories.'

'And you give them their myth in the flesh,' Rosie says.

Traelen studies her. 'Give the people a power couple to root for.'

'Yes,' she breathes, something lighting up in her eyes.

'But that can't be it,' I say. 'We need to know what happens after—I need to know Zenaton or anyone else can never repeat what he's done. What he's created.'

'This won't surprise any of you, coming from me,' Cortane says. 'But while I am onboard with this plan, leaving Zenaton as an option in any election would be a stupid move on our behalf. It's bad enough we may be leaving his party in play—we need a backup plan.'

I share a look with her, a chill running down my spine at the similarity in our thoughts on Zenaton. 'You don't believe the people will vote against him after all the articles go live?'

'I want to believe that,' she says. 'But I am deeply concerned they will prefer to go with the status quo. People don't always like to acknowledge what makes them uncomfortable—face the ugliness head on. And the reality is that, for many, this government hasn't interfered directly in their lives. Asking the average citizen to hold to values that don't always affect their day-to-day life can be a big ask.'

I think of the people around the table in the Defence Committee meeting, my stomach swirling with the knowledge Zenaton wasn't the only person in that room ordering the attacks. How none of them seemed to be against the loss of life on that screen. How easy it was for them to push aside that it was real people they were watching? That Zenaton can't possibly be the only person responsible for the breeding program.

Hard truths that I, too, would have struggled to have believed of our government if I hadn't lived it myself. *Did* struggle with until Nix and River arrived on my island. 'I also want to make sure the Defence Committee are tried before our courts and, if warranted, sentenced to Vana. And, if the people won't remove Zenaton, I agree with Cortane—I think we need to.'

'An assassination is a big step,' Dad says. I know it's not Zenaton he's worried about, but the impact making this call will have on me. In our old life, I would have expected him to argue this plan is fundamentally undemocratic. But now I know he's done more than enough reflection on our current government – perhaps it's a step he already considered necessary.

'One I would prefer we don't have to take,' I say. 'But with Prime Minister Millyn out of the way, Zenaton has effectively made himself the unelected Prime Minister, and is actively shaping and changing policy to suit only the interests of a select few. That's no longer a democracy—and people like Teddy and her family are paying the price.'

'We know the attempted raids on the traitors have increased,' Cortane says. 'Even if we wanted to only take the election route, if we wanted to back away from an assassination, there wouldn't be enough of us left to see it through. Even with the fast-tracked plan,' she says with a look at Traelen, 'there's no way he doesn't come for us.'

Traelen doesn't respond.

'We still need to plan for what comes after,' Bloss says. All eyes turn to her, River's the fastest.

'Apart from cutting off the head of the snake?' Cortane asks, but there's a knowing sitting under her words, an understanding that it won't be that simple.

'Even if we remove Zenaton,' Bloss continues, 'his party will remain in play. We'll be triggering an open election before we've had time to build public confidence in a better alternative.'

'She's right,' Rosie says. 'If you take out Zenaton with nothing to fill the void, something—someone—else will fill it. That someone is most likely to be of the same ilk, potentially worse. As much as he appears to have been driving the current agenda, he can't have been doing it without any support. It's very unlikely, with the ethos that is clearly established in that party, there isn't someone waiting in the wings as his successor.'

The party. The political party that has held sway for as long as I can remember.

I mentally run through the other political parties, but none have ever seemed to have enough widespread support to actually run the country. What would it take to give the people a different option? Even temporarily.

'I think we're forgetting something here,' Dad says. 'Our democratically elected Prime Minister is still alive, and is agreeable to calling an election once freed. Does that not neatly solve our problem, since he's still officially the leader of the party and our government? He can at least prevent the vacuum of power.'

'Yes, but his staff has been decimated, and he can't trust his own party,' Holland says. 'And after being so easily fooled and sidelined, would the people even trust him again?'

Dad nods slowly. 'Either way, he is not without support in the House or among the public. Whether he runs himself or throws his weight behind our candidate—whoever they may be—this cannot happen without him.'

We need someone who knows how the system is supposed to work, then. Knows its flaws, but also how they can be addressed to allow the system to do what it's supposed to do best – support the people of Nuntainia.

Someone who knows what's at stake if it doesn't work.

My gaze is drawn to Traelen like a magnet. He's looking at the others as they continue to talk around us, but it looks like he's thinking hard about something as well as listening. Slowly, he turns his attention to me. The full, quiet intensity of it hitting me in the chest. Teddy is back now – safe. As safe as we can make her. But none of us have forgotten what happened to her. What's been happening to the other women from Tae. Traelen certainly hasn't forgotten.

'I'll do it,' he says quietly, focus still locked on me.

'I don't know if I should be surprised here, but I'm not feeling it. Pretty convenient, isn't it?' Cortane says, leaning back a little to assess him.

Traelen shifts his attention to her. 'I was young when the vote went through. Like in the rest of Tae, Quillian's actual identity was never really known in my village. Just that Ronan King, the unofficial head of our village chiefs, vouched for a new leader with his life. But I knew, however supported you were in Tae, you'd never bring down Nuntainia without intimately understanding how they work. How to ... manoeuvre in politics as well as combat. So, I left my village and became the unofficial other side of your coin. Of Tae's coin.'

I gape at Traelen as all of that sinks in. I knew he'd been in this for a long time, but the enormity of the strategy, the commitment behind what he's spent his life doing ... and none of the traitors even knew.

'So,' he says, 'convenient? No. But planned for, worked for, and sacrificed for? Yes. I can do this. I can lead Nuntainia to a peaceful road with both Coprath and Tae, and I will commit to building an open, official, alliance with the Rebel Prince—and Princess—that will hold Nuntainia accountable.'

It takes a moment for the talking to die away, to realise what's been said, and Traelen doesn't repeat it.

Rosie looks momentarily surprised, but a smile graces her face and she nods. 'You'll need help—and a second representative we can make public,' she says.

Holland frowns. 'Isn't that what Luka and Quillian are for?'

I glance at Quillian, just in case he wants to object, my mind full of the cabin. The one we will need to find. Build. He squeezes my hand.

'Then we should find a second from Tae,' I say. 'Ultimately, our wish is not to be intensely public figures indefinitely. Not after we win this and work through the transition. We understand that could take years, but after that, it's not the life we want. We take the fight public, we support Traelen as the alternative, and if we win—and it holds for long enough—then we want to take a step back. That's a choice we're fighting for, too.'

Holland draws himself up taller, edging closer to Finn, who stiffens but doesn't draw away. 'Then, yes, we need a second in Nuntainia and Tae.'

'Traelen,' I say, 'didn't you have someone in mind for the Warden role? Are they on this side?'

He shakes his head. 'I didn't—I just needed you to believe I did.'

Blossom steps forward, and my heart lurches.

River pulls back a little and runs a hand over his face.

'I'll do it,' she says. Her words echo Traelen's, and it's like two puzzle pieces slotting together. She won't say it here, I know, but I can see on her face this is Bloss's way of honouring her husband.

But it also needs to be for her.

'Are you sure, Bloss?' I ask, conscious of everyone's attention.

Her bottom lip wobbles, just a fraction, and I cross the circle towards her. 'I don't have a profile, but there will be people who remember Frank—people who will support me in turn.'

Finn clears his throat. 'And, if you'll have me, I will be second for Tae.'

Cortane punches him lightly in the arm, and Quillian and Traelen nod. 'You'll be perfect,' Traelen says, and I pretend not to notice Holland narrowing his eyes at him slightly.

'So, what's our plan to get all of this in place?' River asks, looking away and purposefully stepping in front of Bloss, who is trying not to cry.

'If Traelen and Blossom are going to have any chance of gaining the support of the people,' Rosie says, 'they're going to need to have a concrete political stand. If you ... remove Zenaton, it can't be traced back to them.'

I look at her. Even here, she's so composed. She and my father look like two halves of a whole -- maybe they are. It's a whole I never knew about, and the thought warms me.

'I assume you both think this is the right course?' I ask.

They exchange a long look.

'I think ... I wish I wasn't going to say this,' my father says, clasping his hands in front of him. 'Yes. I think it's the right course. Zenaton needs to be removed. *But* we pull out all stops to make the declaration of no confidence stick first, so he can be quietly removed afterwards—and Traelen and Blossom need to be kept as separate from it as possible. At least publicly.' He winces, and I suddenly understand why he was so reluctant to say that out loud – it feels like exactly what the current government would do.

'Their offering to the people of Nuntainia will need to be strong,' Rosie says. 'This is not a time we can put a similar, or weak, party in place. Or we risk being in the same position again in twelve months' time.'

I suppress a shudder at the thought. 'I also think the people need to understand *why* an alternative is needed,' I say. 'That needs to be very clear in our footage—it's not just a sob story that can easily be explained away.'

Cortane's eyes spark a little. 'I think your "sob story" impacted more people than let on, judging by the latest online chatter about it.' I cock my head at her in question, but she doesn't elaborate. 'But, yes, there's more we can make of that still,' is all she says.

I nod, pushing aside the twinge behind my ribs at how easily Zenaton could slip through this plan, and letting my mind fill with all the traitors in the prison—what their stories are. And how many I didn't talk to.

Along with the list of people killed or removed in Tae.

People who haven't yet had the chance to tell their stories.

Stories I am about to tell for them.

'—moving the camp to,' Quillian is saying to my Dad. 'Work with Nix to find at least three suitable options. We may need to split up or move again at short notice. Janly will be back today, ask her to prepare to be as mobile as possible and locate the tents—we may not have the luxury of accommodations for a while.

My skin prickles as Quillian's focus slides to me. 'I don't believe we have time to wait until that move is done to know our exact next step. Cort, what's the update on the Hunters?'

'No time is correct,' she says, with a small shake of her shaved head. 'Our scouts have found them regrouping just to the east. They know we're here, we know they're there. It's just a matter of who strikes first.'

The memory of the Hunters breaching our last camp slams into me and I rub the heel of my hand against my chest. The shouting. The smell of gunfire. The bodies. The bright, white lights that came after.

I shiver as pain seems to shudder from the soles of my feet and into my shoulders.

Quillian's gaze flicks to mine, his fingers clenching and unclenching at his side.

'There are still some families here,' Nix says, his voice heavy, and I think of all the people who were relocated here after one of the initial raids.

'Which is why we can't wait to move them,' Quillian says.

Leaving them to work through how to give a fake location of Quillian to draw Zenaton's forces away, I step with Blossom outside the group. 'Talk to me,' I say, taking her hand.

There are bags under her eyes I can only put down to the huge amount she's been taking on here – healing at the same time as learning her magic, as well as helping run the camp in both mine and Janly's absence. A pang hits me in the chest at the knowledge someone else did this while we were on Zanteera Island, and they are obviously no longer with us.

'I'm good,' she says, with a sniff. 'Really. I just—I guess I never thought I'd have this opportunity. Frank was so ... good at this and, before my duty, it was going to be the two of us. When he died, I lost him and our purpose. As much as I wasn't sure I wanted back into this life, it found me anyway. And now ...' she trails off, looking back at the group who are now discussing some of the immediate concerns of the camp – location, primarily, now the Hunters, and Zenaton, know exactly where we are.

'It doesn't have to be you, Bloss,' I say gently. 'If this isn't what you want—'

'It's what I need, Lu,' she says, certainty creeping into her voice.

I look at her a long moment, wondering what exactly it is she needs from this; perhaps she doesn't know how to articulate it yet either. But I trust that she knows what her heart is telling her.

'Okay,' I say, letting a smile into my voice. 'Does that mean we'll be calling you Deputy Prime Minister soon?'

She swats at me with a small laugh.

'We've got a long fucking way to go before then,' she says, looping an arm in mine and turning us back to the group.

River steps aside to make space for us again. 'We'll need a distraction for the Hunters he'll have with him when we make our move,' he says, 'or we've no chance of getting anywhere near close enough for a public confrontation, or within range to take him out.'

Quillian acknowledges River with a nod. 'Nix and Corvan,' Quillian says, 'you're still on location. Cort—you work with Luka and me on the stories. Film as much as you can. Rosie, you can develop the bones of the election proposal and initial campaign strategy with Traelen and Blossom. But, Traelen, I also need your input on what Zenaton's movements are likely to be over the next week as we amp up our publicity. Finn, Holland, River, and I will start planning for the confrontation and how to draw away his Hunters. We reconvene at the end of the day and give our updates. Good?'

'Nix,' I say as we're all preparing to leave the meeting hall, 'can we talk for a moment?'

He follows me outside and studies me wearily.

'You okay?' he asks.

'Umm, yeah,' I say, not sure where to start. If I should give him what could be a false hope. But he almost died not knowing it was even possible, and ...

'I found records of Villy. Of possible survivors.'

Nix is silent so long, I wonder if he really understands what I'm saying. That there's a list of people who weren't killed in Tae, in Villy. I haven't said out loud that maybe that means his girlfriend survived, but surely, he would know that's what I'm saying?

He sinks to his knees and drops his head in his hands.

I crouch before him. 'You okay? You understand what I'm saying?'

He breathes out heavily. 'Not really, no. But will I ever be? Probably not.'

I close my eyes, the weight of his sadness dragging on me. It's like he's drowning, and my arms won't – can't – move to hold him above water.

'I wasn't sure if I should tell you,' I say gently, leaning into him a little. 'But if there's a chance—if there are other people who need saving—we ... I don't know. I just don't think I can leave it as a list I found that we never look at again.'

Nix purses his lips a fraction. A sign he's heard me. Probably agrees with me, but it's all too heavy for him to voice. Watching him be swallowed in complete defeat presses on my chest so hard, tears spill down my cheeks. Looking at him like this, completely unguarded and devastated, is something I've never seen – the slight shadows that mark under his eyes, the light stubble on his cheeks, the way the light seems to have died in his gaze. Things people wouldn't notice with his cocky grin in place.

But as soon as that grin slips, it's there: his grief.

And I want desperately to take it away. Part of me wonders if I am being naive. Could his girlfriend really still be alive after her village was bombed? But there have been so many lies, so many surprises, why couldn't she be?

I don't know exactly what I expected Nix to do after I told him, but sitting like this in his obvious heartache wasn't quite it.

'What do you want to do?' I ask.

He's quiet for long moments, his hands linked and forearms resting on his knees. 'I just need to sit with it. I have tried for so long to make myself accept that she's gone—they're all gone—no matter what my heart dreams of every night. But ... there's hope, and there's the possibility of breaking all over again. I won't survive it again, Luka—I barely survived the first time. We can't do that to anyone else.'

Giving a little nod, I sit with him on the ground in the soft sunshine and hold his hands between mine. But I can't say 'okay'. I can give him time, we have more than enough to sort out first. But I can't promise I won't go looking, anyway. He may not be able to bring himself to manage false hope, but I need to know about her. And I know I won't be the only one who is desperate to search for survivors.

Cortane and I leave most of the organising and executing of the moving of our satellite camp from place to place to the others, so we can spend as much time talking and recording as possible. We never stay in one location more than one night, and any outside our now slightly expanded core group have been sent to new camp locations to hide.

My bones are weary and I no longer know where we are, but I make myself relive everything I've been through and everything I have learned. Cortane sits opposite me, a camera rolling the whole time. I tell her of the first prison and the luxuries we had there, of Koko's chocolate balls, and the playroom, the aerial yoga, and Zenaton's request for a glass platform in the sky. The weekly cleaning of apartments, and the special drinks, and the string quartet, and the regular banquets and balls. Some of this detail was covered in Rosie's first session with me, but we go through it all again anyway.

Cortane will work with Rosie to edit out what they think is too repetitive, and keep the details – often the smaller ones, Rosie tells me – that will stick with people. Like the luxury of the food and dresses, that I had velvet cushions, and a board for people to request things like changes to playroom rules. The way so many prisoners treated us as if they were gods.

And I tell them of the harder things like child slavery, the trafficking, the sexual abuse.

I talk to her of the prisoners I met in Vana – some who should be there, and many, many others who shouldn't – and everything they told me. I tell her of my torture, of the Hunters, of the man strapped in the dungeon when I arrived, the man who helped my ruined feet, and meeting the true Prime Minister.

I tell her of the lists I found in the archives in Parliament House. What I think that means for the conflict in Tae, that it's obviously a ruse meant as cover for one of Nuntainia's worst crimes. That it's taken lives, and love, and *consent* away. Of the soldiers who are duty bound to make the breeding happen, who are considered traitors of Nuntainia if they don't.

Throughout it all, Cortane's expression changes from resigned to angry and back again, but she's never surprised. Not even at the details I can tell her I have read in the files from Tae. My mind once again fills with the possibilities of what happened to Nix's girlfriend, the wonder if she really is dead.

'Luka?' Cortane's voice breaks into my thoughts.

I stare blankly at her a moment. 'Sorry, what did you say?'

Cortane looks me over. 'Let's take a break,' she says turning the camera off, and I release a heavy sigh.

'What is it?' she asks, her gaze only now flicking around us to the packing and movement that's happening outside the window.

Shifting in the hard, plastic chair, I let myself slump back. 'I can't help but think this—taking Zenaton out of office, having an election, will it be enough?'

She nods. Silently. But I can see the thoughts flickering behind her eyes. The shifting she's doing. And it's this that is most surprising – that I didn't get a quick, barbed response. She's actually considering what I'm saying.

'I think,' she says carefully, 'the last time I felt energised about all of this was when Finn, Quillian, and I made our first pact. When the creed was shared and embodied—it was a powerful time. Every moment since then, and a lot of the ones before, has taken something from us. From me. So ... yes ...' Her hazel eyes seem a little less cold as she talks, opening up to me in a way I never expected, a way that makes me want to remain silent so she doesn't stop. 'I understand it is exhausting, I wouldn't beat yourself up over it. As for the after—that's the bit we all really signed up for. It's just taken us so long to be in a position to *maybe, finally,* crest the summit.'

'What do you want to do … after?'

Her pale pink lips roll together before she releases a soft laugh, a gentleness in the sound that's new. It sounds like the way she looks at Finn and Quillian when she thinks no one is looking. Almost the same look she has for Nix and River.

'Make sure it never happens again.'

'That's it?' I can't help but ask, and her face flashes.

'That's a pretty big fucking job,' she snaps, then sighs, running her palms down the tops of her thighs. 'Maybe learn how to cook properly. There's something quite relaxing in that, I think—not that I get to do it very often.'

I smile, thinking of Koko and Holland.

'You?' she asks, cocking her head a little.

The list runs behind my eyes.

'I think …' I say slowly, unsure how true it is until I consider saying it out loud. 'I want to find the people that have been done so wrong by Nuntainia, and give them a safe place to land. Somewhere they can work out what's next for them without the pressure of having to be … *in* everything again.'

Cortane blinks at me, and I wonder for a moment if what I've admitted is ridiculous. But now the words are out, it feels like they've given life to a fiery desire in the corner of my mind, one I couldn't quite make out the shape of before.

Not that I have any idea how I would do anything even remotely like that, or even where I'd start.

'Sounds like a pretty fucking good idea,' Cortane says, still assessing me. She reaches over and turns the camera back on.

'Tell me about the Defence Committee.'

CHAPTER FORTY-ONE

'Sure you're ready for this?' Dad whispers to me as we prepare to step through Cortane's portal.

The majority of the traitors are now dispersed across both Nuntainia and Tae, mostly in locations that either my father or I suggested. But, however hard I tried to get him and Rosie to go as well, they argued that they hadn't spent the first half of their adult lives inadvertently supporting this government – and the second half to date trying to tear it down – only to walk away now.

Now we're about to take Zenaton down. Together.

The rest of the group murmurs quietly around us, and I'm struck by the almost reverence of this moment. One that feels almost like stepping off a bigger precipice than when Blossom and I jumped off Nix's island.

The last articles followed by carefully timed video follow-ups have continued to build momentum, and the swell of public interest is as high as we're going to get it. It's enough for Zenaton to have been forced to schedule a public press conference, where we plan to confront him today. Publicly, he said it was to 'set the record straight'. But my experiences with him both on the island and in Parliament house mean I don't exactly know how he's going to respond, and the uncertainty of what I'm walking into makes my jaw tense.

My gaze catches on Nix at the thought, the knowledge that the love of his life could still be out there – waiting for him.

'Yeah,' I reply. 'I really am.'

I don't tell him my hands are shaking. Or that my stomach has started a riot.

'Whatever happens in there,' he says, gesturing to the portal. 'Your safety is the number one priority, understand?'

Dad's face is serious when I look up at him. Worried. Fatherly. My chest pinches. It's the same sort of look Claudius would have given me. How did I end up with two father figures who so desperately, even if they came at it differently, wanted – needed – me to end up exactly where I am?

'I'm serious, Luka. Watching you be dragged to Vana almost killed me. I can't do that again.'

I can only nod.

I'm immediately flooded with the raw memories of that prison. Of the message Zenaton had for me.

'Does "hold the line" mean anything to you?' I ask him, and his brows furrow.

'It can refer to a few things depending on the context but, in Nuntainia, it was most commonly used by an extremist military group that went rogue in the name of holding Coprath back from the line at Rite Gorge.'

My stomach sinks. 'What did they do?'

He blows out a breath and takes my elbow, walking me a step closer to the portal. 'It was a group of young, specialist forces – they raided several Coprath villages under the guise of routine military operations, essentially raping and pillaging at will in the night. There were some whispers of them being tried for war crimes, but it was ultimately agreed they were "holding the line" as ordered. I wasn't across the details of how it all unfolded, and I haven't learned more specifics since, but, essentially, I believe they argued that their tactics weakened enemy morale and hastened Nuntainia's victory in key areas of conflict. Why do you ask?'

I stare at him, acutely aware of his hold on my arm as an anchor, as so many things fall into place.

'Zenaton said it to me.'

His face pales. 'Lu—'

'Right,' Cortane says, raising her voice a little to address us all. 'This is it. I have confirmation of teams of Hunters swarming our decoy camp. You know your positions?'

A series of nods and grunts follows, but no questions.

Zenaton will be there when we arrive, making his statement of response, and Quillian and I are to take the stage with him as he's making his speech – a position Quillian will escort me to, flanked by Nix and River. Cortane released the final video about thirty minutes ago, and the interest online is already starting to peak.

But the four of us are a massive target, and I try not to focus on the fact Nix isn't completely healed yet. Try not to think about the fact he seems to tire faster than me now.

So Cortane and Finn will be going ahead to clear the way of Hunters along the path she and Quillian agreed is safest.

Holland and Casey will be with Blossom, my father, and Rosie at the vantage point opposite the park where Zenaton will be giving his statement. Where I hope our declaration of no confidence is met with a swell of support, forcing an election. Exactly how it fits into the legislation is grey to me, but the theory is the people have a voice, and we're going to leverage it.

Cortane has already hacked the system and has our video ready to cut in over his speech when she hits 'play' on the remote I know she carries.

'Stay on comms,' Quillian says, eyeing everyone, including me. 'Nothing goes wrong today. This is as public as we've ever gone, and we know Zenaton has Hunters out here scouring for our locations. Cort has been working to tamper again with the tracking from the wards, but we can't be sure her inference will have any effect. We need to work on the basis they'll know exactly where we are as soon as we step through.'

His gaze flashes as he catches my eye. The memory of the discussion of our future fills my mind. Both the long future we want, and the short future we're likely to have. Perhaps it's just today.

If we don't succeed in swaying the people enough to force Zenaton's hand, it will likely become Zenaton's only priority to find and wipe out every one of the other camps. Now, as we go public as the Rebel Prince and Princess, not only do we risk having the whole of Nuntainia watch us fall, but that we will become the very thing that secures Zenaton permanent leadership of Nuntainia.

No one else says anything, but I watch them check their concealed weapons as I gently press my fingers against Quillian's feather which I've slipped between my breasts.

'Let's go,' I say.

Cortane's portal delivers us into the Academic Quarter, and for a moment I'm transported back in time. A time before my duty, when I was still so sure I would have magic, a notable academic career, and a family. At least I thought a family was in my future, the same as Akira and Zale.

I peek at Quillian, whose mask is so tightly in place I barely recognise him. Except that he links his pinky finger around mine as we begin to walk.

The buildings start to fall away behind us as we wind through the smaller streets and lanes of the Quarter towards the centre park, and with them I sense the final ties to that life stripping away.

And I feel lighter for it.

Despite what I am walking towards.

I squeeze Quillian's finger in return, and my heart thumps in my chest.

'Be safe,' Blossom whispers, looking anxiously between River and me when we pause behind the main library.

My heart aches to leave her, but the thought of taking her anywhere near Zenaton makes acid rise in my throat.

River steps towards her, and I almost expect her to step back. But she holds her ground and blinks up into his face as he comes so close they're almost touching.

'We'll be back,' he murmurs, before gently gripping the back of her head and dropping a soft, slow kiss to her forehead.

I watch her close her eyes as she leans into him, before letting my gaze slip to Nix.

'Goner,' he whispers, the corner of his mouth lifting as he shakes his head at them, and I can't help but wonder what sort of goodbye he'd give his girlfriend if he had a choice.

Quillian's finger slides from mine, and I know instinctively he is putting all of his attention into our next steps. Into keeping us all safe. He exchanges a quick look with Cortane and Finn, but neither of them says anything before they nod shallowly and peel off.

Holland watches Finn go, before turning to Blossom and Casey and jerking his head.

'Casey,' he says, 'you lead. I'll bring up the rear.'

Blossom, my Dad, and Rosie fall into a group between the two former Hunters. A lump forms in the base of my throat as I watch them disappear around the far corner of the library. The last few days I have desperately tried not to think about what the cost will be if we fail here.

But watching my Dad leave—

Watching River kiss Bloss so tenderly my heart aches—

Things, *people,* I know Zenaton would take with a genuine smile on his face.

'Stop,' Nix says gently, bumping my side with his elbow. 'It won't help. The only thing you can focus on now is the very next step. Focus on that step and then what the one after will be—those two things.'

I drag a shuddering breath into my lungs and he grips me, pulling me tight against him, my bag squashed between us a little, and I squeeze him back with everything I have. As if I could squeeze hard enough for it to all disappear.

Nix pushes me back by the shoulders. 'Okay? Two things. That's it.'

I nod, it's all I can seem to do, blinking rapidly at the sudden burn behind my eyes. Am I really about to do this?

Sweat starts to prickle my forehead.

'Luka,' Quillian says, his voice like gravel as Nix stands aside a little to give him room. Then he fills all my vision, blocking out the sunshine and the brick wall of the library we huddle against.

His large brown hand slides along my jaw until his palm cups my face, his fingers in my hair. I press my cheek into his touch and let it soak into my bones. Let his dark green eyes drown me for a moment.

'We do this for all those who prove the colour of their souls,' he whispers.

With those words, it seems like the tattoo down the centre of my chest ignites, lighting up all the resolve I had before we got here. Before I had this moment of doubt and overwhelm, as everyone I love faces significant danger. But that burn reminds me that if not us, then who? Who will bring this to an end? Who will expose Zenaton for his crime and corruption, for electing himself leader of our government, for exploiting Tae and its people, and for covering up for anyone involved in those programs?

'But I also need you to be safe,' Quillian's voice cracks. 'If you want out, Luka, you take it. Now.'

I give him a long look, knowing in my core he means it. That there is no 'loose end' threat to me anymore – that sentiment is long, long gone.

'You started a revolution,' I whisper, my hand sliding up and over his. 'And I'm going to help you see it through—for all of us.' I swallow, turning my face into his hand. 'I promise,' I breathe against his palm.

The brown bricks of the library are warm under my fingers as I run them along the wall to ground me. Zenaton is being introduced around the front, and then his voice starts to echo in the space, making the hairs on my arms stand up.

He starts his introduction with a nod to the research investments he has made into Nuntainia's defence in his role as Minister for Justice. Nothing particularly proactive, just sensible. To be prepared. A common sense approach when there are traitors on the loose. Easy enough to believe.

I know because it's what I would have once believed.

Now, I know it's to build teams. Teams bound by duty contracts, like Nix and River were. Teams ordered to take women from their homes as breeding stock, to train their winged children to fight in a proxy war against Coprath – a country who has done nothing for decades but protect their borders from us.

It's so Zenaton can build the army of Karaylia he's dreamed of.

So he can hold his position as acting Prime Minister unopposed. With our actual Prime Minister in Vana, it's only a matter of time before he takes that role substantively.

So he can *hold the line.*

Unless we succeed today.

The medium-sized crowd is the first thing I see as we round the front corner, meeting no Hunters. There's a small smear of blood on the edge of the brickwork and my stomach turns over. Cortane and Finn have obviously dealt with any Hunters left here and not chasing down our decoy Quillian at the fake camp.

Most of the crowd are watching Zenaton, some stragglers at the back partially watching as they also watch their children running in the grass. Others still picnic on the small rise that surrounds the open park, taking advantage of the shade provided by the full, lush, green trees that ring the park.

I wonder if they planned their day to see the Minister for Justice and acting Prime Minister speak, or if it was an accident they are now here to witness what's about to happen. How many of them have seen the articles and videos we've released so far? What have they thought about them?

At the front of the crowd is the media, most holding small recording devices or their phones towards Zenaton as he talks from a raised platform, two Hunters positioned before him as crowd control. I pay no attention to the words that fall from his mouth as Quillian and I draw near, Nix and River two steps behind. Having seen this man in action on a number of occasions now, I know it will be nothing good. But I try to view him as the crowd would as I let my gaze travel over him – a middle-aged man with broad shoulders and a confident stance, a strong jaw and smart eyes, a no-nonsense way of speaking.

The audience starts to murmur as we progress slowly towards the platform, Quillian and I, side by side.

A gentle wave of whispers races away from us.

'Rebel Princess,' I hear someone say and lift my chin, letting the title drape over me.

'Oh, the Prince is here! Rodney, he's here,' a woman to my right calls.

Zenaton stumbles over his sentence as he finally glances to his right and spots us. His face frozen for a moment, before a deep anger races across his features. He mutters something to the Hunters before him and they turn to us, one of them looking like they issue an order into their comms piece.

My stomach turns over itself.

We chose to leave most of our fighting force behind, not only to save as many from all out confrontation as possible, but to ensure there could be no mistaking our peaceful intent. Now, I wonder if that was a mistake.

Zenaton abandons his speech and turns his full attention on us, standing well above the Hunters below him. He cocks his head, gaze dancing between Quillian and me.

'You're not where you're supposed to be,' he says, pinning me with a grin.

'No,' I say, loud enough for those near us to hear me as well. 'And I'm fairly confident you already knew that. Funny how being unfairly sent to Vana didn't sit well with me.'

The media still, attention bouncing between us.

'Did she say she's been in, and is now *out,* of Vana?' someone asks, their recording devices shifting towards us. 'So it was real, what she said online? And you knew, Prime Minister?'

My spine stiffens at the use of the term 'Prime Minister' for Zenaton. The media aren't wrong, that's the role he currently holds, even in an acting capacity. But he's so close to holding it indefinitely my skin burns.

'That's enough,' Zenaton says, a flash of irritation barely marring his features. 'You're interrupting an important announcement. One that will further our might as a country.' He turns his attention back to the crowd in front of him, lowering his face a little towards the microphones that stand tall from the white lectern.

'Apologies, folks,' he says in a saccharine tone. 'As I was saying, this research will allow—'

'Prime Minister,' a woman with a crisp, blonde bob says, 'can you comment on this apparent shift in Vanan policy? What's changed to mean a prisoner sentenced there can return to the mainland?' Her questions come in rapid fire, but while Zenaton's fingers tense slightly on the lectern, he otherwise doesn't seem worried. A product of extensive media training, most likely.

Quillian steps forward into the silence from Zenaton.

'That's something I can explain,' he says, his voice sure and steady.

Everyone in the vicinity turns to Quillian, a little dumb struck as they process who he must be and what he's saying.

Zenaton's lip turns up at the side as he looks between Quillian and me and the crowd.

He shifts on his feet. 'I apologise for this interruption—'

'Prime Minister, it seems you have *both* the Rebel Prince and Princess here with you, is that correct? They have made claims that both you and your government have vehemently denied, and yet—'

'Can you tell us more about the traitors, Princess?' another reporter asks, their questions starting to overlap. 'What is it you're here for? Tell us about your call for no confidence.'

'Prime Minister!' another one calls. 'Are you fearful for your position, when the Rebel Prince and Princess so obviously stand against you? These two unknowns who are starting to win unofficial polls?'

'Remove them,' Zenaton quietly orders the two Hunters, and they stalk towards us. 'I am not at all fearful,' he says in response to the question, glancing down at us. 'Nuntainia and her people do not abide those who think they can operate outside our laws.'

My blood feels like it starts to crackle in my veins. 'Is that what you told Aiten Gall when he was sent to the island?'

The media pack are silent for a moment before they press closer, questions starting to come rapid fire.

'What's the involvement of Senator Gall?' one asks. 'Was he sentenced to Vana, Prime Minister, or the secret second island prison? Was he not in rehab? So the Rebel Princess's claims *were* correct?'

Zenaton looks at me and covers the microphone with his hand. 'Get the fuck out, and you will live one more day.'

The telltale metallic ringing slices through the air as Quillian's wings come out. Glancing over my shoulder, River's are as well, along with Nix's blades.

'Touch her and die,' Quillian says, not bothering to lower his voice.

A collective gasp races through the crowd. Some people in the front back away slightly, but they watch, transfixed.

'Mumma,' I hear a little voice from somewhere cut through the tension that's drowning the park. 'Is that the Rebel Princess you talk about?'

The Hunters pause. It's clear on their faces they know taking on the three men behind me will not be easy. And to do it so publicly would fly in the face of the image Zenaton is trying to preserve – not to mention risk innocent lives. The Hunters are many things, but mindless killers they are not. They are the force that is supposed to protect the everyday people of Nuntainia.

The blonde journalist shoves herself forward. 'Rebel Prince,' she declares loudly, her gaze calculating, the sharpness of her mind whirling behind her eyes. 'What was your reasoning for serving in the Nuntainian military while loyal to Tae? What message do you want to share with your people?'

Zenaton says something from the podium, but it's lost in the vacuum created as all attention turns to Quillian. Not a single person is now looking in Zenaton's direction. Except us.

He takes a step back, as if he might step off the side of the platform and disappear.

'Zenaton,' I call out, holding up a hand. 'Don't go. You might be particularly interested in what we have to say about the *might* of the country, and what we have to say to the people of *both* Nuntainia and Tae regarding the options they have open to them.'

CHAPTER FORTY-TWO

The Hunters glance at each other before the one closest to us makes way for Quillian and me to take the podium. River and Nix stay at ground level and watch the Hunters. I put Quillian between Zenaton and me as Quillian takes his place at the lectern, the memory of Zenaton's taunting about Teddy, and his confrontation of me on the island, still fresh. I don't think he'd attack me with an audience, not this one, but I'm not going to offer myself up to him either.

'Good afternoon,' Quillian says, and a shiver snakes down my spine. He's so composed. So strong and capable. I can imagine him in this role, leading the country. If I thought that's what he wanted, I'd fight with everything I could to put him there. Instead, my heart warms for this incredible man and the imaginary cottage that now seems within our grasp.

'I'm Quillian O'Daire. Some of you will know me as the recipient of military recognition for Nuntainia. But I am also the former Warden of a prison that isn't supposed to exist—and the Rebel Prince.'

Eyes go wide, a couple of people cover their mouths. A small group at the back start to cheer.

Quillian gestures to me, turning slightly and blocking Zenaton from my sight for a moment.

'This is my partner, Luka Brideoake. You will remember her as the whistleblower for that same prison you were convinced doesn't exist. You might also remember how she was treated for speaking out. Her relationship to me was used to undermine her message, and she was taken to Vana—without charge, and without sentence—because she had the courage to come forward.' A ripple of assent travels through the crowd, several in the media unable to meet my eyes as Quillian continues. 'What you may not know is how long we have been fighting in the background, and why your government went to such lengths to silence and discredit Luka and many before her.' He pauses, looking out over the upturned faces before us.

'Today, we intend to fill in those gaps for you. Expose what your current government doesn't want you to know, and explain how we were forced to transform from innocent, law-abiding citizens'—his gaze shifts to me—'to tortured individuals the world tried to forget.'

I know it's not just me he talks of now, his gaze swimming with memories.

'Step down,' Zenaton grinds out from behind us. But Quillian doesn't even grant him a look.

'We are here, with the support of our *true* Prime Minister, Tomas Millyn, to formally make a declaration of no confidence in this government, and the leadership of acting Prime Minister Zenaton Blake. We invite the people of Nuntainia to support us in this statement, based on evidence, and join us as we call for an urgent national election.' Quillian's voice rings out into shocked silence.

Semi-translucent screens, just like the one at camp one, appear in a circle around the crowd, who all turn in slightly different directions to look at them. A second later, I fill every screen, adjusting in that hard, metal chair as Cortane interviewed me.

I look tired, a bit worn. But I also look determined, and a rush of pride in myself races through my chest.

'I said, step *down,*' Zenaton is behind me now, and I spin to face him. The anger in his voice is mirrored in every aspect of his body. His face. His stance. The way his hands are fisted at his sides.

'How about *you*, step down?' I shoot back. 'Stop this farce and tell the people what you're really doing. Tell them where their *Prime Minister* is.'

I stand to the side so he can see the crowd, the cameras, and the screens across the park, and hold out an arm in invitation. Forcing myself to take a deep lungful and find my calm. 'This is your chance, Zenaton,' I say. 'This is your shot to be something different—be something *better.*'

As I say it, I wonder if it's true. Would coming clean be 'better' enough for him to escape his fate? To be free of the quiet death I know will be coming for him tonight?

But as he snarls at me, I realise I don't have to answer that question. Because he will never come clean. Doesn't want a fresh start to do anything better. He's a man for whom power is a drug, and he will never give it up. Not willingly.

'No,' Zenaton says, his voice sharp and low. 'I do not need a shot to be better, I *am* better. Who do you think has protected you—all of Nuntainia—from the very beginning?'

'What we are about to show you,' Quillian says, still addressing the audience and not Zenaton, 'will shock you—'

'No!' Zenaton shouts, and lunges at me, pulling me into him. 'Let's talk. We'll talk.'

In an instant, Quillian's wings are out again, blades momentarily blinding in the sun, his undivided attention bearing down on Zenaton and me.

'Don't fucking touch her,' he says, his voice lethal. But he doesn't move.

Something sharp presses into my ribs, and I understand why.

'Oh,' Zenaton says wetly beside my ear, 'I will touch her plenty if I fucking feel like it, and there's nothing you can do about it. *I* rule this country. I hold the fucking line and protect Nuntainia from people like you.' His voice is quiet, too quiet for the microphones or media to pick up. 'Now get off my stage.'

The media murmur beneath us. I'm sure they can't see exactly what he's doing. But they can see Quillian.

'Prime ... acting Prime Minister?' a man calls tentatively. 'Is there anything you wish to tell us?'

Zenaton takes a step away, dragging me backwards with him. Quillian mirrors him, as I can only image Nix and River do from below. But I shake my head, just a fraction, the blade so tight against my ribs I can barely breathe for fear of impaling myself. The bell tower in the corner of the Academic Square tolls, the heavy notes vibrate down my spine.

Letting my bag slide off the shoulder that's not pressed into Zenaton's chest, I mouth, *tell them,* before I shout at the crowd. 'He has a knife! Is this how a Prime Minister behaves?'

'Not another word,' Zenaton hisses, lips almost on my cheek.

Quillian is almost shaking with restraint in front of me, but I look purposely to the crowd as Zenaton takes me another two steps away.

Please, I think. *Please, don't let this be for nothing.*

Quillian doesn't move, and I shift my attention to the crowd again. Silently begging the three traitors here with me not to kill anyone with this sort of audience. Not to let this opportunity slip through our fingers.

I grip the arm Zenaton has now locked around me.

'Ask yourself how we know I'm not the first!' I cry out as the blade pierces my skin, and the woman with the blonde bob nods at me, mouth agape and staring. But there's understanding there as well, and I funnel all my hope into the fact she is one person who will not be dissuaded from what she's seeing here.

I watch as Quillian grips the lectern, turning back to the audience as my video starts to play.

'She is not the first,' he says, voice breaking, 'but as he takes her away, she needs to know—on behalf of everyone who has been so wronged by this man and his government—that she will not be erased. That while I want to tear his throat from his neck,' he grinds out, shoulders turning in on themselves, 'what we have all been fighting for, the *people* we have been fighting for ... need a voice on this stage.'

Sick as it is, the people need to see the lengths Zenaton is willing to go to. To be so unafraid of taking me, violently and against my will, in front of so many witnesses speaks volumes to his character. To what he has been willing to do behind closed doors.

And now Nuntainia will see that, along with everything else.

I just hope I don't die in the process.

Because it's abundantly clear that Zenaton now has nothing left to lose.

I stumble as I try to keep up as he quickens his pace away from the stage, and I can't help but look at Nix and River. Nix is clearly talking into his comms, River watching our every move and nudging slightly forward with every step Zenaton takes.

Quillian still talks to the audience, his words punctuated with snippets of my interview with Cortane.

'Who else did you meet in Vana?' Cortane asks.

'The Prime Minister.' My voice rings across the park, then there's silence as Zenaton drags me inside the library and the tinted doors slide shut before me.

He turns, pushing me forward now, and I try to track where we're going in this building that was once so familiar to me – I have no doubt it will be an office or similar somewhere in the back. Somewhere he can lock the doors.

Something unfurls in my gut as he shoves me through a faded green door. Something that makes my fingers tremble and my heart thump wildly behind my chest.

They're here, I remind myself. *They're here and they will find me.*

But will it be in time?

I bite back a sob as Zenaton shoves me again, and I stumble to the floor, hitting my head on the desk. The room swims, but Zenaton still looms in my vision.

'You stupid fucking bitch,' he says. 'I thought that of you on the island, and it's still true now.' He laughs. 'Look at where you've landed yourself because all you wanted to do was chase some winged bastard.'

'Fuck you,' I spit, pushing myself up to seated.

How dare he try to belittle what I've done, what I've found, what I've *been through*.

I think of Quillian's mother, what she endured. Of the little boy who watched her raped and taken. I think of Cortane and the pain that is hidden behind her cold exterior. I think of Nix's girlfriend, and the unknowable horrors she could be suffering.

I think of Teddy, who my heart still breaks for.

And I think of Bloss, who Davorous so blatantly violated and then *laughed* about it.

With Zenaton.

Zenaton. The man prowling towards me.

No. He will not belittle what we've been through, overcome, or been subjected to. Because this path has not been my own. If it were not for all the people before me, I wouldn't be here. I wouldn't be able to make this stand. He will not make me break my promises, both spoken and unspoken, to see this through. To fight, with everything I have, to protect those I love and bring this government, and this man, down.

I drag myself to standing, blinking slowly to try to clear the splitting pain in my head, and slip my hand down my shirt to press my hand against my chest. To steady myself.

Zenaton cocks his head like a predator.

'No, Ms Brideoake, fuck *you*, you little whore. You have done nothing but be a pain in my fucking ass since I met you, and now—you are done. I will not tolerate this nonsense anymore. I had hoped that your time in the House would show you just how much stronger I am than your rebels, that misfit band of traitors, and you would just give them up. Understand what it actually takes to run a country and defend it. Instead, I had to waste my resources to track you down. But it ends now. First with you, and then him.'

He starts towards me.

My fingers trail the top of Quillian's feather, my lips trembling.

Do not hesitate, he'd said when he gave it back to me. *No negotiating*.

I take a breath for every two steps he takes.

I get one and a half.

Then he yanks on the waist of my pants, slamming his body into mine.

The air is forced out of my lungs with the impact, and I slide Quillian's feather out of my shirt. I press my left hand into his chest and push back, just enough so he can watch me race Quillian's feather across the blood on my side and see it turn into a blade in the palm of my hand.

There's no handle, just a short quill that turns deadly sharp, and I have no choice but to grip it hard in my hand as Zenaton's eyes go wide.

Then I drop my arm, driving the blade in and up into his left side.

'What have you done?' he asks, as if in a stupor.

His breathing quickly sounds wet and his grip on my pants loosens.

'Fulfilled my promises, and shown more mercy than you'd get anywhere else,' I say as he sinks to the floor, both hands pressed into his bleeding side.

The door splinters open as Quillian bursts through. He takes in both Zenaton and me, before his right wing flies to Zenaton's throat. Pressing into the skin without breaking it.

'You were never going to walk away from today,' Quillian says. 'But I'm going to enjoy this so much more than I thought.'

Slowly, he presses the tips of his bladed feathers under Zenaton's chin until blood bubbles from his throat. He fumbles weakly at the blades, slicing the pads of his fingers until they fall away as Quillian gives a touch more pressure to his wing.

When Zenaton's gaze finally goes blank, Quillian turns to me. No apology on his face. No question, like when he killed Davorous.

Relief washes through me as he stares at me. Waits for me.

His wings slide away as I throw myself at him, wrapping my legs around his waist and arms around his neck. He holds me tight against him, dropping his face to the soft part of skin between my neck and shoulder, where I can feel his heavy breathing.

Eventually, he lifts his head, one arm still clutching me to him as he presses on his comms piece.

'I've got her.'

CHAPTER FORTY-THREE

ONE MONTH LATER

The prisoners are restless. But, then, it's not every day they find out their torturers will be tried for abuse of power; or that they'll have an opportunity to make their case for an appeal to their sentences to Vana. There were some that were immediately released by order of Prime Minister Millyn, who is now personally overseeing every appeal. While there are others who I'm very sure will never see the light of day again after this, and nor should they.

'Walk with me?' the Prime Minister says as he approaches, and I smile up at him, letting him gently guide me away from the view of Vana across the open, moat-like expanse of grass, and back towards the forest. I let my gaze linger a fraction, before I turn away, to remember that prison. The one that housed so many horrors, but also played a key role in opening my eyes to what was really happening under the surface of Nuntainia.

Its fundamental role in my own traitorous awakening.

'You'll miss it?' the Prime Minister asks with genuine surprise.

'No,' I say as we enter the forest. 'It's right—proper— that it be razed to the ground. With it, I hope Nuntainia's old ways stay dead and buried.'

I feel him glance at me. 'I sense there's a "but" ...'

'Not quite a "but", I don't think,' I say as the shade of the tall trees cools my skin. 'I did wonder if I'd made the right decision about the other prison, though. Whether it should have the same fate as Vana. If saving it—restoring it—was opening the door for it to be reused for a variation of the prison program in the future.'

'But?' he asks, with a smile in his voice, and I laugh.

'*But,* I think taking back what she was intended for is the right thing to do. People, governments, systems—those things can rebuild anything we tear down. It's those governments and systems that need to be structured, the people who need to be taught our true history, so our country can never become so twisted again.'

He stops, and I pull up short to face him.

'Are you sure you don't want to be in government?'

'Absolutely,' I say. 'That job is much better suited to people like Traelen and Blossom. Good, fair people who can see the whole picture, work out all the holes that need plugging and how to go about it.'

He nods thoughtfully.

'I assume he told you I'll take him on as Deputy Prime Minister, should the people vote me back in?'

'And you'll be an advisor to him and Blossom if not. Yes, they told me.'

In truth, it seems like a good arrangement. It wasn't right to rip out the entire current government of Nuntainia and replace it with one of our choosing, despite the damage the previous one has done. And the Prime Minister has lived and breathed how every tiny decision built up to make appalling errors of judgement. So, win or lose, either way he can make sure that it doesn't happen again.

Now – with formal alliances from all government parties in place, as well as Nuntainia with the reigning King and Queen of Tae – whoever the people vote in to lead Nuntainia, we have some sense of safety and security to rebuild Tae.

At the same time, Finn is leading negotiations with Coprath to cease the conflict with Tae and ensure fair and reasonable access to the Rite Gorge for all three countries.

It's going to be a long road.

We fall silent as we walk the dirt path towards my prison – which now needs a proper name. Certainly not one with 'prison' in it.

'I wanted to thank you,' the Prime Minister says after a while.

'You already did,' I say, thinking of his first public address after Holland got him out of Vana.

'To your face this time. Had you not fallen in with the traitors and ended up in Vana, not only would I have rotted away in there, but Zenaton would still be in control down there,' he says, gesturing towards the edge of the island.

'You know I did none of this on my own.'

'I know, but—traitor or not—there are few people in your situation who would have insisted I be released. Not when knowing I was the supposed leader of the government that so badly hurt us – one who should have seen what was happening much, much faster.' He claps his hands together gently. 'But, enough of that. This is an exciting day, and I also wanted to congratulate you. I know you will do good things up here, Luka.'

'Thank you, sir.'

We make the rest of the walk in companionable silence, an experience I once never would have imagined sharing with the Prime Minister. He breaks away with a smile as we reach the concierge gardens, where he heads towards my father.

'Luka!' Blossom waves at me from the opposite side of the gardens, and I let my gaze flick up to the staircases that run up the side. I can still pick Blossom's and mine with ease. The stonework surrounding the window of the Warden's office is still charred with smoke, even though the rest of the building has now been restored. The fire I lit was the worst in there and I know, without having been in it, that room now sits empty.

'Everything is as ready here as I can make it,' Bloss says when I reach her. 'I've given Jan all of my handover thoughts—most of which she was across already—so we're ready for our first guests.'

My chest tightens.

'If we can find them,' I say quietly.

Bloss takes my hands in hers and squeezes. 'They'll find them. Between what you found in the archives and what Traelen has since been able to access, they'll find them.'

I scan her face, unable to stop the quick rise of uncertainty through my gut.

'What if we find some and not ... her?'

A sadness takes her features. 'It's possible, that's true. But Nix knows there is no guarantee, that's as much as you can do now.'

Her face flushes a deep pink, a sign I know River is approaching. It's happened so much more in the last month than I remember at the camp, and I narrow my gaze at her.

'Anything you want to tell me?' I ask, and she swats me away.

'Soon,' she laughs. 'Okay, we'll talk tonight when they've gone.'

'Bloss,' I mock admonish her, 'did you just roll your eyes at me?'

'Shush,' she laughs, her eyes going wide, and I hear River getting closer. I peek over my shoulder to see how many steps away he is.

'You will fill me in on *everything*,' I say, taking her hand and giving her fingers a little squeeze.

She nods before turning her focus to River.

'Hi,' she breathes.

'We're about ready,' River says, and I look between them. The words unsaid are almost tangible.

I pull River into a hug. 'Be safe, please. Keep him safe. And keep me updated.'

River chucks me on the chin as I pull back.

'Of course,' he grins. 'Always.'

I throw Blossom a wink as I leave them to it and head for Nix, Finn, Quillian, and Cortane, who stand together towards the corner of the garden. Near the edge as they are, they could see the open staircase to the marble receiving plane if they wanted. That is an entry point I will *not* be using for anyone from Tae.

Their conversation is animated and purposeful, and even without hearing them, I know they are running over the details of the first extraction again. Between my father, Rosie, Traelen, and the Prime Minister, the breeding program is being wound down. The activity itself has stopped, of course, but it was a huge program of work, and it will take time for the whole thing to be disassembled.

In the meantime, we're not taking any chances and have prepared the prison as quickly as possible to be a refuge for those we can get out of the breeding institutions before any official shutdown of the facilities. The Hunters have all been advised, so there shouldn't be any challenge from them. But if Coprath gets wind that our facilities and resources are no longer as protected as they once were – particularly those in Tae territory – it's possible they will attempt to take what they can before negotiations are finalised.

They have protected their borders against both Tae and Nuntainia for some time, and we don't know how far they will go in retaliation if they think we are weakened in any areas.

It's a small risk, but one that makes my stomach shift uneasily all the same. We've survived so much, there's a limit to how much more I feel like we can risk. But I do know that limit will only come after we've saved as many as we can.

And I'd be lying if I said I wasn't holding onto a burning string of hope that we – they – can find Nix's girlfriend. That, if they do, their love will be strong enough to bring them back together.

The grass is still so green as I pad across it, even though it's much shorter now than when we came back here for the first time. The contrast had struck something in me when we returned. The vast majority of the prison remained intact, but a significant corner bore the fire damage from our escape. Black stones, smashed windows, ash, and half-burnt curtains and apartments. All of it cushioned in a sea of long, vibrant green grass with a smattering of the red flowers I love so much.

'Hey,' Quillian says, tucking me into his side as I join his little group and listen to their final preparations.

It's all well in hand, I know, but it still soothes the simmering nerves in my stomach to hear them so prepared. Organised.

Slipping his fingers in mine, Quillian draws me away a little from the others and cups my jaw in his other hand. His dark green eyes seem more alive up here than they did on the mainland.

'Are you sure you're going to be okay here when I go?' he asks, a crease forming between his almost-black brows.

I lean into his palm. 'I am, I'll have Holland and Casey here, and Bloss. And we still have a lot to do to make sure we're ready for when you come back.'

He nods, but it's clear he's not totally at ease leaving me here without him. 'I know it's something you need to do,' I say, 'and I'm grateful to you for helping him.'

'You know I'm only going for as many extractions as it takes to find her, right?'

My chest swells at the possibilities that lie ahead for Nix, but I tamp them down. It would break part of us all if he loses her twice.

'And then you're never leaving me again,' I say, trying to be serious as I repeat back to him the same sentiment he's told me endlessly the last few weeks. Sometimes, I think he's reminding himself I will be here to come back to.

He brushes the pad of his thumb over my bottom lip as sadness dusts his features.

'My Mum would have loved you,' he says quietly, and my chest pinches. 'My uncle too.'

I reach up and grip the back of his wrist where he holds me.

'I can only imagine how proud they are of you. What you've achieved is ... incredible.'

He pulls me closer until our bodies are flush. 'What *we've* achieved.'

Smiling, I release his hand and loop my arms around his neck. 'What we've achieved,' I agree.

'I have something for you,' he says. 'Something to mull over while I'm gone.' He shifts to take something from the pocket on the side of his thigh, and I let my hands drop down his chest to take it when he holds it out to me.

'What is it?'

'Something I need your input on.' One side of his mouth quirks up. I give him a curious look, but he nudges the folded piece of paper, hurrying me to open it.

Slowly flipping it open, my heart starts to pound as my stomach suddenly feels full of red petals on a windy day.

Sketched out on the paper is a little house. Both the front view, and a floor plan.

'What is it?' I ask again, looking between Quillian and the piece of paper. The drawing of the cottage even has a pot of flowers on either side of the front door that are definitely not jasmine.

His cheeks deepen in colour, but his gaze is steady as he studies me.

'I know you've put a lot into restoring this place,' he gestures to the prison beside us. 'But ... I thought it would be nice to have a place of our own.'

'Here?'

He blinks. 'Well, yes. I know how much you love this island, despite everything, and I didn't think you'd want to be far from the refuge. But ... if you prefer somewhere else, we can do that instead.'

I can't help but grin at him.

'Quillian O'Daire, are you asking me to move in with you?'

He laughs, his head falling back a little as he does, and I stare at him.

'Luka Brideoake, I am asking for so much more than that. I am asking you to build a life with me.'

'Is there somewhere I can hang my painting?'

He quirks his head. 'The partially burned one you told me you hated for so long?'

I laugh. 'Yes, that one. There's just something about that lounging lady that reminds me how far we've come—a reminder of the different things she's represented.'

He tucks a strand of hair behind my ear. 'I'll build you a wall just for that painting ... assuming that means you're saying "yes"?'

'I'm saying yes.' I grin as I fist my hands in his shirt and press up to kiss him.

His mouth is hot when it claims mine, and I press myself against him, sliding my hands through his short hair. He sucks my bottom lip between his teeth and—

'Seriously?' Cortane's voice sounds far closer than I remember her being. But then it's not unusual for Quillian to capture all of my attention. Particularly when he kisses like this.

'Time to move out,' she says, and I keep my eyes closed.

Quillian groans against my mouth before giving me a soft kiss and dropping his forehead to mine.

'I'll see you soon,' he whispers.

I walk with him to the edge of the island where Cortane has her portal ready to go and lean into Blossom as we watch them assemble. The breeze picks up as Cortane steps closer to the portal and gestures them through. Quillian goes first, followed immediately by Finn, and then River. Nix pauses before he steps through and glances back at me, throwing a wink in farewell, and disappears. Cortane says nothing as she goes through, and I smile despite the soft uncertainty I know will sit in my gut until they all return.

The portal recedes in Cortane's wake and I look out at the expanse of blue sky, my breath filling with cool, fresh air—with the flickering of excitement that the possibilities now available to me are as vast as the blueness. But as Blossom sighs beside me as she takes in the same view, I know everything I need, and want, will be on this island I was once so desperate to leave.

And, just beyond, where there is now no trace of the portal, a grey heron, wings spread, banks towards the island, before tucking into a dive and dropping out of sight.

Thank you for reading!

They say it takes a village to raise a child and, honestly, its not dissimilar to create a book. I have a wonderful team that I am truly grateful for – everyone from my critique partner to my editor, beta readers and cover designers. This story tested me (they seem to test me more and more the more I write!) and to have the brilliant minds of all of those involved in its development is an honour.

But, at this stage of my career, and in addition to my family of course, I am just supremely grateful to each and every one of you that picks up (and reads!) one of books. To share my stories with the world is not something I take for granted and I cherish the fact that you read them. I hope I can keep living up to the love you have for them.

AMBER WOLF (DRIARN DUOLOGY, BOOK 1)

FRIEND. GUARD. ORPHAN.

Lish Taylor thinks she knows who she is.

But when her tactical team begins to investigate a series of abductions, the haunting questions she's carried since her mother's murder come flooding back. With the case growing increasingly suspicious, Lish leaves her climate-ravaged city to seek answers, even after she's ordered to stand down—only to be abducted herself.

Captured by the brutal General Siosal, Lish is determined to free not only herself, but also the General's other victims. With the enigmatic cell-guard, Lochlain, as her unexpected ally, Lish's escape catapults her into the hidden world of the Calahi, where magic pulses through the land. But, even with its incredible differences, Lish can't ignore that this world is also suffering.

The threads of her investigation soon draw Lish into a war for a dying kingdom. To survive – and reclaim her future – she must bring those she loves together and prove that healing a broken world begins with standing in your truth.

Amber Wolf is an adult, dystopian fantasy with forced proximity, found family, fated mates, climate themes and hidden worlds. If you love family secrets, slow burn open door romance and epic magic, this is for you.

Blue Pointed Star (Driarn duology, book 2)

A new queen must save the Realm.
But those who would deny her the crown are strong.
Lish Taylor knows that she is the rightful Queen of Airlie. But, before she can officially claim the throne, she is accused of murdering the previous queen – her mother. Forced to retreat to a neighbouring court, the shadow of regicide at her heels, Lish's only chance to regain her throne, and prevent the collapse of both the Human and Calahi lands, is to reassemble the shattered pieces of the Blue Pointed Star.
Underground assassin, Aeyva Kaylneau, is one step closer to fulfilling her lifelong dream of becoming a Sentinel to the Queen. But Aeyva's past allegiances threaten to jeopardise everything she has worked for, and the secrets she keeps have the potential to not only push away the woman she loves, but bring the entire Court of Airlie to its knees.
As the Human and Calahi realms crumble around them, Lish and Aeyva must unite a network of allies across rival courts and the boundaries of magic, to expose a sinister conspiracy that imperils the very fabric of their worlds. As Queen and her Sentinel, they must show that the future belongs to those who fight for more than power.

Blue Pointed Star is the final book in the Driarn duology (sequel to Amber Wolf). Lovers of fated mates, slow burn open door romance, sapphic romance, found family and becoming who you were always meant to be will adore this thrilling conclusion.

When Secrets Beckon

Every secret has its price...

Rubilena Lanmiere can barely remember how it felt to live life for herself. Or what it feels like to live a life in the open. Raising her daughter in a world where it's dangerous to be noticed, her days are spent selling forbidden remedies in her grandfather's shop — and paying her brother Theo's debts in an underground fight den.

When their absent mother returns to gift Theo a mysterious medallion, Rubilena and Theo find themselves fleeing their home in Koamah, hunted by the entire Kingdom and its enemies. With the secrets of the medallion painting a deadly target on her brother's back, Rubilena is forced to seek help from a man who once broke her heart, and her trust.

In search of the mystical witches who can free Theo from the medallion's claim, the group find themselves wrapped inextricably in the tendrils of a prophecy. But as the fight for the ultimate knowledge intensifies, the weight of secrets already between them threatens to tear Rubilena and her allies apart.

And they can't be sure if the medallion is seeking to fulfil a deadly prophecy, or save them from the encroaching darkness...

*When Secrets Beckon is a standalone adult, dystopian fantasy with an epic second chance romance, siblings, clashes with royalty, prophecy, witches and a single mum FMC. If you love your fantasy with forced proximity, touch HIM and d*e, and open door romance, this one is for you.*

TRAITORS' CREED (TRAITORS DUOLOGY, BOOK 1)

Truth makes traitors out of even the most dutiful.

Zanteera Island has a secret: it has two prisons. Vana, the one the world knows and fears, and an unnamed compound lined with comforts.

Serving her National Duty at Vana's secret counterpart, Luka Brideoake doesn't question the unorthodox disciplinary system, or the VIP status of the criminals. But when the Warden offers her a prestigious new assignment in Parliament, she starts to see the prison and its inmates in an uncomfortable new light.

Then, her childhood best friend and his brother show up sentenced to Vana, and Luka is forced to go against every rule she's upheld to seek a dangerous new ally. All the while, the Warden's cryptic advice suggests a political web far bigger than Luka could have imagined.

As inmates start to die and the authorities move in, her path intersects with a man as enigmatic as he is powerful. But how much of the life Luka thought she wanted is she prepared to trade...for the truth?

Traitors' Creed is an adult urban fantasy with an epic slow burn romance. If you like your love interests cold to everyone but the FMC, with wings as sharp as blades (literally) and a touch of forced proximity and forbidden romance, this should be your next read. With political intrigue, high stakes and a found family that will sacrifice everything to save each other, you will love Traitors' Creed.

TRAITORS' PROMISE (TRAITORS DUOLOGY, BOOK 2)

Even the greatest escapes don't guarantee freedom.

With the gilded facade of Zanteera Island's prison smouldering in her wake, Luka Brideoake prepares to make her status as a traitor official. But nothing could have readied her for a summons to a second National Duty. This time, in the heart of Nuntainia's poisonous corruption: Parliament House.

Tasked by Quillian with finding the evidence needed to expose the political tyranny, and armed with an invitation printed with government ink, Luka has no option but to report for duty. Alone.

But as the net of her government's lies closes in, Luka risks returning to the island and the prison she didn't burn—Vana. This time, behind bars. With neither time nor magic on her side, Luka will discover just how much she can endure to reveal a truth that will unseat the highest powers.

Traitors' Promise is the final book in the Traitors duology. Full of an epic romance, open door spice, friends to die for, political intrigue, rebellion and high stakes, this is an adult urban fantasy not to miss.

FIND YOUR NEXT READ

All of Lauren's books can be found here, www.laurenparkerrhodes.com/buy, or at all good bookshops and online platforms.

To stay up to date with all new releases (and inside stories...) subscribe here or at www.laurenparkerrhodes.com

Loved this book by Lauren Parker Rhodes?

I'd love you to leave a review wherever you purchased from or on Goodreads! Just a sentence or two, or even just a star rating, will go a long way to supporting this duology and it would mean the world to me.

After all, without readers, stories go unread and unheard.

Escaping to fantasy worlds is a specialty of Lauren's, either creating her own or reading other people's – providing there's a strong romance, Lauren is all in. Living in semi-rural Australia with her husband and two little wildlings, Lauren tries to teach her children of the wonders of nature. About the impact of all our tiny decisions and that, sometimes, it only takes one person to make a difference. When she's not living vicariously through her characters, or kid-wrangling, Lauren can be found at her second home, the coast; feeding her coffee and chocolate addiction; or trying to fit in a yoga class...even though Archie the labrador would much prefer a walk.

Instagram: @laurenparkerrhodes
www.laurenparkerrhodes.com

www.ingramcontent.com/pod-product-compliance
Lightning Source LLC
Chambersburg PA
CBHW011548190726
48287CB00010B/2793

* 9 7 8 1 7 6 3 7 3 4 6 1 6 *